FIRE BURN AND
CAULDRON BUBBLE

Book **1** of the Jolie Wilkins series

HP MALLORY

Also by HP Mallory:

THE JOLIE WILKINS SERIES:

Fire Burn and Cauldron Bubble
Toil and Trouble
Be Witched (Novella)
Witchful Thinking
The Witch Is Back
Something Witchy This Way Comes

THE DULCIE O'NEIL SERIES:

To Kill A Warlock
A Tale Of Two Goblins
Great Hexpectations
Wuthering Frights

FIRE BURN AND CAULDRON BUBBLE

by
H.P. Mallory

Fire Burn and Cauldron Bubble

Copyright © 2010 by H.P. Mallory

For my son, Finn

Acknowledgements:

First, to my fantastic critique partner, Lori Brighton. Without you, this book never would have been. Thanks for all your help.

To my mother, for all your support. Thank you.

To my husband for giving me the time and space to pursue my writing ambitions.

To my baby son, Finn, just for being.

ONE

It's not every day you see a ghost.

On this particular day, I'd been minding my own business, tidying up the shop for the night while listening to *Girls Just Wanna Have Fun* (guilty as charged). It was late—maybe 9:00 p.m. A light bulb had burnt out in my tarot reading room a few days ago, and I still hadn't changed it. I have a tendency to overlook the menial details of life. Now, a small red bulb fought against the otherwise pitch darkness of the room, lending it a certain macabre feel.

In search of a replacement bulb, I attempted to sort through my "if it doesn't have a home, put it in here" box when I heard the front door open. Odd—I could've sworn I'd locked it.

"We're closed," I yelled.

I didn't hear the door closing, so I put Cyndi Lauper on mute and strolled out to inquire. The streetlamps reflected through the shop windows, the glare so intense, I had to remind myself they were just lights and not some alien spacecraft come to whisk me away.

The room was empty.

Considering the possibility that someone might be hiding, I swallowed the dread climbing up my throat. Glancing around, I searched for something to protect myself with in case said breaker-and-enterer decided to attack. My eyes rested on a solitary broom standing in the corner of the Spartan room. The broom was maybe two steps from me. That might not sound like much, but my fear had me by the ankles and wouldn't let go.

Jolie, get the damned broom.

Thank God for that little internal voice of sensibility that always seems to visit at just the right time.

Freeing my feet from the fear tar, I grabbed the broom and neared my desk. It was a good place for someone to hide—well, really, the only place to hide. When it comes to furnishings, I'm a minimalist.

I jammed the broom under the desk and swept vigorously.

Nothing. The hairs on my neck stood to attention as a shiver of unease coursed through me. I couldn't shake the feeling and after deciding no one was in the room, I persuaded myself it must've been kids. But kids or not, I would've heard the door close.

I didn't discard the broom.

Like a breath from the arctic, a chill crept up the back of my neck.

I glanced up and there he was, floating a foot or so above me. Stunned, I took a step back, my heart beating like a frantic bird in a small cage.

"Holy crap."

The ghost drifted toward me until he and I were eye level. My mind was such a muddle, I wasn't sure if I wanted to run or bat at him with the broom. Fear cemented me in place, and I did neither, just stood gaping at him.

Thinking the Mexican standoff couldn't last forever, I replayed every fact I'd ever learned about ghosts: they have unfinished business, they're stuck on a different plane of existence, they're here to tell us something, and most importantly, they're just energy.

Energy couldn't hurt me.

My heartbeat started regulating, and I returned my gaze to the ectoplasm before me. There was no emotion on his face; he just watched me as if waiting for me to come to my senses.

"Hello," I said, thinking how stupid I sounded—treating him like every Tom, Dick, or Harry who ventured through my door. Then I felt stupid that I felt stupid—what was wrong with greeting a ghost? Even the dead deserve standard propriety.

He wavered a bit, as if someone had turned a blow dryer on him, but didn't say anything. He was young, maybe in his twenties. His double-breasted suit looked like it was right out of *The Untouchables*, from the 1930s if I had to guess.

His hair was on the blond side, sort of an ash blond. It was hard to tell because he was standing, er floating, in front of a wooden door that showed through him. Wooden door or not, his face was broad and he had a crooked nose—maybe it'd been broken in a fight. He was a good-looking ghost as ghosts go.

"Can you speak?" I asked, still in disbelief that I was attempting to converse with the dead. Well, I'd never thought I could, and I guess the day had come to prove me wrong. Still he said nothing, so I decided to continue my line of questioning.

"Do you have a message from someone?"

He shook his head. "No."

His voice sounded like someone talking underwater.

Hmm. Well, I imagined he wasn't here to get his future told—seeing as how he didn't have a future. Maybe he was passing through? Going toward the light? Come to haunt my shop?

"Are you on your way somewhere?" I had so many questions for this spirit but didn't know where to start, so all the stupid ones came out first.

"I was sent here," he managed, and in his ghostly way, I think he smiled. Yeah, not a bad looking ghost.

"Who sent you?" It seemed the logical thing to ask.

He said nothing and like that, vanished, leaving me to wonder if I'd had something bad to eat at lunch.

Indigestion can be a bitch.

~

"So no more encounters?" Christa, my best friend and only employee, asked while leaning against the desk in our front office.

I shook my head and pooled into a chair by the door. "Maybe if you hadn't left early to go on your date, I wouldn't have had a visit at all."

"Well, one of us needs to be dating," she said, knowing full well I hadn't had any dates for the past six months. An image of my last date fell into my head like a bomb. Let's just say I'd never try the Internet dating route again. It wasn't that the guy had been bad looking—he'd looked like his photo, but what I hadn't been betting on was that he'd get wasted and proceed to tell me how he was separated from his wife and had three kids. Not even divorced! Yeah, that hadn't been on his *match.com* profile.

"Let's not get into this again ..."

"Jolie, you need to get out. You're almost thirty ..."

"Two years from it, thank you very much."

"Whatever ... you're going to end up old and alone. You're way too pretty, and you have such a great personality, you can't end up like that. Don't let one bad date ruin it." Her voice reached a crescendo. Christa has a tendency towards the dramatic.

"I've had a string of bad dates, Chris." I didn't know what else to say—I was terminally single. It came down to the fact that I'd rather spend time with my cat or Christa rather than face another stream of losers.

As for being attractive, Christa insisted I was pretty, but I wasn't convinced. It's one thing when your best friend says you're pretty, but it's entirely different when a man says it.

And I couldn't remember the last time a man had said it.

I caught my reflection in the glass of the desk and studied myself while Christa rambled on about all the reasons I should be dating. I supposed my face was pleasant enough—a pert nose, cornflower blue eyes and plump lips. A spattering of freckles across the bridge of my nose interrupts an otherwise pale landscape of skin, and my shoulder length blond hair always finds itself drawn into a ponytail.

Head-turning doubtful, girl-next-door probable.

As for Christa, she doesn't look like me at all. For one thing, she's pretty tall and leggy, about five-eight, and four inches taller than I am. She has dark hair the color of mahogany, green eyes, and pinkish cheeks. She's classically pretty—like cameo pretty. She's rail skinny and has no boobs. I have a tendency to gain weight if I eat too much, I have a definite butt, and the twins are pretty ample as well. Maybe that made me sound like I'm fat—I'm not fat, but I could stand to lose five pounds.

"Are you even listening to me?" Christa asked.

Shaking my head, I entered the reading room, thinking I'd left my glasses there.

I heard the door open.

"Well, hello to you," Christa said in a high-pitched, sickening-sweet and non-Christa voice.

"Afternoon." The deep timbre of his voice echoed through the room, my ears mistaking his baritone for music.

"I'm here for a reading, but I don't have an appointment ..."

"Oh, that's cool," Christa interrupted and from the saccharin tone of her voice, it was pretty apparent this guy had to be eye candy.

Giving up on finding my reading glasses, I headed out in order to introduce myself to our stranger. Upon seeing him, I couldn't contain the gasp that escaped my throat. It wasn't his Greek God, Sean-Connery-would-be-envious good looks that grabbed me first or his considerable height.

It was his aura.

I've been able to see auras since before I can remember, but I'd never seen anything like his. It radiated out of him as if it had a life of its own and the color! Usually auras are pinkish or violet in healthy people, yellowish or orange in those unhealthy. His was the most vibrant blue I've ever seen—the color of the sky after a storm when the sun's rays bask everything in glory.

It emanated out of him like electricity.

"Hi, I'm Jolie," I said, remembering myself.

"How do you do?" And to make me drool even more than I already was, he had an accent, a British one. Ergh.

I glanced at Christa as I invited him into the reading room. Her mouth dropped open like a fish.

My sentiments exactly.

His navy blue sweater stretched to its capacity while attempting to span a pair of broad shoulders and a wide chest. The broad shoulders and spacious chest in question tapered to a trim waist and finished in a finale of long legs. The white shirt peeking from underneath his sweater contrasted against his tanned complexion and made me consider my own fair skin with dismay.

The stillness of the room did nothing to allay my nerves. I took a seat, shuffled the tarot cards, and handed him the deck. "Please choose five cards and lay them face up on the table."

He took a seat across from me, stretching his legs and rested his hands on his thighs. I chanced a look at him and took in his chocolate hair and darker eyes. His face was angular, and his Roman nose lent him a certain Paul Newman-esque quality. The beginnings of shadow did nothing to hide the definite cleft in his strong chin.

He didn't take the cards and instead, just smiled, revealing pearly whites and a set of grade A dimples.

"You did come for a reading?" I asked.

He nodded and covered my hand with his own. What felt like lightning ricocheted up my arm, and I swear my heart stopped for a second. The lone red bulb blinked a few times then continued to grow brighter until I thought it might explode. My gaze moved from his hand, up his arm and settled on his dark brown eyes. With the red light reflecting against him, he looked like the devil come to barter for my soul.

4

"I came for a reading, yes, but not with the cards. I'd like you to read …
me." His rumbling baritone was hypnotic, and I fought the need to pull my
hand from his warm grip.

I set the stack of cards aside, focusing on him again. I was so nervous I
doubted if any of my visions would come. They were about as reliable as the
weather anchors you see on TV.

After several long uncomfortable moments, I gave up. "I can't read you,
I'm sorry," I said, my voice breaking. I shifted the eucalyptus-scented incense
I'd lit to the farthest corner of the table, and waved my hands in front of my
face, dispersing the smoke that seemed intent on wafting directly into my eyes.
It swirled and danced in the air, as if indifferent to the fact that I couldn't help
this stranger.

He removed his hand but stayed seated. I thought he'd leave, but he
made no motion to do anything of the sort.

"Take your time."

Take my time? I was a nervous wreck and had no visions whatsoever. I
just wanted this handsome stranger to leave, so my habitual life could return to
normal.

But it appeared that was not in the cards.

The silence pounded against the walls, echoing the pulse of blood in my
veins. Still, my companion said nothing. I'd had enough. "I don't know what
to tell you."

He smiled again. "What do you see when you look at me?"

Adonis.

No, I couldn't say that. Maybe he'd like to hear about his aura? I didn't
have any other cards up my sleeve ... "I can see your aura," I almost
whispered, fearing his ridicule.

His brows drew together. "What does it look like?"

"It isn't like anyone's I've ever seen before. It's bright blue, and it flares
out of you … almost like electricity."

His smile disappeared, and he leaned forward. "Can you see everyone's
auras?"

The incense dared to assault my eyes again, so I put it out and dumped it
in the trashcan.

"Yes. Most people have much fainter glows to them—more often than
not in the pink or orange family. I've never seen blue."

He chewed on that for a moment. "What do you suppose it is you're
looking at—someone's soul?"

I shook my head. "I don't know. I do know, though, if someone's ailing,
I can see it. Their aura goes a bit yellow." He nodded, and I added, "You're
healthy."

He laughed, and I felt silly for saying it. He stood up, his imposing
height making me feel all of three inches tall. Not enjoying the feel of him
staring down at me, I stood and watched him pull out his wallet. I guess he'd
heard enough and thought I was full of it. He set a one hundred dollar bill on

the table in front of me. My hourly rate was fifty dollars, and we'd been maybe twenty minutes.

"I'd like to come see you for the next three Tuesdays at 4:00 p.m. Please don't schedule anyone after me. I'll compensate you for the entire afternoon."

I was shocked—what in the world would he want to come back for?

"Jolie, it was a pleasure meeting you, and I look forward to our next session." He turned to walk out of the room when I remembered myself.

"Wait, what name should I put in the appointment book?"

He turned and faced me. "Rand."

Then he walked out of the shop.

~

By the time Tuesday rolled around, I hadn't had much of a busy week. No more visits from ghosts, spirits, or whatever the PC term is for them. I'd had a few walk-ins, but that was about it. It was strange. October in Los Angeles was normally a busy time.

"Ten minutes to four," Christa said with a smile, leaning against the front desk and looking up from a stack of photos—her latest bout into photography.

"I wonder if he'll come," I mumbled.

Taking the top four photos off the stack, she arranged them against the desk as if they were puzzle pieces. I walked up behind her, only too pleased to find an outlet for my anxiety, my nerves skittish with the pending arrival of one very handsome man.

The photo in the middle caught my attention first. It was a landscape of the Malibu coastline, the intense blue of the ocean mirrored by the sky and interrupted only by the green of the hillside.

"Wow, that's a great one, Chris." I picked the photo up. "Can you frame it? I'd love to hang it in the store."

"Sure." She nodded and continued inspecting her photos, as if trying to find a fault in the angle or maybe the subject. Christa had aspirations of being a photographer and she had the eye for it. I admired her artistic ability—I, myself, hadn't been in line when God was handing out creativity.

She glanced at the clock again. "Five minutes to four."

I shrugged, feigning an indifference I didn't feel. "I'm just glad you're here. Rand strikes me as weird. Something's off ..."

She laughed. "Oh, Jules, you don't trust your own mother."

I snorted at the comment and collapsed into the chair behind her, propping my feet on the corner of our mesh waste bin. So I didn't trust people—I think I had a better understanding of the human condition than most people did. That reminded me, I hadn't called my mom in at least a week. Note to self: be a better daughter.

6

The cuckoo clock on the wall announced it was 4:00 p.m. with a tinny rendition of Edelweiss while the two resident wooden figures did a polka. I'd never much liked the clock, but Christa wouldn't let me get rid of it.

The door opened, and I jumped to my feet, my heart jack hammering. I wasn't sure why I was so flustered, but as soon as I met the heat of Rand's dark eyes, it all made sense. He was here again even though I couldn't tell him anything important last time, and did I fail to mention he was gorgeous? His looks were enough to play with any girl's heartstrings.

"Good afternoon," he said, giving me a brisk nod.

He was dressed in black—black slacks, black collared shirt, and a black suit jacket. He looked like he'd just come from a funeral, but somehow I didn't think such was the case.

"Hi, Rand," Christa said, her gaze raking his statuesque body.

"How has your day been?" he answered as his eyes rested on me.

"Sorta slow," Christa responded before I could. He didn't even turn to notice her, and she frowned, obviously miffed. I smiled to myself and headed for the reading room, Rand on my heels.

I closed the door, and by the time I turned around, he'd already seated himself at the table. As I took my seat across from him, a heady scent of something unfamiliar hit me. It had notes of mint and cinnamon or maybe cardamom. The foreign scent was so captivating, I fought to refocus my attention.

"You fixed the light," he said with a smirk. "Much better."

I nodded and focused on my lap. "I didn't get a chance last time to ask you why you wanted to come back." I figured it was best to get it out in the open. I didn't think I'd do any better reading him this time.

"Well, I'm here for the same reason anyone else is."

I lifted my gaze and watched him lean back in the chair. He regarded me with amusement—raised eyebrows and a slight smirk pulling at his full lips.

I shook my head. "You aren't interested in a card reading, and I couldn't tell you anything ... substantial in our last meeting ..."

His throaty chuckle interrupted me. "You aren't much of a businesswoman, Jolie; it sounds like you're trying to get rid of me and my cold, hard cash."

Enough was enough. I'm not the type of person to beat around the bush, and he owed me an explanation. "So are you here to get a date with Christa?" I forced my gaze to hold his. He seemed taken aback, cocking his head while his shoulders bounced with surprise.

"Lovely though you both are, I'm afraid my visit leans more toward business than pleasure."

"I don't understand." I hoped my cheeks weren't as red as I imagined them. I guess I deserved it for being so bold.

He leaned forward, and I pulled back. "All in good time. Now, why don't you try to read me again?"

7

I motioned for his hands—sometimes touching the person in question helps generate my visions. As it had last time, his touch sent a jolt of electricity through me, and I had to fight not to lose my composure. There was something odd about this man.

I closed my eyes and exhaled, trying to focus while millions of bees warred with each other in my stomach. After driving my thoughts from all the questions I had regarding Rand, I was more comfortable.

At first nothing came.

I opened my eyes to find Rand staring at me. Just as I closed them again, a vision came—one that was piecemeal and none too clear.

"A man," I said, and my voice sounded like a foghorn in the quiet room. "He has dark hair and blue eyes, and there's something different about him. I can't quite pinpoint it … it seems he's hired you for something …"

My voice started to trail as the vision grew blurry. I tried to weave through the images, but they were too inconsistent. Once I got a hold of one, it wafted out of my grasp, and another indistinct one took its place.

"Go on," Rand prodded.

The vision was gone at this point, but I was still receiving emotional feedback. Sometimes I'll just get a vision and other times a vision with feelings. "The job's dangerous. I don't think you should take it."

And just like that, the feeling disappeared. I knew it was all I was going to get and I was frustrated, as it hadn't been my best work. Most of the time my feelings and visions are much clearer, but these were more like fragments—almost like short dream vignettes you can't interpret.

I let go of Rand's hands, and my own felt cold. I put them in my lap, hoping to warm them up again, but somehow my warmth didn't quite compare to his.

Rand seemed to be weighing what I'd told him—he strummed his fingers against his chin and chewed on his lip. "Can you tell me more about this man?"

"I couldn't see him in comparison to anyone else, so as far as height goes, I don't know. Dark hair and blue eyes, the hair was a little bit longish, maybe not a stylish haircut. He's white with no facial hair. That's about all I could see. He had something otherworldly about him. Maybe he was a psychic? I'm not sure."

"Dark hair and blue eyes you say?"

"Yes. He's a handsome man. I feel as if he's very old though he looked young. Maybe in his early thirties." I shrugged. "Sometimes my visions don't make much sense." Hey, I was just the middleman. It was up to him to interpret the message.

"You like the tall, dark, and handsome types then?"

Taken aback, I didn't know how to respond. "He had a nice face."

"You aren't receiving anything else?"

I shook my head. "I'm afraid not."

8

He stood. "Very good. I'm content with our meeting today. Do you have me scheduled for next week?"

I nodded and stood. The silence in the room pounded against me, and I fought to find something to say, but Rand beat me to it.

"Jolie, you need to have more confidence."

The closeness of the comment irritated me—who was this man who thought he could waltz into my shop and tell me I needed more confidence? Granted, he had a point, but damn it all if I were to tell him that!

Now, I was even more embarrassed, and I'm sure my face was the color of a bad sunburn. "I don't think you're here to discuss me."

"As a matter of fact, that's precisely the reason I'm ..."

Rand didn't get a chance to finish when Christa came bounding through the door.

Christa hasn't quite grasped the whole customer service thing.

"Sorry to interrupt, but there was a car accident right outside the shop! This one car totally just plowed into the other one. I think everyone's alright, but how crazy is that?"

My attention found Rand's as Christa continued to describe the accident in minute detail. I couldn't help but wonder what he'd been about to say. It had sounded like he was here to discuss me ... something that settled in my stomach like a big rock.

When Christa finished her accident report, Rand made his way to the door. I was on the verge of demanding he finish what he'd been about to say, but I couldn't summon the nerve.

"Cheers," he said and walked out.

TWO

"Well, how many people did we have this time last month?" I asked Christa while she studied the figures in the books.

The sun was just starting its descent in the sky and threw itself full force into our windows. I lifted my hand and covered my eyes as a stream of annoyance snaked within me. I'd been thinking about putting some curtains up for a while and cursed my procrastination. A shadow momentarily interrupted the intensity of the glare and upon thinking it might be Rand, my heart flopped around like a fish on the end of a pole. The shadow moved on, and the sun shone through the window again, as if doubly intent on blinding us. My heart stopped palpitating, and I turned to Christa who watched me with quirked brow.

"Double what we've had this month."

This was bad.

I sank into the chair behind the desk, fatigue welling within me. Another shadow passed before the window, but I refused to pay attention to it, lest Christa take notice of the anticipation in my eyes. "Maybe we need to do a better job marketing ourselves," I said, hoping it was as simple as that.

"It's never been an issue before," she answered, meeting my worried gaze. "Jules, if you can't pay me this month, that's cool. I can ask my dad to carry me."

I smiled, resisting the urge to hug her. Christa and I had grown up together, and she'd moved with me from the outpost of civilization otherwise known as Spokane, Washington, to the bright lights of Los Angeles. She was the closest thing I had to a sister.

"Thanks, Christa, but I'll pay you."

Closing the book, she stood and yawned, stretching her arms above her head. The sun's rays traveled across her, setting her brownish-red hair aflame. "Well, I'm going across the street to Starbucks. Do you want anything?"

I shook my head. "Rand should be here soon."

The thought of Rand's impending visit weighed upon me like a mound of bricks, and I couldn't stop thinking about his strange words from our last meeting. Had he come to discuss me? And if so, what did that mean? I wasn't entirely sure I wanted to find out.

I like to keep my personal life … personal.

"Ah, that's right; the hottie is scheduled for today. I don't know why you act so disinterested. It's obvious he's got his eyes on you," she said with a knowing smile.

"Guys like him don't date girls like me." Someone with Rand's looks could be and would be interested in someone equally fetching, rather than girl-next-door Jolie.

Christa rested a consoling hand on my shoulder. "God, you need to stop thinking like that. It's obvious he's okay with the paranormal world, and he's gorgeous, so that should be your cue."

I didn't want to continue this conversation. "We'll see."

"Blah, coffee's calling."

And, with that, she walked out the door.

My thoughts returned to Rand, and if they'd been tangible, I would've locked them away and fed the key to a lion. That said, I still couldn't censor the snippets of bliss that visited me when I considered that maybe Rand did have something for me. Not wanting to think about it, I flipped open the accounting ledger and forced my attention to the numbers that already blurred before my eyes.

I didn't get much time to continue reviewing the financials; the buzz of the door heralded Rand's arrival. Thinking the day had escaped me, I glanced at the cuckoo clock and noted it was 4:00 p.m. on the dot. No sooner did I raise my eyes than the damned clock went off, and the Tyrolean dancers jigged just above Rand's head.

A smile touched the corners of his mouth as he turned and regarded them. He wore dark grey this time—a charcoal long-sleeved shirt and darker pants. My gaze traveled down the length of him and scattered once I reached the bottom of his untucked shirt. I had no business looking *there* of all places.

"Jolie, pleasure to see you," he said in his rich British accent.

His thighs strained against the material of his pants as he strode toward me. He didn't need to turn around for me to know his backside would be just as tight and muscular as his front. I forced my attention to his face as his smile widened, setting off his dimples.

"How are you, Rand?" My voice shook. I was annoyed with myself; Rand's muscular body and dimples were none of my concern.

"Well, thanks."

I stood up quickly, as if I'd been sitting on a thorn. Then my feet decided to go immobile, and I just stood in front of my desk like a moron. When my brain got with the program, I started toward the reading room, Rand behind me. His gait was long and slow as he assumed his seat, swiveling around to watch me close the door behind us.

"I hope you'll give me as good a reading as you did last time." The tone of his voice was so rich, I felt like I could gain weight just by listening to him.

I plunked myself into the seat across from him and motioned for his hands. "Don't get your hopes up. I never know when I'm going to see anything. My visions are very unreliable."

He grasped my hands, and the electric current coursed through me. I resisted the urge to jump and wondered if I'd ever get used to this—not that it mattered since this was Rand's last scheduled visit.

11

"I believe you're more powerful than you think you are." His voice was soft but could've commanded a fleet of ships.

I said nothing but clamped my eyes shut, enjoying the void of blackness. I waited for a vision. Nothing came. I sighed in frustration and opened them again, hoping my naked eye might catch something. All it caught was Rand smiling back at me, and the smile was so disarming, feelings of angst slithered within me. Almost reflexively, I shut my eyes again. I waited. And waited.

"I don't think anything's coming today," I said with finality and opened my eyes, dropping his hands. My own hands hung like dead weights, no longer charged with Rand's electric touch. "Are you sure you don't want a card reading—they can be insightful."

He shook his head. "I'm in no hurry. Let's just sit and talk a while. Maybe something will come."

All I could think about was separating myself from his unsettling company, and he wanted to talk? Well, I guess it was easier than conjuring up a recalcitrant vision. "Okay, what do you want to talk about?"

He paused. "Can you see spirits?"

That was easy enough. "As a matter-of-fact, I saw my first ghost last week—just before I met you."

He nodded, and I noticed the absence of surprise in his gaze, something I would've expected to see. I inwardly shrugged—maybe seeing a ghost wasn't such a big deal. *C'est la vie*, I guess.

"I know—I sent him to you."

I hadn't expected that, and my mouth dropped open accordingly. Now, it may seem strange that I, a psychic, would be so distrusting, but I don't think of myself as anything other than a girl from Spokane who gets visions now and then. Okay, and I can also see auras. But I'm not a spiritual person. I don't do cleansing rituals before or after card readings, I don't hang out with other psychics or meditate, and I definitely don't listen to new age music. My shop looks the part for my customers' benefit—they seem to like the whole mystical thing. I, myself, couldn't care less about it.

"You sent him to me?" I asked, my voice breaking with disbelief. "What do you mean—you sent him to me?"

Rand shrugged as if this were the most commonplace conversation imaginable. He ran a lethargic hand through his hair before returning said hand to his thigh. The distance from his thumb to his pinkie nearly spanned the width of his thigh, and I had to force my attention away. It wouldn't be a difficult feat to kill someone with such ... capable hands.

"Yes, he's a client of sorts. I wanted to see the extent of your abilities, so I sent him to test you."

I'd imagined Rand was a little bit off as most guys aren't interested in the occult. Those who are, in my experience, don't have Rand's gifts in the looks department. Now, I realized my wariness had been spot on. Always trust your intuition as it won't steer you wrong.

12

So Rand thought he had clients that were ghosts. ... "A client?" I repeated, not knowing what else to say.

"Yes. He's a friend of a friend to whom I owe a favor. That's a long story, though, and one we can discuss some other time. I sent him to you to see if you could see him, and it seems you could and did."

I just smiled, thinking I was in the wrong line of work. It must've been a good joke for God or whoever to give me the gift of second sight coupled with skepticism.

"After that little test, I decided to come and investigate myself. Upon learning you could see my life force, my aura as you call it, I was convinced your powers are far greater than you suppose. It's very rare that someone can see the life force of others."

I wanted to call his bluff, but I couldn't help putting the pieces together: the first time I'd ever seen a ghost just happened to be days before I'd met Rand. That, and Rand's aura was different from any other I'd ever seen. Was it possible there was more to this story?

"How do you know all this?" I asked in a small voice, afraid of the answer.

"I'm a warlock."

I didn't say anything for a moment while I replayed the response in my mind.

A warlock?

Frozen in my chair, I wasn't able to form a complete thought and was grateful my body instinctively forced itself to breathe.

"You aren't saying anything," he observed.

I nodded dumbly, and then like a dysfunctional dam, thoughts poured through my head until I was so overcome, I still couldn't form a thought.

"I don't know what to say." How simple. How true.

"A strange reaction in and of itself. Most people might laugh or tell me to leave." He leaned back in his chair and regarded me with an incredibly sexy smile. He looked normal. Scratch that, he looked far better than normal ... hot as hell might be a better description. No one would ever know he'd lost all control of his mental faculties.

Then it occurred to me that maybe it wasn't a good idea to disagree with or mock him—maybe that might incite him? You never know where you stand with crazy people, so it's best to indulge them—then I had a better chance of escaping. And damn it all, Christa was still at Starbucks, so if I happened to get murdered, she wouldn't be around to alert the authorities.

Ergh—bad story getting worse. I glanced at the door, trying to figure out how many strides it would take to reach it. My legs weren't long, so I figured maybe five. Now, the real question—could I make it in five strides without Rand catching me?

I pulled my attention back to the person in question and swallowed the egg-sized lump in my throat. I fought to find my voice. "When you say a warlock, you mean as in a male witch?"

13

He nodded with authority. "Yes."

I pondered it for a moment. A ghost, a warlock ... then it dawned on me and my hollow laugh ricocheted through me like a stray bullet. "Okay, you got me." He threw me a confused frown, and I thought he did a good job playing his part. "Was it Christa who hired you? Well done, I fell for it. Very funny."

He leaned forward. "This isn't ..." he started.

Although I wasn't convinced it was a joke, I decided to go with it. A joke allowed my psyche relief. "The joke is on me. And Christa smartly pretended to get coffee; she could never keep a straight face. She'd have blown the game a while ago."

"You don't believe me?" He wore a mask of injury, as if I'd seriously offended him.

"Give it up, Rand, if that's even your name. Game's up." I stood, trying to figure out how they'd done the ghost. That had looked pretty damn real.

"This isn't a bloody game," he snapped. "No one hired me. I came here because I need your help."

This was becoming tedious. I sidestepped the chair I'd been occupying and approached the door. Settling my hand on the doorknob, I wondered if I should say anything more. Reaching the conclusion that there wasn't anything more to say, I opened the door and turned to him. "You can leave now."

As soon as the words graced my lips, the doorknob yanked itself from my grasp, and the door slammed shut. I shrieked and jumped back. Okay, that was definitely not from the wind! My heart pounded as if I'd just ran up a flight of stairs. I slowly turned to face Rand. He stood. At the same time, the chair I'd been occupying pulled itself out from underneath the table. My gaze shifted from the phantom chair to Rand's seriously irritated countenance.

"You of all people shouldn't be so disbelieving. One who sees the future and spirits should have an open mind."

"I read Tarot cards for God's sake and I've only seen one ghost!"

I could taste my fear. I didn't know what to do and stepped back, feeling the unwelcome edge of the door in my spine. Maybe this was real? He was super pissed off with me thinking it an act. Okay, now ... how to save myself?

"Don't fear me." He said the words in a soft tone, as if realizing his display was a bit on the intimidating side.

Saying nothing, I sank into the open seat before me. I was relieved when it didn't pull itself back up to the table. I felt like I'd been kicked in the stomach and couldn't catch my breath. Panting, I sat there for a moment and was grateful Rand didn't say anything. I guess he realized it all needed to sink in. He stood near me, his arms crossed against a wide expanse of chest. His aura had tinges of purple, something I figured happened when he was upset or angry.

"A warlock, you said?" My voice was strained and incredulous.

He chuckled and straddled the seat across from me. "I assume you've never come into contact with one before?"

I laughed but the sound was tight. "Yeah, that's a safe assumption."

14

He nodded. "Our breed's a dying one. Witches and warlocks don't abound as they used to."

I willed myself to stop trembling. I didn't know if I could handle this. He'd said he needed my help but what did that mean? I tried to remember what, if anything, I'd ever heard of warlocks. I didn't think they ate humans or drank blood or turned into scary creatures. Okay, so far so good ...

"Are you ... evil?" I asked, wishing I hadn't sounded so ... lame.

He cocked his head with a laugh. "I don't think of myself as evil, but no one can say they've led a perfect life. As warlocks go, I'm not half bad."

A respectable answer, so why was I still shaking? "So what do you want with me?"

He considered my question with a lengthy pause. "How about we discuss it over dinner tonight?"

"Tonight?" As a rule, I didn't date, and I definitely didn't go out with warlocks. The idea was extremely dissatisfying. Then it dawned on me that I hadn't had a date in months. Maybe I should go just on principle.

I shook my head, hoping to force the ridiculous thoughts right out of my ears. What in the hell was wrong with me? There was no flipping way I was going out with a psychopath just so I could tell my mom I'd actually had a date.

"Yes, tonight." He was serious.

"Well ..." I tried to think of any excuse in the book as to why I couldn't go to dinner with him. "Okay, dinner sounds great." The words just sort of spilled from my lips of their own accord. Flabbergasted, I'd been thinking there was no way in hell I'd go with him, and yet I'd acquiesced as easy as you please.

"I was responsible for that," he said, in response to what must've been a horrified expression on my face. I swallowed the bile in my throat. Now I knew how Pinocchio felt—I was the puppet to Rand's puppeteer.

Once my heartbeat went from dangerous to as-normal-as-could-be-expected given the circumstance, I faced the ugly facts before me. It seemed there wasn't anything I could do—I had a dinner date with a witch.

~

Thirty minutes later, we awaited a table at Marmion, one of the poshest restaurants in LA I'd never imagined I'd step foot in the place, yet here I was, on a date with the most handsome man I'd ever seen who just happened to be a warlock.

Well, it wasn't so much a date—more a business meeting, I reasoned with myself. I was still wearing my work clothes—a pair of low-waisted denim jeans, a yellow sweater tied around my hips, and a crisp white polo shirt. I'd also insisted we take separate cars which was decidedly undatelike.

"So why do you need my help?" I asked, once an ample roll of rosemary bread, three cubes of herb butter, and a bottle of Perrier found their way to our table.

"I have a job that would require traveling to Chicago to the 1920s. I need you to learn who killed my client, the spirit you recently met."

Okay, I believed in ghosts, and I'd accepted the fact that I'd seen one, and I was beginning to be okay with the existence of warlocks, but time travel? I leaned forward and lowered my voice. "You can time travel?"

He shook his head. "I used that word lightly. You wouldn't be going back in time; your mind would."

I nodded like I knew what he was talking about. "So what does that mean?"

I noticed he hadn't touched the bread. Did warlocks eat?

"It entails a lot of focusing and projection, something I'll have to teach you. It seems that although your powers are plentiful, they need guidance."

Back the mule train up.

"I haven't agreed to go with you," I said.

"I'd make it worth your while."

This appealed to the businesswoman in me. "How?"

"If you accompany me to Chicago for what should take no more than a fortnight, I'll double whatever income you earn at your shop in a year."

"A fortnight?" I could never remember how many days that was. I must've learned it five times in the course of undertaking my English degree, but somehow it never stuck.

"Two weeks." Ah, that's right.

Wow. That was a pretty good offer. I narrowed my eyes—things that sound too good to be true usually are. "For two weeks of work?" I wondered when the terms and conditions would reveal their ugly selves.

"Well, however long the job takes. I don't think it'll take longer than that, but I can't predict it."

I shook my head. When it comes to business arrangements, I'm black and white. Either it's a good deal or it isn't. "No deal. That could mean years."

"Very well … how about we agree you assist me for no longer than two weeks?"

"And if I did decide to agree to this, of course you'd pay me some of the fees up front?"

He nodded. "Half up front and the remainder upon completion."

I was quiet as I considered it. From most angles, it didn't look half-bad. If this guy actually believed I could help him, who was I to argue? Hell, even if it didn't work out, I'd still get paid at least half. No harm done. Hmm, money certainly does talk. This would mean I could relax a bit as times had been tough.

"What if I want to bring Christa with me?" Now that we'd handled the monetary side of things, I should also consider my safety. I'd seen Rand perform some strange stunts, but that didn't mean I believed his story one hundred percent.

"Bring whoever you want. I'll cover her expenses, as well."

The cynic in me raged against the ease of the arrangement. "Why me?"

He leaned back in his chair and toyed with the saltshaker, cupping the cover in his palm while he rotated the shaker up and down. "I've been searching for people with the innate abilities required to perform such a task. I've been looking for months. When I found you, I sent Jack, the spirit, to ensure me of your abilities. Once you passed that test, I came to see you for myself. I must say, I've been quite impressed, Jolie."

"How did you find me?" I asked, noticing I'd been picking at the crust of the bread, and now it looked like a battlefield of littered crumbs.

"The Yellow Pages."

Note to self—advertising in the yellow pages paid off. I nodded, thinking this conversation something out of the Twilight Zone. "You must be pretty powerful yourself?"

I disregarded the smile he sent my way and refused to notice the dimples that lit up his entire face. "I'm considered to be one of the strongest warlocks, yes."

My eyes narrowed. I didn't like arrogant men, although Rand would appear to have more cause than most. "So if you're so strong, why can't you do it yourself?"

That had the desired effect—his irritation.

"It requires two people. I'll be focusing on you, and you'll be focusing on Jack. I can't very well send myself back as I'd have no way of returning."

I'm sure my eyes popped out of my skull. "There's a chance I might not come back?" Maybe this wasn't quite as good as it had sounded. There's always the fine print.

He shrugged off my concern. "No chance, I can ensure your safety, but that's why there needs to be two of us."

I scouted the restaurant, realizing the waiter hadn't ventured near us. "Well the service in this place could use some improvement."

Rand's lips parted in a grin. "I was keeping him away. I wanted to finish our conversation. Do you know what you'd like?"

Yeah, to get the hell away from you. I couldn't help the fear that bubbled up from my gut as I wondered just how powerful he was. Maybe I was stupid and taking my life into my hands. Scratch that, I was definitely stupid.

I blinked, and the waiter was before us, his pen poised on a pad of paper and his eyes riveted on me as if I were a field mouse and he, a hungry eagle.

"The tofu salad please," I said in a spineless voice, repeating the first thing I read on the menu. Once the sentence fell off my tongue, I remembered I didn't like tofu.

Rand scrunched his lips in obvious disapproval. I guess he didn't care for it either. "The prime rib please. I'd prefer that rare." He picked up the wine list and scanned it, signaling he'd found one with a flick of his long fingers. "Chateau Petrus, vintage 1961."

I didn't know much about wine, but I had to imagine anything that old had to be expensive. Once the waiter departed, Rand's attention returned to me.

"I imagine you have many questions."

I nodded, about to deliver one. "So if there are warlocks, are there other creatures we don't know about?"

"Many. They keep themselves well disguised. I'll introduce you to some in time."

That sounded a little too ominous, and I convinced myself that day would never come. "The man I saw in my vision?"

Rand interrupted me. "Oh, yes, that. I sent that vision to you. I needed to ensure we could communicate telepathically and, it seems, we can," he finished with grin.

"You thought of that and sent it to me?"

"Yes. The man you saw in your vision is Sinjin Sinclair, and you were correct in your observation that he's a dangerous man, well, vampire, actually."

I gasped. "Vampire! As in 'I vant to suck your blood?'" I asked, holding my fingers up to imitate fangs.

Rand chuckled. It was a deep and hearty sound. A sound a girl could get used to. If she could wrap her mind around the warlock thing, that is. "Yes, quite so. He's a very old vampire, and I've worked with him upon occasion. And before you ask, no, he won't be in Chicago."

I sighed in relief. I couldn't handle a vampire. I didn't think I could even handle Rand. "How come no one knows about all these creatures?"

"Our goal is to live among people undetected, and we do quite a good job of it. We've had to live in such a way for thousands of years."

The thought left me cold. "Are you that old?"

He laughed. "No, not exactly. I'm older than you'd assume, though. As a warlock, I can use magic to remain young. I was born in Kent, England, in 1843."

I choked on my fizzy water. 1843! He didn't look a day over thirty-four. "How's that possible?"

"That, dear Jolie, you'll learn to stop asking. Never wonder how, just accept it. 'There are more things in heaven and earth than are dreamt of in your philosophy,'" he finished with a sly smile.

Oh, yes, he was definitely English, but Shakespeare was no foreigner to me. "Touché Hamlet," I said with a grin.

THREE

"Are you excited?" Christa asked as she looped one gold hoop earring through her ear. She turned from her reflection in the mirror and studied me, threading the matching earring through the other ear. "It's kinda cool, being in Chicago, ya know?"

"Yeah," I said and turned my attention to the pounding rain outside my hotel window. The drops pelted against the pane as if demanding entrance, the lightning issuing a warning of the coming thunder.

Chicago weather was the pits.

I checked my watch; Christa took eons to get ready. "How much longer?"

She shrugged and returned her attention to her reflection, picking up a tube of lipstick—the color somewhere between magenta and a week-old bruise. She made a pouting sort of expression and painted her lips, taking care to dab them with a napkin.

"The lips, Jules, are the most important part of a woman's face." Her reflection met mine in the mirror. She pursed the most important part of her face and made a sort of kissing gesture at herself. I couldn't keep my smile to myself. She looked ridiculous.

"I thought the eyes were."

She shook her head emphatically. "Nope. The lips."

Rather than get into the world's dumbest argument, I shook my head and glanced at my watch again. "You almost ready?"

Rand had requested we meet him in the lobby for dinner, and I didn't want to be late.

"Yep," she answered, giving her hair one last fluff before turning to face me, epiphany suddenly plastered on her face. "Hey, you think Rand would pose for me?"

Hmm, I wasn't sure what Rand would think about it, but his chiseled face and masculine beauty would definitely make any portfolio shine a little brighter. "I don't know; you can always ask."

My cell phone broke into a beepy rendition of Clare De Lune and halted our progress. I checked the caller ID and sighed. To answer or not to answer, that was the question. Finally, I decided it wasn't right to ignore one's mother and flipped open my phone.

"Hi, Mom."

"Jolie, you forgot to call me when your flight landed." Her voice shook, and I immediately regretted answering the phone.

"We sort of got caught up. But don't worry, I had a great flight and I'm in Chicago."

She paused, and I could hear her turning a washing machine dial in the background. How worried could she be when the call to do laundry was still of prime concern?

"Well, I'm glad to hear it. You know how I worry about you traveling."

She worried about everything, not just traveling. She was the type of person who would rather stay home than confront an unknown world outside her doorstep. To sum up her life: she'd been born in Spokane, and she'd die in Spokane.

I eyed Christa who pointed at her watch. "Sorry, Mom, but I'm sorta busy at the moment. Christa and I are just on our way out."

"Oh, sorry, dear. Tell Christa I said hello."

I dropped the phone from my ear.

"Mom says hi." I pulled the phone back up to my mouth. "Christa says hi back. Can I call you when we're in LA?"

"Sure, love you. Bye bye."

"Love you, bye Mom."

I flipped the phone shut and turned to look at Christa's inquiring smile.

"You still haven't told your mom how you support yourself, have you?" she asked.

I smirked. "She thinks I'm a receptionist at a law firm. You know how religious she is, she'd never be okay with me reading fortunes, and she'd soooo not be okay with Rand."

I'd learned at a young age not to mention the bright colors I could see around people or the strange visions I had that always came to fruition. Multiple holy water cleanses from Father Charles have a way of teaching you when to hold your tongue.

Christa shook her head and laughed, her voice sounding like notes picked on a harp. She was dressed to the nines in a tight black bodysuit that embellished her small waist and broad hips and cheetah stiletto heels that embellished nothing. Her loose dark hair graced her back, and I was sure she'd capture everyone's attention. I envied her nerve.

I glanced down at my lackluster outfit with a sigh—caramel brown slacks with sensible heels (less than two inches), and a nutmeg turtleneck. Christa had pooh-poohed my outfit, saying it was way too conservative. But I could never feel comfortable in the getup she was parading around in.

"God, could I use a drink," Christa said as I pulled the door shut behind us. I was thinking the same thing.

Upon reaching the ground floor, I immediately noticed Rand seated at the bar. My heart did a little flutter when he turned his attention to me, his smile and dimples giving him a sort of boyish quality. He stood up and started toward us, his stride long and purposeful. The dark blue of his suit and grey of his collared shirt lent him a definite business look—I certainly would never use the word "casual" to describe Rand. I suddenly wished I'd taken Christa's advice and worn something a little more daring. But this was work, not play, and I was who I was.

Humph, take that inferiority complex!

Rand gave Christa a cursory glance as she flitted before him like a moth trapped by a flame.

"I made reservations at a Japanese restaurant," he said in his sexy accent.

"Great! I love sushi!" Christa sang.

I guess she figured since I wasn't going to go after Rand, she would. I was quick to subdue the pointed fingers of jealousy jabbing me in the gut—it was none of my concern and what's more, their getting together was probably inevitable.

"Why don't you both wait inside while I hail a taxi?" Rand asked, motioning to the fury of the rain outside.

"I'll go with you, a little rain never bothered me," Christa chirped.

She sidled up to Rand and led him outside while I followed behind. He turned toward me, offering his arm, but I waved it away, not wanting to infringe on Christa's kill. The overhang of the hotel awning did nothing to hold back the rain as it surfed the wind and threw itself against me. I wiped the sting from my cheeks and watched Rand flag down a cab.

The cab stopped before us, and Rand opened the door. Christa crawled inside, making sure to stick her ass out as she bent over. I couldn't keep the frown from pulling at the corners of my mouth. Sometimes she was so obvious. I hazarded a glance at Rand, imagining he'd be mesmerized by the sight before him, but he met my expression with an embarrassed smile.

"This weather makes me feel quite at home," he said with a grin as I climbed in beside Christa and Rand settled himself next to me.

Ah yes, he was embarrassed. When a business partner's friend sticks her ass in your face, discussing the weather is the best line of recourse.

The cab pulled away from the curb, and we were off.

"Is the weather in England so bad?" I asked, knowing the answer would be a resounding yes, but I was just trying to make conversation.

"The sky can be blue and five minutes later, you'll find yourself amid a hail storm."

"That sorta sounds like Washington weather," Christa said and rammed her elbow into my side, apparently annoyed that I was sitting between them. "I've always wanted to go to England," she continued, her voice back to sultry, as if she hadn't just assaulted her best friend.

Rand smiled and I felt the need to throw Christa a bone. "Christa's a photographer," I started. Well, it wasn't really like she was a full-blown photographer—it was more of a hobby, but you've gotta start somewhere.

"Is that so?" Rand asked.

Christa nodded emphatically. "I've been saving up to take a trip abroad, so I can really get some great shots ... you know, expand my portfolio. I was thinking Italy or Spain, but maybe I should try England."

I didn't respond but inwardly shook my head at Christa's lack of subtlety. When the cab slowed to a stop, I looked out the window and found we'd arrived at our destination. The cabbie opened our door, and if he were a cartoon, his eyes would've bulged out of their sockets and his tongue would've unraveled to the floor when Christa stood up before him. I wondered, at that moment, what it must be like to have such control over the opposite sex. Christa was pretty, as I said before, but I think it was more in how she carried herself. I was just as pretty, maybe, but I guess I didn't have any self-confidence. It was a disheartening thought, so I dropped it.

Don't look so sad.

It was Rand's voice in my head. The words were as clear as if he'd spoken them.

My heart stopped then sped up as if it'd just entered the freeway. I nearly tripped on my own feet, and even though they're a size eight, they aren't big enough to warrant tripping over them. Rand's steel grip took hold of my arm, stabilizing me while I tilted my head and looked up into his smug face. Apparently, he thought his little trick pretty nifty.

Then I remembered Rand saying he'd sent me the vision I'd had of the vampire Sinjin. Hmm, okay, so maybe like the vision, he could send me his thoughts? My heart slowed a bit.

If Rand could read my mind, though, that meant he knew I was attracted to him. My heart sped up again.

I'm not sad. Can you read my mind? I thought, hoping and praying the answer was no.

Rand didn't respond, but opened the restaurant door for us as Christa mouthed an exaggerated "thank you." I followed her inside, eyeing him for any sort of sign that he'd received my thought. He just closed the door behind him and approached the hostess, giving his name. Silencing a sigh of disappointment, I turned my attention to the vaulted ceilings, red walls, and black lacquered tables in the restaurant. Hundreds of candles lit the place and threw shadows against the angular lines of Rand's face. Talk about a Kodak moment.

"Jolie," Christa said, and I turned to find the hostess waiting for me so she could lead us to our table. I nodded and brought up the rear. Rand withdrew a chair from the table and Christa took it, her posture as regal as a queen's. I pulled out my own chair and took a seat even though Rand frowned at me. And here I'd thought I was doing him a favor.

Well, I guess reading thoughts only went one way—from Rand's brain to mine. That was a bit of a bummer.

No, I can't read your mind.

I flinched as his voice infiltrated my head again. This was something that would require getting used to.

Well, what do you call that? I thought, hoping my snarky tone would translate.

I caught Rand's grin. *I can only read whatever thoughts you send me.*

A tide of relief washed over me as I figured my innermost secrets and thoughts were still safe. Phew.

I turned my attention to Christa who was chatting away about something. Her hands were so expressive, it looked like she was translating Homer's Odyssey into sign language.

What is she talking about? I asked of my silent friend.

He lifted his menu, and a smile touched his lips. *I have no idea.*

A strange sense of warmth suffused me, and I couldn't help feeling close to Rand, as if our unique ability united us in some way.

Christa then faced me, and I intercepted. "What are you going to have?" I asked.

She frowned and glanced at the menu. "I don't know. I haven't had a chance to read it."

My attention turned to my own menu. My appetite was almost non-existent, and I browsed the menu with indifference. I couldn't help but wonder if my less than stellar appetite had to do with the butterflies that swarmed in my stomach every time Rand looked at me. Butterflies or not, I guess I had to order something.

As soon as I'd decided on an albacore roll, the waiter appeared, and I wondered if this was another Rand mind-control stunt. After taking our orders, the waiter disappeared as quickly as he'd come.

"Let me brief you," Rand started. "We'll leave at eight tomorrow morning to get a taxi to the location of Jack's murder."

"Jack is the ghost," I whispered to Christa, wanting to make sure she was included. I'd made the agreement with Rand, albeit he'd been less than enthusiastic, that Christa should be included every step of the way. I trusted her implicitly, and if I were doing anything that might be considered dangerous, I needed my best friend looking out for me.

"Was he the ghost who came to the shop?" she asked.

"Yes," I answered, "he was killed in the 1920s in Chicago, and Rand was hired to find out who did it."

Christa clapped her hands together with a wide smile. "A murder mystery! I love it!" After a good thirty-second pause, her smile dropped, and her eyes narrowed as she faced Rand. "Why don't you just ask Jack who killed him?"

I couldn't keep the snicker from my lips. That was a great question. Rand frowned and took an extraordinarily long swig of his water.

"Well, Sherlock and Watson, Jack never saw the person who killed him. He was shot from behind."

"Oh, that would explain it," Christa said with an enthusiastic nod.

Rand continued. "Once we're at the location ..."

"Is Jack's house still there?" I asked abruptly.

"Yes, and I've ensured the current residents will be absent."

Christa leaned forward, her eyes wide. "How'd you do that?"

"With the help of a little mental persuasion. They'll wake up feeling as if they need to take a drive in the country, which will turn into a weekend away.

I'm hoping we'll complete the task by the weekend but, if not, perhaps they'll need a longer vacation."

Well, at least he hadn't disposed of them. I was worried such might be the case. It was a scary thought, since I didn't really know anything about Rand. He had incredible power, but I didn't know to what capacity. My gaze slid to his large and sinewy hands. Even without magic, he could easily overpower me. Not like that would be hard to do even if he weren't a warlock, but anyway ...

"We'll carry out the spell in the living room," Rand finished.

"What will I have to do?" I asked, twisting the napkin in my lap. Once I caught myself, I forced my hands to the table, not wanting anyone to realize how nervous I was. I'm definitely not someone who wears her heart on her sleeve.

Rand looked about himself and gave an arrogant nod—to whom I had no idea. Within moments, a waiter was at his side, bent on refilling his wine glass. Both Christa's and my glasses were still full. I smiled to myself as I considered that maybe Rand did have a flaw. My lips widened as I further considered it. An alcoholic warlock ...

"You won't have to do much. I'll carry the bulk of the spell. You'll just need to focus on Jack's spirit, and if the charm works, you'll find yourself as a spectator in 1922 when someone shoots Jack in the head. All you have to do is find out who did it, and Bob's your uncle."

"What?" I frowned.

"Bob who?" Christa asked.

Rand chuckled, and his whole body shook with the effort.

"It's something we Brits say—similar to ... and that's it."

"'The only thing separating Americans and Brits is a common language,'" I quoted with a grin, forgetting exactly who'd said it. Maybe Churchill? I wasn't sure. I'd have to check my quote dictionary when we got back to LA.

Rand's smile was wide enough to touch his eyes, and I wondered if it might turn into a laugh.

"Well, what if the killer doesn't say his name?" Christa asked.

Rand ran his fingers up and down the stem of his wineglass, sending a wash of heat straight through my body. "That's why I wanted a psychic for the job." He faced me. "Jolie, you'll have to use your ability and your intuition."

Reality came crashing down on me like a breaking window, a shard of glass ramming itself into my stomach. Maybe this was going to be more difficult than I'd anticipated. My visions were unreliable at best and now to have so much hanging on them ... it left me uneasy. I guess this was different, though, because essentially, I was becoming one of my visions.

"We'll have more than one go at it," Rand said, as if he was aware of my inner turmoil. "If we don't get it the first time, we'll have more opportunities. I'm hoping we'll have it by the end of the weekend, but again, it's not crucial if we don't. You can take as much time as you need, Jolie."

I relaxed. So I didn't have to be perfect right off the bat. There was a learning curve. Thank God.

~

I woke up in a sweat, my body flushed and an aching need pulsing through my veins. With a groan, I glanced at the clock. It was 1:00 a.m. The dream had been pretty intense, involving me going back in time to help with the mystery of Jack's killer. To my shock, the killer had been Rand. After the discovery, we'd engaged in graphic sex, the threat of his double-sided nature adding fuel to my hormone fire.

I never have erotic dreams—I don't think of myself as an erotic person. Seeing as how I don't have a dating life, I guess it goes hand in hand that I wouldn't be the most sexual person in the world.

I stood up and grabbed a bottled water from the minibar. The water was probably at least seven bucks, but I didn't care. Rand seemed to have no problem with money, so I didn't think he'd mind if I helped myself.

A high shrill interrupted my Evian moment and it took my half-awake mind a second or two to realize it was the phone. I debated answering it, assuming it was Christa. It wasn't rare for me to get a call from her in the middle of the night from time to time—sometimes she drank too much and needed a ride home or maybe she got into a fight with her boyfriend, the list went on. I couldn't imagine what it would be tonight, though, as I'd thought she'd gone to bed when I had.

"Hello?" I answered.

"Jolie." Rand's voice washed over me like a caress.

My mouth dropped open. Dear God! Did he somehow know about the dream? The thought brought a flush to my face, and I wanted nothing more than to hang up.

"What are you doing awake?" he asked, his voice giving nothing away.

My laugh sounded breathless and forced. "Shouldn't I be asking you the same question or why you're calling me so late?"

He chuckled. "Ah, yes, I guess I should've mentioned that I'm able to tell when you're awake and when you aren't."

"And when I've been bad or good so I better be good for goodness sake?" I sort of sang it.

"Pardon?"

I laughed. "Like Santa Claus ..."

"Oh, Father Christmas." Rand chuckled, but I wasn't sure if he actually thought my joke was funny or if he was just humoring me.

"So how are you able to tell if I'm asleep or not?" I asked, suddenly thinking that maybe I shouldn't be joking when what he was telling me was pretty damned weird.

"I send out mental feelers and based on your vibrations, I can tell if your mind is active or asleep."

It took a second for this to sink in and I wasn't sure if I was creeped out or fascinated. Rand definitely had some strange abilities. After a long and awkward pause, I managed to find something to say. "What are you doing up?"

"Warlocks don't sleep much. We need perhaps an hour or two every couple of days. Now, your turn: why are you awake?"

"I had a bad dream." Very, very bad.

"Oh, sorry to hear it. You aren't worried about tomorrow, are you?"

I shook my head and then realized he couldn't see me. "No, I'm not worried about tomorrow."

"You'll do fine."

But his statement did nothing to soothe my frazzled nerves.

"What was your dream about?"

My cheeks colored. "I can't remember," I answered quickly, maybe too quickly.

There was silence on the other end. "Okay, I was just calling to see how you were. I suppose I'll say goodnight."

"Goodnight, Rand." I hung up the phone and dropped back into the warmth of the bed, wondering if it was possible for my dream to pick up where it had left off.

~

My palms were sweaty and itching. As we sat in the living room of what was once the home of Jack the ghost, I thought about the task at hand and wanted to throw up. Forcing my less than attractive thoughts to the deep recesses of my mind, I focused on Rand's Roman profile. Tracing his strong nose and chin with my eyes helped to calm me.

Rand centered his attention on me, and the feelings of calmness exploded, replaced with more primitive and unwholesome thoughts. These thoughts revolved around certain appendages on his person and I don't mean fingers or toes.

I exhaled, hoping the images of a naked Rand would float on my breath and right out of my head. I compelled myself to take note of my surroundings, figuring that might combat my newly awakened sex drive, which was in overdrive.

I turned my attention to the entertainment center—it spanned the entire length of one of the walls and revealed an impressive DVD collection. Photos of the Fords, the family Rand had sent on vacation, smiled down at me. My heart did a strange little jerk. I wanted a family some day—a husband, two kids, and a white picket fence. I wondered, though, if that was the life for me. I didn't have the line of beaus waiting to court me that Christa did.

"Jolie, are you ready?" I turned at the sound of Rand's voice and found him watching me.

I nodded and slipped my hands in his as the now familiar current coursed through me. We sat cross-legged, facing one another. According to Rand, we were to concentrate on each other and envision a circle of energy around us—that was to act as a shield. A shield against what, I didn't know and didn't want to ask.

Jack, the ghost, was nowhere in sight. It seemed a rude thing to be late to your own séance, I thought and closed my eyes once I noticed Rand doing the same.

"When will Jack be here?" I whispered.

"He is here."

My eyes popped open. Glancing around, I didn't see anything. My gaze returned to Rand, who still had his eyes closed.

"He's sitting in between us, right in front of you."

Rand's words jolted through me, and it was all I could do to stay seated. I wasn't sure how comfortable I was with this whole ghost thing. I closed my eyes again and Rand tightened his grip, as if he were letting me know I'd be safe and more so, that I shouldn't be afraid of a ghost.

"Okay, Jolie, I want you to focus on Jack being here in this house, and there's a man who will come through the door. I want you to scrutinize that man, until you know his face. Then use your abilities to find out who he is."

I tried, I really did. I concentrated like I've never concentrated before and … nothing. I opened my eyes and found Christa inspecting her nails. Rand's eyes were still clamped shut, trying to get the charm to work. I closed my eyes again and focused on the ghost, trying to imagine a man shooting him in the head. All I could focus on was the intense heat of Rand's hands on my own.

"Jolie." His voice belied the fact that he knew I wasn't focusing.

"Nothing is happening," I answered with a sigh.

"Try again."

I closed my eyes and focused again, trying to get through the darkness of my eyelids. I wasn't sure what would happen or what I should be looking for but, undoubtedly, I wasn't finding it.

Two hours later, I still hadn't managed to see anything. Christa was napping on the sofa, and Rand seemed quite over the whole thing as well—stifling a yawn and tapping his long fingers on his thighs. I still couldn't see Jack the ghost.

"Okay, let's call it a day," Rand said.

I didn't say anything but nodded and wiped the sweat from my palms on my thighs. Tears of frustration stung my eyes, and I averted my gaze, not wanting anyone to witness the pathetic display.

"Jolie, you did well," Rand said, and his voice was soft, soothing. "I think we need a bit more practice, though."

"Practice?" I asked, not sure what we'd be practicing.

"Yes, I think I expected too much of you. I know you're powerful, but you need to hone your skills."

27

"Sure, sounds good." Even though it sounded far from good. I just hoped this wouldn't mean another two hours of sitting uncomfortably while I focused on nothing and had only my disappointment to show for it.

~

I closed the door behind Rand as my heart sped up. I couldn't say I was comfortable with him, and it didn't help that we were now alone … in my hotel room. I glanced around, my vision coming to rest on the oversized bed in the center of the room. The emerald green duvet beckoned to me, trying to tempt me into its lush, pillowy softness. Taken in, I sat on the bed but then reconsidered and moved to an armchair next to the bed.

Rand watched me with quirked brows. "I won't bite, Jolie."

My giggle was forced. "You leave that to the vampires."

He chuckled and took a seat on the bed. "We need to work on your concentration."

"How do we do that?"

He shrugged and looked around him, at what I had no idea. Maybe Jack the ghost was in our midst again. "See that glass over there?" he asked and pointed across the room. My gaze fell to the unobtrusive, dime-a-dozen glass sitting on the bar. I nodded.

"We're going to hone your attention, so you move the glass across the counter."

Right, good luck. "We are?" The tone of my voice was as dubious as I felt. "How do I even know that's possible?"

He focused on the glass and like a dog with worms, it skittered across the bar. I couldn't mask my surprise and gasped. Rand chuckled. Okay, so it was possible, but maybe just for Rand. I sure as hell wasn't going to be able to move it.

"I need you to focus on that glass, Jolie, and I want you to move it."

I turned to face my opponent, the glass. "Does it help if I'm closer to it?"

Rand shook his head. "Doesn't matter where you are. Now, stop stalling and try it," he said sharply.

I honed in on the glass, thinking: *move glass, I want you to move.* But it seemed the glass was uninterested—it sat there and mocked me as if to say, "I'm only moving for the incredibly hot warlock."

I didn't blame it.

Rand stood up and blocked my view of the uncooperative glass. He crossed his arms against his broad chest and appeared to be all hot and bothered, but not in the good way. Even so, he was still a treat to my eyes.

A frown tugged at his handsome face. "Jolie, witches are very attracted to one another, so you have to move past that."

"Wait, what?" I asked in total confusion. What the hell was he talking about?

"Your attraction for me is interrupting your focus."

28

Okay, did I mention I don't like egomaniacs? I could feel my blood pressure increasing. "My what for you? You think I can't move the glass because I'm thinking about you?"

He nodded, and the volcano that was Jolie's temper erupted. Of all the egotistical, narcissistic bastards! "What a self-centered and ridiculous thing for you to say!" I shot out at him, wishing I could slap the smug smile right off his face.

"I can't move the damn thing because I'm not a witch, not because I'm thinking about you!"

"Focus it on the glass!"

"Fuck the glass!"

Pointing his index finger like he was Death incarnate, he aimed my attention at the glass again, and fury mounted inside me. If I was going to move the damn glass, I needed to do it now. I envisaged all his egoism filling the glass until it was brimming over, bubbles of narcissism and conceit brewing like yeast.

And I moved that glass with my mind. The damn thing actually jumped off the bar and landed with a thud on the carpet. If I hadn't been so livid, I might have been proud of myself but, instead, I was left feeling nothing but empty.

Rand's grin was wide as he took a step toward me. "I knew you could do it."

I held my up my hand to keep him at bay. "Don't come near me, you bastard."

"I said it to get you riled up, Jolie, I needed some energy from you."

I hesitated, my brows snapping together. "You said that so I'd move the glass?" I asked facetiously.

He sighed, as if expending all the air within him. "I needed to give you an outlet. It's true that witches are attracted to one another, all otherworldly creatures are."

Then it dawned on me that I should never have been angry in the first place. "I'm not a witch."

He shrugged. "Call yourself what you will. You can see the future, no?"

"It's called being psychic, and there are hundreds of thousands of people who can claim the same thing," I snarled.

"You can see the life force of others."

"So what? That doesn't make me a witch. I can't wiggle my nose and make the cat litter take itself out. And for that matter, I haven't seen anything that would convince me you're such a great witch. You've moved chairs and slammed a door and moved a glass, but all of that could've been rigged, you know?"

Rand smiled. The challenge was on. "Yes, it could be rigged. What do you want me to do? You name it."

Hmm, this was a good one. What did I want him to do? End world hunger? Abolish taxes? Take off all of his clothes? That last thought brought

29

heat to my cheeks and I dropped my gaze to the floor, reaching for the first thing that next entered my mind.

I brought my gaze back to his. "I want you to levitate." I crossed my arms across my chest and smirked. The time of reckoning was upon him.

He lifted a brow just before his feet left the ground, and he floated in front of me. My smile fell. Well, ask and you shall receive! The cynic in me searched for some plausible reason as to why this was happening, but not finding one, I faced the fact that maybe Rand was a warlock.

If it looks like a warlock, sounds like a warlock … you get it.

"You can come back down, I believe you." Even if I was convinced Rand was otherworldly, it didn't mean I thought I was capable of the same things. "What if I still don't believe I'm a witch?"

There was no emotion on Rand's face as he neared me. "Then you won't be able to stop me from kissing you."

I wanted nothing more than for him to kiss me. I also wanted him as far away as possible because I couldn't fathom the idea of being kissed. I wouldn't be a good kisser. So much though I hated the idea, when he came close, my frenzied mind pictured an invisible bubble surrounding me.

A look of surprise seized Rand's face when he moved in for the kiss and, instead, found himself buttressed by a transparent wall. He backed away instantly, as if he'd been burned. I guess, in a manner of speaking, he had been.

"Rand, wait," I started, my voice failing me at the most inopportune moment.

His eyes were like those of a statue, stoic and revealing nothing. "That's enough practicing for tonight," he said, and his voice was empty. He started for the door before I could stop him, and I stood there like an idiot, not knowing what to do. I was so befuddled, I didn't even get the chance to contemplate the fact that I'd stopped Rand's advances with my mind—with, dare I say it … magic.

The sound of the door slamming behind him ricocheted through me like a bullet and wedged itself right into my heart.

FOUR

Rand's hands tightened on mine. I gazed into the rich chocolate of his eyes and thought I was an absolute moron. I had to be the only woman on the planet who wouldn't allow herself to kiss such an incredible looking man. I closed my eyes against the idiocy of the whole damned thing.

Sitting Indian-style on the floor in the Fords' home, my gaze darted around the room and rested on Christa who sat on the sofa inspecting her nails … again. Then my eyes sought Rand who patiently waited for me to see something … again. And as with the last attempts, nothing happened. I concentrated and tried to get angry, remembering how that had worked when I'd moved the glass.

Nothing at all. Maybe I just wasn't cut out for this.

"Jolie, are you focusing?" Rand asked.

"Yes," I snapped. "If I focus anymore I'm going to focus myself right into a coma!" I hadn't meant for my words to sound so acerbic, but by the smile on his lips, he hadn't taken them as such.

He squeezed my hand. "Okay, just wanted to be sure. Keep going."

I didn't say anything but nodded and closed my eyes again, focusing as hard as I could. I tried to envision the room around me, as it would've been ninety years ago, but still nothing. Course, I didn't really know what was in vogue ninety years ago, so I couldn't make much of a mental picture for myself—just a room with one of those old model radios—the kind that are about four feet tall. And a picture of Clark Gable. Was good ol' Clark even around in the twenties? Sheesh … history lesson on aisle five!

My head began to thud, as if rebelling against the idea of concentrating anymore, and my butt had grown numb hours ago. In fact, my entire body felt strangely numb. Deciding I'd had enough, I opened my eyes.

I was alone.

I turned my head, expecting to find Christa and Rand hiding behind a wall, ready to jump out and scare me, but it was eerily quiet. Where the hell had they gone? Panic began a slow spiral through my stomach, working its way up my throat until I thought I might retch. Needing to calm myself, I forced my attention to the hardwood floors, taking note of every fleck in the wood. The floors gleamed in the light as if someone had just cleaned them, which was odd, as I could've sworn this place had carpeting. My gaze shifted to the curtains, and that was when I realized I'd actually done it.

I was in 1922, and in 1922, this house had curtains instead of blinds.

I breathed in through my nose, out through my mouth, repeating the process until the nausea faded into oblivion. After realizing Rand couldn't be

31

accounted for, I had to suppress the tide of anxiety welling within me. I guess I'd have to find out who killed Jack alone.

I perched on the edge of the sofa while my eyes traced the large floral pattern of the sofa and matching loveseat, trying to find a sense of calmness in the pink blooms. My attention shifted to the coffee table where a newspaper lay in dishevelment, its insides gutted across the table. It was the Chicago Daily Times. I grabbed the section looking most intact. In large black print it read: *What's Wrong With the Criminal Court?*

The strangest feeling of euphoria washed over me as I considered I was living history first hand. Strangely enough, the feeling made my stomach heave again. Not wanting to throw up, I started my breathing exercises—inhale for a count of four, exhale for a count of four. I wouldn't let Rand down.

Now, the only problem … where was Jack?

I dropped the newspaper and stood up, deciding it was time to play detective. I needed to find Jack and preferred to do so quickly—I wasn't sure how long I'd be able to last in this vision. As I walked through the living room, I noted black and white pictures of Jack with a pretty woman and a smiling baby.

In the kitchen, I paused to take in the squat, white refrigerator and the white enamel kitchen range—something straight out of a bygone era. Well, if nothing else, this little expedition was going to end up being quite the history lesson.

At the sound of the front door opening, my heart dropped as if it had been on the top story of the Empire State Building. What would Jack do upon seeing me? Steeling my courage, I ventured into the living room where I watched Jack hang his fedora-looking hat on a coat rack. He walked as if he were en route to the hangman's platform.

He turned, and his cold eyes drilled into me. I tried to come up with a plausible explanation as to why I was in his house, uninvited. He came closer, and if looks could kill, I'd have been pronounced dead on the spot. Jack didn't say a word. Before I could duck out of the way, he walked right through me! It felt like a great wind blowing through my entire being. I braced myself against the wall, having a serious case of Jello legs.

Okay, so I was the ghost in this situation. I couldn't say I was comfortable with that thought but forced it out of my mind, lest it interfere with my mission.

After getting my wits back, I followed Jack into the kitchen. He made himself a chicken sandwich, the whole time banging and slamming this and that. It didn't take a genius to figure out something was amiss.

Then the front door opened, and I peered around the corner of the wall. A woman walked inside. I recognized her from Jack's family photo as his wife. She was pretty with short bobbed hair, wide set eyes, and a trim body. Tears stained her cheeks, and the mascara smudges under her eyes gave her a zombie sort of look. She took her shoes off at the door.

Her small, stockinged feet barely made a sound as she marched right into the kitchen where Jack ate his sandwich. She didn't even bother putting her purse down or taking off her coat.

Before I could comprehend it, she pulled a pistol from her clutch and aimed it at the back of his head. There was no hesitation before she pulled the trigger.

I moved as if waist deep in molasses and tried to push Jack out of the way. As soon as I touched him, the brightest of lights seemed to penetrate through him until it completely encompassed us both. I glanced down and the white ray of light shone right through me, like I was merely a projection. I had to close my eyes against the intensity of the glare. As soon as my eyelashes met my upper cheeks, a jolt sailed through me and I had the vision of energy, of life leaving my body. The hairs on my skin stood to attention. I suddenly felt extremely tired, drained. I felt myself drop. I hit something hard and my eyes blinked open. I was on the floor, the yellow linoleum cold underneath my cheek. Pushing myself onto my hands and knees, I glanced at the wall before me. It looked like someone had thrown buckets of tomato red paint against the otherwise pristine white of the wall. Then I made the mistake of looking at Jack. Half his face was gone, pieces of bone, brain, and other head debris decorating the floor behind him.

Hyperventilating, I pushed myself away from him and clasped my eyes together, hoping the darkness would erase any residue of the hideous scene before me.

You're okay, Jolie, you're okay. Just breathe. I tried to talk myself down but couldn't shake the image of Jack's brain spread out on the floor like spilled cat litter.

I pried my eyes open, glanced down at myself and noticed my figure disappearing. My feet were already transparent and the rest of me was becoming cloudy, as if a fog were twirling up my legs, erasing me as it went. A scream of pure, unadulterated terror cut through the air like a razor blade and it took me a second to realize the scream was mine.

"Jolie!" I heard a deep voice and felt a smart slap to my face.

"Wake up, Jolie! Blast it, wake up!"

I came to with a start, blood pumping in my ears until it sounded like a chorus of demons singing bass. I was on the floor with Rand hovering over me. I sat bolt upright and glanced around, trying to get a grasp of what the hell had just happened. I noted Rand and Christa but I could definitely feel someone else in the room. I turned and found Jack, in his corporeal body, staring at me with his mouth hanging open.

Jack was no longer a ghost.

And, luckily for him, it appeared as if he'd never been shot at all. His head was in remarkably good condition.

"What the ..." I began when it dawned on me that maybe I'd changed places with him and I was now the ghost. A shriek of horror welled up within me, but was gobbled up by Christa who engulfed me in her arms.

33

"Thank God you're alright! I thought you were going to die!"

I pried her arms from my neck. "What the fu ..." I interrupted myself, thinking I should inspect my arms to ensure there was nothing ethereal about them. Nope, I looked as fleshy as Rand and Christa ... and Jack. Then I got angry. "What the flipping hell crap-shit was that?"

As soon as I met Rand's gaze, I knew it was bad—shock on the face of a powerful warlock is not a good thing. "I don't know. You started to scream and then Jack's ghost disappeared and was replaced with ... the real Jack," he said.

I looked up at the person in question and found he was the only one of us wearing a smile.

"I'm Jack," he said, as if we were on a dating game and I'd just selected undead bachelor number six-six-six.

"But he's ... he's dead," I insisted.

Rand frowned. "Was dead. It seems you brought him back to life." Rand was so matter of fact, he might as well have just given the weather report.

"I did what?" I squealed. But that wasn't possible! Like children playing tag, my thoughts scattered as I tried to find a logical reason as to how this could be. How in the hell did I, Jolie Wilkins, manage to bring back a dead person? I couldn't even balance my checkbook! "But that wasn't supposed to happen. I did what you told me to do!" I wailed, my voice cracking.

Rand put his hand on my upper arm. Instantly, the anxiety seeped from my body, replaced with a soft calm. Ah, warlock magic.

"You did everything perfectly, Jolie. I think I underestimated your abilities."

"Well how are we going to send him back?" I asked, still shell-shocked.

"Hell, I'm not going back!" Jack said from the corner. "This is better than I'd hoped for. All I wanted to know was who killed me, and you did one better, you brought me back to life!"

Who killed him? Oh, yeah, about that, I wasn't sure if I could tell him his beloved wife killed him. Perfect time for a little one on one with Rand.

His wife killed him. I'm not sure we should say anything about it.

Rand's gaze jumped from Jack to me and he raised a brow. I wasn't sure if he was surprised due to the situation or the fact that I was teleconnecting with him.

I don't think he's much concerned with it. We can discuss it later. ... Are you alright? Christ, you scared me.

I think I'm okay. Just a bit shocked.

"So is this a success, then?" Christa asked. "Do we go back to LA tomorrow?"

Hmm, that was a good question. Was this a success, or would Rand want to send Jack back? Did this break some sort of rule in the universe? I had no idea. And if Rand did want to send Jack back, how would he? I didn't think he'd just kill Jack, that didn't seem the right thing to do.

"I don't know what to do at the moment," Rand said.

34

"I'm not going back," Jack interrupted, and his gaze rested on me. "That little fox brought me back an' I'm obliged to ya, ma'am." He inclined his head toward me.

Little fox?

What do we do now? I asked Rand.

I don't know. I thought it was going to be a simple matter of finding out who killed him. Now, I'm not sure what I'm going to tell my friend.

Your friend?

The woman who hired me is his daughter.

Well this was quite the quandary—would the daughter be pleased her long dead father was now alive and probably three times younger than she was? Or would I be in a serious pile of crap?

"What are we doin' sittin' around here?" Jack asked. He stood up, then swayed as if he were a bit rocky on his feet and not used to the weight of his body. I guess being a ghost for nearly ninety years will do that to you.

It was just a matter of time before Christa chimed in. I gave her less than five seconds.

"Yeah! We should go out!" It had taken her about two seconds.

"I'm not sure that's such a good idea ..." Rand started, looking at me as if he thought I needed some recuperation time. At least someone was thinking about me.

Jack neared the door and threw off Rand's caution with a wave of his jelly-like arm. Apparently, Jack didn't realize that if Rand didn't want him to leave, he wasn't going to.

"There's a whole city alive out there that I haven't seen in nearly one hundred years ..." Jack began. Christa was right beside him.

I faced the glum countenance of Rand and smiled, thinking I needed a drink. Yeah, that's exactly what I needed—a drink or five.

"What harm could it do?" I asked.

"Bloody hell," Rand grumbled and apparently realizing it was three against one, reached for his coat. So it was set, we were going for a night on the town—quite the motley crew: a warlock, a witch in denial, a badly dressed woman, and a re-animated dead man.

~

I sat in an over-stuffed booth and tried to breathe through the cloud of smoke that billowed out of the nightclub. And I don't mean cigarette smoke. This smoke was white pina-colada scented puffs that served no purpose other than irritating me. Hip-hop blared out of the one-room club, making it tough to hear myself think. There were another four booths that circled the small dance floor that was so packed with people, they only had enough room to sway in place.

To the casual observer, the other four booths would've been entirely more engrossing than ours—their occupants either making out, fighting, or partaking of some illegal substance.

Rand had ordered a round of drinks, and now he and I sat in silence, keeping a sharp eye on Jack, who was dancing with Christa and seemed about as happy as happy could be. As was to be expected, Jack had been shocked by the Chicago of today when compared to one hundred years ago. He seemed to deal with it well enough, though, with the help of a few shots of whiskey and a toast to the death of prohibition.

Rand on the other hand, didn't seem quite as jovial. It'd been a good five minutes that he'd said nothing. He continued to scour the place, as if afraid someone was waiting in the shadows to snatch Jack away.

"So what do you suppose happened?" I yelled, trying to best the volume of the club's sound system. "How did I manage to bring Jack to life again?"

Rand faced me with a small smile, so small I couldn't see his dimples and felt cheated.

I've never seen anything like it before. There was a brilliant light and then Jack was lying on the floor in the kitchen ... alive.

I grinned as I realized I didn't need to scream to compete with the noise of the club. I'd forgotten we could converse through thoughts. *Wow, that's pretty much what happened to me. I saw a bright light too and it felt like energy was flowing out of me or something. When I came out of it, Jack was dead. Then I started screaming.*

And I slapped you. Sorry about that, by the way.

I wasn't concerned with apologies at the moment. I was still caught up in the why and the how of it. Maybe I'd managed to lend some of my own life to Jack? I wasn't sure I liked the sound of that, though. I'd rather keep my life to myself, even if it did make sense. I'd had the distinct feeling, at the time, that I was losing some part of me. And if such were the case, I had to wonder what that meant for me. Would it shorten my own life? I certainly felt fine now, as if it had never happened.

I hate having unanswerable questions.

How do you think your friend will react to us resurrecting Jack? I asked.

I don't know. His daughter is a witch ... a strong one at that and one I don't want as an enemy.

I sipped my amaretto sour, my drink of choice. *And she hired you?*

He nodded. *Sort of. It's more of a favor.*

So if she's a witch, does that mean Jack has special powers?

Rand shook his head, and I imagined we must've looked mighty odd to anyone who hazarded a glance our way. Neither one of us talking, but making gestures as if we were ...

No, Jack was ... well, is a normal human.

Thousands of questions percolated through my head like a swarm of locusts. *Why couldn't she just find out who killed him herself? Seems weird for her to wait so long.*

Rand sighed as if he wasn't in the mood for explanations. *Witches and warlocks all exceed at certain things; we don't all have the same powers. She couldn't have done the spell herself. Perhaps we could've done it together in time, but I don't trust her, never have. I needed someone I could trust.*

So he didn't trust the Wicked Witch of the West, but he trusted me? The thought made me tingle with pride, like the feeling a nerdy kid gets in PE when the popular kids pick him to be on their team.

There was a lull in the music, so I thought I'd give my voice a try.

"Why did she wait so long?"

"Witchcraft is a lot like technology, we make leaps and bounds over the years. Neither she nor I would've been strong enough to attempt something like this forty years ago."

Hmm. That was interesting. So what did it mean that I was able to bring Jack back? Maybe I did have more ability than I thought. That was sort of a nice feeling. I'd never excelled at much in my life. Sure, I'd been a good enough student, but I never stood out. No homecoming queen or valedictorian for me. I was just the girl next door, the one on the sidelines. And now? Well now, I did have something to feel proud about, something infinitely better than homecoming queen or class president.

"Does this mean Christa and I can go back to LA?" I asked, sipping the last of my sour. I noticed Rand was already on his second double Jameson. Apparently, warlocks could hold their alcohol.

The music started up again.

I suppose so. You did the job I hired you for.

The very beginning of a smile tugged at his lips, his dimples just barely cresting. My blood warmed at the expression, and I had to look away. I couldn't say I shared his amusement with the whole situation. The stupid truth of it was that I felt an infinite sadness with the prospect that our little mission was at its end. I downed the remnants of my sour, hoping I'd swallow my gloom at the same time.

It occurred to me I was developing feelings for Rand, and I was definitely not okay with that. Having a crush, or whatever you want to call it, on anyone was dangerous—that whole broken heart thing not sounding especially appealing. But someone like Rand ... I couldn't even contemplate it. True, I was a bit lonely but other than that, it wasn't half-bad. I had a nice house and a reliable car, a cat that needed me, and a best friend. The last thing I wanted was an emotional devastation. Yes, feelings for Rand were not a good idea.

I looked up and found Rand studying me. A flush crept up my neck like a thief in the night, and I faced my drink again, playing with the ice cubes. I blinked and the glass was full. I had to stifle a gasp and looked up with wide eyes.

Looked like you needed another one.

Why'd you buy them the first time around? I thought, taking a sip. It tasted even better than the first—stronger, sweeter.

37

He shrugged. *Best not to arouse suspicion.*

It seems like you're very careful about people's suspicions?

There are rules in this lifestyle and one of them is that we have to blend in with everyone else, not draw attention to ourselves. It wouldn't be a good situation were people to find out we exist.

I nodded, as if I could commiserate. *Well, thanks for the drink.*

I scanned the room, my attention falling on Jack and Christa who were dancing pretty close. Oh no, tell me she wasn't going to go for the newly undead? Christa amazed me. Find a good-looking guy and she was all over him. I was somewhat surprised she'd given up on Rand. He was definitely more the prize than Jack.

What's on your mind?

Hmm, might as well tell him the truth. *I'm just watching Jack and Christa. I'm surprised she's set her sights on him. I didn't think she'd give up on you quite so soon.* I held my glass up as if to cheers him and his incredible looks.

Rand chuckled. *Ah, well, about that ... I put a halt to it. Now, she thinks of me as her brother.*

Surprise pulled on my eyelashes, forcing my eyes wider. *Why'd you do that? Christa's a beautiful girl.*

Yes, she is, but not one I'm interested in. I don't mix business with pleasure.

I couldn't help but recall our near kiss, and my heart suffered as if Cupid was stabbing it with his little arrow. Maybe he'd known I'd pull away? Either way, Rand was right; it was common sense not to mix business with pleasure. I should be thinking the exact same way; I was thinking the exact same way.

Good motto, I thought with a grin.

He nodded, but his eyes held a vacant stare, like a mannequin. He strummed his fingers on the table and continued staring into space. I couldn't say I was enjoying my evening with Vapid Man and my stomach churned with the liquor I'd forced into it. Hmm, maybe Rand's magic amaretto sour was much better quality than its unmagic cousin.

My hotel room started calling my name.

"I think I'm going to call it a night," I said and made a motion of standing, swaying with the effort.

Rand wore a look of surprise. "So early?"

"Yes, I'm not feeling great."

Rand stood and scanned the crowd, his gaze resting on Jack. Then he faced me again. "I'll walk you to your room."

"No need. I can find my way back."

"I insist." It was futile arguing with him. He sure took this gentleman stuff to extremes.

"What about Jack?"

He held my arm, and we neared the door. "I put a charm on him. He won't be able to move from that spot."

"Can you do the same for Christa?"

"Already did. They won't notice a thing."

We walked out of the club, and I found myself in the rain again, the drops plastering my hair to my face until I'm sure I looked like a drowned rat. Rand hailed a cab and opened the door for me as I crawled in. I was careful to keep to my side of the cab, not wanting to give Rand the wrong idea—especially after his comment about separating business and pleasure.

The five-minute cab ride was a silent one. Before I knew it, we pulled up to the hotel, and a squat valet opened the door for me. I ran for the lobby, not wanting the rain to further destroy any semblance of attractiveness I might have left. My hair was beyond repair, but hopefully my mascara wasn't running. Rand caught up with me and the rain dripped down his face, testing my restraint to dab the drops away.

"Well, thanks for getting me back to the hotel," I said.

"I'd like to see you to your room, if you don't mind."

I swallowed my surprise and didn't have a chance to respond before the elevator dinged and opened its doors. Rand took my arm and led me in, hitting the button for the sixth floor as the doors closed behind us.

"Your hands are freezing," he said and rubbed them between his. I didn't respond, and the elevator dinged again, announcing my floor. I stepped out and watched Rand do the same. I guess he was serious about walking me to my door.

"Well, thanks Rand," I started.

"Do you mind if we talk some more?"

I shrugged, secretly delighted he wanted to stay. "Sure. I should start to feel better soon, I hope."

I slipped the room key into the slot and pushed against the door when it blinked green. Rand followed me inside and shut the door behind him. I turned around and had to stifle my gasp when I found him directly in front of me.

"Where do you feel sick?"

I backed away a step. "My stomach hurts."

With no hesitation, he sealed the distance between us, placing his hand on my belly. His other hand went around my back to steady me. Before I had a chance to squirm, wish my stomach were smaller, or ask what the hell was going on, I no longer felt sick.

He backed away then and I breathed a sigh of relief. "Wow, I feel a lot better."

Rand took a seat on a wingchair near the bed. "You can do that to yourself as well. Next time you have a headache, just put your hand on your head, and focus all your energy on removing the pain."

Good to know. "Thanks. What else can I do?"

He kicked his long legs up on the ottoman and I couldn't help but notice how large his feet were. Ergh.

"Whatever you want, you just have to make sure your focus is there, that's all it is. Focusing on what you want to happen and then making it happen."

Wow! This sounded pretty cool. I took my jacket off, contemplating some of the different things I might want to do with this newfound power. Change the curtains in the room? No, not that interesting, and I'm sure hotel management wouldn't approve. My gaze settled on my reflection in a mirror at the far corner of the room.

Perfect.

"Teach me how to change myself."

Rand's brows knitted together as he stood up and closed the distance between us. "Why would you want to do that?"

"I want to see what I'd look like with different hair and ..." His frown deepened. "It's just for fun, Rand."

He shook his head, the beginnings of a smirk toying with his sumptuous lips. Setting his hands on my shoulders, he pushed me toward the mirror. He stood so close behind me I could feel his heat and had to fight the urge to sink into him. His face in the mirror behind me was so perfect, I imagined he'd done some magic work on himself. How could anyone be so handsome?

"Look at yourself and focus on what you want to do."

His breath tickled the fine hairs on my ear and I nearly forgot what I'd set out to do. "I want to change my eyes to brown," I finally managed. I met his gaze, and he mouthed: *focus*. Pulling my attention from his male perfection, I focused. And focused.

"Nothing's happening."

Rand chuckled. "Maybe because your beautiful blue eyes are offended."

Beautiful blue eyes? Wow, had that come out of his mouth? I couldn't help the smile that tugged at my lips. Apparently, Rand caught the smile as his expression changed to one of contemplation.

"Jolie, you're beautiful. You don't believe it, but you should. I don't know why you have so much self doubt, but a successful witch must believe in herself."

"I'm not a witch," I said automatically.

"Maybe not yet, but you're a witch in training. You were born with the gift and now we just need to hone it."

I turned from the mirror and noticed he was only inches away. His proximity caused a sense of breathlessness within me—the feeling you get when surfacing after holding your breath under water for too long.

He needed to understand I was no witch and never would be. I was just a girl from Spokane who could see weird stuff and sometimes see visions of the future. And okay, most recently bring back dead people. But I was no witch.

"I don't want to be a witch."

Rand's brows drew together. "Why? You're very powerful. You have more potential than I've ever seen in anyone."

"Well that's all fine and good, but I like my life as it is."

40

Rand sighed and rubbed the back of his head as if he couldn't grasp the fact that I wouldn't want to be a witch, as if being a witch were like winning the Miss America title.

"This is a calling, Jolie, not a decision for you to make. Witches are born this way, they aren't created."

If witches were born in such a way, then I was definitely not one. My mother was a very religious woman and had no witch anything about her and my father (rest his soul) had been pretty much the same. "Neither of my parents are witches," I said with a knowing smirk, as if I'd bested the warlock.

Rand's lips downturned, and his eyes filled with what I can only term annoyance. "That's a subject for another day."

"You aren't going to tell me I'm adopted, are you?"

He shook his head. "No, nothing as dramatic as that. Your parents don't need to be witches or warlocks. As long as one of them is the descendent of a witch or warlock, they can pass the trait to their offspring, and such is the case with you."

I narrowed my eyes. "So who was the witch or warlock descendant then?"

"How the bloody hell should I know? Ask your mother." Before I had the chance to respond, he continued. "You are a witch as much as I am one."

"But how do you know?" I couldn't keep the edge from my voice.

"You can see auras. So can I. Yours looks the same as you described mine—electric blue."

I got him there. "I've never seen my own aura, so I know that isn't true."

"No one can see her own aura," Rand said with tight lips, clearly not enjoying this argument.

I couldn't say anything to that, so I didn't. In angry submission, I turned toward the mirror again. Rand leaned down, his face parallel with mine. The planes of his face were so different to mine—angular and chiseled while mine were softer, rounder.

"Use your anger, Jolie, focus it, and use it."

I focused and willed my damn blue eyes to turn brown. My pupils dilated until they eclipsed the entirety of my eyes and I looked like some sort of alien. Then the black slowly faded into a rich dark brown. I pulled back and stared at myself. "Did I …"

"You did it yourself," he interrupted me.

I forced myself to concentrate on the mirror again, wanting to continue to test the boundaries of this new talent. What to do next … my lackluster blond hair hung around my face, just begging for an update. I focused on the dull strands and watched as a dark shadow started at the top of my head and like a cracked egg, seeped down the sides of my head, leaving my hair black in its trail. It seemed easier now. Maybe because the task was not a huge one. Changing one's physical appearance had to be ten times easier than willing yourself to travel back in time or inadvertently reviving someone who'd been dead for nearly ninety years.

I faced myself again and thought how odd I looked with brown eyes and black hair. Rand chuckled at the transformation. "Much better fair," he said and with a blink, my eyes and hair were back to normal. Apparently he didn't like the altered me.

"Hey! I wasn't finished."

He focused on me, his eyes narrowing as he bit his lip. "Perhaps some depth to that hair ..."

I looked in the mirror and watched as my hair seemed to take on its own personality, winding itself into tight coils only to drop in billowy waves around my shoulders. So Rand liked longer hair ...

I considered the new look. "Hmm, not bad."

Rand continued to study me; the smile on his lips signifying that he was enjoying this as well. "That lipstick is too red on you."

When I looked from him to the mirror, the red disappeared as if someone had swept it away. In its place, a light pink danced across the planes of my lips. I guess he had a point there. I'd never been good with makeup and just settled for borrowing Christa's colors. And Christa's makeup was ... vivid, like her personality.

"I never thought I was capable of any of this," I said in a small voice as I gazed upon my reflection.

"This is just the beginning."

I didn't respond, but just nodded dumbly.

"Well, Jack and Christa must be tired," Rand said, clasping his hands in an "I'm going to leave now" motion.

Tired? Then I remembered the spell Rand had put on them and figured they must've been dancing for over an hour! "Holy crap!"

Rand waved a hand to calm me down. "They'll be fine. They won't even know there's anything out of the ordinary. Well, I'll say goodnight, Jolie. I had a fun evening with you."

He neared the door and paused, as if he wanted to say something more.

I stood up and followed him. "Thank you, Rand, I had fun also."

He hesitated only momentarily. "I've booked you and Christa on a flight home tomorrow. I'll need to remain here to tie up some loose ends."

My heart dropped and my throat felt like it was closing in on itself. "So I guess this is goodbye?" My voice was an octave or so deeper than it normally is.

"I'm afraid so." He fished inside his pants pocket and pulled out his wallet. My heart took a further dump. He pulled out a folded check and handed it to me. "What I owe you and a ... tip."

I smiled, trying to keep up the appearance of being okay, trying to mask the fact that I would miss him ... I could feel it already—like a scream sounding from the bottom of a long well. I accepted the check and put it on the table next to my bed. Steeling my courage, I forced myself to look into the abyss of his beautiful chocolate eyes.

"Thanks, Rand."

He nodded and seemed as much at a loss for words as I was. "You did an … incredible job. I'm very proud of you."

Tears started in my eyes, and I furiously blinked them away. I knew my voice would crack if I attempted to say anything, so I saved myself the embarrassment and just offered a petite smile. Rand responded by extending his hand. I grasped it, and his electricity pumped through me, saying goodbye in its own way. He dropped my hand and crossed the threshold into the hall. With a quick nod, he started down the hallway. I watched his retreating figure until he turned the corner and walked out of my life.

FIVE

After about a week, I slipped into the usual swing of things and found my life pretty much back on track. It seemed business picked up a bit more, and I suspected Rand had been the reason for my dip in sales, knowing I'd be more apt to accept his invitation to Chicago if I were hard up. I guess I should've been pissed off, but the anger abated once I thought about the tip he'd given me. Let's just say it wasn't standard English etiquette where gratuity is concerned.

"So what are you gonna do with all that money?" Christa asked, leaning her elbows on the front desk.

I shrugged, slumping in the chair behind the desk. "I don't know."

Christa nodded, and I imagined she had some very good ideas as to what I should do with it. "You should buy a new car."

I swiveled back and forth in the chair, thinking there was a definite squeak coming from it. "Why? What's wrong with the Jetta?"

"It's just getting older."

"It's only five years old, Chris. Sheesh!" I had no interest in selling my car. For now, the money could just sit there and build interest.

"Or you could come with me when I take my photography trip."

That was an option.

"Do you even know when and where you're going?"

She shrugged. "Well, not totally. Maybe Italy, maybe England. I've heard Scotland has some beautiful places … and guys."

I laughed. "Been reading more Scottish romances, have we?"

Christa sighed, no doubt picturing a hulking Scottish laird in a kilt and nothing else. "Well, even if I don't know where I'm going, would you want to come with me?"

"I'll think about it. It does sound fun and I'm not sure I'd want you to take a trip like that by yourself, anyway." I was silent as I considered it.

"Well, I did really like Diana Gabaldon's books," I said, thinking maybe Scotland wasn't such a bad idea.

She just smiled and returned her attention to the People magazine before her, humming something I didn't recognize. My gaze fell to the cover of the magazine, and my lips tightened. I didn't know how she could read such crap. I couldn't care less what Brad Pitt was up to or how many times Britney Spears was going to have an emotional breakdown.

"Have you heard from Rand?" Her tone was nonchalant, but she might as well have told me she'd drowned a litter of puppies for the reaction Rand's name had on my stomach.

44

"No." My thoughts immediately painted the picture of my last meeting with Rand, how depressed I'd been at the prospect of never seeing him again. Unfortunately, my feelings hadn't ebbed. To make matters worse, I dreamed of him almost every night, and the dreams were always the same—Rand's lips on mine, the scent of spice thick in the air, our bodies entwined. I'd wake in a sweat, completely unfulfilled. I wondered when I'd get Rand out of my head and prayed it would be soon.

Christa closed her magazine and eyed me as a painter would a potential subject. She chewed on her cheek, and that meant a deep conversation was on the way. I groaned. I didn't like deep conversations.

"Jules ..." Here it came. "You seem ... different since we got back. Like really depressed."

I sighed but knew I wouldn't be able to sidestep this conversation. Since Christa was my best friend, I guess I owed her my honesty. "It's been a little tough getting back into the swing of things since Chicago."

"Is it Rand?"

I nodded, eyeing a pencil on the top of the desk. Grabbing it, I tapped the eraser against my lips, wishing I could cut thoughts of Rand right out of my brain. "I'm peeved that I didn't pursue him when I had the chance."

She agreed with a nod of her head. "He was definitely interested in you."

I laughed, but the sound was hollow, sad even. "I blew it. But, to be honest, if I had the chance to go back, I'd probably end up doing the same thing all over again. I'm a real head case, aren't I?"

"No, Jules, you aren't."

That wasn't the only reason for my depression lately. I was having trouble trying to lead a normal life after uncovering the incredible powers I possessed. I'd sit in front of the mirror for hours at a time, using magic to change my hair and makeup. I even started experimenting with various outfits I saw in magazines, recreating them on myself.

Sometimes I'd concentrate so hard my head would ache, and then I'd have to focus on taking the pain away until I fell into a comatose stupor. But I was honing my craft and getting better and better, finding my fastest time now reduced to seconds.

So here I was the same Jolie, but not quite the same. There was a confidence within me that was truly new, yet I was still too disenchanted with myself to believe such a handsome man as Rand had actually been interested in me. The thought drilled into me day after day ... not that it mattered now since I'd never see him again.

Not enjoying my glum thoughts, I threw the pencil against the table and stood, pacing our small front office. I couldn't bring myself to study the financials, review my appointments for the week, or care about the thin layer of dust covering everything. My mind was absorbed with thoughts of Rand—what he was doing, where he was, if I'd ever see him again.

The buzz of the bell above the door pulled me from my reverie. A woman strode in, her electric blue aura announcing her arrival. I narrowed my eyes, my instincts instantly on the alert. I knew what a blue aura meant.

I'm not sure she was technically beautiful, but she carried herself as if she were the quintessential embodiment of beauty. Her oval face finished in a square jaw and her rosebud mouth would make a rose envious. Her hair had a reddish tinge, and her skin was so perfect, it looked like expensive china, the kind newlyweds register for. So she could be a poster child for Neutrogena, I wasn't envious …

Even with her attractive face and Marilyn Monroe-esque figure, there was a hardness about her, a hardness that somehow seemed familiar. Of course, I'd never met her before, so I attributed the feeling to that weird sense of déjà vu that sometimes hits you like a great gust of wind straight from another life.

She ignored Christa who lifted her hand in greeting. The woman's eyes focused on mine and they were so piercing, my eyes watered.

She hadn't come for a reading.

"Are you Jolie Wilkins?" she snapped.

I didn't want to answer—she kind of scared the crap out of me. I couldn't just stand there gaping at her though. "Yes, how can I help you?"

She motioned to the back of the shop, apparently looking for some privacy. I swallowed hard and led her to the reading room, not missing Christa's raised brows as I closed the door behind us. The woman didn't take a seat.

"I'm Bella Sawyer," she said very matter-of-factly. "You know my father—you brought him back from the dead."

I could taste my own shock. The same flood of emotions that had seized me when I'd reanimated Jack now drowned me.

I nodded. "Yes, about that …" I started, wondering if one should apologize for reanimating a dead parent. Who knows, maybe she was here to thank me? She didn't look grateful though. …

She dismissed me with a wave of her manicured hand. "Never mind apologies, that's not why I'm here. I have a possible job for you—my father told me all about your abilities, and though Rand was less than forthcoming, I know he believes in you as well."

Rand's name piqued my curiosity, and I couldn't subdue the tempest that stormed within my stomach. God, I was in a sore position if merely hearing the man's name did this to me. "Does Rand know you're here?"

She shook her head, but her hair didn't move, every strand perfectly in place like soldiers in formation. "No. He wanted to keep you a secret, but secrets are not possible in our society." I figured she meant the society of witches or maybe otherworldly creatures. "Anyway, of course I'd pay you well," she finished.

My mind wasn't on the job. It hadn't quite gotten past the point she made about her "society" knowing of me. What did that mean exactly? Was I now on the Rolodex of witches, werewolves, vampires, and God knew what else?

"Are you interested?" she asked impatiently, reminding me that she was still standing there. I couldn't say I was interested. With her arms crossed against her chest and her narrowed eyes, she looked like she'd take first place in the World's Worst Boss contest.

"What's the job?"

"I'll discuss that with you later. I'm here to invite you to a party."

A party? I couldn't imagine Ms. Ice Queen would have any reason to befriend ordinary me. The fact that she'd just invited me to a party was so baffling, she might as well have told me she was with Publisher's Clearing House, and I'd just won one million dollars. What I could do with that ...

She reached inside her Prada purse and produced a card with an address written on it. She handed it to me, and her hand grazed mine. I didn't feel any electricity like I had when touching Rand. Interesting ... I filed that note for future reference.

My eyes fell to the card as I admired the curlicues in her writing. Not a nice witch, but she had nice penmanship. "A party for whom?" I asked.

"Just a party. It starts at ten tonight and if you want to come, don't be late." She started toward the door, but stopped and glanced back, a smirk on her face.

"Oh, and I hope you aren't frightened by vampires."

My gaze jumped from the perfumed card to her face as I searched for a semblance of humor in her menacing features. But humor wouldn't live long in a person like her so I reached the conclusion that she wasn't joking. "Um, I think it's safe to say I am frightened of vampires. How do I know I'm not on the menu?"

She laughed an ugly and tinny sound and opened the door, heading into the front room. "Much though vampires love the taste of witches, they'd never kill us. They need us too much." Her smile fell, and her expression turned hard again. "Besides, Rand will be there, and I'm certain he wouldn't allow a hair to be harmed on your pretty little head."

I couldn't picture Rand talking about me with anyone let alone Poison Ivy. What was this woman to Rand, I wondered. "Does Rand know you've invited me?"

She rolled her eyes in exasperation. "No, I've already told you he doesn't know I've come here."

Well she wasn't a warm witch, but if Rand would be at the party, I felt safer. "Okay, I'll be there."

"Oh, and wear a costume. It's a masquerade," she added before turning on her stiletto heel, frowning at Christa and throwing open the front door with a great show of indifference.

Once the door closed behind her, Christa faced me with wide eyes and I just shook my head. "Christa, I have a feeling we're not in Kansas anymore."

~

I glanced at the clock on the dash of my car. Crap. It was five minutes to ten, and I remembered Bella had been very specific about being on time. I narrowed my eyes and leaned forward, peering through the dirty windshield. As luck would have it, I was out of window washer fluid, and the dirt road kicked up a cloud of dust that obscured my view. Maybe this was a bad omen. I shirked off the feeling, knowing full well that my washer fluid is never full. I'm not a very responsible car owner.

My attention returned to the anxious humming in my stomach and I couldn't help but wonder what kind of idiot drives out to the middle of nowhere, alone, to a party full of witches and vampires? I didn't want to answer the question …

Well, idiot or no idiot, I was lost and running out of time. If I didn't see the house in five minutes, I'd take it as fate telling me not to go. Something along the lines of the fox trying to get the grapes and upon not reaching them, deciding they would've been sour anyway.

I rounded a bend, and a twinkle of lights in the distance interrupted the dark night. Depressing my foot from the accelerator, I turned onto a gravel drive. The house before me wasn't old or impressive like I'd imagined it would be. Instead, it was just a ranch house probably built in the seventies. The driveway was long, and attendants were parking cars. Jags, BMWs, and Porsches littered the driveway, making my little Jetta look like scrap metal. But I reminded myself that material things didn't impress me.

The valet opened the door and held out his hand.

"Thanks," I murmured, dropping my keys into his open palm. As fate would have it, the wings of my fairy costume caught in my seatbelt, and I had to battle with both in order to free myself as the valet looked on, trying to choke back a laugh.

About my fairy costume—Tinker Bell would've been proud with my mint green wings and strawberry pink dress, which I will admit, was on the exceedingly short side. Most of the time I'm not too keen about showing off the ol' bod, but when have you ever heard of a fairy in a long dress?

With an exasperated sigh, I jerked on my wings, but they refused to budge. This only further amused the attendant, who openly chuckled. I glared at him and when his attention shifted to my lap, I pulled down on my dress and gave him a scowl. Before I could straighten my wings, another valet appeared.

He reached inside and unhooked my wing from the seatbelt, giving his coworker a this-girl-is-an-idiot smile. I was so pissed off, I refused to take his offered arm and instead, followed him down the steep drive, wobbling in my four-inch pink hooker shoes.

He paused before a set of double oak doors then opened one of the doors and bowed low. I ignored him.

With a sigh, I turned to face the foyer, and my mouth dropped open. It wasn't the great expanse of white marble floor or the Corinthian columns

48

lining the walls or even the ornate tapestries that caused my disquietude. It was the fact that inside, this was a three-story mansion, and upon seeing it from the street, it appeared to be a one-story ranch house.

I forced myself forward, the tapping of my heels against the marble echoing the palpitations of my heart. The vestibule flared into a giant receiving room where jackets and other unnecessary pieces of clothing were strewn this way and that, some lucky enough to have found a hanger. I continued to follow the sounds of music and laughter, wondering what in the hell I'd managed to get myself into this time.

The hallway stopped at a wide set of stairs. Swallowing hard, I started up the steps. At the top of the staircase, I faced the grandest ballroom I'd ever seen—a white baby grand piano played itself, and Louis XIV armchairs and love seats decorated the perimeter of the room, the white marble floor paling against the ornate gold work of the furniture.

There were people (the word *people* used lightly as they were not your average humans) everywhere, and all were in costume. I tried not to stare as a woman walked by, her entire body painted as if she were a snake. I couldn't help my gaze as it followed her … yep, she was only wearing paint.

I pulled my attention back to the main ballroom, my blood rushing through my head, pounding in my ears. Most of the people in the ballroom were dancing and not the type of dancing I'm accustomed to—they were dancing on air, swaying as if an invisible floor were beneath their toes. Others stood along the sidelines, watching the dancers, and no one seemed to be in the least alarmed—as if this was an everyday occurrence and for all I knew, it probably was.

My shock turned to fear.

I slipped behind a marble column, trying to catch my breath. This was unreal, like nothing I'd ever seen before. The entire room seemed to be alive, vibrating with a foreign energy. There was a magic here that astounded me as much as it terrified me.

I forced myself to inhale through my nose and exhale through my mouth until my heart started cooperating. Peeking out from behind the column, I noted the various costumes in an attempt to change the direction of my wayward thoughts. There were plenty of vampire costumes, some pirates, witches everywhere, and other beings I couldn't even begin to categorize. I didn't see any fairy costumes, though, and worried I'd stand out.

I took a deep breath, settled myself, and started down the stairs. Searching the crowd for a familiar face, even that of Bella's would've been welcome at this point. Many eyes followed me, and I wondered if everyone knew I was a stranger and didn't belong. As I met the gazes of those in the room, not one person smiled. A dart of apprehension plunged through me. With their frowns and narrowed eyes, they looked downright hostile.

"Hello, poppet."

The voice next to my ear nearly made my heart stop. I whirled around, nearly losing my balance, courtesy of my ridiculous shoes, and found a vampire smiling at me—that is, a man dressed as a vampire. And a damn good-looking one at that. My hand went to my heart to calm its sporadic beating, and he laughed at my reaction.

"I did not intend to frighten you," he said with an English accent. My stomach flopped—I could honestly say I'd be happy never to meet another Englishman.

He was tall, maybe six-four or so and narrow other than a pair of decently broad shoulders. His black hair was gelled back and almost looked blue when the light hit it at a certain angle. His face was well-defined—high cheekbones and largish eyes that were so light they almost appeared to be white. Upon further inspection, though, they were ice blue. He'd drawn a widow's peak on himself, doing quite the good job of assuming the persona of a vampire.

I collected myself. "You didn't frighten me."

He reached for my hand, smiled as he took it in his, and brought it to his lips. I hadn't noticed until now that he had no aura. His hand was as cold as his eyes. Hmmm … very strange.

"Pleased to make your acquaintance, Miss?"

"Wilkins."

He swept his black cloak forward and bowed theatrically. "Ah, Miss Wilkins, you are ravishing, if I may say so."

"You can call me Jolie."

His expression changed then, and what appeared to be recognition flashed through his predatory eyes. He arched a dark brow and regarded me as if I was a Twinkie and he, a fat kid. "Ah, the witch Jolie, now I am even more pleased to make your acquaintance."

Unsettled by the fact that he knew who I was, my voice was shaky. "And who might you be?"

He bowed again. "You may call me the Count."

I laughed. "Nice costume. You look the part."

He grinned, and his canines lengthened before my eyes. I took a step back as my breath caught, seemingly too frightened to come out of my mouth. So vampires were real—Rand hadn't been fibbing.

I guess I looked frightened because he recoiled his fangs, attempting to set me at ease. His lips turned up in a grin, and warmth crawled up my neck. He was a feast to my eyes and judging by the arc of his brows, he knew it.

"Do not be frightened, I mean you no harm. I have heard of your incredible … talent. I had not heard of your incredible beauty. Although, I must say your frock is quite … brave."

I knew it was short, but there were costumes here that were easily more revealing than mine. As soon as the thought entered my head, a woman walked by sporting nothing more than two black pasties in the shape of witch hats covering her nipples and a pair of black thong underwear. I was dressed like a nun compared to her.

"Brave?" I laughed.

He shook his head and made a tsking sort of noise. "It appears our hostess did quite a lousy job of explaining, poppet."

Why the hell did he keep calling me poppet? If I were correct, it was a pet name in style hundreds of years ago. Well, I guess that answered the question of his age.

I returned to the subject of my costume and Bella's lousy job in preparing me for the party. "Maybe you can fill in where she failed?"

He chuckled and nodded, reaching for my arm to guide me to a vacant settee not far from where we stood. His hand was void of heat and felt odd against my skin—cold. I had to fight the urge to pull away.

"Well, where to begin … this party was given by Isabella, as I imagine you already know. It is in congratulations for the vampires who have now joined ranks with the witches."

I was confused already, and he'd only spoken two sentences. "What?" I managed unceremoniously. Hats off to the Count for not losing his cool.

I took a seat beside him, and he rested his arm behind me, stretching out his long legs and crossing them at the ankles.

"You are quite ill informed. Bella has been trying to unite all the night creatures—all vampires, wolves, demons, fairies—the whole lot of them. The vampires decided it was a good idea, so we joined her union and this party is in honor of that. Bella is hoping word will spread and eventually we will all join her cause."

"For what purpose?"

"Ah … well in the words of your honorable president, a house divided against itself cannot stand."

So the good Count knew of Abe Lincoln—maybe knew him personally. I wondered what all of this could mean—why Bella would even want to unite all the other creatures.

My attention returned to the friendly vampire, and I had to laugh—he was quite the cliché, being everything you'd picture a vampire to be—tall, good-looking, dark hair, light skin and a riddler at that.

"That is why I was saying your frock, er, costume was brave," the vampire finished and looked down at me in expectation.

I'd lost the train of thought and didn't want to appear dimwitted or slow, but it seemed such would be the case. "What was why you said my costume was brave?"

"Well, the vampires are the only ones to have joined ranks with the witches. The fairies have undoubtedly given the union the most difficult time, so it goes without saying your costume requires a certain level of … courage."

Great, so I'd been here for less than ten minutes and I'd already managed to offend everyone. Off to a great start.

I forced my attention back to the subject of the fairies while I thought this night couldn't get any weirder. Not only did fairies exist, but they wanted nothing to do with vampires or witches. I couldn't say I blamed them.

"Well, that would explain the unfriendly gestures in my direction."

51

"Indeed it would. I would not let it chagrin you, though, as I said before, you are quite easy on the eyes."

So now he was flattering me ... well flattery would get him nowhere. I might be slow when it came to the interests of the fairies and the unionized vampires and witches, but I was no idiot when it came to people with hidden agendas, and this vampire had one. "Well, thanks, but your charm won't work on me."

"I know. You are as immune to my charm as I am to your witchcraft." He laughed, the sound deep and rumbling. "I cannot bewitch you, so anything you feel toward me is purely your own desire."

Well, he certainly wasn't lacking in the vanity department. "What do you mean?"

He shrugged. "I cannot use my vampire powers of persuasion on you, love, so whatever you're feeling is genuine."

"How do you know I'm feeling anything toward you?" I asked, my tone biting.

He leaned closer to me, and I held my ground, not wanting him to think I couldn't. He came inches from my throat and inhaled deeply. It took all my gumption to sit there and allow him to do so. "I can smell the desire coming off you, my pet; it is the headiest of all perfumes." He inhaled again as if to prove his point.

I pulled away from him. "Unless you would rather grace someone else with your less-than-thrilling company, lay off."

"No need to grow angry, love."

"I'm not angry," I said, and the lie sounded stupid to my own ears. The vampire just smiled. "So my powers won't work on any otherworldly creatures?" I asked, ignoring him and the fact that he was right, I *was* lusting after him.

He shook his head, a deep chuckle resonating through him. "You are quite a new witch. All of this should have been explained to you. No, your powers will work on others, just not on vampires. We are immune to one another."

I nodded and decided to pay attention to my first mental note, that being trying to find out why Count Dracula had such an interest in me. First things first, find out his real name. "Your name can't really be Count?" I said, hoping he wouldn't riddle with me on that front.

He cocked an elusive brow. "It is not every day I am able to act the part of Count Dracula. What do you think of the costume?"

"I think it's pretty good but not very original."

He pressed his pale hand to his heart, feigning heartache, and I had to give it to him, he'd make a good actor. For all I knew, maybe he'd been one. "If I didn't know better, I'd say you're avoiding the question," I continued.

"Excuse my poor manners, poppet, Sinjin Sinclair at your service," he said with an orchestrated bow.

SIX

My heart fell to the floor. I'd thought there was something familiar about his face. This was the man Rand had warned me about! I didn't know what to do, so I smiled meekly. "Pleased to meet you."

He cocked an elegant brow. "Ah, do not look so disappointed. I suppose my reputation precedes me." He grinned with fangs again.

I was quick to respond, trying to conceal my disquietude. "So it would seem."

"Is the motto of this country not innocent until proven guilty?"

I had to give it to him, he was quick witted and … well, sexy as a son of a bitch. This Sinjin character didn't at all seem the dangerous vampire Rand had warned of.

Speak of the devil, no sooner had the thought crossed my mind than I spotted Rand across the ballroom. He was dressed as a pirate—patch over one eye, red and white striped and ripped pants, short beard, the complete package.

Our eyes met and surprise registered in his before he plowed through the room, looking like every woman's fantasy come to life. Sinjin, apparently noticing my attention was no longer his captive, turned to face Rand. I didn't miss the sigh that escaped his lips or the sag of his shoulders.

"Sod it, here comes the hero," he muttered, sounding like a child who'd been caught with his hand in the cookie jar.

With each step Rand took, the thumping in my chest increased. When he stopped in front of me, I had to catch my breath. He was taller and broader than I remembered.

God, I was a lovesick dumbass.

Ignoring Sinjin, he clasped onto my arm and yanked me to my feet. "Jolie, what the bloody hell are you doing here?" He pulled the patch away, so he could glare at me with both eyes.

"Hello Randall, how are you?" Sinjin asked with the same smile the serpent must have given Eve.

Rand didn't smile in turn. "You know quite well Randall isn't my name," he snarled between gritted teeth.

Sinjin shrugged, studying his fingernails. "Rand, Randall ... what difference does it make?"

Rand's color went from a very attractive tan to a pinkish to an out and out red. His aura vacillated, the tips glowing purple. "For the life of me, Sinjin, I can't figure out what business you have to discuss with Jolie. She isn't a full-fledged witch yet, you know that."

Sinjin grinned at me as a cat would a mouse. Maybe he was dangerous, certainly dangerously sexy.

"Do not be a todger, Randall. I have heard she is a new witch, yes, but I have also heard of her incredible … abilities." He eyed me up and down. "But Bella failed to mention how blessed she is … physically."

Even though he was smooth, I couldn't keep the warmth from seeping through me. I wasn't accustomed to such attention from the opposite sex, and I had to admit it felt good—especially since Sinjin Sinclair was a babe and a half.

Rand stepped in front of me, blocking Sinjin from view. "She's not interested in you, Sinjin, so go find another witch."

I peeked around Rand's back to find Sinjin frowning. It was funny actually—like I was in the midst of the best dream of my life—being fought over by a pirate and a vampire.

"I'm not looking for a row. I was merely making conversation with a beautiful woman." He winked at me.

Rand's jaw tightened, and he turned to give me a discouraging look—had he been Medusa, I'd now be a grinning statue.

"Sinjin, I'm bloody well warning you."

Rand clasped my hand and forced me away from Sinjin. I glanced over my shoulder at the man who could so rile the ordinarily languid warlock and caught his secretive smile—a smile that for all intents and purposes, was for me alone. I'd need to learn more about the history of these two.

When Rand decided we were far enough away from the vampire, he faced me. "Jolie, what are you doing here?" He looked every inch the pirate, and I couldn't stop the whirring of my overactive hormones. Pirates are pretty damn hot.

Then I remembered his salutation offended me. I crossed my arms over my chest and attempted my best glare. "No 'wonderful to see you again' or 'I love the costume.' Instead, all I get is 'what are you doing here?'" I paused to catch my breath. "I was invited."

"Who invited you?"

"Your friend Bella," I snapped. The purple edges of his aura flared up at the mention of Bella.

"Bollocks!"

I hadn't imagined he'd be thrilled to see me, but this apparent disinterest hurt. "You don't have to babysit me, Rand; you can go off and do whatever it was you were doing. I realize you didn't invite me, but I was invited all the same."

His expression softened. "I didn't mean to sound as if I'm not happy to see you, Jolie. I am. But I'm worried about your being here. Bella invited you so everyone would know who you are."

I shifted, scanning the crowd. "Why would she care if everyone knows who I am?"

He stepped closer to me, blocking the crowd from view. "To ensure you won't be able to return to your normal life. If you're known in this society, your powers will be known. Well, for all practical purposes, they already are.

News of your reanimating Jack spread like wildfire. I made a deal with Bella so you could go about living your life, and now I find you in the middle of the lion's den."

"A deal with Bella?" I asked, wishing someone would sit me down and fill me in.

Rand sighed as if the story would be a long one, but he must've known I'd demand answers. Grabbing my hand, he led me down a hallway into a bedroom. He closed the door behind me and motioned for me to take a seat on the bed. My thoughts immediately turned to our near kiss and I blushed like an idiot.

Rand didn't seem to notice. He paced the room, his hands on his hips. "I hoped I could spare you from all of this, but it appears that's not possible now. Bella …"

"Wants to unite all otherworldly creatures, and so far she's just succeeded with the vampires."

He nodded. "I see that bloody bastard Sinjin discussed it with you. Yes, that's so. Anyway, it's Bella's wish to unite all the non-human species."

"Why?" I interrupted.

He cupped his hands behind his head and exhaled. "It's a good plan in theory. There's too much warring between the legions—that is, the vampires kill the weres and the weres kill the fairies, and so on. Bella believes we would be much more powerful if we …"

"Could all just get along?" I interrupted, regretting the cliché and overused statement, but it just seemed to fit. "But for what purpose?"

Rand sighed and stopped in front of me. "Do you recall when I told you witches and warlocks are a dying breed?"

I nodded as he continued.

"About three centuries ago, a group of humans discovered a band of vampires and witches in the woods of Gratz, Austria. The humans attempted to escape, but the vampires defeated and fed on them, leaving them for dead. But some of them weren't dead and they survived the attack."

"Did they turn into vampires?" I interrupted.

"Not exactly. It's not possible to turn into a vampire unless you drink the blood of a vampire at the same time he drinks your blood. Anyway, somehow vampire blood did make its way into some of the humans and although it wasn't enough to turn them into vampires, it gave them extra strength and the quickness of a vampire. They became what we call Lurkers, humans who seek to destroy all otherworldly creatures. And their population has increased over the years. Now, they're the biggest threat to our existence."

And my existence. The thought wasn't a pleasant one.

"So Bella wants to unionize to defeat these humans? What's so wrong with that?"

"In theory, it's all fine and good, but Bella is not the ideal candidate to lead such an effort. She's out for herself and would take advantage of the position it would put her in."

55

I nodded, feeling the situation was finally making sense. "So how do I figure in this?"

"She wants to give everyone reason to join her. You're that perfect reason."

Well crap and a half, this couldn't be good. "Why?"

He shook his head, annoyed I wasn't following him. "There wouldn't be any bad blood between the creatures if you can bring back all their dead. In a way, we'd all start from scratch again, no harm done. That and it replenishes the union. No beings would ever need to die."

"Strength in numbers."

"Yes, so when news spread of Jack, I went to Bella, and I made an agreement with her. She was to leave you alone. I told her you weren't as strong as I'd thought and that I did the majority of the reanimation myself. Clearly, she didn't believe me."

My shoulders slumped, and I stared straight ahead, looking at everything, but seeing nothing. "So that's why Bella invited me to this party?"

"Yes, she wants to announce that you're now working for her."

My mind spun like a roulette wheel, and I wished I'd never agreed to come here. "Are you on her team?"

He shook his head. "No, I haven't yet agreed to anything. I was quite surprised to receive the invitation here tonight. I can only surmise Bella wanted to show me how many have already joined her ranks to entice me to her side."

"I see."

"Having you here tonight was much more important to her than having me join her legion, though. You're the newest and most valuable addition to the unionizing efforts. And now that you've shown your face, you can't return to your old life." There was a finite sadness to his voice.

I couldn't bridge the idea that my being here wouldn't allow me to return to my former life. "I'm not a prisoner. I can just walk away and go back home."

His smirk wasn't an encouraging one. "And she would come for you. An ability like yours won't be ignored."

Clearly, he was upset, and I still didn't know enough of why he was upset to be truly upset myself. "You said to Sinjin that I was just a new witch."

He shook his head and stepped back. "He knows I was trying to protect you. This couldn't have been any worse. I'm going to have words with Bella."

"Well, I could decline the offer."

He laughed as he shook his head. "You don't understand, Jolie, you have no choice. Our society isn't like yours. There's no freedom of choice or democracy. And now if you don't have a protector, you'll be forced to join her union."

I had no idea what he was talking about. God, it sounded like the mob or something. "A protector?"

He sat next to me, which was a relief because I was getting tired of watching him pace. "There are rules in this society, Jolie. Rules I haven't explained to you and hoped I wouldn't have to. I wanted you to return to your old life until you could decide if you wanted to give it up for this one. Now, it seems the choice has been made for you."

"I don't understand," I said, my voice so thick, it barely made it out of my mouth.

"If you don't have a protector in this society, then you have no one to champion you. You'd be forced to join ranks with Bella."

Forced? This was sounding worse and worse. "How does a protector, as you call it, make any difference?"

He stood and started pacing again. "If you have an employer, or a protector, then you're safe. Bella wouldn't be able to force you into her union if someone else has already unionized you. If she wanted you for a particular job, she'd have to go through your employer."

This made a little more sense, but I didn't understand how an employer, as he called it, had anything to do with it. "So, just for the sake of argument, why would it be so bad for Bella to be my protector, since she wants to do so?"

"She's a greedy, selfish bitch." He paused and ran an agitated hand through his hair. "I didn't want to tell you because it's so horrible ..."

My heart forgot to beat for a few seconds. "Go on."

"Once I returned Jack to Bella, and she realized she'd now have to assume responsibility for her father, she killed him on the spot."

"She did what?!"

"She would kill you as soon as look at you."

My stomach churned as if I'd swallowed a gallon of sour milk. How anyone could kill her own father was beyond me. Okay, so working for Bella was not an option. "Why couldn't I just say I'm working for you?"

He shrugged and didn't quite meet my eyes. "I've always been on my own, I've never been protected by anyone, nor have I ever offered protection. I'm not certain I'd be the best alternative. I've not agreed to join Bella, but I'm not enough of a threat yet for her to try to convince me."

"If you aren't protected then how come no one comes for you?"

"I'm very powerful, and it would be no easy feat to get me to bend to someone's will. I answer to no one."

To some his comment may have sounded arrogant, but there was no conceit in his gaze, just honesty. And I believed him. But powerful warlock or not, it was his fault I was in this mess in the first place. So he hadn't invited me to this party, but he'd invited the attention of other people who might wish me harm. As far as I was concerned, he was the first wrongdoer in this tangled web.

"I'm sorry about all this, Jolie," he said, as if sensing my thoughts.

I stood and started for the door, needing to escape. Rand was at my side instantly. "Can we leave?" I asked, my lips tight.

He nodded and opened the door when Bella, dressed as Cleopatra, appeared in the doorway. I stepped back, right into Rand's hard chest. He sidestepped me and let's just say I was glad I wasn't Bella with the look he gave her. Something cross between wishing her dead and wanting to do the deed himself.

"Well isn't this the warm little reunion?" she asked while looping her arm through Rand's. He straightened, clearly uncomfortable. I couldn't understand why he didn't just shrug free of her. Rand didn't take crap from anyone ... right? Something was up.

"I'll have words with you later," he whispered to her.

She just smiled and swept her eyes over me, making me feel as if I were withering in her stringent gaze. It was at that moment that I realized I hated her. Not so much for forcing me into a life I was in no way prepared for, but for her smugness. And for the way she threaded her arm through Rand's—that burned me like all the fires of hell.

"I'm glad you came to my little party, Jolie. You were my honored guest, you know?"

I was done with pleasantries. "Your honored guest? I haven't heard it described like that. In fact, I'd more accurately describe it as your honored prisoner."

She laughed and with a wave of her braceleted wrist, threw aside my anger as if it were day old bread. "Yes, the party was in honor of you. It would've been such a shame had you not shown up. But, alas, I thought our handsome pirate here might cause you to reconsider." She patted Rand's expansive chest.

I blushed at the insolence of the comment and dropped my gaze. She'd known all along I'd come. I felt so naive—so stupid. I'd fallen for her plan as pretty as you please. All it required was Rand as the bait. My injured pride rebelled against the stupidity of my blind desire, which had gotten me into this problem in the first place. Life was so much easier when all you had to worry about was your cat.

"You had no right inviting her here, Bella," Rand said between tight lips.

She trailed her fingers down his chest, and a new wave of anger visited me. Why did he allow her to touch him? Why didn't he pull away from her? Clearly, he hated her—it was written all over his face.

"Oh, I had every right, Rand. She wasn't under anyone's protection so I wanted to graciously extend my own."

Rand stepped away from Bella, his aura looking like it would attack her if he didn't. Then it dawned on me that he must've been trying to preserve the truce between them.

"That's where you're wrong, Bella, she's agreed to be under my protection."

I tried to keep the shock from my face. Wasn't he just saying he worked alone? I didn't get a chance to ponder it further—Bella's aura grabbed my attention as it vibrated with the same violet Rand's did when he was angry.

"You offer no protection, Rand; you're a renegade as everyone knows," she spat between gritted teeth as I waited for a forked tongue to accompany the statement.

"I've offered her protection, and she's accepted. She and I will be working together. I think it fair as I'm truly responsible for discovering her." He smirked, satisfaction drenching his smile.

Bella's nostrils flared, and her chest went up and down like a ship on a stormy sea. If it was possible for someone to burst, she was well on her way. "Is this true? Has he offered to vouch for you?"

So now I had the choice to ally myself with Bella who seemed to be possessed by the devil or Rand who had problems of his own. Still, Rand hadn't murdered his own father … that I knew of. "Yes, it's true. He offered, and I accepted."

Bella gave me a look that said she would enjoy peeling off my skin, layer by layer. Luckily, she didn't attempt it and instead, turned on her heel and walked away. Her hips swayed as if to say she'd have the last word.

"I'm sorry, Jolie, but you're involved in this lifestyle now. I hope you'll be able to forgive me as we're going to be working together very closely," Rand said, his voice low and exhausted.

I couldn't help but think of the irony of the situation. I wanted nothing more than to work closely with Rand, but not like this. "So are you telling me I can't go back to my old life? What about my shop, my house, my cat, and Christa?"

He sighed, and I knew it was bad. "I'm sorry," he said as if that would make it all better.

It didn't. "This is ridiculous. I never agreed to any of this." I'd had enough of being a pawn in this game. These people or whatever you wanted to call them could choose to live their lives according to some doctrine of witches, but I was human and had freedom of choice. I lived in the United States for Christ's sake!

"Actually you just did."

My fingers curled, my nails biting into the palms of my hand. I tried to breathe in through my mouth and out through my nose, but it did nothing to calm me. I was in a house of otherworldly creatures, no one here was human, and what scared me most was that I was now one of them.

Well, I wasn't standing for it. I wasn't going to allow these creatures to dictate my life. I'd show them what they could do with the situation they were trying to force on me. They said I had no free will, no right to choose, well screw them!

I didn't give Rand a backwards glance as I neared the doors. Two enormous men dressed as Egyptian guards, complete with jackal masks, naked chests, and Roman-looking skirts, stepped in front of me, blocking my exit.

"I want to leave," I said between gritted teeth.

"Apologies, but we can't allow that," one of them said and panic welled up within me, choking the air from my lungs. They weren't going to let me leave? Okay, if they wanted to play, we'd play. I focused all my energy on them and willed them to move, forced myself to use the magic Rand had taught me.

I was rewarded with my magic bouncing off them and roaring back into me. Knocked off my feet, I landed with a thump on my ass. My ridiculously short dress rode all the way up my waist. Thank God, I was wearing boy shorts. I watched the guards' attention settle on my panties and blushed as I pushed my skirt back in place.

A hand appeared in front of me, and I glanced up into the face of a very amused Sinjin. I refused his offer and pushed myself to my feet.

"I suppose I failed to mention that your magic will not work here. There is a spell to prohibit it," he said.

I nodded but said nothing as the only thing I could think to say was a few choice curse words. My life was falling apart right in front of me, and there was nothing I could do.

"Are you alright?" he asked. I could only imagine his concern was anything but real. He probably wanted something from me just like it seemed everyone else did.

"I'm fine. My ego is hurt, but that's about it," I muttered.

He chuckled. "Well, if it makes you feel any better, I do not suppose anyone was concerned with your fall, they were more concerned with your pink lace knickers. I, myself, quite enjoyed the spectacle."

I frowned. "Are all vampires so ... sexual?"

He laughed. "We are considered a randy group, I suppose. But then you could say that of all otherworldly creatures. Whereas humans tend to ignore their primitive, baser needs, we relish them."

Great and now, I was among this noble group. The thought made me ill.

"Sinjin, leave her alone, she's spoken for," Rand said, stepping between the two of us.

"The boffin has returned," Sinjin faced me with a sigh. I didn't know what a boffin was, but the remark made me smile all the same.

"Randall always making his presence known when he is least wanted. I know she is spoken for—Bella marked her as her own."

Rand smiled with purpose. "I've marked her for my own."

I swear a growl accompanied the statement.

Sinjin frowned, shifted and glanced at me. "That cannot be, Bella said the party is in honor of the new witch."

Rand stepped closer to the vampire, their muscular chests practically touching.

"I bloody well found her, therefore I have rights to her, and I've exercised those rights. If you want something from her, you must go through me."

I didn't know if I wanted to shout or hit one of them. I felt like the maiden being fought over by two primitive idiots. "I was just leaving," I said and tried to push past them.

Rand's hand clamped down on my arm like a vice. Before I could resist, he maneuvered me away from Sinjin.

"Let go of me," I said, ready to battle him.

"You don't understand what you're now involved in, Jolie. These aren't friendly people here—they're vampires, werewolves, and demons that would kill you as soon as look at you."

Okay, that did the trick. I guess I hadn't been thinking properly. I wanted out and that feeling was greater now more than ever. I didn't belong here—I wasn't like them. I might have unexplained powers, but that didn't make me like them—I was innocent and wanted to stay innocent.

My body began to tremble, and I could do nothing to stop it. "I don't want any part of this. It isn't fair."

"I know, Jolie, and believe me, I wish you'd never come here tonight. Had I known that Bella was coming after you, I would've done my best to hide you. I was foolish—she owed me fealty for you resurrecting her father, and I said we'd call it even if she left you alone."

I nodded—the pieces of the puzzle were starting to fit, but that didn't mean I had to like any of it. As far as I was concerned, I was whisked out of my happy, albeit boring life, but happy all the same, and now I had to fear for my safety. I never asked for any of this, and that was the worst of it. "I just want to go home, Rand."

He clasped my shoulders. "I know, Jolie, but I'm afraid that's not possible now. You'll have to make your home with me."

Live with him? Tears stung my eyes as frustration got the better of me. "I ... I don't e ... even know where you live! I don't even know what your last n ... name is!" When I really get angry, I start to stutter. My stuttering only aggravated me all the more.

He reached out to touch me, but I batted his hand away. I was livid and didn't know if I wanted to scream and tear my hair out or cry. I managed to do neither.

"I live in England and my last name is Balfour," Rand said.

"England!" Then the sobs came. I'd never been abroad and now I was expected to move to England? My mom would have a heart attack! She couldn't even handle me moving from Spokane to LA.

"Shhh, Jolie," Rand whispered, looking about himself for what I assumed was a more private area, lest I have my mental breakdown in the midst of the party. He grabbed my arm and led me into a bedroom, closing the door behind us. He turned on the lights with a nod of his head, and I collapsed against the bed, sobbing.

"I've never even been to England!" My voice broke, but I was past the point of caring. I was being deported.

"I promise to make this as comfortable for you as I can."

I sat up and tried to get some semblance of control over myself. "Why do we have to live in England?" I rubbed my eyes with my arm and sniffled.

"Because that's my territory—witches are broken into covens and each coven mans a certain territory. Bella's territory is here."

"Los Angeles?" I asked while Rand fished inside the pocket of his pirate pants and handed me a hankie. Even though my nose was running, there was no way I was going to blow it in front of him.

"Well, yes, but more than that—she controls the Western states of the US."

I sniffed. "What does that mean, territory?"

"It means I control all otherworldly goings on in England, Scotland, and Wales. If an otherworldly person wishes to move to that area, they must get permission from me—if they wish to work in that area, they must go through me. We're broken up this way so we can cover the most ground and be the most efficient."

"And the vampires and werewolves and demons?" I asked, in shock the statement had even come from my mouth. It sounded so Hollywood movie fake.

"Vampires fall into houses that align themselves with our territories so they're similar in that respect. Werewolves and demons have nothing to do with us—they make their own rules and are becoming more of a problem. We're going to have to figure out what to do with them soon, as there needs to be an established order in our society. The vampires, much though I dislike and distrust them, have at least made the attempt."

My head was pounding like a son of a bitch, and I needed to sit down. The fact that these otherworldly creatures not only existed, but also had a whole government unto themselves was a big bite to chew. I recognized that my life would never be the same. This was the breaking point—the first night of the rest of my godforsaken life.

"Jolie, I know this is a lot to digest. We can discuss more on the plane, and I'll answer whatever questions you ask. I know you're frightened, but I hope you believe you're safe with me. I would never take advantage of you or hurt you. I just hope you realize this is the best case in an otherwise bad situation."

I nodded, but didn't look at him. I trusted he'd never hurt me—he could've had he wanted to. But I just couldn't get giddy about the whole situation. As far as I was concerned, it sucked. Now I'd have to sell my business, sell my house and my car and move to England. I was taking Plum, my cat. I didn't care what Rand thought about that, and if Christa was interested, I was taking her too.

I looked up at Rand and noticed he was unsettled about something, there was worry in his eyes. "What's wrong?"

He rubbed the back of his neck. "I didn't want to tell you, but I see no other way. Bella has challenged me to a duel ... over you."

Okay, this took the cake. "A duel, as in pistols?"

He chuckled without humor. "No, a duel between witch and warlock, using magic. She thinks it unfair I claimed you."

62

I stood up and smoothed my fairy skirts, trying to combat the storm of tears that were just waiting for the okay. "So w … what does that mean? You'll f … fight her with magic? To the death?" I asked, my voice rising as panic overtook me. If Rand lost, I was forever doomed to serving the likes of Bella. I'd rather take my own life than allow that.

He shook his head. "No. We'll fight with our powers, and whoever falls first loses."

"But Sinjin said there's a spell against the use of magic here," I said, sounding like a child pointing out any relevant arguments against the one Rand was making.

He put his hand on my cheek, instantly calming me. "It's easy to break that spell, Jolie."

"Is … is she a worthy opponent?"

He nodded. If he noticed my stuttering, he was polite enough not to comment. "She's a very powerful witch, but Jolie, I'm a powerful warlock in my own right."

"And if you fail?"

He sighed. "Then she becomes your protector."

I burst into another fit of tears. Could this night get any worse? Rand engulfed me in his big arms, and I blew my nose in the hankie, thinking it preferable to leaking on his shirt. I couldn't help but cry harder as I thought my very future depended on his defeating Bella. "W … when will this t … take place?"

Rand pulled away and gave me an encouraging smile. "Tonight. Probably soon. They're drawing up the rules as we speak. Promise me, Jolie, you'll not try anything foolish. Everyone here is far too powerful and you'll be at their mercy. At the conclusion of the dual, you must either go with Bella or come with me. As this is Bella's home, all of these people are her friends, not mine, and I can't account for what might happen upon me winning. I want you to stay close to the door, and be prepared to leave quickly."

"Please don't leave me with her."

He laughed. "Trust me; I'll do everything in my power, literally."

SEVEN

Apparently, the Underworld was as interested in fights as humans—the dancers stopped their air waltz and floated to the ground, looking like petals gliding in a breeze. Everyone formed an amphitheatre around Rand and Bella. This wouldn't be like any duel I'd ever heard of or seen in movies, and I was unprepared for what lay ahead.

I found myself led to the middle of the crowd where I'd be under strict surveillance, lest I attempt to escape. Angst pounded through me, and I didn't even have the wherewithal to notice who pushed me through the crowd. I kept replaying Rand's warning: *Stay close to the door, and be prepared to leave quickly.* I craned my head—the nearest exit was … not very near.

Someone latched onto my arm. I gasped and turned to confront the grinning countenance of Sinjin.

"Come along, my pet, I will ensure you are front and center."

"No," I said quickly, clinging to the image of the door that was now blocked by at least four people. "I'm fine where I am."

"I insist." By the tone of his voice, he wouldn't take no for an answer. A few people blocked our path, and Sinjin did nothing more than glance at them and they scurried out of the way. Before I knew it, I was on the sidelines of the duel and as far from the doors as possible.

Crap.

I jerked my arm free of his grip. "There's no need for you to keep tabs on me."

"I am afraid you're the prize, poppet, and one that cannot be lost," he answered with a grin.

The only type of smiles to graze Sinjin's face seemed to be of the sarcastic or malevolent sort. I couldn't imagine this creature possessed even an ounce of goodness. And the biggest kicker was that even though I could recognize him for the monster he was, I couldn't help my attraction to him.

What a dumbass I was.

"I'll have to report back to Bella that you did a wonderful job of controlling me," I spat out, not wanting to face the fact that I lusted after him.

He shook his head, a grin toying with the ends of his sensual lips. "Bella has nothing to do with this. I came to protect you."

I scoffed—an unattractive sound, but I didn't care. "Seems everyone is out to protect me. But I trust you as far as I can throw you."

His ice blue eyes met mine, and he chuckled. "Think what you want, pet. I am the first to admit my interest in you does not blossom from my own sense of humanity; I have none. You are a commodity, and a valuable one at that."

64

He put his hand on my shoulder, and I shrugged it away. A commodity—that's what they'd reduced me to. These creatures cared nothing for me. I was an answer to their needs, an article of trade, a quid-pro-quo arrangement. At least Sinjin had the courage to tell me to my face.

"I don't care what you think, I still have freedom of choice," I said, knowing my freedom had been ripped from me the moment I'd stepped foot into this hellish place.

"I am afraid your old life is done and gone, love, now you have to face a new reality."

The idea sickened me. "Well, that reality doesn't include Bella or her friends," I said snidely, staring him in the eyes.

His eyes were sharp, deadly. "I am no one's friend."

A chill slipped over my skin. "Then why are you here?"

"Orders," he said succinctly before turning his attention to Rand and Bella. "It appears the show is about to begin, poppet. May the best witch win."

I thought better of making a facetious comment and instead, focused on Rand. He and Bella faced one another with what could only be termed hatred—clenched jaws, narrowed eyes, and fisted hands. Anger seethed from both of them but, particularly, from Bella. She must've taken it pretty hard that I was now under Rand's protection. I guess she was used to getting her own way.

A slender woman dressed as a pirate wench sashayed to the middle of the floor, standing between the two. She threw a flirtatious smile at Rand. But his attention wasn't on her—his gaze fell to me, and he inclined his head as if to say the games were about to begin. I mouthed a terse "good luck."

"This is a feat of magic and strength. Whichever witch drops to the floor first will be the loser. The victor will win the rights as employer to one Jolie Wilkins," the pirate girl said in a deep and throaty voice—the voice sex would have if personified.

Everyone turned to look at me, no doubt questioning the prize. I felt myself shrink against Sinjin who just chuckled, patting my shoulder consolingly. I didn't pull away from him this time.

The crowd fell silent. Rand and Bella stood there, facing one another.

"What's going on?" I whispered to Sinjin.

"Shh." He ran his finger down the length of my upper arm. My skin burned even though his touch was ice cold.

Taking my lower lip between my teeth, I waited impatiently for something to happen. I thought I noticed a thin stream of light emanating between Rand and Bella's fingertips, and I had to blink to ensure it was there. The light grew in intensity until it could be termed a ball of energy. A glimmer of blue engulfed Bella's while Rand's went as white as the first snowfall in Spokane. Just then, I wished more than ever before, that I could go home and forget all of this. Go home to my bland life in Spokane and relish the humdrum safety.

With thoughts of Spokane playing through my head, I wasn't prepared for the combat to begin. When Rand and Bella lunged at one another, throwing the balls of energy, I gasped. Sinjin chuckled and patted my shoulder in an attempt to calm me, but all I could feel was the coldness of his skin, something decidedly not calming.

Each witch sidestepped the energy, and I wondered if it would hit someone in the sidelines. The energy balls twinkled like dying stars and disappeared before doing any damage. I guess the balls of energy weren't the best trick up their sleeves because neither Rand nor Bella seemed at all irritated they'd missed their targets. Instead, they fell upon one another, fighting in a much more primitive and human way—with fists, knees, and ugly words. I winced when Rand got a knee between his legs. He looked like he was about to fall to the ground, and I stepped forward, a gasp on my lips. Sinjin grabbed my arm and yanked me back against the hard length of him.

"Watch it, love," he whispered in my ear.

"I don't need to stand so close to you," I snapped and took a step forward.

Rand righted himself (thank God) and didn't seem to pay any attention to the fact that he was brawling with a woman. Course, I guess Bella wasn't a woman but more a creature. Creature or not, she was powerful. The two of them seemed pretty well matched.

They huffed, puffed and didn't blow either one's house down.

After it seemed neither of them would yield to the other, they separated for a few minutes, each retiring to the far corners of the room, apparently to regroup. Rand leaned over, resting his hands on his knees. His breathing was ragged, his body swaying with the effort it took to inhale and exhale. Sweat beaded on his brow and dripped down his face. I had a feeling this was going to be a long fight.

Then I watched Rand do something that in a word was … incredible. He took a big breath of air and began to … transform. His face and limbs elongated, accompanied by what sounded like bones snapping. Patches of thick brown fur sprouted from his skin like growing grass on fast forward. His back arched until it looked like he might break in half, and then his spine took on a rounded shape as his rib cage doubled in breadth. His lips curled back, his canines morphing into long fangs. Shaking his head, he released an intense growl that seemed full of pain. I could only imagine it had hurt like a son of a bitch to change from a human into a bear.

I shook my head and wiped my eyes, wondering if that might clear my delirious vision, but the bear stood before me and there was no denying it.

Now, I don't know much about animals—I watch Animal Planet on occasion, but I'd have to say this was one of the larger bears out there—maybe a grizzly.

My gaze settled on Bella to see what her reaction would be. I, myself, would've been scared shitless. But apparently, I'm a wuss because Bella just smiled as if to say "you can do better than that." Crouching low to the ground, a long caramel colored tail unraveled from her backside while her fingers stretched into claws, giving me goose bumps as they screamed against the marble floor. Her clothing ripped away as her rib cage expanded, and light brown fur usurped her skin.

Bella was now a lioness. And a pissed off one at that. As soon as her transformation was complete, she lunged for Rand. With a swipe of her paw, she tore the bear's, er Rand's, chest open. The bear roared his outrage as the telltale scarlet of viscous blood emerged from the wound and coursed down his body, pooling on the floor.

Before I could take a step forward, Sinjin jerked me back.

The bear shook his massive head, stumbling backward with another wrenching growl. I held my breath and watched, wondering if Rand was going to die before me.

Sinjin squeezed my shoulders. "Just wait."

The crowd was silent, all eyes on the bear. The beast seemed as if he were about to fall back against the floor but maybe remembering the terms of the fight, he regained his footing and stood, his breathing shallow. Bella circled him and even though she was a lion, she wore the very human emotion of glee in her eyes.

Don't fall down, Rand. Whatever you do, don't fall down. I probably shouldn't have sent him the thoughts—especially when he needed to focus on the fight, but I couldn't help it.

He didn't look at me, but as soon as I thought the words, he ambled forward, blood coursing down his chest. Bella roared. The crowd broke into applause, their cheers vibrating the room, and I thought I might lose my lunch.

I couldn't help sinking into Sinjin. "Why are they cheering?" I whispered. "It's not over, is it? Why are they acting ...?"

"Shh, my pet, it is not over."

No sooner did the words leave his mouth than the bear stood on his hind legs and threw his immense head back, growling the fiercest and loudest growl I'd ever heard. Bella lurched for him at the same time that Rand threw himself atop her.

With a crushing thud, he pinned Bella beneath him and wrapped his jaws around her throat.

"He'll kill her," I whispered. But if he did kill her, would it would really be a loss? I couldn't say I liked Bella ...

"No, he will not," Sinjin said with a chuckle.

Bella whimpered and at the sign of her distress, Rand pulled away. The crowd was silent, watchful.

Even though no one clapped, booed, or did anything, it was clear Rand was the victor. He turned, his brown eyes piercing mine. With long, fluid strides, he started toward me, his grizzly face intent on mine. I swallowed my fear and sidled closer to Sinjin who just chuckled and patted my ass. I was too overcome with the situation to get pissed off.

67

With each lumbering step, Rand's limbs shortened, and the fur began to fade into tanned skin. By the time he reached me, the bear was gone and Rand was back to himself.

Naked.

Completely naked.

My mouth dropped open, and I couldn't keep my gaze from traveling down his chest to his hips and lower still … I'm not sure what I expected after watching two "people" turn into animals, but I didn't imagine they'd be naked. I guess it made sense, though. Changing from a two-hundred pound man to a nine-hundred pound grizzly had to be hard on your clothes.

Needless to say, I found it difficult to take my eyes from Rand's muscled body, glorious in its nudity. Much to my chagrin, it seemed Sinjin caught my interest, and he gave me a little smirk.

I didn't get much of a chance to regain my composure as Rand collapsed at my feet. Then I remembered the huge gaping wound on his chest.

"Oh my God," I whispered.

"I suggest you help him," Sinjin said in a soft voice and pushed me forward as if I needed encouragement.

Someone offered Rand a robe, and I exhaled my relief. Not that I didn't want to see him naked, but now was neither the ideal place nor time.

I stumbled onto the floor.

"Rand," I whispered and rested my hand on his head, willing him to look at me, to let me know he was going to be all right.

Finally, he tilted his head back and whispered a concise, "The door," and that was when I realized we were in a bad situation. He'd won and he was in a house full of people who were rooting for Bella—that and he was hurt. I wasn't sure how bad, but it was bad enough that he was having difficulty breathing.

I slipped my arm around his back and helped him to his feet. Even though he didn't put all his weight on me, it was still enough to make me stumble, and I cursed my damn hooker shoes. A sea of angry faces swayed before us, but I forced my attention to the door in the distance. Trying to walk in stiletto heels with the extreme weight of Rand was like wading through thigh-deep snow while carrying a large television.

The planets seemed to be aligned against me, Bella's guests refusing to budge. Rand leaned into me, and I tripped with his weight. I paused to take off my ridiculous shoes and faced the fact that there was no way I could support him and forge my way through the reluctant crowd. Soft murmurs grew to angry mumbling, and I felt someone rip the wings right off my back. I subdued a yelp as tears of frustration sprouted in my eyes.

Sinjin stepped in front of me, and my heart sped up. Please tell me I wouldn't have to contend with him too? He grinned before turning on his heel and forcing the crowd aside with an encouraging push. The crowd separated for him, and I slowly made my way through the passage. He reminded me of Moses parting the red sea, if Moses was a vampire. And if Moses was hot.

When we reached the door, I faced the next obstacle—those damned Jackal guards. I gave them my best pissed off, you-don't-want-to-mess-with-me look, and I was surprised when they stepped aside and the doors opened of their own volition. Hmm, maybe I'd looked mean enough …

I spotted my Jetta parked across the street, and the vision of my little car had never been sweeter. Now, the problem of getting Rand across the street—he was becoming more and more exhausted, and a dead weight isn't an easy one to transport.

By the grace of God, we managed to stumble across the street. I leaned Rand against the car, smearing the window with blood as I opened his door. He fell into the seat, and I was careful to lift his legs and put them in car. Once he was situated, I hurried to the driver's side and threw myself into the seat, banging my funny bone into the middle console. It wasn't very funny.

"Goddammit to hell!" I fumed, and threw the door shut. Luckily, the keys were waiting patiently for us in the ignition. Starting the car, I pealed out, only too happy to leave the nightmare party behind.

"Where should I take you?" I asked, forcing my eyes on the road, my elbow still throbbing like a son of a bitch. "You need to go to the hospital."

"No, no hospital," Rand mumbled, his eyes closed.

I tried to think of an alternative to a hospital. The dentist? A vet? Yeah, no. The only other option was my house. It would have to do.

As I drove, I repeatedly glanced at Rand, noting his wan expression and the dullness of his aura. Instead of the bright electric blue, it was more of a sky blue.

"What's happening to you, Rand?" I asked

He swallowed hard, his eyes still closed. "Bella … poisoned me."

I thought I might choke on the bile that immediately came up my throat. "She what?"

His breathing was belabored. "When she … turned into the lion … her claws … were poisoned."

The telltale signs of panic rose within my gut—a tightness accompanied with unbelievable nausea. I had no idea what to do in a poison situation—call poison control? Somehow, I figured "poisoned by a witch lioness" wasn't in their repertoire.

"What do I do?" I asked in hushed tone, keeping my head tilted back, lest I vomit all over him.

"Just get me to your house … how much … farther?"

"Maybe twenty minutes. Can you make it that far?" I wondered if I could make it that far.

I didn't hear a response and glanced over at him. He regarded me with a question in his eyes. "Why … are you holding your … head up like that?"

"I feel like I'm gonna puke."

He dropped his gaze. "Just drive quickly."

I couldn't keep thoughts of Rand dying from my mind, much though I grew furious with myself for thinking them. Now that I was inducted into this lifestyle, I couldn't afford to lose Rand. I'm sure that sounds selfish, but sometimes you can't help the thoughts that penetrate your head. I looked at him once more, huddled on the passenger seat. It was humbling and depressing to see such a beautiful, strong man reduced to such a trembling mess.

"Can't you do a spell or something to get us there?"

He shook his head. "I can't teletransport."

Dammit. Well, that just sucked. What I wouldn't have done for a little teletransportation. Where was Captain Kirk when you needed him? Apparently, Captain Kirk wouldn't be assisting me anytime soon, so I drove like I've never driven before. Usually I'm a law-abiding, decent citizen, but I drove as if the devils of hell were on my heels and for all I knew, maybe they were.

When we reached my street, it occurred to me that Rand hadn't said a word in over five minutes. I glanced at him and noted his vacant gaze.

Oh … God.

"Rand, wake up." Terror laced my voice.

"I'm still … here."

Like aloe vera gel on a sunburn, relief coursed through me. I pulled into my garage and didn't waste time in rushing to his side and ripping the door open. Gritting my teeth, I grabbed his arms and hoisted him forward, bracing myself when he fell against my chest. I didn't need to look down to know I was covered in his blood; I could feel the wet warmth soaking through my dress. I tried to maneuver backward and felt like I was going to fall over. It was like moving a refrigerator.

"I need you to help me get you into the house, Rand."

He nodded, and if he attempted to help me, I didn't know it. I had to all but carry him up the steps. I wasn't sure if it was adrenalin or magic that assisted me, but I was thankful all the same. I leaned him against my front door while I fumbled with my house key. Unlocking the door with a curse, I braced myself for my load. He fell into my arms, and I dragged him into the living room. Pushing him against the sofa, he tumbled back into the cushions. His robe fell apart and the angry red gash glared at me. I gave myself kudos for not looking any lower.

"What do I do?"

He said nothing for a minute and seemed to be gathering all his strength. I wondered if the end were close, and the thought made me force my head toward the ceiling while I swallowed the hint of vomit in my throat. I could not allow myself to throw up.

"You can heal … Jolie, you have to focus your powers on me … and heal me."

Once the nausea retired, I leaned close to him, putting my hands just above his wound and concentrated, remembering how Rand had gotten rid of my stomach ache in such a way. I closed my eyes and imagined all of my energy going to the wound to pull the poison from it. I had no idea if this was proper magic protocol, but it was the only thing I could think of, and Rand didn't seem to be arguing, so I went with it.

I nearly screamed when he grabbed my hand. I looked down and had a jolting vision of two people, Rand and I, in a heated embrace. His lips were hot on mine and I could distinctly feel something inside me. It took me a moment to realize it was Rand. I gasped in response, pulling away from him. In a few seconds, it was gone.

"What is it? What did you see?" Rand asked, his voice nervous.

"N ... nothing important."

He swallowed, his jaw clenching. "Was it me? Am I going ... to die?"

I shook my head, realizing I'd have to get over my embarrassment. "No." Well, here goes. "It was you and me and w ... we were ... having sex."

He didn't seem surprised at all and just nodded as though it were to be expected. "Well, then, I suppose I'm not going to die."

I smiled uneasily and with my hands shaking, grabbed a throw pillow from my wingchair, lifting his head slightly while I put the pillow underneath his neck. Then I faced the ugly gash in his chest again. I lifted my hands and settled them just above the wound. Closing my eyes, I could only hope what I presumed were my fruitless efforts were actually doing something. I opened my eyes to judge if my treatment was working—it didn't seem to be, he still looked as pale as ... me.

My gaze moved up his chest, and had the situation been different, I could've appreciated the valleys and mountains of his muscular landscape. Instead, I settled my gaze on his eyes. Fear in a powerful warlock's eyes is not something you want to witness when you're trying to revive him. If I hadn't thought the situation perilous before, it dawned on me now.

What of my recent vision, though? It had appeared that Rand was as healthy as healthy could be. I had to wonder if maybe it wasn't a vision at all but some sort of weird figment of my imagination come to visit me at the worst possible time. God, this newly awakened sex-drive thing was killing me.

"Is it working?" I asked, scared for his response.

"I don't know."

What kind of witch was I? I'd always doubted my abilities but never as much as I did now. I had no clue as to why these beings were fighting over me when it wasn't even warranted.

God, I was useless.

Tears plundered down my face and splashed against Rand's chest, but he didn't even seem to notice. He was pale, paler than I've ever seen another person, and I knew this had to mean his life was slipping away.

There was nothing I could do.

His face was stoic, as if he were prepared for death.

"I'm s ... so sorry Rand," I sniveled. I hated failing him, and this was the ultimate failure. "I'm so sorry I disappointed you."

He shook his head, and it seemed as though it was the only thing of which he was capable—maybe he was so close to death he wasn't even able to speak. My tears increased tenfold as I continued to focus on his wound and attempted to heal it with my ineffectual hands. My tears mixed with his blood and coursed down his side, staining my coverlet beneath him.

I couldn't help the sob that tore at my throat as a deluge of tears bled from my eyes.

Keep crying, Jolie.

I wasn't prepared for Rand's voice in my head and it made my tears subside for a moment as I responded to him. *I'm so sorry.*

Your tears, they're healing me.

I wiped my eyes on my arm and looked down at his wound. The color had somewhat returned to his skin and the blood had coagulated. I couldn't help the smile that stole my lips. Holy crap! It was working!

Don't stop crying!

His voice brought me back to reality, and I had to concentrate on making the tears resume. I couldn't let them up now. I focused and felt as sorry for myself as I could. I thought of the injustice of the whole situation, that I'd had no choice in the matter of my future, that I was terrified of all these creatures who were now my reality, that I still thought I was going to puke, and that I'd nearly lost someone I considered a … friend.

The tears came and I angled myself so they'd land on Rand's wound. The torn skin began to mend itself, as if some invisible doctor were sewing it together. The angry red receded into the growing tan of his skin. A soft pink graced his lips, and his eyes got that magic charm back. And the topper—the sky blue of his aura deepened into the electric blue I'd come to know so well.

I couldn't help the inordinate sense of pride that washed over me as I realized I'd finally accomplished something worth accomplishing.

When it appeared the wound had healed, I pulled away from him and allowed my tears to subside. I wiped my eyes and slumped with exhaustion. I'd been through a crap-load tonight. I felt Rand's hand on my shoulder and tried to contain the tears that threatened to break through again.

"You did it," he said in a small voice. "Thank you. I knew you could."

"I thought I'd lost you."

He shook his head with a chuckle. "I wasn't going out quite so easily."

I stood up and walked to my bathroom, returning with my pink terrycloth robe and handed it to Rand.

He eyed it with raised brow. "Your pink dressing gown?"

I laughed. "It's all I've got, and your robe is stained."

He shrugged and looking down at himself, blinked, and he was dressed in black pants and a white shirt. I'd forgotten about the handy little thing we both possessed called magic. I dropped the pink robe on the corner of the couch, thinking it would've been funny to see him in it.

"What now?" I asked.

He looked around the room, his gaze falling to the clock atop the mantel, and he sighed. "We need to book tickets to England, put your house up for sale …"

"Can't it wait until morning?" He'd just escaped Death's clutches and should be in bed with some chicken noodle soup.

"Perhaps it can wait until tomorrow. I'm not quite feeling myself at the moment." Yeah, I thought, big Duh to that one!

"Why don't you stay here tonight? You can have my bed, and I'll take the couch."

He shook his head. "I'm happy to sleep on the couch."

"I insist," I said and slipped my arm around his waist, helping him to his feet.

I led him to my bedroom, seeing it for the first time—the pink bedding, the lavender and white striped walls, and the five foot, white furry monkey in the corner of the room. God, could my room scream out six-year-old girl any more?

"Lovely primate," Rand said with a laugh.

"Thanks," I muttered and noticed my cat curled atop the duvet. Shooing her away, I pulled the covers aside, helping Rand into the bed. He leaned against the headboard and looked like a giant, his feet hanging off the end of the mattress. The thought of a man, let alone Rand, in my bed was so foreign, it took me a while to even register it was real.

He looked up at me expectantly. "Do I get a bedtime story?"

I laughed and ignored him. "So I really am moving to England with you?"

"I'm afraid you don't have a choice."

"I'm hearing that a lot lately." I took a seat next to him as I thought about the immense chore that moving would mean.

"What if my house doesn't sell?"

"I'm going to ... encourage the first people who see it—they'll buy it with all the furniture and your car too."

Witchcraft had its plusses. "Can my cat come with me?"

"She's most certainly invited."

I nodded, pleased that Rand didn't seem to mind animals. "And Christa?"

I guess Christa wasn't as invited as the cat because he took a while to consider it.

"Does she want to come with you?"

I shrugged. "I haven't asked her yet, but I hope she would."

"Very well, then she's invited also. I want to make this as easy on you as I can, Jolie."

I sighed, knowing this situation was not only frustrating for me, but it had to be for him as well. "I know you are, Rand, and I appreciate it."

He covered my hand with his and the electric current traveled up my arm, its familiarity now like an old friend.

"About this vision you had ..."

It took me a second to realize what he was talking about. When I did, I dropped my gaze, hating the flush that was even now claiming every inch of my body. "What about it?"

He grinned and seemed to be enjoying my discomfort. "Was it real, or did you make it up?"

I frowned. "If you mean did I really have the vision, yes I did. As for whether it was real … I don't know." But I hoped it was.

He chuckled. "Care to describe it for me?"

I pulled my hand from underneath his. "No, I don't. You need your rest."

He laughed again, but his gaze was riveted on me. "It's easy to make you blush, you know?"

I lifted my eyes and found his wide smile and dimples sexy as all get out. I stood up. "You're delirious."

He chuckled, and I started for the door.

"Jolie … thank you."

I nodded and leaned against the doorjamb while I studied him. "You're welcome, Rand. Thank you for … everything you did for me."

He seemed surprised and even a mite uncomfortable. It was pretty funny actually—when I removed myself from the situation. Here I was, a new witch, thanking a nearly dead warlock for disrupting my life and relocating me to England.

Sometimes life is stranger than art.

EIGHT

As Rand, Christa, my cat, and I sat in the taxi that picked us up at Newcastle airport, I was overwhelmed with conflicted feelings. It'd been difficult for me to leave the safety of my life in Los Angeles. My mother hadn't taken it at all well. When I'd told her, she'd burst into sobs immediately, causing me to feel like quite the unfit daughter. Of course, I hadn't told her the whole truth. I'd just said I had a job offer in England that I couldn't refuse. And I'd left it at that. Luckily, she hadn't questioned me as to why England had better legal assistant positions than the States. I hadn't quite thought that one all the way through. ...

With melancholic thoughts and homesickness already coursing through my veins, it was hard to find room for excitement. But that said, I was eager to face the next chapter of my life, even if that chapter was questionable at best. Thoughts of Bella swarmed through my head like angry wasps, but I forced them aside, figuring it would work itself out. Rand knew far more about the situation than I did, so I'd let him handle it.

I glanced across the taxi at Christa who stared out the window, holding her stomach. Pain mixed with carsickness pierced her expression; she'd eaten too many frosted donuts and now reaped the rewards.

I didn't imagine I would've been capable of making such a life-altering change without Christa. In many ways, she was the oak to my sapling—having her with me gave me strength to confront an unknown future. And as for Christa, she'd been thrilled to finally see her dream of traveling abroad to fruition ... and on someone else's dime.

"Ugh," she moaned, her face was pale and beads of perspiration decorated her brow like ornaments on a Christmas tree.

Rand sent an amused glance my way, then turned to face Christa. He slipped his arms around her waist and pressed his hands to her stomach, taking the sickness from her as quickly as it had come. A look of surprise paralyzed Christa's face, and her cheeks colored. She said nothing but thanked him with a small smile and a nod of her head.

A tiny dart of jealousy landed in my stomach, but I plucked it out, thinking such a reaction was ludicrous.

"Just up the way is Alnwick," Rand said with a gesture toward the window. "Where I live."

"How long have you lived there?" I asked.

"Sixty years."

I shook my head, still having trouble imagining he could be so old when he looked so young. What was weirder still was the fact that if Rand looked his age, there is no way in hell I'd be attracted to him. He'd be over one hundred fifty—yuck! I felt my nose scrunching up at the idea and forced my attention outside the window, not wanting to continue picturing the geriatric Rand.

The view did a good job of grabbing my attention. Northumberland was a land of castles, thatched-roof houses, buildings dating to the fourteenth century, and it was right on the coast. The English coastline was entirely different from that of California—maybe more similar to Washington's. The sky was a drab grey, the sun seemingly fighting to break through the shadow of the sky. A light rain had already welcomed us and now sprinkled the rumbling ocean, warning of more to come.

"Hadrian's Wall isn't far from here," Rand said.

"I hadn't realized we were so close to Scotland," I answered and started to get excited. I hadn't done much traveling in my life, and I did have to admit that it was pretty darn neat to see more of what the world had to offer.

"Yes, very close." He smiled, and an image of the Crypt Keeper crept into my mind until I violently shook it away. Sheesh! Just because Rand was over one hundred didn't mean he'd look like a zombie or whatever that hideous thing was.

After driving for maybe thirty minutes, the taxi climbed a long and steep drive. On my right, a rock fence lay in disrepair, speaking of times past. Beyond that, white sheep dotted the landscape and contrasted against the miles of verdant farmland.

"Nearly there," Rand said. I could see why he chose such a remote place in which to live. He was a private person, and one could get as much privacy as one wanted out here—his only neighbors a few sheep and some craggy trees.

As the taxi came to a stop before a stately manor house, my attention turned to the great façade. I inspected it, trying to find an inkling of Rand within the foreboding and immense structure that peered down at me. As mysterious as its owner—its stone face was an exact replica of the stoic strength inherent in Rand's eyes and the stubborn hold of his mouth.

I stepped outside and craned my neck to inspect the majesty of Rand's three-story home. It was something you'd see in a fairy tale—imposing and completely constructed of slate and stone. A wide stairwell graced the front and led to a pair of heavy wooden doors, flanked on either side by two large urns that each housed a yellow blooming rosebush. Two stone gargoyles studied me from their perch atop the third story. Between them and carved into the stone face was "Pelham Manor."

The name fit. I didn't know if Pelham meant anything, but it was as English as the home, the countryside, and the handsome man who owned it. I smiled, breathing in the crisp air and thought my lungs had never inhaled anything so pure.

"Wow," Christa said, already reaching for her camera bag and studying the edifice as if memorizing the angles she planned to capture.

Rand grinned. "Welcome to your new home."

The driver carried our things to the massive front doors, and then returned to the car. Rand assumed the largest bags and left Christa and me to carry the rest, including the cat.

For as ancient as Pelham Manor was, the inside was the epitome of contemporary modernism with large black leather sofas, oriental rugs, and Picasso-looking paintings I could only assume were originals. It appeared Rand enjoyed the most up-to-date of modern conveniences even if his home was anything but. As soon as we stepped into the foyer, he disengaged an alarm and Ravel's Bolero filtered through the house. As if commanded by the music, a fire lit itself in a fireplace so tall I could easily stand in it—on my tip toes. What grabbed me most, though, was the way his home smelled—it shared the same minty spiciness that could only characterize Rand.

I inhaled deeply.

"All bedrooms are on the third floor," he said as Christa and I gaped at the surroundings of our new abode. "Is it to your liking?"

I faced him in disbelief. "I think I need to pinch myself."

He laughed as Christa inspected the fireplace and threw herself into the lush sofa, almost disappearing into the folds.

"Wow, this is the dog's bollocks," she said as I erupted into a fit of laughter.

"Where did you pick that up?" I managed.

"Oh, around," she said evasively.

Rand just shook his head, but couldn't keep the smile from his lips.

Reminded of the weight of Plum in her carrying case, I turned to the wide expanse of stairs and wondered what awaited me in the bedrooms. Rand started up the stairs as Christa busied herself with the television.

"Do I have my pick of rooms?" I asked, following him.

Rand nodded. "Of course. I did have one in mind for you, though."

We strolled down the long and dark corridor toward the eastern section of Pelham Manor. The place was quiet, reflective, yet it didn't feel intimidating in its age and stature. Rand pushed open the last door in the hallway and stepped aside as I entered. An immense canopy bed made of some exotic and dark wood dominated the room. Transparent white panels hung from the bed's wooden beams and gave the room a certain harem-like quality. In the corner, a fireplace erupted into orange and yellow flames as soon as we stepped over the threshold, and the music from downstairs filtered in through a hidden speaker.

My attention turned to the French doors that opened onto my very own terrace. The veranda was complete with a flowering rose that crawled up the ancient face of Pelham Manor, lending the air a sweet aroma.

I didn't bother letting Plum out of her case, but deposited her on the bed and neared the arresting view that beckoned to me from the terrace. A brook weaved its way through an endless grove of ash trees only to disappear on the horizon.

I pulled open the French doors, and a breeze coursed into the room, grabbing hold of a brown silk drape. The drape danced as if the breeze were a long-lost lover. The coy breeze then trailed against my cheek, pushing my hair from my face.

"The rooms on the other side overlook the rose gardens, but somehow, I thought you'd appreciate this view more," Rand said, reminding me he still stood behind me.

"This is … incredible." I turned to face him. "Thank you."

"If you want to see the other rooms …"

"No," I interrupted. "I can't imagine anything more beautiful than this."

Silence reigned as Rand and I met one another's gaze. Like a deer in headlights, I couldn't pull my attention from the beautiful richness of his chocolate eyes. An angry meow interrupted the wonder of the moment, and Rand turned to the cat in her case. He unhinged the door, and she peeked her orange head out, unsure of her surroundings. He scratched her chin, and she purred, easing herself out of the cage.

"I'll keep her in here. I'm sure you don't want a cat traipsing around."

He laughed. "You can keep her on the condition you allow her the run of the place. Little bugger would be bored to tears in here."

The scene before me was pretty touching—a great and powerful warlock completely content to scratch a silly little cat's chin.

"Thank you, Rand."

He smiled, and Plum jumped from the bed, threading herself between his legs as she purred and clawed at the rug beneath her.

"I'm your family now, Jolie; if ever you need anything—I hope you know I'm here for you."

My family now. The words echoed through me, and I fought against them. I didn't want Rand to be my family; I wanted him to be my lover. The realization was clearer now than it ever had been.

"I appreciate everything you've done for me," I managed and forced my attention to the cat. She pulled at the Aubusson rug as if determined to unravel every last stitch. I grabbed the naughty cat before she did any permanent damage and frowned at Rand apologetically.

He just laughed before changing the subject. "I've hired tutors to teach you their craft."

"Tutors?" I asked in surprise, never having considered I might require actual training.

"Yes, the fairies—they're excellent teachers and masters of magic. They taught me everything I know."

I sat on the edge of the bed, scratching Plum as she stretched her paws against my stomach. "Fairies? As in Tinker Bell?"

He chuckled. "Not exactly."

"Do they have wings?"

Rand neared the door with a grin. "I suppose you'll have to find out for yourself," he answered in that elusive way of his.

~

That night, after Christa, Rand, and I had excused ourselves to seek the refuge of our bedrooms, I had another dream. Of course, this one was just as erotic as the others and of course, it featured Rand. The dream was so lucid I felt myself tossing about, and a sigh broke from my lips.

I opened my eyes and found night was still upon me. The moon glowed through my window, casting strange and frightening shadows around the room. I closed my eyes against the shadow of a goblin, trying to think of thousands of sheep all in a line and it was my duty to count them … anyone who tells you to count sheep in order to get to sleep has never tried it.

As I lay in the large bed and thought of the dream I'd just awakened from, heat simmered through my body, pulsing under my skin. I pictured Rand's mouth and how his tongue had tasted me, how his hunger had been ravenous. The sexual tension inside me built to such a degree, I couldn't stop my hand as it traveled down my leg to rest between my thighs at the very place that demanded attention.

I've never been one to masturbate, so I wasn't surprised that at first I wasn't very good at it. I didn't give up, though, and helped myself along by imagining it was Rand between my legs, pleasuring himself just as much as he was pleasuring me.

My hand began an urgent rhythm as my hips jutted upward. I closed my eyes and relished the feeling when the blankets stripped themselves from me. I gasped, my eyes flying open in shock and mortification.

I pulled myself upright and searched for a plausible explanation—maybe I'd pushed the blankets to the side and they'd fallen off the bed? No, something had pulled them off me. Scooting back to the headboard, I couldn't see anything suspicious and wondered if maybe the shadows in the room had been real creatures, come to do God knows what with me. I pulled my nightshirt down over my knees, tucking them to my chest. My pulse echoed in my ears like pounding hooves, my fear holding me immobile. There was something in the room, but I couldn't see it and couldn't decide if it were better to dart for the door or remain where I was.

I waited and nothing happened. I was just about to jump up to turn on the light when I noticed an indentation on the foot of the bed—almost like someone sitting there. My heart began to pound in earnest as I watched the indentation shift and another one, closer to me, take its place—as if someone were on his knees and crawling toward me.

I jumped from the bed, lurching for the light switch.

I flicked the light on and found a man, well, a ghost really, sitting on the edge of my bed and smiling up at me, resplendent in nineteenth century trousers and waistcoat. His sideburns were long, his hair was curly and short with a brownish tint.

My hand flew to my chest as I made the split-second decision not to run screaming from the room.

The ghost didn't look mean or scary, just curious. I inhaled deeply, trying to calm my heart.

"Who are you?" I managed to ask in a mere whisper.

They call me Pelham; I was lord of this Manor.

His voice inside my head threw me off for a second. "Can't you speak?" I asked aloud.

He sighed. *It is more difficult for me to speak in the way in which you are accustomed, so I just converse like this. I hope it doesn't bother you?*

I began to shake my head when I remembered what I was in the midst of doing when this man … er, ghost … interrupted me. I couldn't help the blush that stole my cheeks as mortification got the better of me. *Don't you know it's rude to spy on people*? I thought.

Ah, yes, sorry about that. It is so rare for me to get any visitors here—usually just Balfour.

Balfour? Ah yes, Rand … Rand Balfour. *Well, it was very rude of you, all the same.*

I apologize. What is your name?

Jolie … Jolie Wilkins.

He smiled in his ghostly way and floated toward me, as if to shake my hand. I took a step back until the door pre-empted me from further escape.

Pleased to meet you, he said and the smile on his lips deepened.

Likewise. Are there any other spirits here that I should know about?

The ghost shook his head. *None others, just me. Well, I suppose I should take my leave and allow you to return to your previous occupation.* He gave me a wicked grin.

"Oh my God," I muttered, covering my face with my hands. I couldn't imagine anything more embarrassing. Silence reverberated through the room. I peeked between my splayed fingers to see my surroundings empty; my visitor was gone.

~

"Good morning!" Rand greeted me with a wide smile as I entered the kitchen. Apparently, he was a morning person.

"Where is Christa?"

I shook my head and admired his blue jeans which hugged his rear and his white t-shirt which looked entirely too tight around his biceps. God, couldn't a girl get a break?

"She never rises before nine."

"How'd you sleep?" he asked as he helped himself to a glass of orange juice. "Care for a juice or a bucks fizz?"

"A what fizz?"

He grinned and held up the bottle of orange juice. "A juice and champagne."

"You mean a mimosa. No thanks." I chewed on my lip while I tried to figure out the best way to bring up the ghost. "Is this house haunted?" I guess I'm not likely to win any prizes for subtlety.

Rand laughed. "Ah, you got a visit from Pelham?"

"I did," I said with a frown and took a seat at the table. "Who is this Pelham?"

Rand brought his juice to the table and took a seat beside me. "An old friend of mine, William Pelham. We grew up together and he died in this house ... of cholera. He was only one and thirty. He left Pelham Manor to me."

I smiled at Rand's account of Pelham's age. Sometimes he had a tendency to switch into the language of his time period, and it was amusing. I dropped my gaze to his bare feet and noticed their deep golden tan—it seemed his entire body was kissed by the sun. "How long ago was that?" I asked.

Rand was quiet as he did the math in his head. "Nearly one hundred thirty years ago," he finished with a sigh and took a sip of his juice.

"But you've only lived here sixty years?"

He nodded. "I lived abroad for many years—Paris, Rome, Lucerne. I decided to return to jolly old England about sixty years ago, and I've been here ever since."

"Oh, I see," I said with a smile.

"You met Pelham last night, did you?" Rand prodded me, finishing his juice. He stood up and approached the sink, rinsing the glass. When he bent over to put the glass in the dishwasher, I had a very arresting view of his taut rear.

"Yes, he uh ... he scared me a little."

Rand closed the dishwasher and returned to the table, pulling his chair out and straddling it. "I'm certain he didn't intend to frighten you, probably was just excited to find such a beautiful woman in this house. I imagine he tires of me. I'll have a talk with him."

"A talk with him?" I swallowed hard, heat crawling up my neck as I wondered just how close they were. Would Pelham divulge what I was doing last night when we met? "Good friend? As in, you tell each other everything?"

"Well, certainly, do you think great friendships end with death?" Rand asked with furrowed brow.

"No, I suppose they wouldn't. In your world, anyway."

He balanced the chair on its front legs, looking like a child pretending to ride a bucking bronco. "That's now your world as well, don't forget. We're in this together from here on out."

I nodded, all too familiar with that reality. "So did Pelham tell you we met?" I asked, trying to sound indifferent. The stray thought floated through my head that maybe I shouldn't be so mortified. Everyone masturbated, right? I was a woman, with needs ...

Rand shook his head. "No, he failed to mention it."

81

So my embarrassing secret was safe … for now. Rand excused himself and trotted down the hallway. Moments later, he returned with an old leather album. He opened the jaundiced pages and flipped through them, regarding them with what appeared to be nostalgia. He stopped at one page and rotated the book so it faced me. I inspected the faded black and white picture and recognized Rand in some type of hunting outfit—tight trousers, an overcoat, and a bloodhound at his side.

"Wow, look at you," I said, thinking I'd start salivating any second. Rand looked like something you'd see on the cover of a romance novel. Fabio had nothing on him.

He laughed. "Styles were different then."

My attention moved to the man standing next to him in the photo—William Pelham. I took the book and focused on his companion. He was attractive and it appeared his hair was light in color, maybe brown. It was tough to tell from the black and white photo. His face was angular with a trim moustache and laughing eyes. There was a certain mischief in his gaze.

"Do you miss him?" I asked and handed the book back.

Rand nodded. "He was my best mate."

Maybe I could try to bring Pelham back? As soon as the thought occurred to me, my own sense of fear betrayed it. I'd only managed to reanimate one dead person; that didn't mean I was capable of doing it again. I mean, it had been an accident. Yeah, dropping the idea.

"But you can still talk with him?"

"Yes, Pelham and I continue to be friends though it is more difficult with him in the Underworld."

"This Underworld, is it an actual place?"

"You can think of it as such. It's just another level of existence."

"And does he like being in the Underworld?"

Rand seemed to consider the question, a frown marring his otherwise perfect face. "I don't know. As I said before, my interactions with him are not as they used to be. I might see him now and then and get a feeling he projects to me, but it's not at all similar to you and I standing here and talking."

Hmm, it seemed like Pelham and I had an easy enough time conversing. "Why would your interactions with Pelham be any different than Jack?"

Rand shrugged. "You can't assume what you find to be the case with one entity is the same with all of them. Depending on the person or creature in question, they all have different abilities, different levels in their abilities."

I nodded, satisfied with the response.

"I hope you're ready for your lessons?" Rand asked.

"Yes, I'm ready. What's on tap for today?"

"If by 'on tap' you mean, what you'll be learning today," Rand started with a smile, "I will leave that to Mathilda."

"Mathilda?"

"Yes, you are quite fortunate to have the oldest and wisest of the fairies teaching you some of your lessons. I had to promise Mathilda you were a prodigy, so please don't prove me wrong."

The warning annoyed me, but I nodded in spite of myself. "I'll try to make you proud." I attempted to keep the bite from my voice, but didn't succeed.

Rand's expression softened as he regarded me. "You've already made me very proud, Jolie. No need to worry on that."

The appearance of a newly awakened Christa interrupted us. She rubbed her sleep-swollen eyes and stifled a yawn.

"What's for breakfast?"

~

Well, fairies, for one thing, don't have wings—as far as I could judge by my introduction to Mathilda the fairy. She was a very old one but beautiful in her own right with skin so transparent, it glowed. A few crows' feet and laugh lines marked her years, though I imagined she was much older than her appearance would lead me to believe. Her green eyes, although alight with power, betrayed her age with their depth. Her hair cascaded about her small frame like a sea of silver, and she walked with the air of someone important and proud. Intrigued and self-conscious, I could only hope she'd be proud of her new pupil.

After our introductions, Rand allowed us the privacy of his office and Mathilda neared me, her eyes never leaving mine. She took my hand in hers and covered it with her other hand as if she were reading my soul through my skin.

"Tell me, child, why should I teach you? What makes you worthy of such a gift?"

I was surprised, as I'd thought Rand had already told her why I was worthy and for myself, I couldn't even begin to fathom why I was worthy. I couldn't very well tell her that though, especially in the wake of Rand's none-too-subtle account of how difficult it was for him to get this Mathilda to tutor me.

"Rand believes in me," I said in a small voice, reclaiming my hand when she dropped it. I approached the fireplace and took a seat on an armchair near the fire, berating myself for my stupid answer.

Mathilda laughed, a sound that reminded me of church bells. "That is the answer of one who does not believe in herself."

I sighed and dropped my gaze. Who was I to think I could outwit a fairy and a very old one at that? Better just to tell the truth, potentially angering Rand or not. "I'm not sure I'm worthy, to be honest. Everyone seems to think me capable of wonderful and great things and it seems that everywhere I turn, people … er … creatures are fighting over me and I'm not sure why."

Mathilda's face softened, relaxing the hold of her lips until they unraveled into a smile. "Rand believes you are capable of great things. He has

83

told me extensively of what you have been able to accomplish. Things that we have never seen in any one creature."

"Well, I hope to become great with your teachings." Ugh, I was brown nosing.

"I can see greatness within you, child. I see into you and I see goodness and kindness. That is the best place to breed magic."

"Thanks," I said, not really sure what else to say. Then I felt the uncomfortable drag of silence. I'm one of those people who can't stand long silences, so I think of stupid things to say to fill up the void and I was doing just that as I sat with the formidable fairy.

"What do you see when you behold me?" she asked and interrupted my mind's search for something, anything to say. I was pleased with the interruption.

I wasn't sure what type of answer she was looking for—did she mean physically what did I see, emotionally? Mentally? I figured just to go for the easiest answer first. "I see a striking woman with long silver hair and a petite frame with the most beautiful green eyes I've ever seen." Yep, one hundred percent brownnosing.

She smiled. "You have yourself to thank for that."

I wore my confusion.

"I am whatever anyone wants me to be. To Rand, I am an old woman with a knotted face and limbs and tangled hair. Someone, to him, who represents age and wisdom. To you, I am much more beautiful—someone who represents wisdom and femininity, it would seem."

It took me a second to grasp her meaning and when that second passed, I still wasn't sure I fully understood. "So you look different to Rand?"

"Rand can only see me as old, old but wise. There is nothing sensual or feminine in the picture Rand paints of me. He cannot join the notion of womanhood and age-old wisdom."

I frowned, not sure I was keeping up. "Is he a chauvinist?"

Mathilda laughed, and the bell-like cadence was music to my ears. "No, certainly not. He believes in you above all else. He sees you as the embodiment of feminine sensuality and beauty. He believes you are the Savior of the species, child."

I gulped, pleased I was seated as this was certainly information to take sitting down. Savior of the species was a hefty title and one that shouldn't attach itself to me. "How do you see me?" I asked.

"Young and naïve, but capable of incredible things. You need to grow and trust in the magic that is inherently part of you. You will be torn in different directions and you must trust the witch within you to show you the correct path."

So this is what Luke Skywalker must have experienced upon meeting Yoda. It was almost as if she were speaking a different language. I just couldn't understand what her ambiguous words meant. Not wanting to encourage this line of garbled insight, I changed the subject.

84

"So people see you however they want to see you?"

She nodded. "That is the beauty of fairy magic. We can be whoever you want us to be. You should take that as a lesson, child; you too can be whoever you want to be. As a witch, you can choose to be great or good. It is all up to you."

I smiled and appreciated my first lesson—believe in myself and I could achieve anything—it was like an after school special.

NINE

 T wo weeks later and I'd somewhat managed to adapt to my new circumstances. I had an English bank account now, and Rand had added to it generously. I knew he owed me wages, but I was convinced he'd overpaid me when I received my first bank statement. Trying to argue with him was futile and in the end, he told me to spend the extra money on a vehicle, something I'd need if I were to have any sort of independence. I wasn't sure how he did it, but he managed to convince me and before I knew it, I was the proud owner of a silver Range Rover Freelander, a smaller and less expensive version of his black Range Rover.

"You should just marry Rand," Christa said as we took the car for a test drive.

I slammed on the breaks. "Marry him?"

"Umm, hello, you're in the middle of the road."

I glanced in the rearview mirror. Fortunately, we were on a lone country road with only a few cows to show their disapproval. Getting used to driving on the left side of the road was hard enough and having Christa as a passenger made the overwhelming task even more daunting.

"He's loaded. You'd never have to work another day in your life."

I snorted, thinking of married life with Rand. Ridiculous. He'd be controlling, demanding, sexy as hell … I shook the useless thoughts from my head and looked to my right for oncoming traffic. Then remembered I should be looking to the left.

"Well, first of all, Rand is hardly the marrying type, so it's ridiculous even to have this conversation."

She turned on the radio and sifted through the stations, settling on techno. The insistent thudding from the speakers acted like a rat gnawing away at my nerves.

"I was just saying," she said defensively.

"There's no point …" The music gained in intensity, reverberating through the car like a stray bullet.

"Oh my God, Chris, can you please turn that off? It's going to make me have an accident."

Christa groaned, but turned the volume down, and my entire body breathed a sigh of relief. "I bet Rand's good in bed, too," she continued with an impish smile.

"What makes you think that?" Images of a naked Rand flashed through my mind like a bad porn. Not something to be thinking about when you're trying to learn to drive on the wrong side of the road.

Christa shrugged. "I don't know … he just has that certain something about him. I wonder if he'd be naughty …"

I laughed. "Do you realize you can't go for more than a day without talking about sex?"

"That's what makes me so popular with the boys," she answered with a little giggle. We pulled up to the driveway of Pelham Manor, and I parked the car, relieved we hadn't hit anything or anybody.

"I bet he's super naughty."

"Oh, God," I said with a frown and watched as the subject of our heated conversation neared us, his dimples in full effect.

He opened the door for Christa and once she'd stepped outside, poked his head in with a grin. "How are you finding the car?"

I returned the smile. "I love it."

He nodded. "If your afternoon is free, I wanted to teach you your next lesson myself."

I was thrilled with the idea, being infinitely more comfortable with him than I was with any of the fairies. So far, I'd been tutored by Mathilda and another fairy named Gor who taught me spells of nature—how to see with your natural eyes, those untainted by human society. Upon using my natural eyes, I was able to perceive all sorts of woodland life. There were pixies of all kinds—those that live in flowers, those that prefer bushes and trees, and even water pixies who swim about in slow moving streams or in puddles.

I opened the door, and Rand took my hand. The contact sent heat spiraling through my body. Swallowing hard, I followed his lead into the forest, wondering if my poor nerves would ever get used to him.

"Today I'm going to teach you how to find your inner beast."

I started to laugh, thinking it sounded ridiculous, when I remembered Rand changing into the shape of the bear at Bella's party. The laugh dropped right off my lips.

"Every witch has a sister beast within herself and in times of danger, it can be best to revert to the shape of the beast," he continued.

"How do I know what mine is?" I asked. "Or will I be a bear too?"

Rand didn't answer right away but unlocked the decrepit wooden gate that led into the wilderness bordering Pelham Manor. The squeak of the hinges sounded like a witch cackling.

"No, your beast won't be a bear. Your creature will choose you, and it will come to you in time. It takes a great deal of patience and …"

"Focus," I interrupted him with a grin. "Your favorite word—focus."

He laughed. "Yes, focus. Sometimes it's easier to bring forth the beast when you're in its natural domain. I find it much easier to draw forth the bear in the forest, and I imagine it will be easier for you as well."

Leaves crunched under my feet as I followed him further into the woods, the sun splaying against his hair until it appeared almost chestnut in color. The further we walked, the more the sun fought to get through the umbrella of tree branches. Finally losing the battle, we were bathed in an umbra of shadow.

We settled in a meadow, and I noted a few pixies as they danced upon a blade of grass, using it like a trampoline. They didn't seem to pay any attention to Rand or me and instead, just bounced up and down, giggling to one another.

I couldn't help the awe I felt at being able to see them. Without Gor's lesson, I'd never have been able to. "Look at the pixies, Rand," I said in a whisper. Rand noted them with disinterest—a quick nod of his head. I glanced at the pixies that were now facing both of us, one of them with her little hands on her hips, apparently not appreciating Rand's dismissal.

"Careful, they have a mean bite," he said with a smile.

Pixies and fairies were distantly related, think second cousins or cousins removed twice—whichever is farther apart. As I mentioned before, fairies (as far as I could tell after meeting Mathilda and Gor) don't have wings and are human size. Pixies, on the other hand, have beautiful ethereal wings that beat as quickly as a hummingbird's, so you can only see them when they're still. And pixies are rarely still. They reminded me of ants—each one set on her own mission and all appearing very busy. They're about the size of my thumb.

"Now, think of all the beasts in nature and allow one to choose you," Rand said, pulling my attention from the pixies. "Your beast will come forward to claim you; just allow it to do so."

I nodded and shut my eyes, imagining all the animals in the animal kingdom. I pictured Noah's ark and the pairs of animals he'd brought aboard his ship, and then my mind moved to National Geographic magazine. I started thinking of animals you find in the Sahara, but that didn't seem at all suitable since we were in England ...

"Has your beast chosen you?" Rand whispered.

I shook my head. "I can't focus."

"It might help if you picture a line of animals. Just tell the one that's yours to come forward."

I imagined all the animals lined up. It was a funny picture, thinking of cats and dogs lined up next to elephants and monkeys. And what about insects, should I have been imagining them to? Hmm, the idea of turning into a giant cockroach or praying mantis didn't thrill me. Yeah, nix on the insects.

Pretty soon, I had an expansive list of animals, but none were coming forward. Was I that pathetic that none of them wanted to be my other half? As soon as the thought left my head, a small red fox stepped forward. Her attention riveted on her paws, she seemed embarrassed. She turned her attention to a great hippo just next to her and dropped her gaze to the ground again.

"A red fox," I whispered.

"I should've known. You have something of the fox about you."

I was too enamored of the fox to pause and wonder what in the hell Rand was talking about.

"She seems very shy," I continued as I watched the fox come closer. Rand took hold of my hand, but I didn't dare open my eyes for fear of losing my fox.

"I'm going to help her."

I ignored the warm strength of his hand and focused on the quivering fox. The thick fur of a bear slipped between my fingers. The bear looked up at me and almost appeared to be smiling. I wasn't sure if he was only in my thoughts or if he was actually next to me, but I didn't open my eyes to find out. It took some getting used to, but I petted his head, slightly intimidated by the giant beast. He licked at my hand, and I bent down, so I was on his level. He lapped at my face, and the little fox came forward.

The closer the red fox came, the more the animals in the background began to fade away, and the more I realized the fox was my partner in crime. Rand, the bear, neared her cautiously and rubbed against her as she came closer to him.

Before I knew it, the fox was at my feet, and I maintained my hunched position, so as not to scare her. She came right up to me, sniffing and inspecting me, maybe to be sure I was, in fact, her witch of choice. Rand butted me until I started petting his head again while the fox licked my other hand.

I opened my eyes, and the vision shattered. My fox and the bear were gone. I found Rand staring at me with a smile on his handsome face. I guess it had all been in my head, which threw me because it had seemed so real.

"You found your little fox it seems."

"Yes, I have," I said, wondering if my fox was the best animal to have selected me. She wasn't large like Rand's bear or menacing like Bella's lion. But I guess she was better than a rat or a frog or something.

Rand drew up his knees and leaned back against a tree. "The fox is a very powerful ally to have, Jolie," he said, as if reading my thoughts. "She may not look like much, but she's quick and wise. I'm very pleased with this pairing."

I was pleased that Rand was pleased. "She's cute, too."

Rand chuckled. "Now that you've found her, you need to learn how to harness her power. You'll need it especially when you're in the natural world. You'll do much better as a fox than a human."

I leaned against the tree next to him. "How do I do that?"

"Call to her and allow her to take control of you. She'll know what to do and she'll help you."

I nodded and closed my eyes, calling for the fox in my mind. This time she came right away. "She's here," I whispered, not daring to open my eyes.

"Tell her to take control of you."

I allowed her to come very near me, and then I opened myself as best I could, envisioning a white light emanating from my body as I reached toward the fox.

At the exact moment I turned into a fox, I can't say it was painful at all. It was more a feeling of lightness—as if your soul is floating to the very top of your head and then floats out of you. It happened immediately and when I opened my eyes, the foliage had gone from green to yellow as well as the tufts of grass that peeked from the base of the trees. The orange tulips, too, had lost their color and disappeared into the yellow of the background.

It was like looking at a landscape through extremely thick glasses when you, yourself, have good vision. Everything appeared to be distorted and further away than it actually was. And the smells! The scent of water droplets on the leaves was as powerful as newly mown grass. When I turned my head, I caught the definite whiff of something dead that now lay rotting.

I didn't have time to inspect anything further, the pat of a bear's paw sending me careening. Landing on my rear, I yelped but was up and on my feet in the bat of an eyelash. The bear was just behind me, his paw raised as if to repeat the performance. But as a fox, I was notoriously quick, so I didn't miss a beat.

I sprinted around Rand and grabbed his fur with my teeth. He roared when I got a bit too much, but I knew it was all in fun and wasn't frightened of him. Once we grew tired of harassing one another, we began scouting the forest, our noses leading us in our exploration. I uncovered a den of newly born foxes and scampered away when their mother grumbled at me. A mouse darted from one bank of daffodils to another and I was about to go chasing after him when Rand growled. I turned to face him, and he shook his great head—apparently, he wanted me within sight.

Finding too much fun in taunting Rand, I took advantage of a momentary lapse in his ever-vigilant watch and hid behind a tree stump. When he lumbered around the stump, I jumped at him, grabbing a mouth full of his fur. His thunderous growl met my ears as he reared around and we tumbled into a yellow broom bush. The tumble broke my concentration and before I knew it, I was human again with an enormous bear lying atop me.

And I was naked.

Leaves stuck to my back, and the flowers of the broom bush dotted the landscape of my body, making me look like the queen of the fairies clad only in yellow blossoms. The bear's fur tickled and irritated the sensitive skin of my breasts. In a split second, the bear's fur disappeared, only to be replaced with the soft sprinkling of dark brown hair on Rand's glorious chest.

My cheeks colored as Rand stared down at me. There was a heat in his eyes that terrified me as much as it excited me. He didn't move away but rather, pulled himself up, so he could see every unclothed inch of me. He reached down and dusted the yellow blossoms from my breasts, his fingers grazing my nipples, which instantly stood to attention. A flush of heat stole across my face as his gaze traversed my breasts, my belly and the junction of my thighs. It was all I could do to grab his face and yank it back up to eye level.

"What …" I started.

90

His mouth on mine preempted me from finishing my sentence. His lips were full and warm. Shivers tore down my spine when I felt his tongue caress my lips, as if begging entrance to my mouth.

He pulled back just an inch, his warm breath fanning across my lips. I wrapped my arms around him and explored the sinewy muscles of his back as he shifted. Something hard pulsed between my thighs, something decidedly male. I closed my eyes, resisting the urge to open my legs. When I dared to open my eyes again, I didn't say anything, but pulled his head down to mine and kissed him as he groaned into my mouth. Then like a flash of lightning, he pulled away.

"Bloody hell, we can't do this," he said, but his husky voice would've suggested otherwise. He refused to look at me.

I didn't know what to say as he'd just gone from boiling hot to frigid in a matter of seconds. "Why?" It seemed a good question.

"Because I'm your employer and it's my duty to protect you ... not blasted well seduce you." He stood up, leaves stuck to his knees. But it wasn't his knees that captured my attention. It was his erection. With a nod of his head, he denied me the pleasure of looking upon his nudity and clothed himself in a black t-shirt and jeans. I couldn't help the obvious slump of my shoulders.

I said nothing, but thought of a white sundress and felt the material flow over my naked skin. I inwardly smiled as Rand's gaze traveled the length of me. The dress was short and just skimmed the tops of my thighs, and I'd imagined it with a couple of buttons undone down the front, so the junction of my breasts was exposed. Hey, all's fair in love and war, right?

"Goddamn you," he growled and turned away from me, his hands fisting at his sides. "You know how hard this is on me."

He started to walk away, leaving me wondering what the hell had just happened. I stood up but didn't make any motion to close the buttons. Instead, I clasped my hands together which made my cleavage almost buoyant within the dress.

"You don't think it's hard on me? You make no sense. In Chicago, I could barely keep you away from me."

He turned as quickly as a snake that had been trodden on and his eyes were just as venomous. His gaze went directly to my breasts, exactly where I'd intended. Goddamn, this was just too easy. He seemed to struggle to bring his eyes up to mine and I couldn't help the sense of pride that suffused me. Somehow, I was managing to throw the normally staid warlock into a sexual frenzy. Jolie Wilkins ... sex kitten ... hmm, I liked the sound of that.

"That was different," he said and his chest panted with the effort.

I smiled as I noticed how short his sentences were. I supposed a man, when trying to defeat his libido, reverted to caveman talk.

"How is that different? You could kiss me there, but not here?"

"That was before you worked for me ... long term."

His hands hadn't quite relaxed at his sides—still balled into fists. He immediately released them as if he'd been writing a five-page letter and was taking a break to exercise his cramped fingers. My attention shifted to the proof of his obvious excitement, stirring in his pants. I quirked a brow while he frowned and covered the bulge with his hands.

Then I remembered the whole situation pissed me off. "So you would've screwed me in Chicago and left with no remorse?" I asked, forcing the amusement from my voice.

"You're blowing this out of proportion." He shook his head and started to walk away again.

"Wait."

He stopped, but didn't turn around to face me. "Jolie …"

"No, dammit, what happened?" I caught up with him and grabbed his arm, insisting he look at me. "You can't just leave when …"

As soon as I touched him, he turned on me with a vengeance. I was almost frightened when I saw the lust swimming in his eyes. He pushed me none too gently, and my back came up against a tree. The bark bit into my skin as he pushed his body against mine and nudged his knee between my thighs. Spreading my legs, he rammed the bulge of his erection against my pelvis. The sting of thousands of needles ebbed within me, and my mouth fell open—I couldn't seem to get enough air through my nose.

God, how I wanted him.

His mouth was demanding when it found mine again. This time there was no gentle attempt to gain entrance; he thrust his tongue between my lips while his lower body continued to pump against mine. His hands slid down my arms and grasped both of my hands, pulling my arms above my body. He pinned them there and held them with one hand while the other started a descent, pausing just above my breasts.

As I wondered what he would do next, he pulled away from me and brought his attention to my chest. I followed his gaze and noticed that one of my breasts had already freed itself from the halter top of my dress. He looked upon it as if he was starving and it was a smorgasbord of gourmet delicacies.

I closed my eyes as soon as his hand plied the delicate skin of my breast, euphoria burning in the pit of my stomach. My eyes shot open when his tongue flicked my nipple, and I tried to bring my hands down, to run them through his hair, but he unapologetically kept my arms pinned above my head. He squeezed my breast and continued sucking on it while I felt as if I were dying the sweetest of all deaths.

With a low growl, he tore the strap from my shoulder and the dress pooled around my waist. I gasped as his mouth fell to the other breast, and he sucked it violently.

His free hand delved between my thighs and as soon as he touched the obvious proof of my excitement, he threw himself away from me. I opened my eyes and found him before me, hunched over and panting. His eyes were livid, like a rabid dog's.

"Fuck!" He ran an agitated hand through his hair. "Bloody fuck!"

He took another step away from me as if I were going to throw a net over him and force him to suck on my breasts again. He turned away from me and paced back and forth before turning his angry expression on me.

I thought it a good time to button my top.

"I thought I made it clear. I can't do this with you. Not when I'm your employer. We need to keep things strictly platonic."

"Umm, you just attacked me," I said, with a great show of put-outedness.

He threw his arms up in the air and continued pacing. "I can't help it, Jolie. Goddammit, can't you see that?"

"I want you too, Rand." It seemed like a simple math problem—if Jolie wants Rand and Rand wants Jolie, then, logically, that should equal sex. "Why not go with it?"

He looked at me like I'd just sprung another head. "Because we're living together now, and we're in a business relationship. Those two things are reason enough for us not to have sex." To drive the point home, he kicked the stump of the tree as if it had spurred the whole sexual business.

I wasn't sure if I should feel disappointed or offended or what. I managed not to feel anything at all and, instead, returned his glare, self-consciously smoothing my dress. "Whatever, Rand."

He looked like he was about to say something, but the words must have escaped him because he just grunted, gave me a look of pure annoyance and trudged off.

~

At the end of the week, I was pleased with my lessons and with myself. I'd learned to harness the power of the fox, to see beyond the periphery of human vision, and Mathilda had taught me to change my likeness, something she insisted I'd use at some point in my witch career. All in all, my lessons were progressing well and my abilities becoming more and more pronounced.

But Rand, well that was another situation entirely. To maintain our employer-employee relationship, he made himself scarce. He seemed preoccupied with travels and finances, but I was sure it was just an excuse to avoid me. I did have my own friends, though. I spent much of my time with Christa, and I formed a friendship with the unlikely person of Pelham who spent many of his evenings with me.

Pelham had lived quite a life—he'd been born the only son to a wealthy landowner. Living the esteemed life of an affluent young man, he courted many a beautiful girl and never worked a day in his life.

What a useless existence! I thought with a grin.

Pelham sat at my vanity and regarded me with annoyance, his ghostly lips caught in a severe line.

Quite a wonderful existence, actually. A life filled with the pursuit of art and literature. I would hardly call it useless.

93

I enjoyed the rise I was getting out of him. *What have you done for humanity? Nothing. Never worked, you don't know the meaning of supporting yourself. That's what I call useless.*

He crossed his arms over his chest and glared down his nose at me, looking like an irritated Lord Byron. One thing I'd noticed about Pelham was he didn't take criticism well.

Rubbish. I don't care to argue with you. Why are you in such a foul mood?

I sighed and shook my head, throwing myself against the multiple pillows that crowded my bed. Pelham, apparently liking the image of me stretching out on the bed, floated to the frame of the canopy, wrapping his ethereal hand around the post.

Sorry for being so moody. I just have things going on right now and I'm stressed out.

Pelham frowned and took a seat on the bed, appearing to lean against the post. *What things?*

Rand and I aren't getting along. I knew I couldn't say much more than that. Pelham wouldn't understand and wouldn't like the fact that I had feelings for another man. Even though I told him time and time again that I couldn't develop romantic feelings for a ghost, he wouldn't take no for an answer.

Pelham was quiet for a few seconds. Well, he was always quiet—I guess it's better to say my brain was silent for a few seconds. *Rand can be difficult. I've known him for many years and though he is like a brother to me, he is definitely the most stubborn person I've ever met.*

I smiled. *Well thanks for listening to me.*

No worries. He leaned forward on his elbows and looked like he was about to disappear into the billowy duvet. Instead, he traced my naked legs with his ghostly hand and stopped short where my skirt met my lower thighs.

What are you doing? I asked, sounding amused more than annoyed.

He frowned. *Please give me a touch, just one? I haven't had a woman in so long.*

I just laughed. *Piss off, Pelham.*

He righted himself and did his best impression of thoroughly offended. I laughed again. *You know neither of us would feel anything anyway. You'd go right through me.*

That's what she said, I thought to myself and smiled. Of course *The Office* humor was lost on Pelham.

You always spoil my fun, he said.

I said nothing, but shook my head as I considered how ridiculous it was that I couldn't get one man to have sex with me if I paid him and yet, another one was just dying to do the deed … no pun intended. I stifled a yawn and glancing at the clock on my mantle, realized it was late.

I think I'm going to go to bed.
Very well. Adieu.

94

He was still annoyed—it was in the sharp cast of his shoulders and the droop of his mustache. He didn't give me time to consider it further, but faded into the recesses of my duvet, floating down through the floor to do God only knew what.

But even as he vanished, I knew I wouldn't sleep. I wasn't tired—I'd just said it because I needed some time to myself. Like an animal in a cage that's much too small, I paced the perimeter of the room. My thoughts were a tempest—all revolving around Rand. They swirled around my head, running headlong into one another until I wanted to scream. Something needed to be done. I couldn't continue to live with the man, knowing he wanted me and knowing I wanted him. Something had to give.

Thinking my throat felt like the desert, I decided to take a walk downstairs for a glass of water. I threw open my bedroom door and started down the hall when a light emanating from Rand's bedroom caught my attention. I hadn't seen him at all in the last week. It was time to reconnect. I lightly knocked on his door, and my breath caught when he opened it.

"Jolie, is everything alright?"

He was dressed in a pair of plaid boxer shorts, and I had to pull my attention from his well-defined chest. Some women like a man's ass best or maybe his back, but I've always been a chest girl. Not that I've had many to admire … Anyway, Rand's was certainly one worth admiring. Looking upon his nearly naked form now, I couldn't help but recall how feral and passionate he'd been in the woods.

This was a bad idea.

I nodded and prayed my voice wouldn't fail me. "I was on my way downstairs for a glass of water when I noticed your light was on. What are you doing awake?"

He leaned against the doorframe and regarded me coolly. Clearly, his mind was still on what had happened in the woods as well. "Couldn't sleep. You?"

"I'm just headed to bed now as a matter of fact," I answered. "After I get my glass of water."

He rubbed the back of his neck and my attention fell to his shorts, searching for a sign of his interest—hoping his mouth was saying one thing, but his body another. Nothing. I couldn't help the disappointment that surged within me.

"Good … good …" he said absently.

"Where have you been all week?" I asked quickly.

"I've been seeing about some jobs we've been requested for."

"Jobs?" It had been the last thing I'd expected to hear.

"Yes, if you recall, I told you about the relationship between employer and employee …"

I vaguely remembered that conversation. I believe I'd been more interested in my own safety as Bella had marked me as her own, there was the

95

vampire Sinjin to contend with, and then Rand nearly died. Employer relationship discussion?

"Vaguely," I lied.

"Well, it takes quite a bit of money to upkeep Pelham Manor ..."

"Why don't you just use your magic, so you don't have to work?" Why work when you can control the cosmos?

Rand laughed at my supposed naiveté. "There are rules within our society that you will learn in time. One of those rules is that we are prohibited from creating our own money ... inflation affects witches just as much as humans."

"It seems funny that witches would bother themselves with inflation." I was pleased just to have an avenue of conversation that wasn't a threatening one. Although I burned with the need to touch him, if talking about inflation would prolong the sight of him in his boxers, so be it.

"Who makes these rules and who enforces them?"

"The rules have been around for as long as I can remember. They're within the charter of the witches, the creed by which we run our lives. And as far as someone enforcing them, we do have our own police force of sorts—something more akin to your idea of a hit man. Needless to say, we don't challenge them."

"Going back to the jobs you were discussing ..." I said, not wanting to think about warlock hit men.

"Right. Well, there are a couple of jobs that have come my way. I'm just trying to decide if you are ready yet."

I couldn't keep the surprise from my face. When he'd started talking about jobs, I hadn't even considered that I might be involved. I guess it was a stupid oversight on my part. There had been that whole conversation we'd had at Bella's party where Rand had said I was now working for him. I'm not sure what I'd been expecting.

"I'm supposed to do the jobs with you?"

Rand laughed and his dimples usurped his face, painting a glorious picture. "Well, of course, that's the point of me hiring you, you realize?"

I nodded absentmindedly. With his unshaven face, dancing eyes and beautiful smile, my legs were the consistency of soggy cereal. I was surprised I was even still standing. God, did I have it bad.

"Oh yeah, I guess that makes sense. What are the jobs?"

"The first job is breaking a spell that was put on a demon ..."

I was ripped right out of my pity party. "Wait just a second! Demons?"

Rand ignored my outburst and placed a hand on my shoulder. Although he meant to be calming, all it did was send a jolt through me that lodged right in my lower stomach. I lacked the ability to respond.

"The second is placing a spell on someone's neighbor," Rand continued.

Finally, I was able to find my voice. It helped that he'd stepped away and taken his hand with him. "That sounds easy enough ..."

96

"The third job is reanimating a dead werewolf," he finished and eyed me speculatively.

"And let me guess which one pays the most …" I started, angst bleeding through my voice.

"You can imagine which I'm most tempted to accept? After all, we do need to test your acumen for bringing creatures back, don't we?"

A rhetorical question if ever I'd heard one.

I sighed as I thought of the daunting task ahead. "How do we know this is something I can even do again? Maybe it was just a fluke."

Rand shrugged. "Could be, and I've warned the client as much, but they still want to give it a go. They've agreed to pay half the money up front and if you aren't able to reanimate the wolf, we're still able to keep the deposit … and I'll give it to you, either way."

Rand was generous.

"Are werewolves dangerous?" I asked with a frown.

"They can be, but that's why you'll have me," he answered with a smug smile.

Generous and arrogant.

TEN

It seems nothing is ever as you expect.

"They're the werewolves?" I whispered to Rand, my attention falling on the pack who looked like a bunch of scraggly humans—longish hair, shabby outfits, and a generally nomadic appearance. They were about as ferocious and terrifying as the pixies I'd seen in Rand's garden.

Rand didn't respond but led me to a chair near the blazing hearth of his dining room. The wolves assembled themselves around his imposing twenty-person dining table and reminded me of a bunch of homeless people awaiting Thanksgiving dinner. I felt like the turkey as they watched me walk across the floor, their intense eyes unblinking. I forced a smile on my lips.

"Hi, I'm Jolie."

All different ages, there were three women and five men but, apparently, the actual pack was much larger and they were the chosen eight. If they were the chosen, I hated to see the rest of the troop.

I'd say they tended to have a bit more hair than humans did and Rand explained their hair grows at three times the rate a human's does. Any hairdresser would consider a werewolf to be a cash cow.

Before I had a chance to take my seat, I was surrounded.

"So nice to meet you," a woman with an American accent and flame red hair said.

She patted my arm expectantly.

I was a little taken aback by the contact. "Oh, okay thanks …" I started.

A man patted me on the back, shaking his head in what I thought was wonder. "Incredible powers you have." He sounded American too. I guess these werewolves were from the States. They sure had traveled a long way.

It was my turn to shake my head. "Well, I'm not sure you should expect too much …"

"Absolutely amazing," someone who looked like Jerry Garcia added.

They continued to fuss and buzz about me as if I were a great messiah. I hoped I'd not disappoint them as I had every doubt concerning my ability to bring back their leader. For one thing, we weren't even at the locale where he'd met his fate. Rand thought my powers strong enough that it wouldn't matter but, to me, it sounded like it was fated for failure.

And to make this enormous task even more impossible? There was no ghost. How I was to reanimate a dead wolf when there was no ghost, and we weren't anywhere near the place where he'd died, was beyond me. Rand wasn't so pessimistic and seemed to think if we had an article of clothing or something of a personal nature, we might be able to get enough "essence," as he called it, to bring the wolf back.

About their dead leader, his name was Trent, and he'd been killed by a rival werewolf pack about four months ago. It seemed he was the be-all-end-all of pack leaders as the small group couldn't elect a decent vice-werewolf to take his place and instead, decided to reanimate him.

The wolves, not wanting to miss any part of the performance, decided that Rand and I should sit on top of the table, in the middle of everyone, so they could see what was going on. After Rand assisted me to the tabletop, I sat cross-legged when one of the wolves shoved a t-shirt in my hand.

"It was Trent's," the man offered with a hasty nod.

I faced Rand.

"Shall we?" he asked and reached for my hands.

Before I closed my eyes, I hazarded a glimpse at Christa who gave me the thumbs up. She would serve as interpreter to the werewolf pack, explaining everything I did.

I closed my eyes and focused on the shirt. The image of a man popped into my head, and air caught in my throat. I could only assume it was Trent. The quickness of the vision shocked me. I was accustomed to having to wait, focus, and wait some more until any inkling of a vision would come. Now, I merely closed my eyes and Trent was before me. The fairy lessons must've been paying off!

Trent was not quite what I'd imagine a werewolf to be—he didn't at all resemble his pack although he did have a plethora of dark hair atop his head. He was dressed in a suit and looked just like your average, run of the mill businessman—neither tall nor short.

He was of a good age to be a pack leader, maybe in his midthirties. He was broad and stocky as you'd envisage a werewolf to be, and attractive with wide set brown eyes, high cheekbones and a full mouth. He had a generous nose—some might even say it was big. He smelled of men's aftershave.

How he was the leader of the ragtag group was beyond me. They looked as if they were one-step from homelessness but Trent was a suave, and for all intents and purposes, debonair businessman.

His cell phone went off, and it wasn't one of those annoying ringtones. You know the ones that attempt to sound like a good song, but in the world of phone rings, sound more like the soundtrack to Pong or maybe Pac Man.

He answered it with a terse "hello" and the voice on the other end was a woman thanking him for "the other night." He was quick to hang up, and I figured he was a womanizer. I wondered if she was also a wolf. The more I thought about it, the more I wondered if maybe she was sitting around the table tonight—maybe his ladylove was Big Red?

Trent must've died in or near his work because suddenly I was in an office. He plopped his briefcase on the seat next to him and began listening to his messages. Halfway through the first message, he brought his head up and seemed to be studying the door. After deciding a door couldn't be so engaging,

I realized he'd caught the scent of something. He paused and looked like someone stuck in freeze frame—one foot before the other as if he were about to walk away, but no motion accompanied the attempt. His nose was in the air, like he was trying to discern what the smell could be.

Once in motion, he followed the scent to a cupboard in the corner of his office. He opened the door and growled. He tore from the office so quickly, I had to sprint to keep up with him.

I never did find out what was in the cupboard.

As I followed him downstairs and outside, he darted into an alley behind the office building. I rushed around the corner, and was hit with the foulest of all smells. Is there ever a nice smelling alleyway? Forcing my attention from something that smelled cross between old fish and vinegar, I found a wolf standing before me.

Werewolves are nothing like movies depict them. They're bigger than your average wolf and brawnier, think the wolf's larger and bigger cousin. But they don't have any of that Hollywood horror that you usually think of when you hear "werewolf"—no salivating from the mouth, or walking on two feet (with ridiculously muscular legs), and no flaming red eyes.

Steeling my resolve, I took a hesitant step forward. Trent, the wolf, raised his back and growled, his canines glistening. A black wolf appeared out of nowhere, and my breath caught in my throat. The other wolf growled at Trent, his hackles raised. I watched, transfixed, as the two wolves lunged at one another.

They were something to be reckoned with, that's for sure. Lots of growling and grunting and gnashing of teeth. They nipped at one another, but it didn't look as if either was doing any permanent damage ... maybe just some bald spots here and there. But I didn't want to mislead myself—Trent had to die somehow and soon—it just didn't look like this wolf was going to be the bearer of that death sentence. No sooner did the thought cross my mind then a man stepped from a hidden corner in the alley, a gun aimed at Trent. The other wolf seemed to understand some hidden cue and disengaged himself as the human fired.

I needed to interfere somehow with the moment Trent died in order to bring him back. I had nothing to go on other than what had happened when I'd brought Jack back, so I just dived in front of Trent and grabbed a tuft of his fur. Immediately, that same intense light that had visited me when I'd reanimated Jack blinded me. I couldn't keep my eyes open against it. Whereas the faintest humming of energy had surged through me when touching Jack, I now felt a stream of electricity, like I'd been hit by lightning. It tore through me, from head to toe, and then stopped. Before I had the chance to feel any sort of relief, I could feel my own energy separating from me, a part of myself pulling away from me. Suddenly panicked, I screamed but the feeling was already gone.

I groaned when I felt my cheek hitting something hard and unyielding. Opening my eyes, I realized it was the table I'd been sitting on. I looked up and found Rand leaning over me, his brows drawn in concern.

"She's coming out of her vision," Christa said in explanation as the wolves around the table nodded enthusiastically. She reminded me of a docent giving a bunch of kids a tour of a museum.

"Is he here?" I asked, feeling drunk. It took me a second to shake off the reaction.

"She wants to know if your leader is here," Christa said as she eyed each of the wolves.

"He's not here," Rand said and shook his head.

I turned to the others to find their expressions crestfallen. I forced myself upright. I couldn't understand it. "I did exactly the same thing I did before, Rand."

He shook his head and looked at Trent's shirt in my hand. "Maybe there just wasn't enough to go on," he said.

"There just wasn't enough to go on," Christa repeated, shaking her head. She was driving me nuts.

Rand took my hand, his grip strong and warm. I gave him a wavering smile in thanks as he helped me down from the table.

I had failed.

But I wouldn't let my despair show. Smoothing my hands down my jeans, I thought frantically of what to say, my attention traveling over the wary group. How did one begin to apologize for not being able to reanimate their pack leader?

That's when I saw him—just beyond our small group, standing in the doorframe of the dining room. He started limping toward us, looking like he'd just been to hell and back. The lamplight hit his familiar features and I gasped, throwing my hand over my mouth. It probably didn't look good for the powerful reanimator to be surprised with her own success, but oh well.

"Trent!" Red called out—yeah she was definitely the one on the answering machine. At her call, they were all on their feet, knocking their chairs this way and that in order to tend to their recovered leader.

The dead wolf was back, but he didn't look happy.

"What the hell …" Trent started. Luckily someone nearby had the wherewithal to hand him a towel with which he covered his nudity.

"What happened?" he asked, pushing the throng of his followers away from him.

I took a step back, right into Rand's hard body. His arm went around my shoulder and chest, pulling me into him as if instinctively protecting me.

A very enthusiastic bottle-blond approached Trent, a huge smile on her face. "We hired the witch to bring you back."

His attention sought the "witch" and landed on me when his people gestured in my direction. "You, come here," he said and motioned toward me. His accent sounded faintly American, but with hints of something else.

101

I took a step forward, but Rand's arm tightened around me, pulling me back. He sidestepped me, being careful to keep a decent distance between Trent and me.

"Your pack hired us to reanimate you," Rand began before I had a chance to say boo.

Trent nodded, never taking his eyes from mine. "I see," he said and continued to study me. "I've never heard of this being possible, you must be some witch."

I said nothing, but shrugged as Rand took over.

"It seems we've done the job you asked of us. If you'd please provide the remainder of the balance, you can be on your way."

One of the minions neared us and fumbled with his wallet, giving me ample opportunity to invade Rand's thoughts. *That was pretty rude of you. Usually you're the poster boy for English manners. If you're so keen to get rid of them, why invite them here in the first place?*

Rand didn't look up from watching the younger man sort through his wallet, dropping receipts and sticks of gum.

Rude or not, I had no choice but inviting them here. Wolves can't be trusted and I've reinforced Pelham Manor with a protection spell. We're safer dealing with them here than we would be in public.

The scruffy young man finally found a money order and handed it to Rand. I thought it funny that a werewolf would bother himself with something as human and silly as a money order, but there it was. Rand took the proffered check and folded it, putting it in the breast pocket of his long-sleeved shirt. I had to stifle the smile threatening my lips as the young man returned to his pack—he looked like Ron Howard and was as intimidating.

Sometimes Rand was just ridiculous.

"Witch," I turned to see Trent take a few steps toward us. "Thank you."

I said nothing, but nodded and watched Trent turn and lead the rag tag group out of the dining room. Christa and I followed Rand to the balcony and watched them shuffle down the staircase and exit through the front door. They looked like they were on a field trip—all single file.

"So this time you just touched his fur?" Christa asked.

I nodded and retreated back into the dining room, Christa beside me. "Yes, I think that's the crucial part—I must make physical contact at the time of said creature's death."

"Do you know how you're able to do it yet?" Christa asked.

I shook my head. "No idea. The same thing happened to me this time only five times stronger. Like I got hit by lightning or something."

I took a seat at the table, watching Christa take one opposite me. Rand leaned against the wall behind Christa and eyed me.

"Interesting," he noted and strummed his fingers along his chin as if in deep thought. "Probably because werewolves are creatures of Underworld. Jack was just a human."

"Could be," I said. But it was all conjecture. I didn't imagine I'd ever really learn how I was capable of bringing creatures back. I guess I was now keeping company with Stonehenge, the Egyptian pyramids … hmm, what else has never been explained? Ah, every episode of *Lost*.

"You did a good job, Jolie," Rand said.

I just smiled and dropped my gaze—I've never really mastered the whole being good at taking compliments thing. I'm probably better at taking criticisms.

"Were you scared?" Christa asked with wide eyes.

"No, not really," I said, thinking to myself that otherworldly creatures had a bad rap. I had no idea what demons were like, but now that I'd met some werewolves, I could honestly say they weren't half bad. They seemed to love one another and balance successful careers (if Trent was any indication). And as for vampires, Sinjin was all I had to go on there. And in a word, he was just scrumptious.

"They didn't look like werewolves you see in the movies," Christa said, cocking her head as if trying to bring to mind a werewolf you see in the movies.

"More like a regular wolf, but bigger and burlier," Rand finished.

"So what did you think of the leader?" Christa asked with raised brows and I knew she'd found Trent attractive. Come to think of it, he seemed just her type—burly and entirely masculine.

"He was nice looking," I said with a laugh, "for a wolf."

"Nice looking?" Rand asked with incredulity. "I would think him a bit too coarse for your tastes."

I frowned. "Oh really, and how would you know what my tastes are?" Jerk-head.

"Well, I suppose I don't," he said and shifted uncomfortably.

"I'll go and cash the money order first thing tomorrow," Christa interrupted our embarrassing exchange, and I was only too happy for her to do so.

She and Rand had arranged that she would serve as his secretary. She seemed ecstatic about the position—she'd only had two jobs in her life—one was working for me, and the other had been working at a video rental store in Spokane. She was understandably excited to be working for Rand—he paid much better than the video store or I.

~

Two nights later, I was still high from bringing back the wolf. With what had become a permanent grin on my lips, I strolled to the French doors of my terrace, opening them wide while humming *Think of Me*, from the Phantom of the Opera. The moon was full and looked like a glowing orb amid the velvet darkness of the night sky. There weren't many stars out tonight, or maybe the moon just overpowered them with its milky rays.

I leaned against the railing, letting the fragrant breeze cool my skin. Pelham floated through my wall, and I started to face him when I noticed a flash of movement below my balcony. I stiffened and leaned forward, hovering over the railing. Had it been a dog? Maybe a fox? England was certainly full of them. Nope, it was a wolf. It stepped into a shaft of moonlight and the redness of its coat burst to life, a coat I recognized as belonging to Trent.

Why is that wolf pacing outside? Pelham asked.

A very good question and one I was wondering myself. *I think he wants me to go down there.*

Are you mad? He could kill you very easily.

I shook my head. Pelham was like having an incessant voice of doom always at the ready. I wasn't in the mood for it tonight. *I'm not so sure he could kill me easily. I am a witch, you know?* I pushed past the ghost and started for the door.

Are you going out there?

I nodded. *I don't think he'll go away unless I do.*

Then I am going with you.

I laughed. *What will you do if he attacks? Scare him?*

I fail to see the humor in that.

I didn't respond and instead, grabbed a coat and headed outside with Pelham floating at my heels. The thought occurred to me that maybe I should get Rand, but I hadn't seen him all day and anyway, I was a witch and capable of taking care of myself.

Once outside, I headed toward the wolf and watched as he neared the forest, apparently not comfortable visiting me in full view of the house.

This is madness. Pelham continued and was beginning to annoy me. Clearly, he thought I was in more danger than I did and I wasn't sure which of us was right.

I turned on him with my hands on my hips, doing my best pissed off expression. *Go back home if you're going to carry on. I won't be gone long.*

Fine. His feelings were hurt. *You do not want me here, so I will leave you to be eaten by that wolf.*

Before I could respond, he disappeared, and so I turned to the task of finding out what Trent could want with me.

"Witch."

I wheeled around at the sound of his voice. He stood in front of me, naked except for a pair of boxers. A flush stole my cheeks as I took in his olive chest covered with wiry dark hair. His muscles were broad and well defined. I forced my eyes to his and suddenly had the funniest glimpse of a wolf with a pair of red boxer shorts in its mouth.

"Why are you here?" I asked, cutting to the chase. I guess I wasn't in a very affable mood tonight. It seemed I was snapping at everyone.

"I came to talk with you."

I could've deduced that much. "So talk."

He chuckled, but continued. "I wanted to thank you for what you did …"

"Rand makes the decisions on jobs we take, not me, so you should thank him."

He cracked his knuckles and gave me a broad smile. "Well, I daresay it was you who did the work? At least that's what my people told me."

"We share in the responsibility."

"What's your name?"

"Jolie."

He nodded as if my name could only be Jolie.

"Well, witch Jolie, I came to tell you my pack is forever indebted to you and we've sworn ourselves to protect you should you ever need it."

I was taken aback. I'm not sure what I'd been expecting, but I'd been on edge since first seeing him. There was just something about him that spelled danger. Maybe it was just his bad-boy persona. I relaxed. "Thank you."

"Can you whistle?" he asked and thoroughly confused me.

After a moment of wondering why he'd ask me this, I shrugged and figured I might as well answer. "Yes."

"Please do so."

I was sure I looked as perplexed as I felt, but whistled in spite of myself. Trent seemed to hang on the sound when I remembered dogs have excellent hearing and maybe werewolves even more so.

"I'm committing the tonal vibration to memory," he said and paused. "Whenever you need me, just whistle and I'll come."

I wanted to make a joke about whistling while I work, but held myself back. I didn't imagine the wolf would appreciate it, and he was being civil, after all.

"What if you're far away?" I couldn't help asking the obvious.

He quirked another debonair smile—one I'm sure he'd used to win over many women. This guy just breathed player. "We're creatures of the Underworld, right? We have powers that transcend human abilities. Whistle, and wherever you are, I'll come for you."

It wasn't every day a girl had a sworn protector even if he was a hairy wolf who probably got around.

"Thank you."

"One other thing," he began.

"Yes?"

"When I died," he hesitated and I imagined it must've been a weird sentence to say. "Did you see who killed me?"

"You were fighting with a wolf," I started, trying to remember exactly what had happened. "And a human stepped out from the shadows and shot you. I couldn't see his face because his back was to me."

Trent bobbed his head, as if remembering himself. "The wolf was from a rival pack of ours. Do you remember what the man looked like?

"Normal height with dark hair … sorry, that's all I remember." I guess I should've been paying more attention, but the man had jumped out of the shadows so quickly. Then he'd fired his gun, and I had to worry about touching Trent at the moment of his death … it was over before it started.

He nodded, and I thought maybe he'd leave. But he hesitated. "Would you care to go to dinner with me some night?"

Maybe it was the way he said it—with none of the machismo and conceit I'd seen him display otherwise. He actually sounded nervous—like I might turn him down. Me! Someone who hadn't had a date since … anyway, my lips parted in surprise. A sworn protector and a date? My night was off to a good start.

"I'd be happy to go to dinner with you," I answered, still a little bit shocked that he'd asked me. Aside from Rand, I couldn't remember the last time I'd actually had a date. And really, Rand and I never had gone on a real date. So I guess that didn't count.

Trent smiled, and I felt as if I could get used to such a charming expression. He wasn't exactly what I'd call my type at first glance—maybe he had a bit too much of the playboy thing going on. Of course, I wasn't even sure what my type was, as I didn't date. True, I had something for Rand, so if he was the control, then Trent was nothing like my type.

He was shorter than Rand and stockier and seemed to be hairier, but he had a nice face and a strong, capable body—well everything in view anyway. There was something about him—a certain charisma that was attractive, and I could definitely understand why women would pursue him, as I'm sure they did.

"Great. I will pick you up on Saturday evening at eight o'clock if that suits you?"

"It's a date!" I answered and watched as Trent assumed his wolf likeness and with a canine grin, trotted off.

I couldn't help the smile that stole my lips as I made my way inside and upstairs. Maybe being involved with the Underworld wasn't quite as bad as I'd thought. I definitely wasn't accustomed to such attention from the opposite sex, and it made me feel good, feminine. I pushed open my bedroom door and couldn't help the surprise that landed like a grenade in my gut.

Rand stood in the center of my bedroom, his arms crossed and a frown marring his handsome face. "What were you doing speaking with that damned wolf?" he demanded.

I closed the door behind me and removed my coat, taking a great while to respond. Who the hell did he think he was, eavesdropping on me and in my own room, no less? "Just that—talking. Why were you watching me?"

He ran an agitated hand through his hair, and I had to fight the urge to run my own fingers through the unruly waves. God, why did the bastard have to be so damned hot? It wasn't fair!

"Pelham alerted me that you'd gone down to talk to him."

Damn the nosy Pelham. I'd have words with him later about this, but for now, I had to face the angry countenance of one perturbed warlock.

"What did he want from you?" Rand demanded.

"To capture Cerberus, the guardian dog of Hades." I paused for dramatic effect. "And using no weapons."

"Goddammit Jolie!"

I held my hands out before me in a play of submission. "Okay, okay. God. He wanted to thank me, tell me he's forever indebted to me, and I can rely on him and his pack to protect me should I ever need it," I finished with smug satisfaction.

"And that was it?" he asked, his shoulders loosening as he appeared to calm down.

"That and he asked me to go to dinner with him," I added with a grin.

The anger returned to Rand's face and his aura began to tinge with purple. "And of course you bloody well said no."

I took great care with pulling the French doors closed and locking them. Then I wiped my fingers along the panes and noted they were covered in dust. "Why would I say no? He's very good looking, and I have no plans for Saturday," I shrugged, feigning indifference.

"Why would you say no?" Rand repeated, his gaze focused on my fingers as I rubbed them together trying to wipe away the residue of dirt. "Because he's a wolf!"

"What's wrong with that? Are you racist?" I asked with a smile.

"There are things you don't know about the other creatures of the Underworld, Jolie. You have much to learn and shouldn't be taking chances with a wolf. They're renowned for being less than honest, and they take what they want."

I frowned, thinking I didn't need this lecture. Trent seemed anything but dangerous. I was beginning to wonder if Rand was just paranoid. "Well, I guess I'll have to find out for myself."

His mouth caught in a tight line. "You're making a mistake."

"Are you finished?" I asked and turned away from him.

"I don't want you going to dinner with that wolf," he said through gritted teeth.

I turned to face him, ire building within me. Who the hell did he think he was? "Last I ... I checked, you weren't my father."

Dammit, I was starting to stutter. It only infuriated me more.

"Perhaps that's what you need," he responded and stepped so close to me I could feel his breath against my cheek. I didn't back down.

"D ... do you know what I think, Rand?" I asked in a low voice and didn't wait for his response. "I think you're j ... just jealous because you want nothing more than to be in his place. You're so afraid of ruining our relationship b ... because I mean nothing but money to you that you won't act on your feelings."

I was proud I was able to stand my ground and even with a few stutters, I spelled out in no uncertain terms exactly what I felt. Rand said nothing, but continued to glare at me, and I wasn't sure if he was going to kiss me or

107

scream. I returned his murderous gaze. Finally, without so much as a goodnight, he excused himself and left the room.

ELEVEN

"You look lovely," Trent said as he withdrew my chair from the table.

Mentally, I had to second his notion as I'd spent hours slaving over my appearance. With a little help of witch magic, I'd recreated a black sparkly dress Jennifer Aniston had worn to some awards show. I'd found the picture in one of Christa's craptastic magazines. The dress hugged my curves, stopping just short of my knees. It plunged down in a low v in the front, revealing just enough cleavage to appear sexy but not slutty. I wore my hair down but ensured it was full of wavy curls and completed the elegant look with a pair of diamond earrings I'd borrowed from Christa.

"Thank you, you look wonderful yourself," I said and gave him the once over. He was dressed smartly in dark green slacks and a sweater the color of coffee—the kind with no milk. It looked like he'd gotten a haircut for the occasion and now wore it with a certain spikiness at the top.

"I was surprised you agreed to have dinner with me actually."

"Then why did you ask me?"

He shrugged and relaxed into the chair across from me. "No one can fault me for trying," he said with a laugh before continuing. "I'd thought you and the warlock might've been involved."

The mention of Rand left me a bit cold as he and I hadn't spoken since our altercation in my bedroom two days ago. He'd avoided me since then. He was becoming habitual about getting pissed off and then disappearing for at least a week. It annoyed me—when was I going to get over the jerk? I refocused my attentions on the handsome man before me and thought maybe he might be a solution to my problem.

"He's my employer ... that's it."

The waiter approached us and I couldn't help but think that had I been with Rand, the waiter never would've ventured forth when we were in the midst of conversation. Ugh, I had to catch myself again.

"We'd like a bottle of Chardonnay and the Bruschetta to start off with," Trent said. The waiter took note and disappeared as Trent's attention returned to me. "I hope you like Bruschetta and wine?"

I downplayed the sense of irritation that snaked through me. It would've been nice if he'd asked me earlier, but I was determined to make this a successful date and wouldn't hold it against him. I just nodded.

"Where are you from?" I asked abruptly, trying to force my thoughts on calmer topics. I'd noticed upon first meeting Trent that he wasn't from

England—his accent was distinctly not English, but it wasn't quite American either.

"I'm originally from Russia, but moved to the US when I was very young."

"Ah, I thought you weren't from the States."

Trent reclined in his chair and steepled his fingers in his lap. He regarded me coolly, his lips slightly upturned at the ends. "I thought my accent would've faded away after all these years. I ..."

"Do werewolves live forever like vampires?" I interrupted.

Trent's smile combined with the low candle light caused a flurry of butterfly-like activity in my stomach. I could get used to that sensual smile.

"No, I'm afraid we're not so lucky, or unlucky, depending on how you look at it. We age much slower than humans do, though. The average lifespan of a werewolf is about one hundred thirty years."

"How old are you?"

He glanced down at his steepled fingers before returning his bedroom eyes to me. "Thirty-five."

I laughed, actually pleased with the fact that he wasn't much older than I was. Any difference from Rand was a good one. "Sorry for interrupting, please go on."

He obeyed with that same sexy smile. "My pack and I only recently migrated to England to escape the clutches of Bella."

I straightened, my ears perking at the mention of Bella. "What do you mean?"

"Well, it seems the league of witches, now that they've joined the vampires, is getting more and more angry that the demons, fairies, and wolves haven't joined ranks with them, and they've been hunting us out."

I glanced around the small, intimate restaurant. Only a few patrons sat scattered about and none seemed interested in our conversation. I leaned forward and lowered my voice. "Hunting you?"

His hands broke from the steeple and turned into fists. "Yes, trying to set an example by imprisoning us and in some cases, even killing us." His tone was so cold, I waited for his words to fall from the air, landing crystallized on the plate before him. "Their recruitment methods leave something to be desired."

I couldn't suppress the chill of fear that seized my spine. "And have their tactics worked?"

"Some of the wolves joined them while others migrated." He quirked a brow. "I believe the wolf that attacked me was sent by Bella."

I instantly pictured Trent and the wolf that had lured him into the alley when he'd been shot ... and killed by the human lurking in the darkness.

"Sent by Bella?" I repeated.

"Yes. She was holding me captive, but I managed to escape. Needless to say, she didn't take it well that I'd outwitted her, so she sent her pack after me." He frowned and tapped his fingers against the table, almost looking anxious. "No creatures can track quite so well as werewolves."

I was shocked to hear this, as I'd not thought Bella would resort to such violence. Apparently, she was set in her mission, and it made me wonder what this would mean for Rand and me. Bella still wanted me to join her—I was sure of that.

I slowly turned my water goblet, watching the clear liquid slosh up one side, whirl in the middle, and slosh up the other side like a mini typhoon.

"So you came here to escape persecution?"

Trent nodded. "Word spread that your employer isn't allied with Bella and therefore, his territory is safe. I believe we aren't the only pack to migrate—there have been many others and will continue to be many others."

"I see."

I couldn't control the racing of my heart. This was no little Underworld quarrel, but was shaping up to be a full-blown WWIII on the verge of erupting around me. I'd thought Bella had gone her separate way but now, it seemed she was of the belief that all creatures needed to join her union or suffer the consequences.

"I believe you, yourself, are in danger as well—that's why I offered my protection, and I meant it. Once I learned of your extraordinary power, I figured it would be a matter of time before Bella would want you for herself."

"She already made that known."

"Yes, well, I don't suppose she will let it rest either. I don't want to frighten you, but it's best to be prepared. If you ever need me, don't hesitate."

I nodded although I felt anything but sure. "Thank you."

"I'd hate to see her get her hands on you," he said with a lascivious wink and it wasn't hard to guess whose hands he'd love to see on me.

I mentally pushed thoughts of Bella into the dark recesses of my mind. I'd need to revisit them later, which caused me chagrin. Recently I'd been pushing so many thoughts aside that I'm sure my mind looked like a closet stuffed to max capacity.

"Are you flirting with me now?" I asked, figuring I'd give it a try myself.

"I believe it could be construed as such."

"I bet you have quite a few lady friends?" I decided I could be as blunt as I liked with Trent. He seemed to wear his heart, or more pointedly, his libido, on his sleeve.

"I just haven't found that perfect one yet."

He probably liked sorting through the many in search of the one. "Don't you think that perfect one would be a wolf?"

He shrugged. "That's what the elders would have me think, and they encourage us to mate with one another, but that cuts off a huge amount of very beautiful and eligible ladies, such as you."

Hmm, I wasn't sure how I felt about that. Mate? It sounded so animal kingdom. I'd need to protect myself—I didn't want to be another notch on his

111

bedpost. "Maybe you should know that I'm a bit more traditional. I'm not interested in one night stands." I thought I'd give him an easy out.

He just smiled. "You didn't need to tell me that—I already knew. You're a lady and I, myself, am not interested in one night stands either—not with you anyway."

I'm not an idiot, and this wolf didn't know me so why was he feigning so much interest? Was he telling me the truth or was he just really really smooth? "So I should believe the playboy has changed his ways?"

He nodded. "I'm up for the challenge, if you are." As if to prove he was up for it, he leaned over and clasped my hand in his.

Hmm, was I up for the challenge? It wasn't as though I had a line of dates ready to go. I'd just need to guard myself, play it safe, so I wouldn't get hurt.

"Does this mean you're asking me for a second date?"

"I believe I am. When can I see you again? Tomorrow night?"

I laughed. "You're certainly eager. I think I'm free tomorrow night."

~

Four hours later I was in my room, sitting at my vanity and replaying the events of the evening in my mind. Conversation with Trent had been easy and interesting and even if he was a risk—being a player in every sense of the word—if you don't take risks, you don't see rewards, right? Part of me thought statements like that were just a load of crap, and that part of me had a really loud voice.

I pressed my fingertips to my lips as I thought of his goodnight kiss. For the first time ever, I'd been comfortable in kissing someone. I guess I had Rand to thank for that. I enjoyed kissing Trent, maybe not quite so much as kissing Rand, but I enjoyed it nonetheless.

I sighed, shaking thoughts of Rand from my head. It wasn't a fair comparison. Rand was nothing other than my employer, and it appeared he'd never be anything more than that. The sooner I got him off my mind, the better.

Easier said than done.

I slipped Christa's diamonds from my ears and laid them on the table. They caught the overhead light and erupted into a prism of color.

The door squeaked open.

"Well, how was it?" Christa asked, peeking inside.

"I had a nice time," I said with a smile and motioned for her to come in. She shut the door before sitting at the foot of my bed, dressed in her cowboy PJs.

"Oh, come on, you have to give me more than that. Did you sleep with him?"

I giggled and instantly caught myself—killing the giggle, lest it rear its annoying head again. "Of course not. It was only the first date."

"So what," she said, rolling her eyes. "Everyone always pooh-poohs the first date, but it's the best time to decide if you have any real chemistry."

I frowned. "Well, anyway, I had a good time. He was every ounce the gentleman, and he asked me out again for tomorrow night.

"Wow! Good going, Jules. You're finally dating again."

I laughed as I thought about it—I, the one person who hadn't had a date in over six months, was finally back in the game. It felt great, I had to admit. I'd thought a life with only a best friend and a cat would suffice, but now I realized how much it lacked. I needed companionship and if that companionship was in the form of an attractive wolf, so be it.

"Does he have any friends?" Christa asked, and it dawned on me that she hadn't had much of a social life since we moved here. She was probably dying for a good date.

"I'm sure he does, I'll ask him."

Christa sprawled against the bed, and my attention fell to her pajamas. They were something you'd see on a five-year-old-boy—cowboys with lassos and Indians with tomahawks against a brown background with a couple of tumbleweeds. And I was the one who could never get a date? I shook my head.

"And make sure his friend's cute—none of those people who were in his clan or whatever they call it."

"Pack," I corrected her. "So what did you think of Trent?"

She was silent for a moment as she looped a tendril of hair around her finger. "I think he's pretty hot," she finished. "He has something about him; I can't quite put my finger on it. But he just oozes sex."

I had to laugh at that although I seconded it. He did just ooze sex, and it made me nervous. I just hoped he wasn't sharing the ooze with someone else. Okay, that sounded pretty gross ...

"Got some pent-up frustrations?"

She sighed. "There's not much to do around here. Rand is nice to look at, but all he thinks about is work ... and you."

The statement surprised me and I couldn't suppress a heated flush of pleasure. I knew the truth, though, and trampled the flush until it died a slow and painful death. "He doesn't like me that way, Chris."

She stuck out her tongue in mock denial. "Blah, of course he does. He won't admit it maybe."

I sighed and felt a great pressure on my shoulders. Whenever I thought about Rand, it depressed me. I guess I had it bad for him. And it's never easy when you have a crush and the subject of your crush doesn't return your affections ... or does return them but is such a dumbass that he won't act on them.

"We've been down that route and whatever his reasons, he's keeping his distance which leaves me the chance to date Trent."

Christa nodded, and her eyes lit up. "I wonder what sex is like with a werewolf. He'll probably tear your clothes off and ... doggie style all the way."

"Doggie style? Oh, God!" I laughed. "I doubt it. He doesn't seem to be that different …"

"I'm sure he is," she interrupted before changing the subject. "Jules, I have nothing to wear tomorrow night. Will you use your magic and invent something for me?"

I was sure Christa had ADD. She was Ms. Tangent and couldn't focus on any one thing for more than about five minutes. It was one of the things I loved about her.

"Sure. Let's worry about it tomorrow." Then I stopped myself and shook my head. "I don't even know if he has a friend to set you up with."

"Well, hopefully he does," she said, glancing at the clock on my mantle as she stood up. "I guess I should get to bed now."

I nodded and dropped my gaze to my lap, thinking I should be getting to bed too. I just felt as if there was so much swimming in my head. Thoughts of Rand, Trent and everything he'd told me about Bella.

"Okay, out with it."

I looked up and found Christa gazing back at me. "Out with what?"

She propped her hands on her hips and gave me her best serious expression—narrowed eyes and a frown. "Jolie Wilkins, I've been your best friend now for what, over fifteen years? I think I know when you have something on your mind."

I smiled and shook my head, knowing I wasn't getting out of this one anytime soon. "Trent told me Bella was his reason for moving here."

Christa fell back against my bed and returned to twisting her hair around her finger, something she did when deep in thought. "What does that mean?"

"I don't know. I didn't think Bella would force creatures to side with her. It just worries me because I thought we'd be okay here, but now I wonder. Trent made it sound like she'd come after me."

Christa brought her knees to her chin and encircled her legs with her arms, rocking back and forth. "Rand would never let her near you."

"I know. It just worries me."

There wasn't anything Christa could say that would take the worry away. I was well aware of Bella's abilities, and if what Trent said was true, it was just a matter of time before the situation came to a blistering head.

~

I was exhausted. As I trudged down the hallway, in search of Rand, I couldn't help the yawn that claimed my mouth. Today's lesson with Gor had been a really tough one. He'd taught me how to cast protection spells which basically required pulling some of my own magic and lending it to the person I wanted to protect. Using Christa as my study, I built up enough protection around her to last a year. I, on the other hand, felt as if I needed a nap. I almost regretted the fact that we had a double date this evening.

I found Rand in his massive library, studying Quicken on his laptop.

114

"I have news for you," I said as I closed the door behind me.

Rand didn't even look up from his computer. "What?"

Anger bubbled up within me like lava. The jerk still hadn't forgiven me for going out with Trent. I imagined Pelham had informed him of my second date tonight. Ugh, the two of them were like old meddlesome women with nothing better to do then stick their noses in my business.

"I can only assume you know of the migrating werewolf packs to your territory?" I began, crossing my arms over my chest. The tone of my voice dripped with sarcasm.

"Of course," he said nastily and made a big show of typing like he was Mavis freaking Beacon.

I took a step closer. Damn interrupting him. "Why didn't you mention it?"

His eyes never left the computer screen, but I didn't miss the redness that claimed the tops of his ears. He was as pissed off as I was. "I didn't want to worry you."

My hands fisted at my sides. "T ... to hell with not worrying me. If we're to be partners ..."

He finally looked up, his eyes flashing and his jaw clenched. "We're not partners. I'm your employer."

His words were like a smart slap to the face and echoed through my head. "So that's h ... how it'll be between us then?"

He returned to perusing his finances, but there was no slack in his jaw and his eyes were as narrowed as they'd been a second ago. "Yes."

His lips were so tight, they formed a white line across his face.

"Then maybe I should join Bella," I said, immediately regretting how immature I sounded.

Rand didn't go for it. "Maybe you should."

The fiery dance of anger welled within me, my breathing shallow and irregular as I watched Rand pretend to be entirely divested in his accounting books. I closed the distance between us and grabbed hold of his shoulder, intending to force him to take notice of me.

"Rand, this is serious."

He slapped his laptop closed, jerked away from my hold and stood up, towering over me like an enraged titan. I told myself I wasn't afraid of him, but took a precautionary step back anyway.

"Trent told me I might not be safe," I said in a mouse voice.

Rand started a bit at the mention of Trent, but I couldn't help it—I had to tell him what I knew.

"I'll protect you," he said between gritted teeth. You could have fried an egg on the tops of his ears.

"Do you think Bella will come for me?"

He was silent for a moment, seemingly weighing a potential response. "Yes."

My knees felt as if they might give at any second. I leaned my arm against the wall and thought about what this meant. Bella was planning an attack and both Trent and Rand were well aware of it. I'd been living in a fairy tale since I'd arrived at Rand's. I had been stupid, so very stupid. Of course Bella was going to come after me, she needed me. I was an arrow in her quiver. Suddenly my attention turned to the lessons I'd been taking lately and like a horrid troll pulling aside the canvas of a beautiful landscape only to reveal a brick wall, realization dawned on me.

"And is that why I'm taking all these lessons—to learn to protect myself?"

"I wanted you to be prepared."

"And our taking the case of the werewolves, was that to try and recruit them to our side?"

He laughed, but there was no mirth in his voice. "You're quite the ingénue, Jolie. The werewolves are a very strong force to reckon with. I thought it helpful to have them on our side. I fear we'll need to create our own battalion against Bella ..."

With the epiphany, fury bit at me. I wasn't so much angry that he'd done all these things in preparation—it was for everyone's own good. I was perturbed that I'd been left out and more so that I'd been too dumb not to realize his plans earlier.

"So you thought if you could show what I'm capable of, we'd win recruits." He nodded and a new tide of ire crested within me. "You've had this all figured out all along ... how to use me in your s ... stupid war."

"No, that's not it at all." He shook his head as if to further emphasize his point. "Stop being foolish, Jolie."

"Foolish? It sounds like that's been your plan all along," I spat out as I breathed in through my nose, out through my mouth, and managed to silently count to ten all the while. There was no use in being angry now—not when I needed to find out the entirety of the situation. I could be angry later.

"When do you think she'll make a move?"

Rand frowned. "I have no way of knowing. It's just a guess that Bella will even make a move."

"So we just wait it out then?"

"Yes. This is why I was wary about you leaving my protection with that bloody wolf," he started. "I wanted to tell you ..."

"Trent has sworn to protect me."

Rand's aura began to tinge with purple again as he cupped the back of his head. "The wolf is nowhere near as strong as I am nor as strong as Bella."

"You can't expect me to live my life boxed up in here," I interrupted and couldn't help the edge to my voice.

He stepped closer to me. "When you came here, you knew you'd be living with me ..."

"Yes, but had I known you'd dictate when I come and go, I'd never have agreed."

"It's for your own protection, Jolie."

"If that's so, then why aren't you upset when I go with Christa to town or when I take walks around here? What you're angry about is me being alone with Trent."

His brows met in the middle of his forehead. "I can't deny that. I believe the wolf should pursue his own. He can't understand you, Jolie. You're a witch and you belong with your own people."

I laughed, and the sound was cold. "You'll never admit your jealousy, will you? If Trent were female, I bet you'd have no qualms with my spending time with him."

"You call it jealousy; I'm not convinced that's what it is. Do I hate the idea of his hands all over you, yes," he said, his lips tight, his eyes as piercing as a blade.

"That's jealousy Rand. I wish you'd just admit it," I snapped and turned to walk away.

He grabbed hold of my hand and reeled me back around until I faced him. "Don't walk away from me."

"I have a date and ..."

The look in his eyes stopped me—anger mixed with a pinch of jealousy. It must've been a few seconds that we stood staring at one another. The lust in his eyes was palpable, and I gave my best "don't you dare even think about kissing me" look. Apparently, my expression wasn't convincing enough because his mouth was on mine instantly. His lips were strong and his tongue forced its way inside my mouth, mating with my tongue. I did nothing to encourage him, but neither did I fight him, so he continued to explore me, his hands plying my breasts above my blouse.

I had to suppress the urges that flowed through me—that told me to wrap my arms around him and meet his plundering tongue. I closed my eyes against the temptation.

I would not give in.

I wouldn't give Rand the benefit of my interest. Not when he had done this to me before and where had that gotten us?

Nowhere.

He pulled away and his eyes had a glossiness to them. "Stay with me tonight, Jolie, and I'll make love to you until morning," he whispered and my stomach dropped, the idea was so appealing.

"W ... what of our work arrangement ..." I began, my stutter this time having nothing to do with anger, but more with the nervousness slithering within my gut like multiple snakes.

"Fuck the work arrangement. I've wanted you since I met you, and it's eating me alive."

His words echoed in my head, and I felt as if he'd consume me right then and there. How I wanted him and had always wanted him, but had Trent not decided to take me out and spurred Rand's jealousy, he'd never have made such a move. That and I was still pissed off that he'd lied to me about his

117

motivation to use me in this burgeoning Underworld war. It seemed every time I turned around, I was a pawn in someone's game.

I was so freaking sick of it.

I pushed his hands away. "It's t … too little too late, Rand. I have a date I need to get ready for."

I didn't wait for a response, but stormed out of his office, slamming the door behind me.

I thought it might be time I moved out.

TWELVE

I'd never been on a double date and after experiencing one, I'd recommend it to anyone. It seemed to remove any pressure or nervousness you might feel during the course of a regular date where you have to think of witty conversation and watch your table manners. Well, you have to mind those things during a double date, as well, but it seems much easier when you have a close friend to tell you if you have any food stuck between your teeth.

Luckily, Christa's date was as fetching as Trent and in no way represented one of the group of followers whom we'd previously met. When we learned he'd been among their number, we were both surprised to say the least. Christa a bit more pronounced in her surprise than I.

"You were there that day? Wow, I'd never have recognized you—you all looked so …"

"That's interesting," I interrupted, trying to subdue a potentially embarrassing situation. Trent and John noticed and laughed at my effort.

"When Trent was killed, we were all so overwhelmed we sort of stopped functioning—hence our less than civilized appearance," John explained and to his credit, he didn't seem embarrassed or annoyed in the least.

"A pack entirely relies on their leader," Trent continued, resting his arm on the back of my chair. "When a leader succumbs to death, it would be a sign of non-allegiance for the pack to continue as if nothing were out of the ordinary."

"Well, you sure clean up well," Christa said, her admiring gaze darting between the two of them.

I had to second that. Trent seemed more handsome than I remembered, and I wondered if such were the case or if he was just growing on me. As I studied him across the dinner table, I could see the wolf in him. It was there in his eyes, a fierce sort of animal quality that was arresting but dangerous. There was also something wolf-like behind his slow smile, his olive complexion, and five o'clock shadow.

John was not half bad, either. John was lighter than Trent in his skin and the color of his hair. I wondered if his wolf coat were more on the yellowish side than Trent's almost mahogany coloring. John had a nice enough face though—broad with high cheekbones and rich dark green eyes. Christa certainly seemed pleased with him and ran her hand down his arm, as if checking the hide of a horse before agreeing to purchase him.

"We have to say the same about you. You both look lovely," Trent said with a grin in my direction. A wolfishly devilish grin.

119

The beauty of the moment was shattered when the thought suddenly occurred to me that maybe Trent preferred Christa to me. It was like Juno had dropped a package of jealousy right into my lap and like an idiot, I'd opened it. I've never been a jealous person, maybe because I've never had reason to be jealous. If you have no love life, then what's there to be or get jealous over?

My leg started shaking as it does whenever I get nervous, and I slammed my hand down on top of my knee, forcing it to stop. How I hated the thought! And I wasn't certain if I more hated the thought or the humility that accompanied it. I decided I shouldn't be concerned with comparing myself to my best friend. It would only be natural that a man should find her sexually attractive. He'd have to be blind not to ...

"Christa, what is it you do?" Trent asked her with a simple smile, and my stomach fell.

"I do all the accounting for Rand, our employer. And I'm a photographer."

"A photographer," Trent said, his smile wide. "Wow, that's impressive. I'd love to see your photos some time."

Something in my gut turned sour, and I felt the immediate need to retreat. "I ... I need to go to the ladies room." I stood as if a dog had just bitten me in the ass. Before anyone could respond, I rushed toward the back hall, showing myself into the restroom. I was elated to find it empty and leaned my hands on the sink, staring at myself in the mirror.

What the hell was wrong with me? I was acting like a total imbecile.

Taking a step back, I smoothed the invisible wrinkles in my brown miniskirt while I tried to get a firm grip on whatever sanity I had remaining. I faced my reflection again. My hair hung in loose waves about my face and even though I could recognize how pretty my reflection was, I didn't feel it. I've never cared much about my looks, but at that moment, I would've sold my soul to be the most beautiful woman alive.

If this was what dating did, I wanted no part of it. True, I hadn't had much of a social life prior to becoming a witch, but now that it seemed other beings fancied me, I wondered if I were changing and not for the better.

I needed a breath of fresh air to settle myself. Opening the door to the ladies' room, I slipped around the corner into the hallway. I spied Trent and Christa leaning close, their faces alight with laughter. Resisting the urge to gag, I turned in the opposite direction and hurried down the hallway, praying for a door leading outside.

My prayers were answered in the form of a black door covered in scuffmarks that simply said "exit." Pushing the door open, I collapsed onto a bench overlooking the back of the restaurant. No sooner did my butt meet the wooden bench then a swarm of anxious thoughts battered my already flustered mind ... So what if Trent preferred Christa to me, what did I care? It'd be better to find out sooner rather than later. Did I want to be with someone who was interested in my best friend anyway?

120

Like a distraught landlord, I begged for the uncooperative tenants in my head to move out.

"I've wanted to get you alone all evening," Trent's thick voice interrupted my ridiculous inner monologue, and I gasped in surprise. I turned around to face him and stood, wondering how long he'd been standing behind me.

His arms went around my waist, and his lips touched my cheek. Thoughts of Christa disappeared, replaced with more intimate and unwholesome thoughts.

"You're not enjoying yourself?" I asked, my voice trembling. Hopefully Trent thought it due to the cold evening air and not the argument I was just having with myself.

His lips continued their descent down my neck, and his breath burned my flesh. "I'm enjoying myself now."

I thought I'd melt in his presence. Wolves tend to run hotter than humans and his body felt as if it were on fire. When he kissed me, his lips burned against mine, and I relaxed into the heat of his body. His hands splayed through my hair as his tongue lapped at my own. When he pulled away from me, there was fever in his eyes.

"God how I want you," the beast within him groaned.

"We still have a date to get back to," I said, not able to meet his eyes and the desire that danced within them like devils before a fire.

He chuckled and kissed me again. "What do you think about getting a place of your own?"

"I was already contemplating it."

"Good. I can't imagine Rand would welcome me with open arms."

I laughed. "You're a good judge of character."

"You find yourself a nice little place to live and I'll pay your rent," he said and bounced his index finger on the end of my nose. If his statement wasn't enough to make me sick, the show of his finger on my nose definitely was. What did he think I was—a kept woman? I forced my reaction down, imagining it wasn't the way he intended it. At least, I hoped it wasn't the way he meant it.

"No thanks, but I appreciate the gesture."

He laughed. "You're quite the independent woman."

Well, whatever I was—witch, newly jealous harpy ... yes, I guess I was still every ounce the independent woman.

~

Christa giggled as I opened the front door of Pelham Manor.

"John was such a good kisser, and he was so hot ... I mean literally."

I laughed and closed the door behind us, thinking I'd definitely had a good time on our date. Granted I'd had a bit of a mental breakdown, but I could honestly say I'd enjoyed myself ... most of the time.

"He was cute, didn't you think so?" Christa asked as she started up the stairs to her bedroom.

"Yeah, really cute," I answered and headed up the stairs behind her, stifling a yawn. It was dark in the house, and I had no idea what time it was, but I was definitely tired and looking forward to my soft bed.

"Jolie, can I speak with you for a minute?" Grabbing hold of the banister, I turned to see Rand standing in the hallway. I glanced up at Christa who just gave me a small smile and disappeared into her room. Facing Rand again, I gave him a quick nod and started down the stairs.

When I reached the ground floor, Rand turned on his heel and headed down the long hallway into the kitchen. Left with no option, I followed him.

The lights in the kitchen came on as Rand stepped over the threshold. He opened the refrigerator and pulled out a bottle of white wine.

"I have another job I want you to consider," he started. He held up the bottle of wine in offer, and I gently shook my head.

"Okay, what is it?" I took a seat on one of the barstools, throwing my purse atop the black granite counter top.

He leaned against the counter and crossed his arms against his chest, looking like a model straight out of GQ.

"Another pack, a larger one than Trent's, wants us to bring back some of their members who were killed by Bella."

"Okay." I could probably handle some more werewolves, if the last pack was anything to go on.

"It might be a bit more difficult because it will be more than one wolf you're bringing back." He took a sip of his wine, and it left a slight moustache on his upper lip. He licked his lips, and I had to drop my gaze, lest I appear too interested.

"I think I can handle it."

He nodded, something else obviously on his mind. "Did you have a good time tonight?"

I sighed, knowing an argument was about to rear its ugly face. I knew his feelings toward Trent and I imagined he wouldn't be at all happy to have the wolf frequenting Pelham Manor. Maybe he was kicking me out.

"Yes, thanks for asking."

He hesitated, his jaw clenched, and he put the glass of wine down. He came closer to me and my breath froze in my throat as I awaited the words. He leaned his elbows against the counter of the bar, and I straightened my posture, not wanting to be so close to him.

"I wanted to apologize for getting involved with your personal matters. I should never have done so."

I was surprised to say the least, imagining I was about to be read my rights. "Oh, thanks," I said dumbly.

He eyed me up and down until I felt as if I were withering in his insistent gaze. "You look lovely."

Okay, what the hell was wrong with Rand? I was better prepared for the arrogant, angry, and stubborn warlock I was used to.

"Thanks ... are you feeling alright?"

He chuckled. "Yes, I'm fine."

I didn't know what else to say. It definitely seemed like something was up with him ... he had that look of someone who had lots to say, but didn't quite know where to start. I wished he'd get on with it, so I could go to sleep. Glancing at the clock above the stove, I noted it was already 2:00 a.m. Way past my bedtime.

"You've changed quite a bit since being here," he said softly.

"Is that your first drink of the night?"

He laughed that same innocent, *I don't know what you're talking about* laugh. "Yes, it's my first of the night."

I shook my head, but smiled and decided to play his game. "Okay, how have I changed?"

He smirked and leaned farther across the counter, crossing his ankles behind him. "Look at you. Wearing a tiny skirt and a tight pink sweater. Showing off your breasts and legs."

My mouth dropped open. "I'm not showing off my boobs and legs!"

He chuckled again. "Come now, Jolie, look how much leg your showing and I bet I could guess your bust size just by looking."

I feigned offense and dropped off the bar stool, grabbing my purse. "Well, I don't think it's such a bad thing for a woman to be confident ..." I started.

He quirked his brows and a smile pulled at his lips. He sipped his wine again. "I'm not saying it's bad. You're beautiful—so are your legs ... and your breasts."

I swallowed against the desire that threatened to make me a stumbling idiot and tried to hold his gaze. "Well, thanks, I guess."

He saluted me with the glass of wine and that was when I realized I needed to see my thoughts about moving out to fruition. I couldn't live with Rand anymore. I just couldn't handle it. "I ... I wanted to tell you I think I'm going to move out."

He pushed away from the counter and put the glass down so violently, it sloshed onto the counter. "Move out?"

I took a deep breath. "Yes, I think it'd be for the better. I don't want to overstep your generosity and kindness in having me here, but I feel as if I can't come and go as I please."

He clasped the back of his head with interwoven fingers and walked four paces forward only to turn around and walk four paces back. Clearly, Rand had a difficult time saying what was on his mind.

"I don't want you to move, Jolie; it will be too hard to ensure you're safe."

I couldn't help the smile that tugged at my lips as I watched him pace the kitchen. He looked like an ad for a new fridge or something: *is your current refrigerator getting you down?* I shook thoughts of Rand and his commercial right out of my head.

"I won't move far—maybe a small place in the village. Not more than ten minutes."

Rand frowned and stopped walking, his attention centered on me. "Ten minutes could mean life and death." He started pacing again. "Couldn't you be comfortable here? I won't interfere in your personal life again. You have my word."

I shook my head. "I think I need my own space, Rand."

He sighed and collapsed against the counter. He strummed his fingers along the granite as if he were playing every chord of my guilt. I couldn't feel bad about my decision though. If I were to have any sort of dating life, Trent aside, I couldn't have it while living underneath Rand's roof. And I was determined not to remain a spinster forever; I needed to make up for lost time. I needed to get Rand off my mind.

"There's a small house on the property here that served as the butler's quarters when the house was built. It has a separate entrance, and I believe you'd be happy there. It would be a compromise because I'd feel more secure knowing you were closer than the village."

"I'll consider it. Can I see it tomorrow?"

"No one has occupied it for over forty years and it's currently being used as a shed so it'll need a bit of repair, but it's yours if you want it, free of rent."

I smiled and watched him remember the wine spill as he pulled out a cloth and mopped it up. "Thank you, Rand, that's very generous, but I'll pay you something. You aren't much of a business man, are you?" I asked with a grin, hoping to elevate his mood.

His face remained serious. "Not where you're concerned. It seems I have a bit of a soft spot for you."

My smile fell. If he had a soft spot for me, I had a gaping wound for him. "Let's visit it tomorrow. If you don't mind, I'm a bit tired, so I think I'll be on my way." As if to prove my statement, I started for the hall. I didn't need to turn around to know Rand was directly behind me. I faced him and his lips parted as though he was going to say something, but he stopped. And I realized I wanted him to say something. Anything. If he'd just admit his feelings, I'd stay in Pelham Manor, I'd forget Trent.

He said nothing.

"Goodnight, Rand."

"Jolie, I hope you know you can trust me?" It seemed an odd thing to say and I suppose my confusion showed on my face. He stepped closer to me, biting his lip.

"If that wolf, Trent, ever hurts you, I hope you'll come to me."

"I'm sure he won't hurt me, but if he ever he does, I'll come to you."

He smiled and with a nod, leaned back against the kitchen wall. I recognized my exit cue and took it, knowing he watched me all the while.

~

Two weeks later and I had a new place to call my own. I couldn't admit I was completely pleased with my decision—I'd miss being so close to Rand, seeing him every day, eating our meals together. And I was a little jealous that Christa was still his roommate. Not that I thought there would ever be anything between them—I knew Rand's feelings toward Christa were merely platonic and she'd been happily dating John for a while now. But, still, there was definitely a part of me that would miss Pelham Manor.

So now, I sat in my very own breakfast room complete with new furniture and a blazing fire in the hearth. Plum returned from the bedroom and crawled into my lap. I petted her in long, languorous strokes as I thought how easy it was to be a cat—what a wonderful and simple life they led. To worry about the occasional mouse interloping in your house, sleep whenever it pleased you, and never be concerned with warlocks.

Oh, to be a cat.

It was exactly one week since I'd last seen Trent. He'd been out of town on business, but was due back in a day or so. I couldn't wait to see him. I'd missed him, which was strange, because I hadn't thought myself so emotionally attached—something that was exciting but also scared the bejeezus out of me.

The rain had been threatening all day and now it began in earnest, pattering against my slate roof like diamonds falling out of the sky. I curled up on my new sofa and opened a romance novel I'd been meaning to start for a few weeks. I didn't get through page one before a knock sounded on the door.

I shooed the cat from my lap and wondered who would be calling in the pouring rain. Upon opening the front door, Trent smiled down at me, his white shirt wet and clinging to his muscled chest, his dark hair plastered to his head. My gaze moved down the length of him to the bouquet of roses in his hand. They were soaked too.

"Special delivery for Jolie Wilkins," he said in a cartoon voice and held up the bouquet. I accepted it and opened the door for him. Once inside, he took hold of me and spun me around, his lips imprisoning mine as soon as my feet touched the ground.

"I missed you," he groaned in my ear.

"I missed you too." The truth of it was that I'd counted the hours until his return and had found little diversion in anything else.

"I wanted to take you out tonight," he said with a smile. "Shall we go?"

"Where are you taking me?" I asked, thinking I was still in my loungewear and wouldn't mind applying a dab of makeup or two.

He shrugged and the grin on his face deepened. I guess this one was going to be a surprise.

"Get your coat. I'll start the car and get the seats warm for you." I watched him turn and head back toward his red Audi.

Figuring I didn't have any time to change, I eyed my sweats with a sigh and grabbed my coat from the peg behind the door. Stepping outside, I locked the door behind me. I didn't see Trent's car, which was odd, as he'd just parked in the driveway. Covering my face to avoid the teardrops of the heavens, I started up the drive, wondering where he'd gone.

A low growl vibrated through the night.

My steps faltered, as I doubted whether I'd actually heard the growl. It could've been thunder. I turned at the sound of rustling leaves and saw a white wolf in the driveway.

The wolf turned to face me, its hackles raised, the raindrops coursing down its mouth, looking like drool.

I took a step back.

"Trent!"

The wolf came nearer.

"Trent, are you out there!"

The wolf pawed the ground and watched me, edging ever closer and closer. I could try to get back inside the house, but by the time I pulled out my keys and unlocked the door, I'd be wolf bait.

My mind was such a mess, I couldn't even think of a spell to use on him. I just kept my eyes on his and backed up slowly. The wolf, apparently growing impatient, lunged at me as I turned on my toes and ran as quickly as I could. My ballet flats combined with the puddles of rainwater made it exceptionally difficult to get any sort of traction and I nearly lost my balance a few times.

As if I had eyes on the back of my head, I knew the wolf was nearly on my heels. Like a shard of glass straight through my brain, the memory of Trent telling me to whistle pierced my swollen thoughts. But the idea of trying to whistle while running as fast as I could was ridiculous not to mention impossible.

All I could think of was panicking until a little voice in my head reminded me to use the help of the fox, my inner beast. I headed for the trees alongside my little house and with the wolf on my heels, I called to my beast. No sooner did the thought enter my head when that familiar feeling of lightness overtook me and I felt myself drop to the ground.

It took me a second to shake off the after-effects of my metamorphosis. Realizing time was a luxury I couldn't afford, I galloped for the undergrowth of the forest which would offer prime protection. Wondering if the wolf was still on my tail, I made the mistake of glancing behind me and stumbled headlong into a large rock. Luckily, my paws hit it before my head did which allowed my instincts to kick in and jerk my head back before it, too, came up close and personal with the rock.

The wolf took advantage of my moment of stupidity and threw his body on mine, nearly crushing the life from me. With a squeal, I was back to myself, naked with a growling wolf on top of me, his eyes aimed at my throat. The rain continued to pound down on us, and I had to close my eyes against the onslaught. The wolf shifted, and I pulled one hand up to clear the errant drops from my eyes.

As I looked into the very human eyes of the beast atop me, I could only wonder if it was one of the wolf henchmen that had teamed up with Bella. If so, I didn't imagine he'd kill me—Bella wanted me very much alive. Even with that somewhat relieving thought, I couldn't stop the fear that ate through me like maggots on a corpse.

The growl of another wolf interrupted my gruesome thoughts, and I prayed it was Trent. The wolf atop me cocked his ears and turned his long face, apparently to see where the growl came from. No sooner did he incline his head then the other wolf leapt on him, pushing him off me. Newly freed, I wasted no time in clothing myself in jeans and a sweatshirt with a blink of my eyes. Then I scurried to a nearby tree, and turned my attention to the two wolves.

I recognized Trent as one of the wolves, his reddish coat giving him away. I had to wonder at who would best the other. They seemed to be of the same large stature, their canines and upturned muzzles intimidating by any account. They continued to growl and circle each other, as if daring the other to make the first move. The white wolf sniffed Trent's rear and Trent did the same. I guess this was the wolf way of saying: "You talkin' to me?" If I hadn't been so damned scared, I might actually have found that little ass-sniffing bit amusing.

Trent pulled away from the other wolf and raised his head, howling into the bitter and wet night. Then he leapt on the other wolf, wrapping his paws around the white wolf's neck and bit him right on the nose. Blood welled from the bite immediately and coursed down the wolf's white coat, looking like a piece of white cake with a flowing river of cherry filling.

The white wolf yelped a high-pitched wail and Trent separated himself, allowing the wolf to retreat. Trent didn't permit him relief for long, though, and threw himself on his opponent again. The white wolf whimpered as it dropped to the ground, rolling to its back. Trent wrapped his canines around the wolf's neck and I wasn't sure if he was going to rip the wolf's throat out.

The white wolf whimpered louder, as if begging Trent not to kill him, while his bushy white tail cemented between his legs. Trent continued to growl, but stood aside, allowing the wolf to change to his human form. The wolf's facial features shortened as his hair disappeared, replaced with milky white skin. The man who appeared was a pretty young werewolf—maybe in his early twenties. He was extremely pale with a long forehead and a large mouth. The bite on his nose continued to bleed, running down his cheek and chin until it puddled in the mud below him. He didn't appear to enjoy playing captive to the growling Trent and I'm sure it didn't help that he was as naked as the day he was born.

Trent changed into his human form much faster than the other wolf had—in fact, it was so quick, I blinked and found Trent before me. He continued to stare at the other wolf, making no attempt to free him. It was kind of funny actually, watching two naked men glaring at one another.

"Who were you after?" Trent growled out.

127

The young wolf refused to answer until Trent pummeled him in the stomach. Then he was quick to groan: "You."

"Who sent you?"

The wolf didn't wait for the next onslaught of fists in his rib cage. "Bella. I was to bring you back. Once I saw … the witch, I wanted to bring her back also."

"You go back to Bella, and you tell her the next time she sends a creature after me or this woman, I will kill her myself."

The young wolf looked like he might laugh but, apparently, thought better of it and nodded as Trent stepped aside and allowed him to pass. The man bolted for the trees, the sound of rustling heralding his departure. Trent turned to me, grabbed me by the shoulders and jerked me forward.

"Did the wolf bite you?" he demanded.

I held my attention to his face, not daring to take in his naked body. "Nope, why is it true what they say about werewolf bites—that I'd turn into one?"

Trent smiled and engulfed me. "Absolutely."

I forced my gaze on his face and away from his incredible and incredibly bare body. "Are you okay?" I asked.

He nodded and pulled back with a frown. "So you're dressed and I'm not."

"I prefer you in your birthday suit."

The rain pounded against us, soaking my clothing and trailing down Trent's muscled body. He grabbed my hand and led me from the umbrage of the forest. Not finding my house key, I used a bit of magic to unlock the door and let us inside.

As soon as I shut the door behind us, Trent pulled me to him, holding me as if I were the most precious thing to him. Damn, did it feel good.

He grabbed a throw blanket on top of the couch and took hold of me, wrapping both of us in its warmth.

"I'm sorry, Jolie. I'm sorry you had to get in the way of that."

"Where were you? When I came outside, I couldn't find your car."

He shrugged. "When I was getting in the car, I thought I noticed a wolf at the end of your driveway, so I went to investigate. I guess the wolf found you before I found him."

"Yeah, I guess so."

"Do you know what the good news is though?" he asked and I looked at him in doubt as he continued. "You're scared and I can comfort you…naked."

I laughed as he set me away from him and studied my face, taking my lips captive.

The thought entered my head that this would lead to sex. Here we were, in my house, Trent was naked and kissing me. It seemed like time stood still as I weighed the question of to have sex or not to have sex. Was I ready? I wasn't sure.

I'd only had sex once and it had been with an exchange student in the tenth grade … in the back of my mom's station wagon. And it had been quick and painful—the guy basically pumping in me like a horny Chihuahua on your leg. Then he'd jerked as if he'd been shot, screamed something in Italian, and collapsed on my chest. It took me a good six months to redevelop a liking for Italian food.

It's difficult to try and weigh a situation at the same time you're kissing someone. Finally, I made the decision that I wasn't ready. I didn't love Trent and the stupid truth was that I was saving myself for someone I loved. Not marriage … I'd just settle for love. That was good enough for me.

"Are you nervous? You're shaking," he said as his lips seared the flesh behind my ear.

There was no use in lying. "Yes," I responded as he pulled me closer to him. "I'm just not ready."

"We don't have to do this, Jolie."

I smiled, silently appreciating the fact that he was making this easy on me.

"Can you do something about some clothes for me then?" he asked with a chuckle.

I smiled and imagined him in a pair of khakis, nothing else. I opened my eyes and he stood before me, inspecting the pants with appreciation.

"Not bad. How's the quality?"

I laughed. "Pretty good. I could give Banana Republic a run for their money."

He kissed me again. The heat from his naked chest seemed to emanate through me, insulating me from the cold draftiness of my house.

"Can I stay here tonight?" he asked. A bolt of lightning lit the sky followed by a round of thunder. If I hadn't known better, I would've thought Trent had choreographed the whole thing.

"Of course, you can even sleep in my bed … as long as you behave yourself," I added with a smile.

THIRTEEN

It sounded like a brigade of soldiers was pounding on my front door. So much for sleeping in.

"Damn it," I snapped and smiled apologetically at Trent who lounged in my bed. "I'll be right back."

"I'm counting on it."

I threw my pink robe over my Victoria's Secret PJs and hurried into the living room. It could be one of two people, Christa or Rand. Dear God, please let it be Christa. Flipping on the outside light, I found Rand standing on my doorstep, rain trailing down the harsh planes of his face.

He was the last person I wanted to see. I pulled the robe closer around myself and wished I'd closed my bedroom door, not wanting to draw any attention to the half-naked man currently lying on my bed. Cracking the front door open, I poked my head out, wondering what in the hell could be the matter. Before I could say a word, he took the liberty of pushing the door wide and stepped over my feet.

"What the bloody hell happened to you, Jolie? I took a walk through the grounds and found this." He held up a piece of tattered blouse. It was the one I'd been wearing before turning into my animal form had shredded it to bits.

I didn't get a chance to wonder why Rand had decided to take a walk on my side of the woods, which was at least two miles from his property, and in the pouring rain, no less.

"I got into a little trouble and had to call on my fox."

If I could've paid someone five hundred dollars to clear Rand out of my living room, I would've gladly paid it. Crap, I would've paid a thousand. And in pounds …

"What sort of trouble?" he asked with raised brow and narrowed eyes.

"Werewolf trouble," Trent answered, strolling toward us, still dressed only in his pants.

My stomach dropped at the sight of him. Why couldn't he have stayed in my bedroom and minded his own damned business? I shook my head and faced Rand again, noting the surprise that registered in his eyes.

Even though Rand had a good four inches or more on him, Trent seemed just as dangerous. Rand's nostrils flared slightly and his hands curled into fists. He looked so incredibly angry, it wouldn't have surprised me if steam had come out of his ears. Angry or not, he was quickly deducing what had just gone on—with Trent standing half-naked and me in my PJs and robe, it wasn't difficult to guess. His aura began to tinge with purple.

I wanted to tell him that nothing had happened, that we'd just slept in the same bed, but I knew I couldn't. Besides, my love life was none of his concern. Let him think Trent and I had had sex, maybe it might even be the impetus we both needed to truly consider one another as only employee and employer.

"I see," he said, clearing his throat. "I didn't realize you had company."

I hazarded a glance at Trent and he wore his smugness as if it were the newest in men's cologne. His arrogance irritated me, and I dropped my gaze to the ground, not especially thrilled with meeting the ire in Rand's face either.

"I'm alright, Rand. The wolf was after Trent, not me," I said apologetically, realizing that I wasn't apologizing so much for the fact that Rand had found my blouse, but more so, for the situation. Then I chided myself for acting in the least bit repentant. I didn't owe Rand any sort of apology.

"Then why did you have to shape shift?" he asked with tight lips.

"The wolf was after me, as she said," Trent answered and Rand's body was tight. "But upon seeing our little witch here, I imagine he decided it'd make Bella extra proud if he brought her back as well."

Trent draped a casual arm around me, and I instinctively leaned further away. Rand flinched at the mention of me as their "little witch," but didn't miss a beat before he was on to his next question.

"And the wolf? Is it dead?" His gaze rested on me even though Trent had assumed the role of responder.

"No, Trent let him get away," I said and shrugged out of Trent's hold, grabbing Plum as she lazily walked past Rand. The cat was so surprised, she didn't even get the chance to meow in resistance.

The purple in Rand's aura had now usurped the blue. "You bloody well let him get away?" he repeated, and by the tone of his voice, I supposed letting the wolf go hadn't been what he wanted to hear. "Now he'll return to Bella and tell her where Jolie lives."

Trent took a seat on the arm of the sofa, one side of his mouth quirked in a smile like he thought he was Elvis or something. "I wanted the wolf to deliver a message—if he comes after me or Jolie again, I'll come after Bella."

Apparently, Trent thought that was a good rebuttal as he wore a certain defiance that stretched from his narrowed eyes to his crossed arms. It sounded dumb to me. I figured it sounded really dumb to Rand.

Rand laughed, and the laugh said that Trent was a dumbass by all measures. "You could never defeat Bella, she's too strong for you. What a foolish …"

Before this became wolf vs. warlock, I thought I should intervene. "It's done, Rand, and Bella would've found out where we were inevitably. You said so yourself."

"I didn't imagine it would be this quick," he snapped and then paused before turning toward me. "Jolie, may I have a word with you please?" His gaze returned to the barely-clad Trent. "In private?"

"Whatever you have to say to her, you can say in front of me. She's my woman," Trent answered in a constricted tone, his face taking on a reddish hue. The cat started complaining, probably because I was holding her too tight, but I made no motion to release her. My thoughts were still trying to digest what Trent had just said. His woman? It reminded me of something Tarzan would say.

After the initial shock wore away, I was left to ponder it. We'd never discussed our relationship. I guess it made sense though—we'd only been dating each other—well, again, that was a guess. I'd only been dating him and hoped he wasn't dating anyone else. Maybe I was his woman? His Jane?

The news didn't sit well with Rand who, at this point, was fuming, his ears beet red. The cat continued to undulate in my arms, but I paid her no heed.

"For Christ's sake, let the bloody cat go!" Rand all but yelled.

Shocked, I put the cat down, and she retreated to the far corner of the room, looking at me like I was the worst of pet owners. Rand's murderous gaze returned to Trent.

"Regardless of what she is to you, she is first and foremost my employee, and our business doesn't involve you."

Before Trent had the opportunity for rebuttal, I stepped between the two of them and faced Trent. "I'll just be a second. If it's work related, it's important."

Even though he didn't look happy about it, he nodded, his eyes never leaving Rand's. I took Rand's hand—more so to remove him from my house than as a show of affection. I led him back outside where the rain had begun to let up and now just bathed the ground in a light dew.

"Did you have to be so rude?" I asked as soon as we were alone.

"Rude? I wasn't being rude. I was concerned for your safety and …"

"Well, regardless, you weren't friendly," I interrupted, wrapping my arms around myself. England was damn cold.

"And what the hell were you doing traipsing through the forest in the rain anyway?"

The anger melted out of his gaze and was replaced with a cold embarrassment as he seemed to struggle to find an excuse. "I was taking a walk."

I shook my head as a smile played with my lips. "In the middle of the pouring rain? I've never seen you take a walk before …"

"Yes, I decided to get some fresh air!" he interrupted, and his voice was back to being angry—I guessed he wasn't comfortable with the fact that I could see through his alibi like a pair of shorts with a hole.

"Okay, okay."

Rand looked like he was about to argue, but then thought better of it and swallowed the sentiment. "It's true what he said—that you're … his?"

Ah yes, that meant he caught on to the "Me Tarzan, you my woman" conversation. It was a good question and one I hadn't really decided myself. It would've been nice had Trent consulted me, but I guess I didn't object to being his girlfriend, or his woman as the case may be.

"Well, I guess so, I mean we never talked about it, but I guess it's true."

Rand was quiet for a moment, and then his expression turned into one a librarian would give a noisy child. "Then you have disregarded my advice that the wolf can't be trusted. He's bloody well put your life in jeopardy ..."

"Bella would've come after me anyway," I muttered even though I doubted the intelligence of Trent's actions myself.

"Jolie," he looked away, and his jaw was tight. He faced me again, and I could tell it was taking his entire wherewithal not to scream at me. "Sometimes you are so stubborn."

I laughed, but it was a hollow and caustic sound. "I'm stubborn? You, Rand, are the most stubborn person I've ever met."

He sighed in what I figured was frustration. "There's no use arguing with you. I hope you just keep your eyes open and don't trust him." When it appeared I was going to bicker with him, he intercepted. "Anyway, I'm sorry I disturbed you as I didn't think you had company."

He turned on his heel and started to walk away. I was about to call after him, to attempt to reconcile any damage I'd done, but I realized it was fruitless. I needed to let Rand go. He needed to know I was with someone else. But watching him walk down the driveway, I didn't feel especially good about my decision.

~

One week later and it seemed Bella's preparations for a unionized front of otherworldly creatures were coming down to the wire. Now, it wasn't just werewolves who were seeking refuge in England—a multitude of creatures sought haven in the neutrality of Europe.

Every time I turned around, I heard news of a new pack of wolves or a group of vampires—a gaggle of vampires?—making their home in Rand's territory. The fairies still kept to themselves, playing it as neutral as Switzerland, and I hadn't learned of any demons who were heading this way.

Trent and I sat across from two werewolves who'd escaped from the US to join ranks with Trent. In a matter of days, Trent's pack had tripled in size. While the new numbers had pleased him to no end, I hadn't been as excited. My time with Trent was rare enough as it was, and now he was so busy, I felt like I didn't even have a boyfriend.

The two wolves with whom we were having dinner were old friends of Trent's from a pack he'd known since childhood. They were a brother and sister, Jeffrey and Anne, both dark in hair and eyes and nice looking. Anne had a heart shaped face with a bit of a wide nose and large looming eyes. Her dark hair fell down to her waist and like most wolves, it was thick and luxurious. Jeffrey also shared the same thick and dark hair and though his wasn't quite as long as his sister's, it still graced his shoulders and required a band to keep it out of his face.

133

From the look of it, Anne seemed to be harboring quite the affection for Trent—it was there in the way she watched him with her doe eyes and how she giggled after everything he said, funny or not. I wasn't jealous, maybe a little bit, but only by the fact that she knew him far better than I did. That and she was spending a lot more time with him than I was. Of course, it was all in the name of building a solid pack, but still … I didn't have to like it.

"How many more wolves are migrating over?" I asked as I sipped my drink, feigning interest in the conversation. My mind was swimming with thoughts more along the line of this woman, her relationship with Trent, and exactly how well acquainted she was with him.

Trent faced me, and his hand went to my thigh, squeezing it.

Take that werewolf girl, I thought, and then got annoyed with myself for being so petty.

"We have no way of knowing until they get here, but it seems they're either siding with Bella or seeking refuge here. There's no in between," Jeffrey said.

"Meanwhile the Lurkers have struck again," Trent said with a frown.

I watched a fire ignite behind Anne's eyes as she watched him. I would've bet fifty bucks she had no idea what he'd just said. I could almost read her thoughts and they all centered around what a catch Trent was, now that he was leader of a very large pack.

"They were the group of humans sworn to destroy all creatures of the Underworld?" I asked, forcing my eyes from Anne, lest she notice the anger that sparked in their depths.

Trent nodded, his arm going around my shoulders.

"Great, more good news," I muttered, playing with the ice in my glass.

"Where?" Jeffrey asked, ignoring my comment.

"Arizona. They killed two vampires," Anne finished. Wow, so she had been paying attention. I guess I'd have to eat humble pie.

"Do you think it's a good idea to separate ourselves from Bella's forces when there seems to be a larger threat looming above us?" I asked. Even though I didn't have the warm fuzzies about Bella and recognized her for the witch (ha ha) she was, it seemed a dangerous proposition to separate ourselves when the Lurkers could attack again at any time. We would be much stronger as a collective force.

"Of course it isn't the best situation, but we don't have an alternative. Bella's made her intentions clear and she's playing by her rules. We'll have to face her and then the Lurkers," Jeffrey said.

Luckily, it seemed the Lurkers weren't organized in their attacks. They were more guerilla warfare style, taking out random creatures here and there with no military precision whatsoever. Not that I was up on military tactics at all … only a few years ago I'd learned guerilla warfare had nothing to do with monkeys.

"Looks like it'll be war," Trent finished and downed his drink.

The mention of war left my palms clammy. Wars were one thing when you learned about them in history class or watched a news reporter in some godforsaken place via the TV. But when you, yourself, are thrown into the middle of a brewing one, it's not an enviable position. And fighting against vampires, wolves, and demons? I'd rather rent the movie, thank you very much.

Anne finished her drink and placed it on the table with a thud. Her glazed eyes and swaying body bore testament to the fact that she was inebriated. "I'm tired of talking about a pending war. There isn't going to be any war with Bella—pretty soon we're all going to have to face the Lurkers, and that's going to be a war."

"Why don't you think there will be a war?" I asked, grabbing onto her words like they were a life preserver, and I was drowning in the middle of the Pacific.

Trent rolled his eyes, as if annoyed that I'd even broached the subject. Apparently, he thought there was going to be a war. Anne didn't seem to notice.

"Because when it comes down to it, we aren't going to be foolish enough to fight each other when there is a bigger enemy out there."

I nodded, thinking she made a good point.

"Anne, it has nothing to do with being foolish. If Bella attacks, what are we going to do? Welcome her in with tea and crumpets?" Jeffrey asked, his voice soft as though trying not to be harsh on his sister.

I thought the tea and crumpets line was pretty funny and hid my smile in the sleeve of my shirt.

"How do we even know she's building an army?" Anne continued, apparently annoyed at being ganged up on. I didn't know enough of the situation to take sides.

"What else do you think she's doing? She's building an army—I'd bet my life on it," Jeffrey finished and his lips were tight.

"Enough talk about war," Anne said. "Let's go dancing. I haven't been to a club in ages."

Trent faced me. "That could be fun. Are you up for it?" He gave me a little kiss on the tip of my nose.

I didn't want to be the party pooper although I was tired and hoped to have a nice evening with Trent ... alone. "Sure," I said, thinking I was quite the party martyr.

Two hours later, I was drunker than I'd ever been. After my fourth amaretto sour, I'd lost count. There's a point when you drink too much—past the point of the room spinning. That's where I was and after dancing to what I could only class techno music, I slipped into a chair and watched as Trent, Anne, and her brother danced together. Werewolves are physically stronger than humans are and can, therefore, dance longer than we can. And though I'm a witch, I still have that very human trait.

135

My gaze steadied on Trent as I watched him move to the rhythm of the music. I couldn't help the tingle that ran up my spine. I frowned as Anne interrupted my focus. She was dancing very close to Trent and didn't have his gift in the moves department. She threw her hair behind her shoulder, trying to draw his attention to it.

Give it up, Rapunzel, I thought.

As I watched Anne attempt to flirt with Trent, my head started spinning and I caught my breath, hoping I wouldn't pass out. I felt like I was on a techno merry-go-round, and it was all I could do not to fall off. The room stopped spinning, and I found my gaze resting on Anne and Trent again. I could see why she'd be attracted to him—he had a presence about him, a certain *je ne sais quoi.*

I wasn't in love with him, I was sure about that, but I cared a great deal for him. I did find myself wondering what our future would hold for us, though, as I figured his pack wanted him to date a wolf. As pack leader, he'd be expected to marry among his own kind and reproduce and he'd only be able to do so with another wolf.

This was one of the birds and bees conversations I'd had with Mathilda. She'd explained the natural order of things and while it'd been one of the oddest conversations we'd had, I'd learned a lot.

Apparently, witches and warlocks could reproduce together, but it was difficult for a witch to conceive. I wasn't sure how I felt about that. I certainly wanted a family someday, but because that day seemed as far off as possible, the thought that it might be tough for me to conceive wasn't as earth shattering as it otherwise might have been. And who knew, maybe it was just hard for me to conceive with another witch. I'd neglected to clarify that little point with Mathilda.

Vampires were technically dead, so there was no bun in the ovens for them; fairies had an easier go of it and they could reproduce with anything—humans, witches, whatever. I guess they were like the rabbits of the Underworld. Demons could reproduce with witches or other demons; I'd yet to meet a demon, but somehow, the idea of reproducing with one left me cold.

"How's your night going?"

I turned, feeling like I was underwater and faced a man smiling down at me. He was strange looking, and dopey—sort of like Gomer Pyle. I didn't say anything and before I knew it, he was sitting next to me.

"The name's Bradley," Gomer said. "You having yourself a good night?"

"It's going. How's yours?" I asked even though I couldn't care less about him or his night.

"Better now." His grin was toothy—it was like a donkey was sitting there and smiling at me.

"Ha." I managed as he scooted closer to me. I wasn't discreet when I moved farther away from him. He didn't notice. He must've been one of those people who required a bomb dropped in his lap with a note attached to it reading: *I'm not interested*!

"What are you drinking?" he asked as I took a ride on the merry-go-round again.

I dropped my forehead into my palm and closed my eyes, praying the room would stop spinning. "Nothing more, thanks," I said and pulled my head up. Nope, my prayers hadn't been answered—the room still spun like a record player.

"I saw you sittin' here all on your lonesome."

I rubbed my index fingers on my temples and tried to make the room hold still. I was amazed I was even able to continue the conversation. "I needed to sit one out."

"I like blonds."

"What do you want, a medal?" I felt like adding I'd never liked the Andy Griffith Show, but held my tongue. The dumbass wouldn't get it anyway.

He laughed as if he also liked rude women. "What's your name?"

"Her name isn't your concern," Trent's voice interrupted us and I turned to see him glaring at the drunk man.

I smiled up at Trent. "Hi, babe, this is Gomer."

The man gave me a quizzical look.

"It's Bradley, actually," he said.

"Great, Bradley, were you on your way somewhere?" Trent said, and his eyes issued a silent warning.

Bradley dropped his donkey smile and stood up as if he'd been sitting on hot coals. Trent shook his head, laughing as the man figured out what was good for him and vacated his seat. Trent watched him walk away before he took the empty seat.

"I can't leave you alone for a second," he said and nibbled on my ear.

"Looked like you were enjoying yourself with your wolf friend." I regretted sounding so concerned.

Trent laughed. "Is my little witch jealous?"

I shook my head and returned his kisses. "No, I'm not jealous."

"Looks like you're drunk."

I nodded. "Yes I am."

Trent didn't appear to be inebriated in the least, and I wondered if werewolves could handle their liquor better than humans could. It seemed Rand handled his liquor with aplomb. Maybe all creatures of the night did? If so, I had to catch up, as I was the epitome of a lightweight.

Trent excused himself to answer a call of nature. As soon as he left, Anne took his place. I couldn't say I was excited to see her, but I guess she beat another Gomer.

"This is a great club," she said.

The club was one I'd never been to before—called Interlude. It was overrun with people who were on the younger side of thirty. It seemed those frequenting it were of the drug persuasion—some seriously strange dancing giving me a clue. And though the music was okay, I couldn't get into techno much. I'm more an eighties fan. Give me some George Michael or INXS and I'm good to go.

"So you and Jeffrey have known Trent for a long time?" I asked, attempting to make small talk and praying I wouldn't lose my stomach.

"A very long time. My brother and he were always good friends and now that they've joined packs, they'll be even closer, I think."

I frowned—if her brother was going to be closer to Trent, then the same went for her. A sense of foreboding washed over me, and I wondered if Trent would eventually bend to the needs of his pack where I was concerned.

"How long have you and Trent been dating?" Anne asked nonchalantly, but I knew enough to realize she was hanging on my response.

"Maybe a month or so."

She nodded and dropped her gaze, tracing the mouth of her glass with her index finger. "He seems to really like you.

I frowned. What did one say to that? Sorry, that I'm in a relationship with him when it's obvious you wish you were? "I really like him—he's a good guy."

She stopped tracing the mouth of the glass and downed the rest of her drink. "Yes, he is a good person. Thank you for what you did for him."

"What I did for him?" I asked, clearly not following her. I was too busy trying to defeat the threat of an upset stomach.

"Bringing him back to life. You don't know the service you did for us; we can never repay you for that."

I downplayed it with a wave of my hand; acting as though I'd lent him some sugar, not reanimated him. Hmm, I guess in a manner of speaking, I had lent him some sugar. With an inward smile, I reached for my drink and brushed against Anne's hand and gasped.

I was so drunk it took me a second to realize I was having a vision. Once it dawned on me, I closed my eyes and focused. It was Anne and she was in trouble—cornered by a werewolf and an adversarial one at that. I could see the fear in her eyes as she attempted to push the wolf away from her. I didn't know why she didn't just turn into a wolf, herself, but I didn't get time to contemplate it as the vision disappeared just as quickly as it had come. What remained was the bitter aftertaste that the wolf had been sent by Bella.

Anne could see the change in my demeanor and paled. "What did you see?" she whispered.

I debated on telling her and decided not to. "It was a quick vision, Anne. Just be … sure you don't go anywhere alone. Always have Jeffrey with you, okay?" I wondered if she noticed that I left Trent out of that sentence.

Anne nodded. "Was it bad? Was it Jeff?"

This is always the tough part when you know certain things that you shouldn't know. When it's good news, that's easy. Everyone is happy and I'm always pleased to be the bearer of good news. Bad news is a different animal altogether.

138

"It was you and another wolf."

She seemed as though she were trying to make sense of my stupid statement. I just couldn't quite bring myself to extrapolate.

"Did I get killed?"

I snorted and wished I hadn't sounded so unladylike. "No! It was just a wolf and it was cornering you and growling. That's why I said just don't go alone anywhere."

I had no idea what was going through her head. I tried to imagine what I'd be thinking if I were her and in my current state, I couldn't think of a damned thing.

"Do you have any idea when it will happen?" she asked.

I shook my head. "No idea. I just see things and I never know when I'm going to see them. As far as when these things happen, I don't know. It could be days, months, or even years."

She seemed deep in thought. I regretted telling her. It was a huge thing to put on someone's shoulders—knowing that something bad was going to happen to them, but not knowing the when or where or how of it.

"Thanks," she said in a small voice. I just nodded and thought it ironic that she'd be thanking me for dropping a bomb right on her doorstep. I lifted my drink and downed the remnants of melted ice.

Luckily, Trent returned. "What do you say we get out of here?" he asked with a secretive smile and tapped me on the butt.

I stood up, swaying with the effort. Trent was immediately by my side. I made the mistake of glancing at Anne who was wearing her worry. I should never have told her anything—I should've just made something up. My anger was so palpable, I could've choked on it.

I threw my gaze back to Trent, knowing browbeating myself was useless. Then my thoughts turned to the nature of the vision itself. I wasn't sure why, but this latest episode really got me. Maybe it forced me to face the fact that a battle between the species was not just a faraway dream but was becoming a definite reality with each day that passed.

139

FOURTEEN

One week later and I found myself in Christa's bedroom bemoaning my breakup with Trent. I'd managed to keep a boyfriend for about a month and then boom, he dumped me.

"I'm not going to cry about it," I said with reserve. I hadn't cried yet, so why start now? Christa sat on her bed and looked at me as you would a cat that's lost all its limbs, teeth, and fur and was trying to hobble over to you for some attention.

"You can cry about it, maybe you should."

"I don't want to give him the satisfaction of my tears, the miserable jerk." The truth was that I wasn't sure Trent was in fact a miserable jerk. After another wolf attack, he'd told me he couldn't see me until he was sure he wouldn't threaten my safety. But it was easier to blame and dislike him, so I stuck with it.

Christa pulled her hair into a loose ponytail. "He was only looking out for you."

I threw myself back on her unmade bed and stared up at the ceiling, the only tidy thing in the room. "That's what he said, but I think it's all a front. He said he was only looking out for my safety and because he cares about me so much, he couldn't see me for a while."

Then the tears came, but they weren't tears of missing Trent, more tears of humiliation and those were okay to shed. I wouldn't cry over my destroyed relationship, but I could cry over the fact that I'd been dumped. I could only imagine he was already gracing the bed of some unfortunate woman. Anne's face immediately surfaced in my tormented mind and I had to beat the image away.

At least Rand wasn't home to witness my pathetic display. He'd been gone all week on an errand near London, what errand he hadn't told Christa and I had no idea, as he hadn't talked to me since the spectacle with Trent at my house. Usual Rand form.

"Why don't you stay here tonight?" Christa asked, leaning over to pat my hand reassuringly. "We can have a girl's night since the boys are out."

I wiped my tears on my sleeve and sat up. "You don't have plans with John tonight?"

She shook her head. "No, I told him tonight was for you, I thought you might need it."

"Well, I hope you didn't say I was depressed—you know that will go straight back to jerk-face."

Christa laughed and mimicked zipping her lips closed and throwing away the key. "I didn't say a word."

I nodded and traced the pattern of her matelass'e quilt with my fingertip. "How are things with you and John?"

A Texas-sized smile lit up her face. "Good. I really like him."

I tried to feel happy for her, but it was tough given the fact that my love life sucked balls. I'm sure that sounds insensitive, but at least I'm honest.

"That's good," I said and stood up, trying to detect the carpet through the mound of clutter littering Christa's room. Dirty clothes formed a pyramid in the center of the floor and she had enough dishes lying around to piss off the kitchen.

"I haven't seen his car up here in a while," I finished.

She plopped down in an armchair next to the marble fireplace, not bothering to move the dress and wad of socks already sitting there. "That's because Rand made a rule that no wolves are allowed in his house ever again."

"Even John?"

She nodded. "He was upset about you and Trent, I think. He left the next morning for London, and all he told me was that he was on business and would be gone for a week. I haven't heard from him since."

"Has it already been a week? Do you think we should call him?" I asked, worried that Rand was in trouble somewhere.

Christa shook her head. "No, I think Rand is about as safe as safe can be. Who's going to threaten a warlock?"

I nodded, thinking she made a good point. Rand was at the top of the food chain. Then my thoughts strayed to his recent banning of all wolves from his house. "I don't know what Rand's issue is with me. He seems to want me when he can't have me. God, men are so frustrating."

"Yes, they are," Christa agreed and then fell silent. I felt her eyes on me, and my suspicion flared.

"What?" I demanded, and threw myself back on the unmade bed, as if to show her that I wasn't planning on budging until she came out with whatever was on her mind.

"Rand had a woman over the other night," she said, looking like she hadn't wanted to tell me but thought she should all the same.

Like a punctured balloon, my entire being deflated with the news. I'd thought I was over Rand but, apparently, such wasn't the case. It was as if fate had conjured up a little vat of jealousy dust and blown it in my ear. I thought I might be sick. "A woman?"

"She wasn't as pretty as you are."

I had to laugh at Christa and her good timing. That was the first thought that had entered my head—that I hoped the woman wasn't beautiful.

"I think she lives in London," Christa continued.

"Hence his visit down there now," I finished for her, with a sigh. It felt like a tiny part of me died, and I hated myself for my reaction. The sooner I realized there was nothing between Rand and me, and there never would be anything between us, the better.

"Ugh, what is wrong with me?"

Christa shook her head. "You're a woman."

"God, Chris, I thought I was over him. Moving out and dating Trent—I really did think I was over him." Tears pooled in my eyes and Christa jumped up from her chair, throwing her arms around me.

"For all I know, he could be on business," she said, suffocating me with the smell of her baby powder deodorant.

I patted her hand, thanking her for her reassurance. "It isn't any of my business anyway."

Christa nodded and although she allowed me my space, she still sat close by in case I needed another dose of her lovesickness remedy.

"True, but you can't escape the fact that you both have always wanted one another, but just never acted on it. I guess it's for the best since these types of things always end and then where would your work relationship be?"

"Nowhere," I answered, thinking that our work relationship was always the reason we never acted on anything, and I was sick and tired of thinking about it. If I could have taken our "work relationship" out back and shot it full of bullets, I would've done so in a heartbeat.

I tried to wade through the crap on Christa's floor, feeling the sudden need to pace the room. I stopped next to her desk and threw myself into the desk chair, noticing some of her photos sticking out beneath a pink dress. I shifted the dress and picked up the photos. They were all eight by tens. One was a photo in black and white of Pelham Manor. With its gothic façade and gargoyles, it reminded me of Wingfield Hall, Mr. Rochester's home from Jane Eyre.

The next photo was Rand's rose garden; the color of the blooms so vivid, it seemed that in just touching the picture, I could rub the redness off on my fingers. "These are beautiful, Chris."

She smiled. "Thanks. I showed the thumbnails to Rand and he asked me to blow them up so he could hang them around the house. I was going to frame them for him ... like a surprise."

If I hadn't remembered the spell Rand had put on Christa, which made her feelings for him lean more towards brotherly love than physical love, I might've thought she had the hots for him ... again. But I knew better.

"He would love that, I'm sure."

I flipped to the next photo, which was a stylized portrait of Rand in sepia tone. He was dressed in a long sleeved shirt and dark pants. Sitting on a stool, with one leg stretched out before him, he was so rigid, a light breeze could've blown him over. And the small smile on his lips looked like he'd been going for the Mona Lisa but never quite got there. He appeared to be completely uncomfortable. I couldn't help my grin.

"He wanted to frame this one?" I asked.

She shook her head and giggled. "That's a joke. I threw that one in because he looks so funny. Talk about the worst subject. He was more uncomfortable posing for me than you are."

I laughed and went to the next photo. It was of me and I was sitting cross-legged on my veranda, Plum in my lap. I was wearing blue jeans and a white t-shirt. My hair splayed against my shoulders, on one side a breeze playfully lifting it. I remembered Christa taking the photo, she'd snapped it just as I was telling her not to. I looked happy, a laugh in the process of stealing my lips.

"What are you doing with this?" I asked, holding it up.

Christa dropped her face just the smallest fraction as if shielding a secret. "That's for Rand. He didn't want me to tell you."

"He wanted to frame it?" I couldn't keep the shock from my voice.

She nodded. "So much for keeping his secret," Christa said with an unapologetic smile. "He said it was just so … you."

"Wow." I dropped the photos back on her desk. I didn't know what to think, so I chose to think nothing at all. "Those are really good, Chris. I'm really impressed."

She smiled. "Thanks, I think I might start taking some photography classes … sharpen my skills a little, you know?"

I suddenly felt like a very bad friend. I hadn't been super supportive of her talent. Hell, I hadn't even been around. Had I been so involved with my own life that I'd totally ignored my friend? The answer was pretty obvious. "God, Chris, I've been a bad friend lately. I … I'm really sorry."

She waved my concern away. "Jules, you've been so busy with stuff. I can't even imagine how tough it is to be you right now. Don't feel bad. It's just a couple of pictures."

"No, Chris, I shouldn't have been so caught up in my own life. I'm really sorry."

She just smiled. "What do you say we break into a bottle of wine?"

A bottle of wine—just what the doctor ordered. Numbing myself with alcohol. A motto that I tried not to live by, but what the hell, desperate times call for desperate measures.

"Amen to that." I checked my watch. "It's eight o'clock, it's late enough."

Christa stood up, and I trailed her downstairs into the wine cellar where we approached endless rows of bottle rear ends. Neither one of us a wine connoisseur, we just stood there in silent indecision.

"Do you think he's saving any of them?" Christa asked.

I shook my head. I didn't give a crap if he was or not. "Who cares?"

Christa laughed. "I like your attitude, Jules." Her hands hovered over the bottles as if she wasn't sure which one to go with.

"Close your eyes and pick one," I said with a grin.

She shut her eyes and reached out like someone playing pin the tail on the donkey and grabbed a Merlot. She opened her eyes and eyed the bottle before returning her gaze to the wall of bottles.

"Maybe a couple more?"

I laughed, thinking the more the merrier. "Sure, couldn't hurt."

After loading ourselves with four bottles of wine—a Merlot, a Chardonnay, a Pinot Grigio, and a Syrah for good measure—we retired to Christa's room. She turned on her CD player and some new age type music came pouring out.

"What the hell is this?" I asked with a frown, taking a seat on her bed while she followed suit.

"It's my meditation music."

"What? Since when do you do that?"

She raised her brows and pasted an indignant smile on her face. "John says it's good for the soul."

I rolled my eyes. "Oh, God."

The meditation music wafted out of the speakers, sounding like something you'd hear in an elevator in a cheap hotel somewhere in the Midwest.

"We forgot glasses, didn't we?" she asked, pulling my attention from the "music." I nodded while she leaned across her bed and pulled open a drawer, retrieving a corkscrew.

"You keep one in your drawer?" I asked with a laugh.

"You never know when you're going to need one." She popped the cork on the Merlot and swigged from the bottle, looking like the quintessential wino. Wiping her arm across her mouth, she handed the bottle to me.

I held up the wine. "To drinking four bottles with no glasses while listening to the crappiest music I've ever heard."

Christa grabbed the Pinot with a giggle and popped the cork, holding it up to imitate my salute. "Cheers."

Two hours later and we were both hammered. I hadn't realized just how much I needed a girls' night. But after talking about Spokane and what our lives used to be like, boyfriends and breakups, I'd realized exactly how much I'd missed a little estrogen in my life.

"You want some more?" Christa asked, her right eye drooping like an old lady's pantyhose. It was the sign that Christa was drunk. She said it was a form of lazy eye; I just thought it was hysterical and laughed although I tried to hide it with an inconspicuous cough.

"Count me in." I thrust my hand out, and she rammed the bottle of Chardonnay into my palm. "Which bottle are we on?"

"Um, three I think." She hiccupped.

I downed the remnants and let the bottle drop to the carpet, watching it roll across the floor until it butted into a pile of People magazines.

"What time is it?"

Christa never wore a watch so she grabbed her cell phone from her pocket, squinting at it with her droopy eye. "Nearly midnight."

"I feel sick," I said and tried to stand up, using her shoulder to get to my feet. "I gotta go to bed." Once I managed to stand on my own for a few seconds, I turned and started for her door, my feet like flippers.

Christa hiccupped again. "Are you going home?"

I shook my head and grabbed hold of the top of her chair as the room started spinning. "I'm too drunk to walk. I'll just crash in my old bedroom."

Christa waved and crawled into her bed. I was jealous, not wanting to travel the five hundred feet to my bedroom. "Night."

"Night, Christa, and thanks. I needed this."

She smiled as I stumbled across the threshold. With a wave, I closed her door and headed for my old bedroom. The view of my canopy bed was a sight for drunk eyes. I kicked the door closed behind me and made my way to the windows, enjoying the warmth that rushed over me at the familiar view. A full moon bathed the lush grounds of Pelham Manor in rays of blue.

You finally decide to come back.

I turned at the sound of Pelham's voice in my head and smiled at my friend. *I guess it's been a while.*

He joined me at the window, trying to see what I was looking at. *The wolf went his separate way?*

I guess you were spying on Christa and me all night?

What else have I got to do?

I laughed and faced him, thinking how odd it was that I could see him so completely and yet he was a ghost, energy.

Pelham, why haven't you ever asked me to bring you back to life? I thought as I nearly tripped over my own feet.

Pelham looked like Thinking Man as he sat above the bed, his chin in his palm. *I have been like this for so long now, I cannot conceive of what the outside world must be like.*

You're afraid? I asked and thought if I were in his shoes, I'd feel the same way ... probably.

Perhaps. The desire is just not strong. Everything I care about is within this house. He smiled but it looked sad. *Now, the wolf ...*

Not a subtle change of subject but I respected it all the same.

Yes, he dumped me, so you can rub it in.

Pelham shrugged. *Why would I want to do that? I imagine you are already rubbing it in yourself. Is that why you're inebriated?*

I laughed. What a perceptive ghost. *Yeah, I guess so. It was one of the many reasons.*

Well, the wolf is a fool to have let you go. A beautiful woman like you ...

If you were alive, I'd kiss you!

Don't let my current state stop you, he said and I just shook my head.

Thanks anyway.

Pelham sighed and attempted to put his arm around me. He went through me, but I appreciated the gesture all the same. *I should go to bed. I have a terrible headache,* I said, stumbling back into the room and thinking I'd had way too much to drink.

Can I watch you undress?

I rolled my eyes. *You will anyway.*

He nodded with a wink. I searched through the drawers, hoping I'd left something to sleep in. I'd already learned that being drunk didn't equate to magic working properly, so there would be no creating my own nightshirt tonight. And the headache? That would have to stay too.

Not finding anything and not wanting to wake Christa, I decided to head into Rand's room and look for a t-shirt. I hoped he wouldn't mind and then scrubbed the thought, he wasn't here anyway so what did it matter?

I opened the door and breathed deeply. Rand's scent lured me inside, heating my body with that particular spicy male aroma. It was a masculine room, with dark cherry wood paneling, oversized and deep brown furniture, and an enormous bookshelf. I'd never been in Rand's room before and being here now, by myself, almost made me giddy with the inclination to snoop.

A bottle of wine sat on the side table next to the largest bed I'd ever seen. Cal King Schmal King. This thing had to have been custom ordered. Images of him in bed and drinking wine with the woman in London coursed through my head, and I braced myself against the mantle, thinking I might pass out. When the dizziness subsided, I decided to help myself to the bottle and took a generous swig. Then I turned to the task of finding something I could wear to bed.

Rand's closet was full of clothes, all organized according to color. Figured he'd be the OCD type. I found a white t-shirt and couldn't help bringing it to my nose as I inhaled the scent so completely Rand—a scent of laundry detergent with notes of his cologne. God, I made myself want to vomit.

I thought you were coming back?

I looked up and found Pelham on Rand's bed, facing me. Of course, he wasn't going to miss the chance to see me in the buff. *I didn't have anything to wear to bed, so I wanted to borrow a shirt from Rand.*

Ah, I see, well go ahead, put it on.

I pulled off my shirt, draping it over the side of one of Rand's plush bedroom chairs. Pelham's eyes were glued to my every move and in my drunkenness, it actually made me feel good, attractive. I slid off my pants, laid them atop my blouse, then undid my bra, and watched as a smile lit the corners of his mouth.

Very nice.

Then I pulled Rand's shirt over my head and Pelham frowned. *What about the knickers?*

Those aren't coming off. Now go away and leave me alone.

146

With his lips pulled taut, he faded away and I shut the door, so he'd know I didn't welcome his return. I wanted some time to myself to snoop around Rand's room and to finish the rest of the wine.

There were pictures of Rand with various people all over his room and finding one, I picked it up, inspecting it. This one was Rand in what looked like the Alps—snowy and steep mountains. Rand was dressed in blue snow gear, his ski mask perched atop his head, throwing his hair in disarray. He smiled broadly, his dimples in attendance and accounted for. A young man stood next to him, but I had no interest in him.

I took the photo with me to his gigantic bed and climbed in the middle as I grabbed the bottle of wine and downed a few swallows. I sank into the bed, the mattress as warm and welcoming as a hug. It felt as if I were in a cloud of feathers—feather mattress, feather duvet with feather pillows. Thank God I wasn't allergic to ducks.

I downed the remnants of the wine and put the empty bottle on his bed stand as my attention returned to the photo in my hand. Rand was the best-looking man I'd ever seen. I leaned against the headboard and tucked the picture up against me, imagining how nice it would be to be in bed with Rand this very moment.

~

"Jolie, wake up."

The voice was distant and the pounding in my head forced me to ignore it, so I could return to the solitude of my dreams. I'd felt the warm sun through my eyelids for a while now, but I just couldn't bring myself to wake up and face the steady ache in my head.

"Jolie," the voice persisted and I groaned out my discomfort, pulling the covers up higher.

The covers pulled themselves back and I stirred from the cold air that whispered over my legs. I opened my eyes. The dark paneling, dark green paint on the walls was unfamiliar. There was an empty bottle of wine in front of me and something sharp jutting into my chin. Before I had a chance to register what it was, Rand leaned down and pulled his photo from my arms. My head ached too much for me to feel any sort of embarrassment. He replaced the photo on his mantel over the fireplace before facing me with an inquisitive grin.

"What are you doing in my bed?" he asked, returning.

I sat up and regretted it as my head throbbed with the effort. His shirt twisted up above my waist, and I jerked it back down over my legs, so as not to appear entirely indecent. At least I had panties on, otherwise I would've given Rand quite a show. I wiped the corner of my mouth after noting it was wet and then realized I'd drooled all over his pillow.

Nice going, Jolie, really nice.

"Um, I don't know why I'm in your bedroom," I said with a sheepish smile.

147

He didn't look angry, maybe more amused than anything else. He sat down next to me. "I must say the last thing I thought I'd find is you half-naked in my bed."

"I came over to see Christa last night, and we drank your wine and talked about my break up with …"

"You broke up with the wolf?" Rand interrupted, his face growing serious.

I grabbed my head, willing it to stop aching. "I think it's more fitting to say the wolf broke up with me."

Rand nodded. "Are you alright?"

"I'll survive. I didn't have anything to sleep in, so I came in here to borrow a shirt, then drank the rest of your wine and … fell asleep in your bed. Sorry."

"And drooled all over my pillow." He laughed. "No need to apologize. It appears you have quite a hangover."

I nodded. "Yeah, a nasty one."

He motioned for me to put my head in his lap and when I did so, he laid his hand atop it and set on removing my headache. I set on removing my morning breath by picturing a drop of mint spreading on my tongue. I swallowed a couple of times, tasting wintergreen.

"Rand, why are you so good to me?" I asked him, still drunk enough to raise the question.

He chuckled. "I have to ask myself that over and over."

His hand on my forehead felt heavy, warm, and soft. I smiled as I studied his incredibly handsome face above me. "Even from this angle, you're still damned hot."

Rand shook his head, a smirk playing with his lips. "Well, from this angle you're pretty damned hot yourself."

Using my drunkenness as an alibi, I decided to ask him the question I'd always wondered. "Rand, do you use magic to … look the way you do?"

His chuckle rang through the air loud and clear. "Bloody hell, I can't believe you're asking me that. No!"

I smiled and squirmed in his lap. "You told me a long time ago that all witches are very attracted to one another."

His smile fell, and he was back to looking serious. Slowly, his fingers slipped through my hair, teasing the strands. "Yes, but what I feel for you goes beyond that, Jolie."

Heat stirred in the pit of my belly and it took me a second to realize what he'd just admitted. Maybe I needed to get drunk and sleep in his bed more often. "I feel it for you also. I always have."

He nodded, as if weighing the thought. "I think it's best we don't act on it. It just confuses things."

I resisted the urge to scream and forced the tears away. I would not cry, but at the same time, I had to know why. "Why?"

"In light of recent events, I think it best we keep our distance and make our relationship business," he finished.

"What recent events?" I wondered if he meant Trent's and my relationship. That was so yesterday.

He shook his head. "We just can't."

I sat up, but he wouldn't look me in the eyes. He always gave the same lame-as-hell answer. I wondered if he'd ever give in to his feelings, ever allow himself to care for me the way he wanted to—the way I wanted him to. Then the thought dawned on me that maybe he was in a relationship. I couldn't bring myself to broach that subject, afraid of how my stomach might react.

"That's what I thought you'd say." I stood up and braced myself against his bed as my stomach heaved, and I thought I'd be sick. "I drank too much wine."

He stood and placed his hand on my belly. My stomach muscles quivered, heat spreading from his palm as it curled through my stomach and up my body. The feelings of sickness faded into obscurity. I couldn't help it as my arms went around him and I hugged him, needing to feel close to him. He hesitated for a moment and then returned the embrace, kissing the top of my head.

He sat down again and motioned for me to put my head back in his lap. I'm not sure why I did—maybe I was just too tired and hung over to protest.

"I was in London meeting with one of the largest of the wolf packs," he started. "There are more and more wolves migrating to England as Bella pushes them out of the States."

"So what Trent said was true. They're all seeking refuge with you," I said as I thought about what this meant. Bella was making fast headway in deciding who was with her and who was against her. It'd only be a matter of time before she came for me. I was the winning lottery ticket in her pocket and sooner or later she'd come for her winnings.

"Yes, I've been deciding how we build a team of forces ourselves," he finished.

"You mean do what Bella's doing?"

"She hasn't given us a blasted choice. She's building an army and her plans are to force us to join her or kill us. And I, for one, will not go down without a fight," Rand finished as he ran his fingers through my hair, catching them in a knot. He then went about loosening the knot, and I closed my eyes, loving the feel of his gentle hands.

"So what was in London?" I asked, only too aware the answer was a woman. I could've slapped myself for asking.

"A friend of mine, Gwynn, she is an old and powerful witch, and she just happens to be half vampire."

And she also just happens to be having sex with you, I thought to myself. I disliked her already. "What will she do for us?"

"Her coven controls Ireland and she has an ally in the warlock who controls Scandinavia, so we have those areas covered. Since she is part

149

vampire, she has a special relationship with the vampires and many have joined her already."

Rand worked the knot loose and began separating my hair into sections, as if to braid it.

"So she will be our liaison to the European witches and warlocks?"

"Yes and with all the newly arrived werewolves in England, I'm going to make the mandate they either join us or move on. We have to take the stance that if they aren't with us, they're against us."

"This is really happening," I muttered, feeling sick all over again.

"Yes it is, and we have to be ready for it. I've called a meeting in a week's time and all the witches from Europe will be joining us as well as the leaders of the werewolf packs and some prominent vampires. We need to begin recruiting against Bella's army. I want to show them we have a weapon that Bella doesn't."

I felt the weight of his words and sighed. It seemed the entire universe was counting on me. I wasn't much of a hero. "I don't know how good of a weapon I am, but I'm happy to be there for you."

Apparently, he wasn't good at braiding as he gave up and ran his fingers through my hair again. "And just so you know, Trent will be there."

Great, so I'd have to see the wolf that dumped me as pretty as you please and as an added bonus, I'd get to meet the witch who was warming Rand's bed.

Lucky me!

FIFTEEN

Upon visiting London, I decided I didn't like it. Sure, it was beautiful and had the best stores I'd ever seen in my life and the Tower of London was all fine and good. But everywhere I turned, something reminded me of the woman who lived here—the woman who'd somehow managed to capture Rand's interest.

The woman who wasn't me.

I couldn't keep the frown from stealing my lips as I looked out the window of Rand's Range Rover. We were on our way to meet said woman. Had I the option to A. meet Rand's current flame or B. chew off my own toe, option B was sounding pretty good.

Christa was in much better spirits. Even though she was going to miss John while we were on this trip, she was overly excited about sightseeing, like a kid at Disneyland excited. I could think of nothing worse than going on a tourist trip of London.

"Madame Tussaud's is supposed to be an excellent wax museum," Christa said as she eyed some obnoxious brochure she'd picked up in the city. "Do you think we'll have time to see it, Rand?"

Rand seemed as disinterested in seeing wax figures as I did. He smiled and feigned ignorance, keeping his eyes on the road like a good driver. "Ask Jolie if she wants to go."

I frowned, but tried to keep my aggravation in check. "Let's see how much time we have."

We were on a tight schedule and hopefully that would be my alibi. Rand had said we'd be in London for the weekend—for our grand meeting with the creatures who might team up with us against the evil legacy that was Bella. I wanted to get our meeting over and done with so I could get back to the safety of my little house. There no one would bug me and I could drown away thoughts of Rand and Trent with some good ale.

We arrived in front of an ornate townhouse in what I learned was the most expensive area of London, Kensington Square. So not only did the stupid woman have claim to Rand's heart, but she was rich on top of it.

When it rains, it pours.

Rand parked in front of the three-story, white Victorian mansion and faced me expectantly. "We're here."

I managed a smile and undid my seatbelt in record-breaking time, record-breaking slow time. Christa, on the other hand, hopped out of the car, alight with non-stop chatter and buzzed around me like an insistent mosquito.

"Are we going to dinner?" I asked with a frown.

Rand shook his head. "Gwynn said she had something prepared."

Oh, even better. Now I'd have to suffer through the flirting, the lustful eyes and all in the less-than-humble abode where the Gwynn-Rand seduction was taking place.

Vo-mit.

I followed Rand and Christa up the numerous steps. He knocked on the door, and I could hear the soft pitter-patter of heels on hardwood from inside. Then she opened the door.

That was when I realized Christa hadn't been forthcoming in her description of the witch; Gwynn was beautiful. She was taller than I was and thinner and that was as far as I'd let myself make a comparison.

"Rand!" Gwynn said with an Eastern-European accent. She engulfed him in a hug and kissed both of his cheeks. He responded in kind.

"Gwynn, this is Christa," Rand said, introducing Christa first as I was lollygagging behind them. He took hold of my shoulder and encouraged me forward.

"And this is Jolie." There was a certain note of pride that accompanied his voice ... I think.

"Charmed," Gwynn said with a smile and opened the door wide, granting us entrance. I smiled as best I could and took in her long platinum blonde hair, wide hazel eyes, Nicole Kidman nose and instantly was depressed again.

She led us to her dining room and en route, I noticed the ridiculously high ceilings, the ornate crown molding, the priceless art and sculptures (I imagined they were priceless, but I'm not an art connoisseur, so what do I know), and the heavy velvet of the curtains.

Taking my seat at the expansive dining table, Christa took the one next to me. Gwynn, of course, sat next to Rand, and I had to unclench my teeth, lest I appear to have lockjaw. Like something out of a movie, Gwynn picked up a small silver bell and rang twice. No sooner did she put the bell back on the table than a flurry of servants entered the room and began filling glasses, offering hors d'oeuvres, and generally making themselves useful.

My attention returned to Gwynn and Rand. Thank God, they displayed no sort of affection with one another in front of us; that would've been enough for me to lose my lunch. They were very matter-of-fact, instead, and one would never have known they had any sort of romantic affiliation.

"How many people will be there tomorrow night?" Christa asked.

Rand shrugged and glanced at Gwynn. "I believe the count is one hundred fifty?"

Gwynn nodded. "Not bad, but we'll need to expand our numbers if we're to go up against Bella. One thing we can promise those who do join is that we can bring back their fallen compatriots."

It took me a second for this to sink in, and then it dawned on me: who'd be the person bringing back the fallen? "So that's where I come in?" I asked, sounding less than enthusiastic.

"You're our secret weapon, Jolie," Rand said.

I frowned, thinking they had a better chance with a gun, some silver bullets, a cross, and maybe Van Helsing. "That sounds like a huge number of creatures to bring back. Do you think I'm capable of that?" I asked, clearly thinking "no" was the answer.

"It will be very time consuming, but it's imperative you do this," Gwynn answered, and her tone was one a parent would use with a child. My hands curled in my lap as if they were so affronted by the tone they couldn't help but wither in disgust.

"Where do I sign up?" I asked with a facetious smirk.

Gwynn ignored me and cemented the fact that neither of us cared for the other. I could see it clearly in her ash hazel eyes. I only wondered if she could see my feelings for Rand as clearly in mine.

She turned to Rand and plastered a smile on her lips. "I'm pleased you'll have the opportunity to meet Ryder, finally."

"I've heard much of him and look forward to it."

Christa wore her confusion. "Ryder?"

Rand nodded. "Ryder is a vampire. He's Gwynn's creator."

"There is a very special relationship between a vampire and his brethren. The bond is a strong one," Gwynn explained although no one had asked her.

"Oh," Christa said, nodding as if she had a clue as to what Gwynn was talking about. I had to hide my smile.

"Ryder has decided to throw in his lot with us," Rand continued before facing Gwynn again. "I look forward to finally meeting him."

Gwynn just batted her cow eyelashes at him. Rand's mouth quirked into a grin—one that seemed aimed at Gwynn alone.

This was going to be a long goddamned night.

~

The next day passed slowly, and I found that Christa and I were left to our own defenses as Rand and Gwynn planned for the festivities of the evening. When the night of the "Halloween Rally," as Christa dubbed it, was upon us, I wanted nothing more than to get it over and done with.

"I wonder what demons look like," Christa said as she donned her flame red lipstick, gazing at her reflection in the mirror of my hotel room.

"Well, you'll find out soon enough," I answered, smoothing the non-existent wrinkles from my evening gown. Apparently, the creatures of the Underworld took public appearances seriously; this evening was a black tie event. I was dressed in a black satin, strapless gown that was so long, I knew I'd trip on it before the night was through. My hair was fastened in a chignon at my neck and felt about as tight as the damned dress.

"How do I look?" Christa asked as she turned to face me. Her red evening gown hugged her curves and ended just below her knees. I was the short one and Rand had stuck me with the long-ass gown, now tell me that makes any sort of sense?

"Great."

"Rand did a good job of picking these dresses out for us," she continued, prancing around as though she were a princess.

I didn't agree with her as I thought my boobs were going to come popping out of my top any second. I guess I didn't much like getting dressed up ... period. "I wish I could at least have a shorter dress."

Of course, I was pleased that I probably looked better than I'd ever looked. Especially with the prospect of reuniting with Trent this evening.

Christa turned her attention to me and frowned. "You look so beautiful, Jules. Try to snap out of your depression. Think about how many eligible bachelors will be there tonight. We're going to meet all the big wigs of the Underworld, and now that you're single, you can have any one of them!"

Christa would have made a very good motivational speaker. But I wasn't concerned with eligible bachelors. I was dreading the whole night—dreading having to see Trent again, dreading having to witness Rand with Gwynn, dreading the whole crappy thing.

"You ready?" Christa asked.

"I guess so."

I followed her out the door, finding it difficult to walk—the dress was so tight, it only allowed for Barbie doll sized steps. At least the stupid party was in our hotel and wouldn't require any traveling to get there.

"I wonder if this will be fun?" Christa asked as she pressed the call button on the elevator.

"I doubt it."

Christa smiled sadly and dropped her gaze as we stepped in the elevator. We didn't stop at any floors along the way down and arrived on the ground floor within seconds. I took a deep breath and attempted to gather my courage for the evening. It was going to take a load of it.

"Here goes." Christa opened the door to the reception room, and the sound of mingled laughter and soft music met us.

One hundred fifty creatures of the night in one room is a bit overwhelming. Auras of all colors created quite a rainbow, and there was a stirring in the evening air that bespoke of the magic within the walls.

We weaved our way through the crowd. A couple parted in front of us, and my eyes met Rand's. He was sitting at the head table, wearing a black tuxedo that hugged his muscled body and acted like acid on my heart. I gave him a small nod as I settled in the chair next to him. His scent enfolded me with its notes of cardamom and man. I breathed deeply, trying to concentrate on Christa's mindless chatter.

Rand and Gwynn had done a good job organizing the whole thing, and if I'd been an outsider looking in, I would've thought someone was having a wedding reception. There were fourteen tables, all covered with white linens. Apparently, this was going to be a dinner service as place settings decorated the tables and included nametags for each creature. My nametag said: Jolie Wilkins, Witch. How original.

"Hey," Christa nudged me in the side. "Did you hear me?"

"What?"

Christa frowned. "I said, does it look like I have deodorant stains? I didn't notice it in the room, but now it looks like …"

I tried to pay attention to Christa's deodorant stains, but had my own ADD moment. My attention centered on the table before me which included Rand, Gwynn, Christa, and two people I didn't recognize. One was an elderly man, and upon seeing his nametag, I learned he was Grimsley Jones, a warlock who controlled Sweden, Finland, and Norway. Sitting beside him was Ryder Colden, the swarthy vampire who'd turned Gwynn and who'd already committed himself to joining Rand's ranks.

As soon as my gaze landed on Ryder's wide and unattractive face, my pulse quickened and the breath in my nose ran back down my throat. There was something about him—he was vile—in everything from his face to his clothes to his body language. I'm not sure why, but I was terrified of him.

My gaze shifted to Gwynn who sat very closely to Ryder and must have had poor eyesight because she clung to his every movement as if he were beauty personified. The thought of becoming some sort of half vampire was not in the least appealing, and I couldn't help but wonder what was involved in such an ordeal. One thing that was clear—there was some sort of special relationship between turner and turnee. Gwynn treated Ryder with an admiration and awe she bestowed on no one else. Ryder didn't seem as intrigued with her, though, and regarded her and the rest of the room with indifference, boredom even. I decided I didn't much care for Ryder.

Rand stood at the head table, a microphone in his hand. It seemed he was waiting for all the late stragglers to find their seats.

"Look who's here," Christa whispered in my ear and jabbed me in the ribs. I turned in the direction she was pointing.

My heart dropped as I recognized Trent, the bastard, and who should be on his arm, but Anne? The two of them were enough to make me spit fire. I jerked my gaze away and met Ryder's eyes. The bastard actually smirked, cocking a brow. I figured my history with Trent was obvious by the expression on my face. Ryder resumed his bored expression and looked away as a rush of heat claimed my face. I hadn't even been introduced to the vampire, and he was already mocking me and my past relationships? Yes, I definitely didn't care for Ryder.

"Thank you all for coming," Rand began, and the room quieted. "I'm certain you all know why you are here and how important it is to keep Bella from building an army that will eventually come after all of us."

If I hadn't realized Rand was a well-respected warlock in the Underworld community, I realized it now—the room hanging on his every word.

155

"Word has spread there's a new witch under your protection?" A fat man with no aura asked. He must have been a vampire.

Rand nodded and turned in my direction. "I was waiting to uncover our newest addition to my coven, but now is as good a time as ever. Jolie, will you please stand?"

Christa squeezed my hand as I got to my feet, feeling like livestock at auction.

"This is Jolie Wilkins," Rand continued. "And the rumors you've heard about her incredible powers are all true. Jolie has the unique ability to reanimate the dead."

There was a round of oohs and aahs and heat went straight to my face. Just as I was about to take my seat again, there was another comment from the crowd.

"We've heard she's a new witch."

Great, I thought. This was when the second-guessing started.

"She is a new witch, but that doesn't change her incredible gift," Rand responded, steeling my strength with an emphatic smile.

I had to admit I was proud of him—he was an excellent public speaker and answered all questions with eloquence and informed persuasion.

"How many has she reanimated?" another audience member threw out.

So now I'd have to stand here and pretend I wasn't extremely uncomfortable as they tried to disprove my credibility. "Two," I answered, to which there was much discussion among the room and feeling as if I couldn't stand trial any longer, I took my seat with a great deal of disdain.

"Quiet!"

No sooner did I sit down then I heard a voice I distinctly recognized, and I raised my head. Trent.

"I was dead," he started and looked straight at me. I diverted my attention, feigning interest in the silverware.

"She brought me back. I'm living proof of her abilities."

There was more discussion from the crowd and Trent sat down. Rand took control of the audience and made it known I'd be very available to answer any questions at the end of the dinner service. But I was barely aware of his speech. My stomach churned, my head ached, and I wanted nothing more than for the floor to open up and swallow me whole.

This was going to be the never-ending night; I could see it already, and now I'd have to answer a bunch of inane questions when all I wanted was the solitude of my house and the company of my cat.

"I didn't realize you was the witch," Ryder said, his gaze settling on my bust.

Apparently, not all vampires could speak the Queen's English, I thought and smiled to myself. For as much as I disliked Ryder from the start, sensing his holier-than-thou attitude, his diction bothered me all the more.

I thought of saying something rude, but then thought better of it. "That would be me," I managed.

"I'm Ryder Colden."

"I know, it says so on your name tag."

He grinned, the light glinting off his fangs, and I noticed Gwynn watching us like a hawk. Ryder didn't respond but leaned back in his chair, returning his attention to Rand, who was now wrapping things up. Once Rand finished his speech, he returned to our table as everyone clapped.

"Nice job," I said.

"You're going to be quite busy tonight," he responded with a grin. "I hope you're prepared to answer numerous questions."

I shrugged. "I guess I'm as ready as I'll ever be."

Rand turned to the old man at his left, Grimsley, and said something in some Scandinavian language I wasn't even going to begin to guess. I figured he was translating what he'd just said to me because Grimsley nodded in my direction. So Rand could speak more than one language ... was there a limit to what this man could do? And why were his abilities such a turn on? I tried to remember back to high school—had I ever had a crush on any of the foreign language teachers? Hmm ... no.

"Two creatures, eh?" Ryder asked.

He was as ugly as the sneer that arrested his lips. He was a burly looking guy or vampire—it wouldn't have surprised me in the least to find out he was a biker—he had that sort of look. Everyone had dressed up for this affair with the exception of Ryder who wore blue jeans and a leather jacket. But I wasn't going to be the one to point out his faux pas.

"I believe the count is two so far."

He chuckled. "We're puttin' alotta weight on someone who only had two successes."

"Jolie has incredible powers," Christa said and Ryder made a humph sound.

Apparently having witnessed our conversation, Rand stopped talking to Grimsley and faced Ryder. "Two out of two, Ryder, she hasn't failed yet."

Ryder nodded and continued to inspect me, his inspection centering on my bust until I excused myself and hurried to the ladies room. I imagined this was what I'd be up against all night—creatures second-guessing me, wanting to make sure they were making the right decision by joining us. And the supreme kicker was that I was right there with them, doubting my own abilities as much as they were.

I turned a corner and Trent waylaid me en route. I resisted the urge to curse.

"Jolie," he began, lifting his hand as if to take hold of me.

I stepped back, crossing my arms over my chest. "What do you want?"

He seemed deflated, his shoulders sagging visibly. "I wanted to talk to you."

I sighed—crap, I didn't have the time nor the interest for this. "About what?"

"You look beautiful," he said, and eyed me up and down, grinning appreciatively.

"Thanks," I said with great put-outedness. "I'm sure that isn't what you wanted to talk about though?"

Trent paused and glanced around him before his eyes settled back on me. "Can we go somewhere a bit more private?"

There was no way in hell I was granting him the favor of going anywhere more private. Whatever he had to say, he could do it right there in the hallway. "No," I said. "We can't. What is there to talk about anyway?"

"About us."

I shook my head, little bursts of anger heating up my blood. "There is no us, Trent."

He paused and shifted uncomfortably as a woman stepped between us, on her way to the ladies' room. I envied her, wishing I could escape just as easily.

"I wanted to tell you I've missed you."

Was he insane? I couldn't imagine why he'd even bother talking to me when he was the one who dumped me. Couldn't he leave me alone and allow me to lick my wounds with dignity? "It's a little bit late for that now, don't you think? Or have you forgotten the part about you dumping me?" I said, not caring if I sounded pissed off or not.

He sighed and tried the quarreling with me route. "I knew you wouldn't understand and you'd take it the wrong way."

"Trent, I'm not a dumbass, so don't treat me like one." I started past him.

He grasped my upper arm, stopping me. "I did it for your own good. I didn't want to see you get hurt."

I laughed and it was a caustic sound. "That's a good one. I'm up to my neck in the same crap you are." I yanked my arm out of his grip.

"Well, let's give it another shot, then."

"You aren't serious?" I asked with a slight facetious laugh, before the smile fell off my face. "Let me rephrase that ... have you lost your fucking mind?"

Trent shook his head. "No, Jolie, you don't understand."

"I think I understand perfectly well," I snapped, my gaze settling on Trent's table and the discomfort in Anne's face as she awaited his return. "How would Anne feel about that?"

"It's not like that between us."

I frowned, feeling I was close to my boiling point. "Do you really expect me to believe that?"

Before he had a chance to respond, Rand appeared.

"Is everything okay, Jolie?" he asked, stepping close to me. The feel of his warm hand on my lower back provided me with the comfort and strength I needed. Well, and some excited hormones, which I guess I didn't need ...

"Yes, Trent was just saying hello, but he has to get back to his table now," I answered, my lips tight. I glared at Trent so he'd understand I was serious. There was no way I'd ever consider getting back together with him. I wouldn't make the same mistake twice.

Trent frowned. "Actually, we were in the midst of a private conversation."

Even though I imagined Rand wouldn't take that as his exit cue, I grabbed his hand to ensure he'd stay. "Trent, I have nothing more to say to you, so either you go or we will."

Trent gritted his teeth and merely stared at me for a moment, a moment that felt really freaking long. Finally, with a perfunctory nod, he walked away. I took in a deep breath and realized I was still holding Rand's hand. His grip was strong, sure. I didn't want to let go. I squeezed his fingers to show my appreciation and then forced myself to drop his hand.

"Are you okay?" he asked.

"I'm fine. Thanks for checking on me."

Rand quirked a brow and frowned. "I hope he wasn't doing what I thought he was?"

I couldn't keep the wry laugh from my lips. "Well, I'm not sure what you thought he was doing, but he just asked me to get back together with him as if he'd never dumped me in the first place." I shook my head. Men.

"Well, he came to his senses and realized the mistake he'd made ... you did say no?"

"Did I say no?" I scoffed. "Of course I said no!"

My attention fell to our table and it occurred to me that Gwynn was sitting especially close to Ryder. I wondered if Rand had noticed it as well and if it bothered him. He didn't seem upset—he seemed the same levelheaded Rand he always was.

"Seems that Gwynn is quite taken with Ryder," I said, trying to sound nonchalant.

Rand turned his attention from me to Gwynn who was now leaning in to whisper something in Ryder's ear. "It follows that she would be. There's a very special bond between vampires when one turns the other."

I nodded. "Does it bother you?"

Rand laughed and furrowed his brows. "Why would it bother me?"

I shrugged, confused. "I thought you and Gwynn were ..."

Rand frowned. "Whatever gave you that idea?"

"Well, you've been in London quite a bit and ..." my voice trailed as I tried to think of the reasons I'd thought he and Gwynn were an item. It didn't help that he was considering me with complete amusement. "W ... well, that's what Christa said."

"I've been in London making plans with Gwynn for this evening and we've been meeting to chart our progress with our own union ..."

I sighed, not in the mood for long-winded explanations. "It's none of my business anyway. I was just concerned that if you were d ... dating her or maybe you weren't dating her but ..."

Rand grabbed hold of my shoulders and forced me to look at him. "I am not and never have dated Gwynn, Jolie. She's not my type."

I couldn't meet his gaze as I wondered what his type was. "Oh." Gwynn was blond, I was blond ...

"Were you on your way to the powder room?" he asked.

Ah yes, the restroom.

I nodded and he turned my shoulders in the direction of the ladies' room and gave me a friendly shove forward. With a chuckle, he returned to the table.

I hurried to the restroom so I could catch my breath. I must have sounded like a stuttering moron. Even though I was embarrassed, I couldn't help the happiness that welled up within me. I stared at my reflection, noting the flush of color, brought on no doubt by the fact that Rand and Gwynn weren't an item. Slowly, my lips split into a wide grin.

When I returned to the table, I noticed everyone starting in on their dinners. Christa smiled up at me and I was relieved to have her by my side. I took my place, but nerves and excitement shredded any appetite I might have had. I picked at the vegetables, but just managed to move them around the plate. Giving up on eating anything, I looked about the room at the people who would comprise our union. I wondered how many of them would join us and how many would move on or worse, join Bella.

"When does the bar open?" Ryder asked Rand with a sneer.

Rand didn't look up from his plate. "I imagine after we've finished our dinner."

Ryder pushed his untouched plate away. "I'm done."

As he stood and moved toward the bar, I noticed how big he was. Talk about a menacing looking person. Even though he was incredibly rude, he did bring back two bottles of wine for the table and upon offering me a glass, I welcomed it wholeheartedly.

"Is anyone teachin' the witch self-defense?" he asked the table and settled back into his seat.

I wasn't even aware he was talking about me until Rand glanced at me.

"No, we've been focusing on other matters," he said.

"What do I need self-defense for if I have magic?" I asked.

Ryder leaned back in his seat and eyed me as he took a long and exaggerated gulp of his wine. "Your magic ain't gonna work on me or any other vampire. If I was attackin' you, I'd break you in half."

Shocked by his response, I said nothing, but looked at Rand for reassurance.

Rand smiled at my reaction. "You have a valid point."

Not exactly the reassurance I wanted.

Ryder nodded. "I could teach her self-defense."

"No," I blurted and everyone regarded me with surprise. There was no way in hell I wanted anything more to do with this horrid creature. "I meant, I have tutors who could teach me."

"What, the fairies?" Ryder snorted. "I eat fairies for dinner."

Shocked, I said nothing and turned to face Rand, but the jerk was actually smiling!

"Ryder is a self-defense expert," Rand said, as if in explanation to why he was wearing that damned smile.

It was Gwynn's turn to argue the idea. "Yes, but he's going to be busy working with me on the unionizing efforts. I'm certain someone else can train the witch."

While I didn't appreciate being referred to as "the witch," I agreed with her one hundred percent. "I really wouldn't want to be a hindrance," I started.

"If you're so important, I can make time to train you," Ryder responded.

I really wanted to say that I wasn't important but just dropped my head and faced the pile of food before me. God, I was so pissed off. And what bothered me most was that Rand seemed to champion the idea. Could this night get any worse?

You are awfully quiet.

It was Rand's voice in my head. I looked up at him. *Why would you agree to let him train me? He's horrible!*

He's the best person to train you—he's right, you do need to learn to defend yourself.

But I don't trust him!

Did you really think I'd leave you alone with him? I'll be right there with you.

That made me feel a little better. *How many times will I have to meet with him?*

Until you can adequately protect yourself.

I didn't respond, but turned my attention away from him, put out with the whole thing. The sound of music met my ears and I turned to watch as people began nearing the dance floor. I thought it was a waltz if I had to guess, but I wasn't too familiar with classical music. This had to be the weirdest night of my life. Surrounded by creatures of the Underworld and now a waltz?

I downed the remnants of my glass and Ryder refilled it. I didn't say anything but nodded my thanks, noting Gwynn hanging on him like a toupee on a bald man. If she was attempting to talk him out of training me, I wished her much success.

He pulled away from her and leaned in closer to me. "You'll thank me one day."

It would be a cold day in hell before those words ever spilled from my lips.

Christa finished her glass of wine and accepted another from Ryder. I wished I could teleconverse with her to see what she thought of the bastard.

161

The waltz ended and Bon Jovi's "Living in Sin" came on, making me think this night couldn't get any odder.

Christa grabbed my hand when I thought she would and with a great big smile, she led me to the dance floor. I was only too happy to appease her in order to escape the confines of the table and Ryder's insistent gaze. I'd taken my glass of wine with me and downed the remnants, giving myself a little liquid courage.

After dancing three songs, I started feeling better. At the start of the fourth song, I decided I needed a rest and returned to the table. It was empty aside from Rand who leaned back in his chair, regarding the scenery around him with interest.

I took the seat next to him and watched the throng of dancers pulsate to the rhythm of the music.

"Aren't you a dancer?" I asked.

He shook his head. "I prefer the old style of dancing." He turned his attention to me and I dropped my gaze.

"You look beautiful tonight, I didn't get to tell you earlier."

I offered a small smile in thanks as thoughts of reflection coursed through me. My life had changed in ways I'd never have imagined. Even though there had been bad moments and my future was uncertain, I'd have to say it had changed for the better.

"It's funny where you end up in life," I said, reaching for a glass of water.

"How so?"

"A year ago, no, six months ago, if someone were to tell me I'd be dancing with a bunch of witches, wolves, and vampires, I'd say they were crazy."

Rand laughed. "Destiny is a funny thing."

"Do you think that's what it is?"

"I do," he answered as Neil Diamond's "Sweet Caroline" came on. This only happened to be one of my favorite songs, and so I stood up and reached for Rand's hand.

"It's not a waltz, but it's slow enough, come on."

Rand took my hand and as we walked to the dance floor together, I caught Christa's eye. She waved as she mouthed the words to the song—this was one of her favorites too.

Rand grabbed hold of my waist as we started dancing. I had to give it to him, he wasn't half bad.

"I actually like this song too. I liked it when it first came out," he whispered in my ear and I laughed.

It was wonderful being in his arms, being so close to him. The scent of his aftershave hit me and I had to inhale, thinking it the best aphrodisiac. He twirled me around and caught me even more closely than he'd been holding me before. For a moment, I could pretend there was no tension between us, that we could admit our feelings for one another … that we had admitted them.

"I should teach you to waltz sometime, I imagine you'd be wonderful," he whispered.

I didn't notice that another song had started until it was almost halfway over. I did notice that Rand was now holding me against him, very closely. I closed my eyes and settled my head against the crook of his neck. Melting into him, I could feel every hard plane of his chest, every muscle.

"You make our work relationship very difficult on me," he said as his hand began stroking my waist

"These are your rules we're playing by, not mine," I answered with no amount of apology.

"I second guess them every day." He squeezed my waist. I lifted my head just in time to see Trent grabbing Rand's collar. Before anyone could stop him, he yanked Rand from my grasp and punched him across the face. Rand, completely unaware, fell to the ground, but was up an instant later, his lip busted and bleeding. A few women screamed, and I wasn't sure, I might have been one of them.

Realizing I had to do something, I jumped between the two of them and grabbed Trent's jacket, trying to keep him from going after Rand again. "What the hell is wrong with you?" I screamed as he turned his attention to me with a sneer.

"That bastard has been after you all along," Trent said and grabbed hold of my waist, pulling me into his hard body.

I pushed against him, but his grip was iron strong.

The entire room was silent as everyone's attention centered on Rand, who was facing Trent with an anger the likes of which I'd never seen before. He wore the façade of calm, but his eyes were raging, his hands fisted. His aura was doing its own dance of ire, billowing purple against the rage and humiliation Rand must've been feeling.

"Let go of her," Rand seethed.

Trent tightened his grip on me, and I dug my nails into his arm, pushing against him.

"You're making a drunk fool of yourself," I seethed.

"If you don't bloody well let go of her now, I will kill you," Rand warned and his eyes were deadly serious. Dear God, he would.

Even though Trent was far down my list of favorite people, I couldn't say I wanted to see him dead. I glanced at Rand's determined countenance and his eyes spelled it out in no uncertain terms. Trent was lucky he was still alive.

"Don't be a moron, you can't defeat him," I whispered, hoping Trent would back down. Then I remembered I was a witch and imagined a powerful burst of electricity coursing through Trent, not something too potent but just enough to wake him the hell up. Trent jumped and I stepped away from him.

"Go then," he growled, the hairs on his arm all standing to attention—hmm, maybe I'd jolted him with a little too much energy.

"I want you to leave," Rand said and I could see he was subduing himself. He'd always hated Trent and I imagined it was all he could do to keep himself in check.

Trent laughed and made a move for the door, but being the bastard he was, had to get the last word in. "Jolie, when you get sick of the warlock, you know where to find me."

SIXTEEN

As I sat in my room and removed my earrings, I couldn't help but play back the events of the night. What had Trent been thinking? God, I was almost embarrassed I'd dated him considering what an idiot he'd turned out to be. I was surprised Rand hadn't killed him on the spot.

Rand.

I couldn't suppress the heat that started at the top of my head and coursed through my entire body. I'd been seriously misled to think Trent had in any way dissipated my feelings for Rand. I was as crazy about him now as I always had been. Trent had just been a minor interlude in the symphony known as Rand.

I shook my head against the onslaught of emotion that claimed my already fragile temperament and faced myself in the mirror. I, Jolie Wilkins, never imagined it possible that two men would fight over me; things like that just didn't happen to me. Well, I guess now they did.

I sighed and turned around, thinking I should get undressed and go to bed. The thought held no temptation—I wasn't tired, even though it was late and I'd spent enough adrenalin to wipe out a small army. There was an insistent hum alive in my head that would prohibit me from sleeping—a hum of thoughts regarding Rand: if he were sleeping, how his lip was, if he was mad at me.

I suddenly remembered Rand telling me in Chicago that he could tell when I was sleeping by sending … mental feelers, I think he'd called them. Hmm, maybe it was worth a shot. I closed my eyes and imagined Rand, but from there, I wasn't sure what to do. After a few seconds of getting myself all hot and bothered as my dream Rand happened to be naked, I opened my eyes.

In a moment of spontaneity, I slipped my feet back into my four-inch heels and grabbed my room key that had been ogling me from the bed stand all night. If the damned thing were capable, it'd be smiling and winking at me about now, knowing I was headed for the elevator that would take me to Rand's floor.

Once in the elevator, the muzak floating through the walls made my stomach clench, and I had to talk myself out of hitting the button to take me back to my room. The dinging of the elevator doors announced Rand's floor and interrupted the doubt clouding my mind. I didn't separate myself from the wall and just stared at the hallway as if a three-headed gorgon awaited me at the end of it. The doors started to close, and I prohibited their marriage with my arm.

I was on his damn floor; I had to get out. I took a step forward, feeling like I was wading through drying glue. Would Rand tell me to get lost? Maybe he wanted to be alone. Maybe he was angry and blamed me for the incident? I guess if anyone should be blamed, it was me—it was my fault I'd dated the bastard Trent in the first place.

If I could have yelled at myself, I would have. There was no way this was my fault—I was just looking for an excuse not to knock on Rand's door. Well, the doubts in my mind wouldn't win. I raised my hand with authority and aimed my fist to strike the door when it opened.

"Took you long enough."

Rand stood before me and just like that, my confidence leaked out of me as if I were a sieve. Feeling as ineffectual as a bowl of spaghetti, I hesitated, cursing myself for coming up here in the first place. I faced the hallway before me and thought if I took off my shoes, I could probably run and get to the elevator before he stepped foot in the hall.

"I … how did you know I was standing here?" I said, and my voice wavered.

I tried to keep my gaze from traveling down his white t-shirt and boxers. Obviously, he hadn't been expecting anyone. The spacious width of his pectorals protruded through the thin fabric of the t-shirt, and I could just make out the dusting of hair atop them.

His face, Jolie, focus on his face, dammit!

"I could sense you from the elevator."

I swallowed the butterflies that were forcing themselves up my throat. My attention shifted to the amused smile alight on his lips, and I had to force down the flush threatening to steal my cheeks. His lip had healed, courtesy of his magic. He didn't say anything right away but stood looking at me while I tried to make my mouth work.

"I wanted to make sure you were alright," I blurted haplessly.

"Come in." He held the door open, and the darkness of the room seemed to fight the light of the hallway. A lone yellow glow from the corner of the room leant the darkness a jaundiced sort of feel.

I took a step forward until he and I were parallel, then I hesitated. "Well, I don't want to interrupt you …" I started, suddenly realizing it might look as if I'd come here to have sex with him. That hadn't been my goal. I'm not sure what had been.

Rand chuckled and settled his hand on my hip. With a gentle nudge, he pushed me over the threshold. "You've already interrupted me, so no harm done."

I timidly stepped inside as the subtle notes of "Rhapsody in Blue" twirled around me, as if dancing with my breath. When I turned to face him, my attention quickly swept over his muscular and tan legs. How he was able to maintain that golden color year-round in England was beyond me. That had to be warlock magic. I dropped my gaze, finding it too difficult to look upon him in his current state of undress.

"I wanted to apologize," I said, not wanting him to think I'd come for any other reason. He closed the door and turned toward me.

"Why? It wasn't your fault."

I shook my head. "I should've listened to you about Trent." I'm one of those people who has a tough time saying I'm wrong. But once the words were out, I was proud of myself. I guess, in a weird way, it felt good to say I'd royally f'ed up.

He neared a small kitchenette area and poured two glasses of wine, handing one to me. "You needed to find out for yourself."

Hmm, so he wasn't going to play the part of: *I told you so.*

I shook my head. Now that I'd come out on a limb and admitted I was wrong, I didn't want him to take that away from me. "I should've just listened to you, and I can't help but think that it's my fault you got punched." I took a sip of the wine, wishing it were an elixir of fortitude and courage.

"How's your lip?"

He whetted his lip with his tongue, and I thought it the most erotic thing a man had ever done. "Healed," he said as he pulled a bar stool out and perched atop it. Swirling the wine in his glass, he studied me. "It's the wolf's fault that he punched me. It had nothing to do with you."

"Well, I did date him."

Rand chuckled, the wine in his glass swirling up the sides as if echoing the sentiment. "Okay, you win, I suppose I can fault you for that."

I couldn't help myself as I stepped closer to him, needing to feel his warmth in the same way a junkie needs his next fix. Only inches away, he dropped his smile and merely watched me as I put my wine glass on the side table. I stepped between his legs and nearly lost my nerve when I felt his hot breath against my bare shoulders.

"Let me see your lip," I said and tilted his face down, pretending to inspect his mouth.

I ran my thumb across his plump bottom lip, and he closed his eyes, his long black lashes gracing the tops of his angular cheeks. My heart pushed against my ribs, pumping so much blood, I almost felt faint. I knew what I would do, maybe I'd known even before I'd come up here. I leaned down, replacing my fingers with my lips. The kiss was tender, only skimming the surface of his mouth with my own. He didn't flinch or demand more. He let me explore him. I ran the tips of my fingers down the sides of his face, noting how soft his skin was, how the merest indication of stubble grazed my fingertips.

Suddenly overcome with the biting need to gaze on his exquisite face, I pulled away, my index finger perched at the bottom of his cheek. "You're beautiful," I whispered.

Rand opened his chocolate eyes. I could almost see the tempest of emotions flooding his gaze—how he fought against himself, knowing we shouldn't want one another but also realizing the futility in thinking it. He set his glass of wine down next to mine and wrapped his arms around my lower waist, imprisoning my torso against his chest. I smiled down at him and braced my arms on the counter, on either side of his head.

"Did I tell you how stunning you were ... are tonight?" he asked.

I nodded. "You did. I believe that was right before you got punched."

Rand quirked a brow, but it was the only sign of emotion on his face. "I can't keep fighting this, Jolie." He sighed. "I just want you too bloody much."

With his words, bliss showered down on me, each droplet of delight sinking into me until I felt the need to cry or scream with glee. I leaned down, and he lifted his head to meet my lips. His hands roamed down my back, resting on my bottom as my tongue worked its way into his mouth. He pulled me into him as if he couldn't stomach the idea of any air separating us.

A tiny internal voice of doom interrupted the dance of our tongues and whispered that I was becoming dangerously gone, on the brink of not being able to stop. I reminded myself that I hadn't come to have sex with him. With a groan, I broke the seal between us. I licked my lips, wanting to get every last taste of him. He chuckled but didn't loosen his grasp around my waist.

"I enjoyed dancing with you tonight," I started, looking into his eyes. They were different now, heavier in their chocolate brown, darker with lust.

"As did I. It would've been perfect if that fool hadn't hit me."

I traced his hairline as I laughed. "That was rather unfortunate."

He reached for my face and pulled my lips back to his as his tongue invaded my mouth again. I moaned and sank into his hard body. How badly I wanted to let go, to tear the t-shirt from him and explore the wonder of his naked chest with my mouth. His hands cupped my bottom, and he was insistent this time, pulling me against his hard arousal.

My breathing was shallow, like a doe that's been shot. When his hands traveled up my back and around my waist, only to settle on my breasts, my breathing picked up. He dropped his face into my cleavage and kissed the mounds of flesh that ached to be free.

I'm not sure how I did it, but I flattened my hands on his chest and pushed back. He regarded me with a bit of surprise and even more disappointment. "I didn't come here to have sex with you," I said, commanding as much courage as I could.

"What did you come for?" He wasn't angry, more curious.

I dropped my gaze. "I needed to be near you." I was a bit embarrassed after I said it, thinking it sounded sort of melodramatic and emotional. Rand wasn't much of an emotional guy.

Rand didn't say anything but leaned into me and began toying with the zipper on the back of my dress. His eyes never left mine as he peeled the dress down my chest and let it pool at my hips. His eyes traversed my naked stomach as his hands coaxed the dress from my hips, until it piled at my feet. I shivered, clad only in my strapless bra, panties and heels. I stepped away from the mound of fabric at my feet and wrapped my arms around myself, feeling entirely too exposed.

Rand pulled the t-shirt over his head. I couldn't stop my gaze as it raked his very muscular chest. His pectorals were broad and well defined and his abdomen was tight, revealing rows of defined muscle. I didn't want to count, but I think he was verging on an eight pack. Dark hair lightly dusted his chest, and I wanted nothing more than to run my hands through it, to see if it were soft or wiry. Thoughts like that would get me in trouble, and I forced my attention back to his face, searching for something to say.

"Wow, I guess you work out." I winced as I thought how stupid I sounded.

Rand smiled, apparently enjoying the fact that I'd taken notice of his incredibly sculptured body. "It's important to be fit in this line of work."

"Do you use magic to ... maintain your physique?" I asked, wondering if maybe I could do the same.

He shook his head, and disappointment coursed through me. God, I didn't like working out. I guess I was lucky I didn't really put on weight. I wasn't very active and ate pretty much what I wanted, but I imagined a good workout every other day would have me in great condition. I glanced down at myself, trying to see me as Rand did. Did he think I was pudgy?

"Get in my bed," he commanded and stood up, pulling my attention from the muffin tops of my hips that seemed larger than I'd ever thought them before.

"Rand, I'm not ready to have sex with you ..." I started, eyeing the king bed before me with hesitation.

He put his index finger against my mouth and grasped my waist, nudging me backward. "We aren't going to have sex, Jolie. You came to be near me, you can be near me in bed."

He continued pushing me backward, his hands grasping either side of my waist, until I met the mattress with the backs of my knees. I didn't sit down but allowed Rand to run his hands down my hips. He hesitated once his fingers scaled the line of my panties. Then he traced the elastic band across my lower stomach with one index finger. I closed my eyes against the assault, feeling every nerve ending in my body come to attention. I opened my eyes and found him smiling at me. He reached down and pulled the duvet cover aside then pushed gently on the tops of my shoulders until I took a seat on the bed.

"Thank you ... for understanding," I said in a shaking voice.

"You should be thanking me," he answered with a laugh and walked around the bed to the other side. He pulled the duvet aside and hefted himself in next to me. "I'm about to have a very restless night attempting to sleep next to you."

He bounced around a bit, trying to get comfortable and then draped his large arm around my waist, pulling me into the curve of his body. I closed my eyes, soaking in his strength and warmth. This was the closest to heaven I'd ever been.

"Are you tired?" I asked.

"I'm asleep," he mumbled.

169

I giggled as he ran his fingers down my side. "So would you have had sex with me tonight?" I asked.

I felt his body tighten at my words. "I'm trying to keep myself from having sex with you now."

"Would it be so bad?"

Rand chuckled. "Make up your mind, Jolie, do you want me inside you or don't you?"

My heart fluttered at his choice of words, and I fought to find something to say. "I didn't mean that, I meant would … us be so bad?"

He was silent but exhaled a long and telling breath. A sigh after the question I'd just posed wasn't a good response. I tried to prepare myself for the rejection that was about to come my way. I would've given anything to be able to read minds at that moment.

"Being connected to someone is dangerous."

"You aren't connected to me now?" I asked, feeling offended. I was certainly connected to him, connected wasn't even the word for it. Head-over-heels would be more apropos.

He groaned. "More than I ever planned or wanted to be." He pulled away from me and leaned against the headboard. "Turn around."

I did so and faced a warlock deep in contemplation. "I think it's a yes or no answer, Rand."

He shook his head. "Unfortunately it isn't that easy. I can't give you what you want right now, Jolie, what we both want. Not with our precarious future looming above us."

I nodded. "I understand." Although I'm not sure I did understand. Rand was one of those people who seemed to make everything more difficult than it actually needed to be. He reminded me of some sulking hero who constantly had to challenge temptation, lest it get the best of him.

"No, I don't think you do. I care deeply for you, Jolie. Do I love you? I'm not sure, but I can't let it progress to that stage. Love between witches is not the same as what humans consider love or a relationship to be."

"Why not?" I couldn't imagine that a relationship would be all that different from the type I was used to … or wasn't used to in my case. But going on my relationship with Trent, it hadn't been so different to those I saw on TV or read about in books. It started off with a date and ended with … getting dumped. Maybe a relationship wasn't such a good idea, after all.

"A relationship between a witch and a warlock is forever. There is no marriage, there is no divorce. It runs deeper than that. It's a connection of souls."

A connection of souls sounded pretty serious. Hadn't I just been asking about dating? "I didn't ask you to marry me, Rand."

Rand shook his head, apparently thinking I wasn't on his wavelength. "If you and I were to get involved, it would be a deeper connection than anything I'm prepared for. It might not be the relationship I just described, but it would lead to that."

170

I started to argue with him, but he silenced me with a shake of his head. "It wouldn't be casual, Jolie, not between us."

I didn't know how I felt about this. On the one side, I was thrilled that his feelings ran so deeply for me, but what was the point if he wouldn't act on them? "So it would have to be all or nothing?"

He nodded. "Neither one of us can afford to even think in such a way. Not with Bella and the Lurkers threatening our lives."

"That's why you've been fighting it all this time?" I asked the question, but it was more an observation.

"Yes."

"Why didn't you just tell me?"

He shrugged. "I didn't want you to take it the wrong way."

I wondered if maybe I might have taken it the wrong way. Maybe I was taking it the wrong way now. "And just sex between us?"

He chuckled. "Would you ever be happy with that?"

My body would be happy, but my heart would sing a different tune. "No, I wouldn't."

"Neither would I. It wouldn't be enough for either one of us." He paused. "That and the jealousy of seeing you with other men would tear me apart."

I didn't even want to contemplate the notion of seeing him with other women. "Do you think you'll ever ... let yourself love someone, for lack of a better word?"

He was quiet as he considered my question. "I don't know. I've been alive for one hundred sixty-five years and in that time, I've never considered it. I've dated casually, of course, but never anything as finite as what I've described to you."

"That sounds very lonely," I said in a small voice, hating the idea that it would be my lonely existence as well. If love were as complicated and involved as he pictured it, either all of my relationships would be casual or a bonding of souls? What was the point of dating at all? Ugh, I was back where I'd started from.

I started to get angry with the whole scenario. Just as I was finally enjoying some male attention and actually had men vying for my affections, this landed in my lap. Well, maybe I'd just need to avoid witches. I guess I could have a normal relationship as long as it wasn't with one of my own kind. So who did that leave? Wolves? No thanks, been there done that. Vampires? I wasn't sure how I felt about dating the undead. An image of Sinjin popped into my mind ... hmm, vampires might not be such a bad option. Demons? They just sounded dangerous. Maybe it was back to ordinary humans for me. Yeah, good luck—like that had worked at all in the past.

"It can be lonely. You have to get used to it, Jolie. You're a young witch, but in time, you will have to make some fairly tough decisions. Love is one of the toughest because it's all consuming."

"What does that mean, all consuming?"

171

He groaned and raked his hands through his hair. "It means you become one with each other. The magic bonds between the two of you cement you as one. You can read each other's thoughts, your magic increases tenfold because you share one another's magic. But you also become susceptible to the same problems. I've seen witches die when their lover dies."

Yeah, definitely not dating another witch anytime soon. I was quiet as I laid my head back on the pillow and thought this night had taken a different direction than I'd planned.

"I care for you deeply, Jolie," Rand's whisper in my ear caused shivers down my spine. "I care for you more than I've cared for anyone in a very long time. It scares the shit out of me," he finished.

"I understand now," I said with finality. I got the picture, the whole enchilada.

"Perhaps someday ..."

"Shh," I interrupted. I couldn't stand to listen to apologies. It was what it was. I'd have to live with it in the same way that Rand had lived with it for over one hundred years. Whoever coined the phrase 'life's a bitch and then you die' hit the nail right on the head. "Don't say anymore. Let's just have this night."

He pulled me closer to him, and I couldn't keep the tears from rolling down my cheek.

~

Ryder was just as horrible as I'd remembered him. There was something about the vampire that was malevolent, an intangible evil that lurked in his eyes.

"Let's see whatcha got," he said, crossing his burley arms and leering at me.

It was my first lesson and Rand, Ryder, and I were in Rand's workout room. Rand had removed all the workout equipment, and in its place, the floor and walls were covered with thick padding. It was an ominous thought as to why he felt it needed all that padding.

"Go easy on her, Ryder," Rand warned from the sidelines.

I walked onto the floor, dressed in leggings and a sports bra, hoping my sporty look would equate to a decent performance.

"Just come at me like you would if I were gonna attack you," Ryder said.

I shrugged and neared him, noting his bull-legged stance. There was no way in hell I was going to do any sort of damage to this oaf, but I had to try. Steeling my resolve, I lunged for him, thinking maybe I could deliver a blow to his face. No sooner did I raise my arm, than I found myself on my back, the air completely deflated from my lungs.

Ryder stared over me with a sneer. "Gotta do better than that."

172

I didn't think I'd be able to get back up, feeling like I'd just been hit by a train. I took a moment to catch my breath.

"Are you alright, Jolie?" Rand called out.

I nodded and turned over so I was on all fours as I forced myself up. "Clearly, I can't take you down. Maybe this is where you should start teaching me," I snapped.

"I'm gonna grab you 'round the waist."

He came up behind me and wrapped his arms around my waist. With a quick jerk, he pulled me against him, and I frowned, thinking the proximity not necessary. His cold breath against my neck made my stomach churn.

"What do I do now?"

"You just think to protect your ribs and make sure I ain't gonna lift you. Anyone who grabs you like this is gonna pick you up an' throw ya on your ass to hurt your hips or back."

"Okay, so what do I do?"

"In one move, push down on my wrists and squat, then once you do that, you gonna stomp on my foot or try and wrench my fingers."

This sounded impossible. I was thinking it would be better to try and find a stone with which to take down the mighty Goliath.

"Try it, Jolie," Rand said.

Ryder separated himself from me and then came at me without any sort of hint. He grabbed me around the waist, hoisted me up, and then threw me down. I landed on my hip with a thud, biting into my lip with a cry. A shard of pain coursed through my side and traveled all the way to my lip.

"Christ, Ryder!" Rand yelled as I righted myself.

I stood up and tasted blood. Unfortunately, Ryder noticed it as well and his expression changed from one of amusement to one of hunger.

Crap.

My heart plummeted. He was a vampire and I was bleeding.

He didn't pounce on me, thank God, but came at me slowly, his attention riveted on the blood seeping from my lip.

"Ryder, stay the hell away from her," Rand yelled as he forced himself between the two of us. He pushed Ryder, and by the fact that Ryder somewhat lost his balance, I realized how physically strong Rand was.

Rand touched my lip and the blood stopped. I licked the area where I'd bitten into it and found it healed.

Rand nodded. "Good as new."

I snuck a glance at Ryder, and he was no longer like a deer in headlights. He didn't seem embarrassed either, but faced me in his sinister way.

"You didn't grab my wrists like I told you."

"I didn't realize you were coming at me!" I yelled, my hands on my hips in the most put-out stance I could muster.

"You won't know when someone's gonna attack you either, so you gotta be quick on your feet. Try it again."

Luckily, I was saved by the ringing of my cell phone. I lunged for it and answered it before Ryder could protest.

"Hello?"

"Hi, dear." It was my mom.

I smiled at both Rand and Ryder and mouthed "it will be a while." Rand frowned while Ryder shrugged and turned to doing pushups on the floor.

"Hi Mom, I'm just in the middle of ... working out." I wasn't sure how she'd react to know I was sparring with a vampire while a warlock looked on. Mom had no idea she'd spawned a witch. Better to keep her in the dark.

"That's good to hear, darling. I just wanted to call and say hello and see how England is treating you."

I continued making small talk, trying to give Rand and Ryder a reason to call our lesson off, but after ten minutes of meaningless chatter, they were both ready to give it another go. I was less than ready.

I hung up the phone and tossed it back against my towel as I turned with a groan and braced myself for Ryder's next attack.

An hour later and my lesson was finally finished. I was sore all over, and I'd been thrown against the floor so many times, I'd lost count. The entire hour had been spent in perfecting my response to the around,the waist attack and by the end of it, I'd at least been able to grab Ryder's wrists. I hadn't been able to do much more than that. Vampires were damn fast, and they were incredibly strong.

As far as lessons went, I preferred those of the fairies—at least they didn't involve a scary vampire, blood, and pain.

SEVENTEEN

"Throw yourself into it," Rand yelled as I struggled against Ryder, my feet slipping on the dew-soaked grass.

It was my fifth self-defense lesson, and I was making no headway. I just wasn't cut out for this crap. I wasn't what I'd call a sporty person—I'd been to the gym maybe five times in my life, and I hadn't gone willingly.

Ryder tightened his hold, pinning my arms securely behind my back like he was a cop arresting me. My plan was to bend forward and kick my leg up behind me, which hopefully would land squat between his legs. Well, it sounded like a good plan in theory, but when I put it to the test, the bastard just laughed and released me, shaking his head at my apparent inability.

"Jolie," Rand started.

I lifted my hand to silence him. "I'm not in the mood to hear it. Defending myself against a vampire is impossible." I sighed. "The whole thing is the dumbest idea on the goddamned planet. Just give me a freaking gun and when one attacks me, I'll blow his head off."

"That's fine an' good, but a bullet to the head won't kill a vampire," Ryder said, grinning with exposed canines … just to piss me off. Well, I was already pissed off, as I had a tendency to be when faced with my lessons. Ryder was a craptastic teacher, and I guess I wasn't much of a shining student.

I turned toward him, just then wishing I had a gun to test his theory. "I'm sure it would slow you down!"

Tonight we were sparring outside. Even though the night was ice cold, sweat beaded on my forehead, trailing down my face until it interfered with my vision. A cold wind sailed through the trees and made the sweat against my skin sting like ice.

Ryder had thought it a good idea to vary my surroundings. Luckily for him, he was dead and couldn't feel heat or cold, so he couldn't care less if we were battling in the elements or in the heat of the desert. And as for me, I'm not really sure if there was much of a difference between getting my ass kicked inside or outside, but there you have it.

"Again," Rand said from the sidelines.

I gave him a look that said I was anything but amused. He either didn't notice it or ignored me. Sighing in frustration, I faced Ryder again.

He moved around me. "Just walk and I'm going to jump out at you."

The moonlight fought to get through the clouds as my gaze went to Rand. He stood with his legs braced apart, his arms crossed. He looked annoyed. Hell, I didn't blame him. I was annoyed as I'd yet to improve my skills. Ryder had thrown me five times already.

A cloud obscured the moon, and I was left in total darkness, wondering when Ryder would force me to the ground, so I could eat some more dirt.

"I can't see a damned thing!" I yelled.

"If a vampire attacks you at night, you'll have to be …"

"I know!" His argument was always the same: it'll happen in real life, so you better be ready for it. Well, vomit on Ryder and the whole vampire race.

"Listen for him, Jolie," Rand called out. "When he moves, you'll hear it in the air. Rely on your ears, not your eyes."

I threw a glare his way, hoping he could see it in the dark, wondering when he'd bust out with the 'young grasshopper.'

Steel hands wrapped around my throat and slammed me against a tree, the bark biting into my cheek. Frantic for air, I clawed at his arms as my legs flailed, hoping to connect with him but to no avail. Just when I started to feel woozy, he let go. Cool air rushed into my lungs, and I stumbled forward. Thank God, the asshole was giving me time to recoup. I closed my eyes to compose myself, when a howl pierced the calm night air.

"Jolie," Rand snapped. I didn't waste time rushing to his side, not at all excited about the prospect of standing on my own when a possible werewolf or something worse lurked in the foliage.

Ryder just stood there, staring into the woods like the idiot he was.

The howl sounded again, this time louder and closer. It was definitely the call of a werewolf. My heart jumped into my throat, and I had to resist the urge to grab onto Rand as I wondered if the wolf was Trent. I couldn't imagine he would be idiotic enough to come for me when Rand could turn him into wolf shish kabob as easily as blinking. But what other wolf would have any reason to be here?

Rand looked directly into my eyes. "Don't move." Before I could question him, he slipped into the forest, hidden by foliage and darkness.

"Rand!" I called, worried that he might not come back. Then I checked myself, he was a warlock. I should be more worried for the wolf.

"I wonder what the hell that was?" I said, turning to face Ryder.

Ryder's fist interrupted my vision as it connected with my face.

Then there was the blackness of nothing.

~

I felt like I was swimming.

Swimming through the blackest ocean, but it wasn't an ocean at all, more like oil, thick and unyielding. I fell underneath the wave of black and crested again, sputtering.

I could hear something; it was the faintest sound of a voice calling to me in the distance. I just had to swim through the sludge to get to the shore, a seemingly easy deed that proved extremely difficult.

I didn't have the stamina to stay afloat. My limbs ached with the intense agony of swimming in a limitless sea with no horizon in view. I went under again, and the voice called to me, encouraging me to swim through the wave.

I opened my eyes and saw white. I blinked, trying to focus. Slowly, the white took the form of a ceiling, a brown water stain spreading from the middle of the ceiling to one corner like a great big spider with one leg stretched out.

I was in a bed; I could feel the fluff of the pillow underneath my neck. I tried to turn my head, to take in my surroundings, but as soon as I moved, pain stabbed the back of my skull.

Magic.

It would take the headache away. I attempted to bring my hand to my head, but I couldn't move my arm—something held it firmly in place, something cold. I pulled against the restraint again, and the sound of metal grating metal caused my eyes to pop open. Even though I knew the pain would fight me, I turned my head and looked down.

Each of my wrists was handcuffed to the metal railing of a cot. I turned my face forward again and closed my eyes against the onslaught of panic that was already visiting me.

My head ached like a bitch. But it wasn't the pain that disturbed me the most; it was the sudden exhaustion that visited like a bolt of lightning. It was a fatigue the level of which I'd never experienced before—like I hadn't had a thing to eat for two days and had just run a marathon—that sort of exhausted. Course, I've never run a marathon, but if I had, I'm sure I'd feel as tired as I now was.

I forced my attention back to the present, back to the riddle of why I was cuffed to a bed in a room I didn't recognize.

"She's coming to." I recognized the voice. I couldn't bring myself to open my eyes, though—invisible weights hung on the end of every one of my eyelashes.

I fell back into the tide of black water.

I don't know when I awoke again. It could have been minutes or days, but I suddenly found myself conscious. I opened my eyes and my vision floundered for a minute. My gaze settled on the same white ceiling. Not a sound interrupted the silence of the room. It was quiet, too quiet.

Was I dead? I paid attention once more to my body and pulled against the cuffs that were still in full effect. If I were dead, I imagined I'd gone south because this certainly wasn't the treatment of the saved.

I didn't feel any pain, which was a relief. My vision blurred as I trained it to focus on an empty chair in the corner of the room. A feeling of nausea washed over me, like I had the worst case of the flu.

Once my eyes were capable of focusing again, I turned my head to take in the rest of the room. It was small and uncluttered. There was the cot I was occupying, a small bedside table, as well as two chairs, one on either side of me. Both were empty.

Knowing enough of my situation now, I began to worry.

Foreign room + cuffed to bed = bad situation.

I closed my eyes and breathed in through my nose and out through my mouth, trying to calm the fear that stampeded within me. My fear wouldn't do me any good.

Think, Jolie, remember what happened ... I told myself.

All I could remember was practicing my self-defense lessons with Ryder outside, and Rand was there. I was pissed off about something ... God, what was it? I couldn't remember. Then I recalled the howl from the trees, and Rand had gone to inquire.

Oh, God, Rand ...

A scream sounded within my ears but never birthed itself on my lips. What had happened to Rand? I just couldn't remember. I shook my head against the images that visited me—thoughts of Rand being killed by a wolf. I opened my eyes, hoping to dispel the horrors playing underneath my eyelids.

Then I remembered Ryder's fist. I closed my eyes against the fury that seized my heart and threatened to squeeze the life out of it. Tears burned the corners of my eyes.

"Are you hungry?"

I gasped as my eyes flew open and it took me a moment to focus on the face smiling down at me. I knew that face. Dark hair, blue eyes, handsome aquiline features. Yes, I definitely recognized the face, but my muddled mind couldn't put a name to it. It wasn't a face that caused me any sort of fear; actually, it was quite the opposite. The man was extremely attractive, and his smile helped to subdue the anxiety warring within me.

"What's wrong with me?" My voice sounded foreign, and I wondered if I'd pass out. This had to be what someone on drugs felt like—only partially aware of her surroundings and in control of nothing.

"You are being subdued," the man continued as he sat in the chair closest to my cot. "You need to eat." His voice echoed through my head as if there were valleys and mountains between my ears. I fought to maintain my focus on him. He kept fading in and out, as if projected on a screen that someone kept moving.

I shook my head. "I'm ... not hungry."

"You have not eaten anything in three days, Jolie."

He knew my name. A flurry of wasps attacked my stomach and I had to close my eyes against the wave of exhaustion that rode over me. "How do you know my name?"

"You do not remember me now, but you will in time." His voice was so deep, so baritone, and there was something different about it—an accent maybe? I kept my eyes closed, imagining it too great a task to even attempt to open them.

"Your memories will come back to you soon."

"Tell me ... what's wrong ... with me."

"We had to subdue you so we ... drained you."

178

Drained me. ... I couldn't quite grasp what that meant. I could only focus on the timbre of his voice, how it reminded me of waves crashing against rocks. Somehow, I thought I should pay attention to the part of the conversation where he'd said someone had drained me, but I just couldn't.

He said something more, but his voice was unintelligible and before I knew it, I was laying in a field of the greenest grass, with a gnome whispering in my ear.

~

When I came to again, I wasn't alone. I opened my eyes to see the dark haired man. I glanced down and found myself still cuffed to the hospital cot, a white blanket covering my lower half.

"How long was I out?"

"Perhaps an hour," the man answered. I turned and noticed he was still holding the untouched soup. "You need to eat. Are you peckish?"

I had to imagine that meant hungry. But I wasn't much concerned with food at the moment—I was more thrilled with the fact that I actually had awakened with a bit of energy. "I want answers."

He shook his head. "You eat and I will answer your questions."

I sighed, but nodded and parted my lips as he spooned the now lukewarm soup into my mouth. As soon as the first bit went down, my body came to attention, my stomach clenching with hunger. He brought another spoonful, and I swallowed it quickly, licking my lips where some escaped.

"You must eat it slowly or you will be ill," the man said and pulled the spoon away from my mouth, depositing it in the bowl.

There was a certain kindness in his blue eyes. I didn't know why, but instinctively, I wanted to trust him. As soon as the thought dared assault my brain, I rebelled against the lunacy of it. What the hell was wrong with me? There was nothing good about this man—he was holding me against my will and then there was that whole drained business.

I'd lost my goddamned mind.

"You said you drained me, what does that mean?"

The man dropped his gaze. "You were going to fight us. We needed to ensure we had complete control over you, so we drank from you."

I thought I might wretch up the soup I'd just consumed. Drank from me? The sudden need to search my neck for signs of puncture wounds overwhelmed me, and I strained against my bonds. "You're a vampire?"

"Yes. And before you ask, no, you will not become one of us ..."

"I already know that," I snapped, feeling exhausted. "Why does drinking from me make me feel like this?"

"You do not have enough blood in your system to operate fully."

Shock and fear surged through me, as if hell bent on waging a war, but I realized it was no use. I was completely alone, cuffed to a bed in a foreign and

179

unfriendly place with a vampire keeping watch over me. A vampire who'd already helped himself to my blood.

God, where was Rand?

Then I remembered I could speak to Rand with my thoughts. I closed my eyes. *Rand ...*

It felt like someone stabbed me with a lance straight through my eye. It was so quick and unexpected, I cried out against the pain and pulled against the cuffs that held me tightly in place.

"You cannot use magic here. You are under a spell to prohibit it. I suppose I should have told you earlier."

I squeezed my eyes against the tears that threatened to explode underneath my eyelids. I wouldn't allow myself to cry. "Am I going to die?"

The man laughed. "No. In a few days, you will be fine. That is, if you do not fight us."

"Who are you?" I opened my eyes again and focused on the man, trying to remember where I knew him or how I knew him.

The corner of his mouth lifted, but the would-be smile never reached his ice blue eyes. "Sinjin. We met at a party, do you recall?"

Icy realization crystallized in my blood. That smirk, those eyes, I should have known. "Yes, I recall." I'd harbored a soft spot for Sinjin and to think he was keeping me here against my will and ... drinking from me. Then I realized the fruitlessness of it all. It didn't matter that I felt angry or hurt by what I perceived as his betrayal. Those feelings would do nothing for me now. "Why couldn't I recognize you before?"

"You did not have enough blood in your system—it causes a concussion."

A concussion? I had to swallow the bile in my throat and closed my eyes, warning the tears to keep away. I would not cry in front of this ... monster.

"It seems last time we met was under ... better circumstances," he said.

I refused to look at him. Refused to admire the ocean blue of his eyes or the jet black of his hair and the shadow that covered his chin and cheeks. "I have nothing to say to you."

He stood and made a motion to leave. "Very well, I shall leave you to your rest."

Then I realized I was being stupid. I needed answers to my questions. "How did I get here?"

He sat back down. Picking up the soup once more, he held it to me. "Swallow a few more bites, and I will tell you."

I acquiesced, and he blotted my lips where some of the soup escaped. Amazingly enough, I could feel my strength returning with every bite. It only steeled my will to learn what I needed to know from Sinjin in order to get out of here ASAP.

"Ryder brought you to us."

The bastard! So he'd been a spy all along. Hatred pooled in my gut as I thought how much I'd love to run a stake through his heart …

"Is Rand okay?" I blurted out, thinking I couldn't handle the possibility that Rand might be injured or worse, here.

"Yes, he is fine."

"Did you capture him as well?"

"It was you we were after."

"And Ryder, is he here?"

"Yes, but I am your assigned keeper."

I sighed, relieved because between the two of them, I'd prefer having Sinjin for company. At least he could put a sentence together. "I assume that when you said Ryder brought me to 'us,' you meant Bella?"

He nodded, but didn't say anything more.

I remembered Bella's territory included the US and my stomach dropped. Maybe I wasn't even in England anymore. "Am I still in England?"

"I cannot answer that question."

I felt tired again. "Have you been feeding on me?"

Sinjin shook his head. "Ryder did."

Bile traveled up my throat and I had to swallow it back down. The thought that Ryder had fed on me left me cold, and I immediately regretted eating any of the soup for fear it might revisit me.

My limbs ached as I attempted to shift in the bed. "Can you release me from these please?"

Sinjin hesitated. "Please," I begged. "I can barely even lift my head let alone attempt to escape from you."

Apparently seeing my point, he chuckled and leaned over to uncuff me. Once my hands were free, I rubbed my wrists, trying to relieve the pain. But the pain in my wrists was barely noticeable when I thought of Ryder feeding on me. Swallowing hard, I reached for my neck and noted the telltale puncture wounds. They felt like two tiny hills protruding from my neck, both concave in the middle.

"How long will these take to heal?"

Sinjin leaned into me. Shocked, I pulled back from him, but his grasp was strong and he easily held me in place. Oh God, not again! I opened my mouth to scream, but no sound came out. I didn't feel his teeth—only the soft caress of his tongue on the puncture wounds.

He pulled away from me. "It is healed."

My heart pounded and heat flushed my cheeks. I smacked my hand against the side of my neck as I searched, in vain, for the two marks. "They're gone. What did you do?"

Sinjin shrugged. "Ryder, the fool, forgot to close you. If you seal the wounds with vampire saliva, they fade away to nothing." My wide eyes met Sinjin's and he smiled, licking his lips. "You taste wonderful."

I started trembling. "You stay away from me."

181

He laughed. "You will soon come to realize I am the only friend you have here."

I'd thought he was the closest thing to a friend at Bella's party and look where that had gotten me. "What does Bella want from me?"

"She wants you to join her side."

"And if I refuse?"

"You will not refuse."

I didn't get a chance to argue as he stood and took hold of my arms. I had no energy to fight him. He reached for the cuffs and pinned my wrists in each one as I looked on helplessly.

"I am going to get you more soup."

I closed my eyes, praying this was all a dream, a terrible nightmare that plagues you, but always promises escape simply by waking up. But I knew such thoughts were hopeless. This was no dream. This was reality, cold and stark.

The door opened and Sinjin returned. He wasn't alone. Ryder strolled beside him, acting as though he was late for one of our lessons, not as though he'd punched me in the face and then kidnapped me, or witchnapped me as the case may be. My stomach clenched at the sight of him, and all I could think about was that thing, sucking the life from me.

Ryder wasn't shy about his disloyalty. He strolled to my bedside and looked as if he were ready to bite into my neck the moment I came into view.

"Keep away from her," Sinjin growled.

Ryder grunted, but backed away, taking a seat in the chair beside the bed.

So it seemed Sinjin was the alpha vampire between the two of them. I wasn't sure who'd win if you pitted them against one another. Sinjin was taller, but Ryder was as thick as a wall and I'm not talking about his intellectual capacity.

"I'm hungry," Ryder groaned, never taking his eyes off me. "An' she tastes real good."

"You are not to touch her again. You nearly drained her completely."

I felt utterly and completely invaded. I couldn't help but wonder if Rand had any idea what had happened to me. Had he seen Ryder abduct me? Where was he, and was he trying to find me?

"Ryder, come here," I said with as much authority as I could muster which wasn't much considering I was the one cuffed to a bed and on death's door.

Ryder chuckled. "She wants more."

"I want to ask you some questions."

"Be careful what you answer," Sinjin warned the big and stupid oaf.

Ryder neared me and leaned in too close. I could see the hunger in his eyes and prayed that Sinjin wouldn't leave us alone. Ryder would kill me, I could see it as clear as day in the void of his eyes.

"What happened to Rand?" I asked, forcing my mind off the devilish look in his gaze and his elongated canines.

"He was busy with a wolf."

"Did you hurt him?"

Ryder shook his head. "No, I didn't do nothin' to him. My orders was to get you an' that's what I did."

So the bastard didn't know what had happened to Rand. I could only hope Rand was safe. My second hope was that he was looking for me.

Just as Ryder was about to assume the seat next to me, Sinjin pushed him out of the way. Ryder left the room, muttering something under his breath. Sinjin took the seat in question and spooned a portion of soup from the bowl, blowing on it with his cold breath. He fed me gingerly, and I was surprised such a horrid creature could take such care.

"Are you just going to keep me here?" I asked, once I'd had enough.

"Bella will decide when she thinks you are ready."

"Ready for what?"

"You have your work cut out for you," he said with a malevolent smile. "There is a waiting list of creatures who need to be brought back to life."

I laughed, a mirthless sound. "I'm not going to help her."

Sinjin frowned. "It is life or death, poppet, you would be wise to do as she asks."

I faced him with ire. "Don't call me that name ever again."

"If I recall correctly, it did not bother you at Bella's party."

I gritted my teeth, hating him with all my being. "If it never bothered me before, it bothers me now."

Sinjin seemed deflated somehow, and it surprised me. If I didn't know better, I would've thought my opinion of him actually mattered. But, of course, I was fooling myself. This creature was incapable of any human emotion.

"Where's Bella?" I demanded.

"She will come to you when you are ready."

"I'm ready now. Send her to me, so I can tell her she'll have to kill me before I'll ever help her or you."

Sinjin frowned. "Be careful what you say, poppet. If you do not help her, she will kill you."

"Well then, do it now because I'll never help her."

"Do not be foolish."

"You think I'm not serious?"

"I think you need to keep your courage to yourself. You do not know what Bella is capable of. If you knew what was good for you, you would do as you are told."

I narrowed my eyes. "I've had enough to eat for today, you can go."

Sinjin stood and left the unfinished bowl of soup next to my bed. He started for the door before he seemed to remember something and turned to face me. "Be careful, Jolie, I would hate to see something bad befall you."

Then he closed the door.

EIGHTEEN

I knew my respite from Ryder wouldn't last long. With only Sinjin and Ryder watching me, it was a matter of time before Ryder would attend me alone. And unfortunately, that day had come. At the site of him, my entire body stiffened, and I pulled against the cuffs that held me in my prison.

"What do you want?" I seethed.

I didn't allow the fear to take control of me and instead, forced myself to be angry, livid.

He balanced a tray and slammed the door shut with the heel of his thick, black boot. The sound of the door slamming reverberated through my head like the dull blade of an axe. The walls of the room seemed as if they were closing in on me and although I've never been claustrophobic, I suddenly understood the anguish of those who are.

"I've brought you somethin' ta eat."

"Where's Sinjin?"

Ryder smiled as if he were privy to information I was not. "He had business with Bella."

His smile unnerved and irritated me. "Send it back. I don't want you here."

Ryder laughed an ugly and abrasive sound that wreaked havoc with my nerves. He straddled the back of a chair. "Looks like you don't have much choice. My orders are ta make sure you eat all o' that 'fore I go back."

I narrowed my eyes, thinking that whether or not those were his orders, he'd use it as his excuse to stay. If I wanted him to leave, I'd have to eat whatever he brought and do so quickly. "What did you bring me?"

He looked at the plate and rattled off the list of uninteresting items. "A sandwich, a pickle, an' some chips."

As he was listing my night's dinner, it occurred to me that maybe I could get some information out of him. He wasn't sharp like Sinjin, and I might be able to use that to my advantage. I glanced at the food, feigning interest. "What type of sandwich?"

He shrugged. "Turkey, looks like."

I nodded. "What type of mustard? American or English?"

He sighed and lifted the bread. "You sure are picky. Looks like English ta me. Got them little brown kernels in it."

I had him now. "Well, how did you find that? Must be tough to get English mustard around here."

He looked at me as if I were stupid. Wasn't that the pot calling the kettle black ..."We're in England."

"Oh."

My heart swelled with flowers, chocolate cake, birds singing …
anything else that's heaven on earth. This was the only good news I'd had.
Rand would have a better chance of finding me if we were still in his territory.
I couldn't suppress a smile as it crawled out of my heart and landed on my
lips.

"You gonna eat or what?" Ryder asked, still eyeing me as if I were a
ding-dong.

I motioned for him to bring me the plate and peered over the edge. The
food was just as bland as I'd thought. I couldn't say I was a fan of English
food.

"I gotta feed you, you know?" Ryder asked with a wicked smile.

"Hurry up."

He picked up the sandwich and held it in front of me. I went to take a
bite, and he pulled it away with a demonic laugh. I swallowed against the
outrage burning in me.

"What are you, five?"

He shrugged. "So touchy."

He brought the sandwich back and didn't pull it from me when I moved
in for a bite. I chewed the lump of food in my mouth and couldn't say I tasted
it. I could've been chewing cardboard for all I cared. The food was just a
means to an end. I needed to get rid of Ryder and this was the only way. Once
I'd swallowed, he picked up the pickle and held it in front of me. I took a bite
then motioned to the glass of water on the bedside table. He dropped the pickle
back on the plate and took hold of the water. I leaned forward and allowed him
to empty the remainder of the glass into my mouth.

"Why'd you do it?" I asked.

"Do what?"

"Betray Rand and me?"

"I was workin' for Bella all along."

I nodded, I'd figured that much out already. "And Gwynn?"

He grinned, his fangs threatening. "She works for me, too."

I steeled myself against the worry that gnawed my stomach. Rand had
considered Gwynn to be one of his closest allies. I could only hope he'd
realized she was no good. He had to know she was no good, I reasoned with
myself. He'd definitely realized Ryder had taken me, and Rand was the one
who'd told me of the incredible bond between a vampire and his progeny. He
knew.

"I don't want anymore," I said.

"I'm 'sposed to make sure you eat everthin' on that plate."

I shook my head, suddenly becoming furious. "Tell them I refused. You
can go now."

Ryder nodded, but didn't leave. He put the plate next to my bed and
focused on my neck, making me shift uncomfortably under his intent gaze.

"You look like your health is comin' back," he said with a sneer. "You lookin' mighty good."

I knew where this was going. For as feeble as I'd been when I'd sparred with Ryder in the past, I would be one hundred percent helpless in my current state. The only way I'd be able to defend myself would be with ugly words, and I didn't imagine that would do anything to thwart him.

"I will scream if you touch me." My voice was as cold as a tombstone.

He laughed. "I'll just cover your mouth."

He stood and pushed aside his chair. It clattered to the floor, sounding like a skeleton collapsing. I tugged against my cuffs as the emotionless steel just chafed my wrists. I had to face the fact that Ryder would do whatever he wanted with me.

So I played my last card. "I'll tell Sinjin if you touch me."

He leaned close, so close I could smell his breath—a bitter smell like walking into a damp closet that's been sealed off from fresh air for years. It was the smell of death.

"Then I'll come back when you're asleep and I'll kill you myself."

He grabbed hold of my head and yanked it to the side, his eyes roving my exposed neck. I whimpered, trying to pull my head down, but his brute strength was too much for me. He leaned down and inhaled, as if smelling my blood through my neck. I was about to wail out when his hand cupped my mouth. His hand was so big, it covered my nose and mouth, and it was all I could do to get a breath.

He leaned down, and I closed my eyes tightly. I thought he'd bite me, instead, his cold tongue darted out and licked my neck. I shivered in disgust, and he pulled away, smirking down at me. "I can't leave no mark else Sinjin gonna know what I did."

My eyes widened, and a glimmer of hope lit within me. Did that mean he was leaving? He wasn't going to feed on me? He pulled his hand away from my mouth. "Stay the hell away from me," I whispered.

Ryder laughed and leaned over me again. He grabbed hold of the bottom of his shirt and ripped it, his shirt screaming against the brutal treatment. I'd fare much worse. He approached me with the long piece of fabric, and I made the mistake of opening my mouth to scream. All it did was made the job of gagging me that much easier.

Knowing it was futile, I strained against the handcuffs anyway. He jerked the blanket away from my lower half, and fear beat a wild path through me. My entire body trembled as I glanced down at myself, noting my sports bra and stretch pants. I wasn't wearing much and my lack of clothing would make Ryder's job that much easier, whatever it was that he intended to do.

He lunged for my legs, but since they weren't restrained, I kicked at him with all the pent-up frustration and fear that had been living within me these last couple of weeks. I kicked out with such strength that the cot bucked up. Ryder took a step back as an evil smile captured his broad and ugly face. When he came after me again, he was prepared and grabbed one of my legs, forcing it down with intense pressure until I thought he might break my ankle. I managed to land the free leg right into his nose, and he reared back, his hands covering his face.

That was when I knew I was in deep crap. He dropped his hands and his canines were longer than they'd been a minute ago. His eyes glowed with a fierce and unnatural quality as he faced me with pure hatred. "You gonna bleed for that."

He was lightning fast. Within a blink, he had hold of my stretch pants. It only made me realize that he'd been playing with me earlier—toying with his prey before landing the deathblow. He pulled and the material was quick to rip under his immense strength. Angry tears boiled in my eyes as I attempted to bring my legs together. He held them easily, his fangs exposed, lips snarling, and eyes alive with hunger and lust. "Stop flinchin' around. When we drink, we get mighty horny."

I closed my eyes against the tears. There was nothing I could do. The bleakness of my situation beat down on me, and I couldn't control the river of tears that streamed down my cheeks. Ryder didn't seem to notice, or if he did, he didn't care.

He lay atop me and pushed my legs as far apart as they'd go, sinking his head between them. I felt the pierce of his teeth as they broke through the skin of my upper thigh and the resulting sting as my body protested his assault. He began to suck, making grunting and moaning sounds as if he were having sex with me.

I screamed out against the gag, my shoulders heaving with sobs. I tried to fill my mind with as many thoughts as I could muster, just so I could ward away the sound of him drinking me and more so, the sound of him enjoying drinking me.

I refused to look at him, but I could feel his eyes on my face. He enjoyed the pain he was causing me.

I whimpered at the sound of him tearing at his belt and the zipper of his pants.

Then I heard the sound that saved me from Ryder.

The sound of Sinjin yelling for him.

Ryder jerked away from me, stumbling to his feet while he threw the coverlet back over me, as if covering the evidence and tore the gag from my mouth. A thin trickle of blood coursed down his chin.

My blood.

Ryder faced me, and his eyes promised he'd pick up where he'd left off. Before I could say a word, he left, zipping up his fly as he went. My will to remain strong crumbled away, and I sank back into the cot, thinking only of my desperate situation as tears bled from my eyes.

~

"Good morning, sunshine."

The voice interrupted my dreamless slumber and forced me to face the ugly world beyond the safety of my closed eyelids. "You certainly are sleeping late." It was Sinjin's voice.

Relief washed over me. I opened my eyes and never would've known it was morning—the room had no windows and was lit by a single lamp, leaving the whole place in relative darkness.

"Aren't you supposed to be hibernating?" I mumbled, barely able to get the words out.

Sinjin laughed. "Vampires can be up any time of the day or night, as long as we are not in the sunlight."

"Oh."

His brows drew together, his gaze flashing over my body. "You are overly tired this morning?"

I nodded, staring at the ceiling and hoping he'd read nothing in my eyes. The door opened, and I craned my neck to see Ryder casually stroll through it. My stomach dropped and my pulse increased.

I hated him.

"I'm to take over watch. Bella wants you," he said, facing Sinjin.

Sinjin looked at him with a sneer of disgust.

"Don't leave me with him," I blurted out before I could stop myself.

Sinjin turned to face me, his eyes riveted on mine. "Why? I will only be …"

"Please," I begged, a sob choking my throat. I couldn't fathom being left alone with Ryder. "If Bella wants me to help her then you can't leave me alone with him."

Sinjin's jaw clenched and for the first time I saw true anger flash in his eyes. It wasn't a pretty sight—it was a damned scary sight. "Why are you so afraid of him?"

I made the mistake of glancing at Ryder who promised to kill me in no uncertain terms. The threat of retribution was in his eyes. "I … I just don't trust him." I couldn't bring myself to go into the how and the why of it, having promised myself I would never revisit yesterday's events. I would wipe them from my memory and pretend they'd never happened.

Sinjin frowned. "It will just be a moment, love …"

And he started for the door. All I could see was Ryder's smug smile and although I'd tried to blind myself against them, images of his head between my legs flashed before me. "Please, Sinjin, he bit me!"

Sinjin stopped. For one long moment, he didn't say a word. "I did not see any marks on your neck and Ryder always leaves marks."

His jaw clenched tight, his eyes issuing a warning of their own. The anger in his gaze scared the life out of me. He thought I was lying. Crap, now I had two vampires to worry about? Well, either way, I wasn't lying. "He didn't bite me there," I said in a small voice.

Ryder shifted, his beady eyes darting to the door. Sinjin was at my side so fast, I didn't see him move. "Where?"

189

I motioned down my body. "You'll have to remove the blanket. At the junction of my legs … and my body," I said as the heat of embarrassment claimed my cheeks.

Sinjin tore the blanket off me. His face took on a reddish glow when he noted the tear in my stretch pants. Thank God I'd worn underwear, otherwise I'd be entirely exposed. Much to my chagrin, Sinjin shifted the rip around until he could adequately see the bite marks on my thighs.

He met my gaze, and I was stunned by the remorse I saw there. Then his expression turned deadly. At the emotion in his eyes, my heart dropped, and I wondered if he would attack me. But he wheeled around and leapt on Ryder with a growl.

I pulled against the cuffs until they bit into my wrists, but I was immune to the pain, my eyes transfixed by the sight of Sinjin and Ryder. Sinjin had him by the throat and slammed him into the wall. The entire room vibrated until it felt like an earthquake.

"What did I tell you, you bloody clot?" Sinjin growled in a voice that was so laced with hatred, I barely recognized it as his. "Am I not your elder?"

Ryder didn't respond, but sunk his teeth into Sinjin's shoulder, biting a mouth full of flesh with an obvious smile. He pulled away from Sinjin as blood dripped from his fangs. Sinjin dropped his hold around Ryder's neck and glanced at his now bleeding shoulder with disinterest, as if a fly had landed on him. Then Sinjin's eyes became entirely white and with a low growl, he launched himself at Ryder, thrusting his fingers into Ryder's arm and shredding his flesh.

I had to turn away at the site of bone and found myself hyperventilating, tears drenching my face. If I hadn't realized how immensely strong vampires were before, I realized it now. They were basically going to tear each other apart. And the crapper was that I was stuck here as an unwilling audience.

"You disregarded an order from your elder," Sinjin continued, his eyes like those of a crazy person as his hands tightened around Ryder's throat again. He lifted him ever so slightly and pitched him against the wall.

"I am a master vampire, or have you forgotten?" Sinjin demanded.

Ryder landed, making the same sound a felled tree would. "I'm sorry," Ryder said the words as if they were venomous to his tongue.

In a flash, Sinjin had him by the throat again. "If you touch her again, I will tear your heart out and suck every last drop of blood." He lifted Ryder and pinned him against the wall while Ryder's feet dangled beneath him. He looked like a man in the process of being hanged.

"I apologize, master."

I was surprised by the appellation, but Sinjin seemed to accept it as he pulled his hand away and Ryder dropped to the floor. His blood marred the wall where his raw shoulder had rubbed against it. Without a word, the younger vampire fled the room.

Sinjin turned and I shook my head as he neared me, tears running from my eyes.

"I am not going to hurt you," he said and his voice was calm.

I wasn't. "Y … you s … stay the hell away from m … me."

Sinjin kept coming. I tried to pull against the handcuffs and could feel them cutting my skin. I didn't care.

"It had to be done. Ryder disrespected me and I am his elder."

"I don't care who y … you are. You stay away from m … me."

He slowed and lifted his hands in a show of submission, but my attention centered on the bite in his shoulder, which continued to squirt blood until it was flowing like a river down his arm. A few seconds later, the wound appeared to be healing itself.

"Jolie …" he started forward again.

"Please!"

He stopped and his usually plump lips worried into a straight line. "I was protecting you."

I didn't know what to say and still couldn't catch my damned breath, so I said nothing, but watched Sinjin take a seat on the chair next to me.

"Do you want me to heal the bites?" he asked and I realized what that would mean. His head between my thighs.

"No."

He smiled and looked hesitant, unsure of what to say. "I will not allow him alone with you again. I apologize for what happened. He will be severely disciplined."

Will be? I'd thought he'd just received the tail end of a severe punishment. I wondered how much more of this I could take. I hadn't been up and about in what felt like weeks, although I imagined it was more like days. I needed to make my move sometime; I needed to get out of this situation one way or another.

"When can I see Bella?"

He seemed surprised to hear my voice. But the surprise on his face didn't last long before his usual arrogant countenance returned. "She will come to you. I do not know what else to tell you, my pet."

I closed my eyes against the term of endearment. How it rubbed me the wrong way. "If Ryder finds me alone, he will kill me. I know he will."

Sinjin nodded. "I will not allow him near you. You have my word."

"Your word means nothing to me," I spat.

Sinjin gritted his teeth, and I wondered if I'd gone too far. He seemed to be the only protector I had here and maybe I needed to make the most of it. "I suppose actions speak louder than words."

~

Four days later and Sinjin had been true to his word; I hadn't had any more visits from Ryder. I did, however, have a visit from Bella. The sight of her made me want to scream. If I hadn't been cuffed to the goddamned cot, I would've lunged at her to let her know exactly what I thought of her.

"What am I doing here?" I already knew the answer, but I needed to hear it.

Sinjin followed her and sat in a chair in the far corner of the room, regarding me with what appeared to be concern. Bella settled in the chair next to my bed, taking time to smooth her long, blue skirts.

"I should have won the rights as your employer a long time ago," she started.

"You lost fair and square even though you poisoned Rand. He was the better witch." I wasn't going to mince words. I might be stuck here, but that didn't mean I had to be polite about it. Her aura vacillated with purple edges, and I smirked.

Surprisingly, she kept calm. "Regardless of what you think, you are now working for me. You either do as I tell you or I will kill you."

"Then kill me." As soon as I'd said the words, I gave myself a second to reflect upon them and thought maybe it wasn't such a good idea. For all I knew, maybe Bella wasn't bluffing. She had killed her father, after all. Killing me would be like taking out the trash.

Sinjin shifted, drawing my attention. He gave a slight shake of his head. Well, screw him.

"Don't forget I know where you live. I know how to get to Rand if need be …" she said, her eyes narrowed like a cat's.

"Rand is way too strong for you to ever take him unaware."

"That is debatable," she said, trying to mask her fury. "But what of your friend … the one I met at your shop?"

My stomach dropped. Bella could and would kill Christa easily. There comes a point when you have to admit your defeat. If Christa was a pawn in this game, I'd lost. I could not and would not endanger my best friend.

"If I do as you say, you'll leave her alone?" I asked, realizing I'd just given up all my freedom if ever I'd had any.

"You have my word."

"Just say yes or no," I demanded, angry that she'd even offer her word.

"Yes," she snapped.

I nodded and inhaled deeply, preparing myself for the fact that I was now Bella's slave. "I want out of this bed."

"Sinjin, attend to her," Bella said, watching him hungrily as he moved across the room and bent over me. But Bella wasn't a bloodsucker, so the hunger in her eyes was of another sort. I smiled inwardly. So Bella was lusting after Sinjin. Interesting. Another note to file away for future reference.

Sinjin undid the cuffs around my wrists, but before I could pull them free, he massaged the inside of my wrists with his thumb. The touch was so personal and out of the blue, I didn't even have the wherewithal to pull my hands away. I eyed Bella, but she was too focused on the comeliness of his ass as he bent over me to even notice the exchange between us.

Sinjin pulled away from me and returned to Bella's side of the room as I breathed a sigh of relief. I didn't want him so close.

"I need a shower," I said, rubbing my wrists. Now that I'd made the decision not to fight them, I had some demands of my own. "I haven't had one since I've been here, and I need some new clothes. I'd create some for myself, but I've learned my magic won't work here." I couldn't help the anger that laced my last sentence.

Bella smiled, but it wasn't sweet. "Whatever you require, we are happy to oblige."

"The witch will room with me," Sinjin announced.

"No," I started.

"Why?" Bella asked, jealousy resonating in her tone. I wanted to avoid her jealousy like the wrath of God. I was in a bad enough situation as it was, and I didn't want to add to it by fueling the flame of contempt Bella was already displaying toward me.

"Ryder is still a threat to her safety. If we lose her, we lose everything we have strived for," Sinjin argued and eyed me as if he were purchasing a new car.

"So kill him," I interrupted.

Fire burned in his ice blue eyes. "We need him. If we kill him, Gwynn will pull her support."

Bella nodded. "Yes, we can't dispose of him."

"I want a room to myself," I continued though no one was paying any attention to me.

"You will room with Sinjin," Bella said, obviously annoyed she couldn't find a decent argument against it. She faced me and issued a warning with her eyes—a warning not to mess around with her man.

I said nothing, but glared at Sinjin, and he gave me a cursory nod. I didn't know what to think about being his roommate. He'd definitely protect me against Ryder, but who would protect me against him?

NINETEEN

The darkness of the room enveloped me, and I was overcome with the smell of something sickeningly sweet ... the scent of sickness, of infection. It was the stink of a rose that had been sitting in stale water for too long—the smell of death, rotting and sugary.

I forced myself forward, forced myself to approach the four-poster bed. In the darkness, I could make out a small woman engulfed in the center, her long gray hair matted in clumps, sweat pouring from her brow.

A small lamp sitting on a side table burned yellow against the pitch darkness of the room. It cast strange shadows against the woman's face, making her deathly pallor even more pronounced. I wasn't sure if the brownish stain on her pillow was from sweat or something worse. The high neckline of her nightgown reached her chin, making her look like a turtle. The covers were strewn around her, as if she'd been tossing and turning.

I fought the need to open a window and clear out the deathly odors that hid in each corner of the room. The air was so thick with stale mustiness, I could bite it.

The old woman's eyes were closed, but I imagined they'd be colorless. One as old as she wouldn't have effervescence in her eyes. They'd be dull and void, life having distilled any vivacity from them.

I neared the bed, fully aware she couldn't see me.

I was here to bring her back to life. To bring her back to the land of the living, so she could serve the undeserving person of Bella. I was here to reanimate an enemy. The irony lined my throat like mucus.

The woman wasn't a werewolf or a ghost, so I couldn't really rely on past experiences for guidance on this one. The woman was a prophetess, at least that's what Bella had called her. Apparently, a prophetess was someone who could see the future. I didn't know how that differed from a psychic, but didn't care enough to ask any questions. I wasn't sure what this meant for me, if bringing back a so-called prophet would make my job any different, any harder.

She was over eighty, if I had to guess, and sickness hovered around her like a fog. Being the late 1800s when leeches were considered good medicine, it wasn't going to be long before her maker came for her. Or I intervened.

Then it suddenly dawned on me; how would I know when Death arrived? In all my other experiences, it was obvious when the time of reckoning was upon the person in question. This was entirely different. There was no gunshot, no angry wolf ... this was sickness, slow and unreliable.

I moved closer to the bed, willing myself to breathe through my mouth, so the sickening scent of infection wouldn't cause me to retch. Her eyes were clamped shut, her breathing shallow and ragged—like the sounds you hear as a kid when you're supposed to be asleep, but you're convinced there's a monster breathing in your ear. I wondered how long it was going to take her to kick it. I didn't want to wait around all day. Not like I had much to get back to—a pissed off witch and a vampire who was making it very difficult to hate him.

I angrily shoved thoughts of Sinjin away. I couldn't deal with them now. I sighed and broke away from the bed, wandering around the barren room. It was like being on a tour of some museum house where you aren't allowed to touch anything. I frowned and touched every piece of furniture.

"Who's there?"

Her voice shocked me out of my boredom. I couldn't see anyone else in the room, and it took me a second to realize she was talking to me.

"I can't see you," she continued, her fingers clutching her bedspread. "But I know you're there."

I neared the bed again and noted her old and dull eyes were open wide with fear. She gazed around the room, but her eyes never focused on me. I wasn't sure if she was blind or what. After watching her for a few more seconds, it looked as if she could clearly focus on the door, so she wasn't blind …

"Speak!" she insisted.

I was at a loss for words. What was I supposed to say? Hello and how is your day going? Were you planning on dying any quicker? "Can you hear me?" I said, thinking it the next best question.

She closed her eyes and swallowed. "Who are you?"

My mouth fell open as shock waged a mini battle within me. I guess this was what was different about resurrecting a prophet. She could hear me where none others could. It sort of weirded me out.

"I'm here to save you," I said, thinking I sounded like an idiotic super hero.

She laughed. Apparently, she thought my answer idiotic too. Her laugh turned into a racking cough and my hands curled as I waited on pins and needles for her to die, so I could dive in and stop it from happening.

"You can't save me," she said, once the spasm of coughs escaped her. Her voice was gravelly. It sounded dehydrated. She opened her eyes again and searched for me in vain. I stepped up closer to her.

"I can save you," I said, though not completely convinced.

"Are you a spirit?" Sweat poured from her brow, making it look like her forehead was crying. It grossed me out, and I had to look away, the need to open a window as demanding as eating something sweet when you're on a diet.

I shook my head and then remembered she couldn't see me. "No."

"Why can't … I see you?" She closed her eyes and inhaled deeply. I couldn't help but wonder what the hell she was sick with. Hopefully it wasn't

195

airborne. Not that it mattered anyway—as a witch, I could heal myself. Apparently, such was not the case with prophetesses. Maybe she was just sick with old age.

"I don't know."

"What are you?" She frowned and grated a trembling, gnarled hand across her brow. Her hand was so old, you could mistake it for a tree root.

"I'm a witch," I started. "From the future."

As soon as I said it, I realized how ridiculous it sounded and felt like laughing myself. A witch from the future. ... If it was me, I'd think I was dreaming. It surprised me that this woman didn't consider the same thing. Course, maybe she was.

The old woman sucked in a breath, her eyes widening. "You," she whispered.

"You ... you know me?" Wait, that couldn't be right. She was delirious. Great, I didn't have time for this crap.

"Ah, I remember."

I sat on the edge of her bed. But after imagining her sickness crawling along the bed, up my arm and into my nose and mouth, I quickly stood. "You remember what?"

She cleared her throat and reached for a glass of water on the side table, her hand shaking like she had palsy. "You are the prophecy. I never believed it, but it ... must be true."

My heart slammed against my chest as I wondered what in the hell she was talking about. "What prophecy?"

"We were ... told that you would come. The woman who ... can bring with her everlasting life. I ... I never believed it."

She looked as excited as someone could who's nearly dead. I didn't know what to think, but I couldn't stop the angst that welled up within me. A prophecy? It seemed implausible that she should know about me hundreds of years ago, but it unsettled me all the same.

"I don't bring everlasting life," I said, trying to disprove her belief for my own sense of well being.

"Are you here to save me from dying?"

I nodded and caught myself again. It was hard being invisible. I had a new level of understanding for Pelham. Pelham ... the thought that I might never see his ghostly handsome face caused me more chagrin than I wanted to admit. Of course, that thought led to ones of Rand, and I had to abandon them before I became a blubbering mess. "Yes, but ..."

"You can't save me."

I was annoyed. I wasn't sure if it was so much due to the situation or the thoughts of Rand which had thoroughly depressed me. "Why not?"

"You can only save those who wish to be saved." A smile played with her lips—almost like she was pleased she could throw a wrench into my plans.

"I have a job to do, and that job is bringing you back with me, regardless if you want me to or not."

Her smile widened, revealing tarnished and yellow teeth—four to be exact. God only knows what had happened to the rest. I could never understand why people held such a reverence for the past. No doctors and no dentists ... I was very happy to be part of the twenty-first century, thank you very much.

She pointed toward the vicinity of where I sat. "I know why you ... are here. I will not go ... with you."

There was no point in arguing with the old fart. Once she started to see the light, I was grabbing her and taking her with me. I backed away from the bed and stretched my arms above my head. God, she was taking forever.

"I won't join Isabella," she said in a small voice.

That grabbed my attention like Rand in a pair of tightly fitting pants, and I neared the bed again. "Why is that?"

She turned her head to the side and seemed to focus all her energy on a single rose bloom that stood in a tall vase. There was no water in the vase and the rose looked wan with thirst.

"I have looked forward to my ... freedom for so long. I refuse ... to be her slave any longer."

Hmm this was interesting. "Bella seems to think you're pretty important. You were on the top of her list."

"She is mistaken.

I sighed. "I didn't come here to argue with you."

The old woman laughed, an empty sound that grated on my nerves like a Celine Dion song. "You do not serve her."

I frowned. "I work for her, it's the same thing."

"No, you do not. I can sense it from you."

She started coughing again and I inched closer, thinking she couldn't last much longer. "I'm dying," she said as if to validate my thoughts.

"I'm taking you with me."

She shook her head as her breathing became very ragged. "Tell Isabella I will ... see her in hell."

I grabbed hold of her shoulder as she exhaled and her eyes popped open.

"You are no witch," she said, her eyes wide. "You have ... no idea ... what ... you ... are."

Then she died.

Before I could fully understand her words, I was rushing through a tunnel. A flash of light burst in front of me. I opened my eyes and found my cheek against the itchiness of cheap carpet. I peeled myself off the floor and sat back on my thighs. I shook my head, trying to shake off the after-effects of mind traveling.

"Jolie..." Sinjin said, worry gnawing at his otherwise handsome face.

Bella gave him a scowl before her eyes fell on me and the scowl turned deadly. "Where is the prophetess?"

"She refused to come with me," I said, thinking the truth was the best response. "I grabbed her arm when she died, but it made no difference."

Bella's eyes narrowed as color rose in her cheeks. She stood up and towered over me, her hand twitching like it wanted to lash out and smack me. "You're lying!"

"I'm not lying," I answered between gritted teeth and stood, angry that I still had to look up into her eyes. Being small had its shortcomings … no pun intended.

"Perhaps we should try it again tomorrow," Sinjin interrupted, taking Bella's hand. I'm not sure why, but the image of him holding Bella's hand pissed the hell out of me. I had to drop my gaze lest either of them see the angry flames lashing from my eyes.

"She won't come back with me. She knew I was there for her, and she knew it because of a prophecy," I said, instantly regretting my diarrhea mouth. I didn't want to give Bella any useful information. I wasn't sure how useful this tidbit was, but I needed to watch my mouth.

"What prophecy?" She eyed me.

I sighed. "The woman said she'd known I was coming for her. That's all I know, so don't ask me anymore about it."

Bella frowned, and I could see the hatred in her eyes. I guess she wasn't used to people talking to her in such a way, but I didn't care. She could force me to do her bidding, but that didn't mean I had to be happy about it.

"I've listened to enough of your drivel. Sinjin, get her out of my sight before I do something we'll both regret."

Sinjin reached for me, but I avoided him. "Don't touch me dammit …"

"Jolie," Sinjin interrupted me, his jaw so tight I immediately shut up. He grabbed my arm, and his grip was none too gentle as he led me down a long and dark corridor. He threw open the door to our bedroom and deposited me in the room with a shove as he slammed the door behind us. "You need to watch yourself."

"Screw you."

He took a seat on his bed. "Bella will hurt you if you drive her to it."

I refused to look at him and even went so far as to sit on my bed, my back facing him. The mattress was squishy beneath me, completely different to the hardness of the cot. Tonight would be my first night in my new abode. I knew I wouldn't sleep a wink, not if Sinjin was in here with me. And he would be—he'd made it his business to be my keeper.

"I don't care."

"You care what she does to your friend?"

I dropped my face and eyed my lap. He had me there. "Okay, you've proven your point. You can go now."

He materialized directly in front of me, and I thought I'd choke on my gasp. "It is impolite to turn your back on someone," he said with a smile.

"I don't care."

"I have killed men for less," he continued, and if he was trying to intimidate me, it was working.

"What do you want, a gold star?"

198

Sinjin laughed, and I enjoyed the sound, much though I wanted to kick myself with the realization.

"You are very fortunate you are a woman and a beautiful one at that," he finished, eyeing me up and down as his tongue caressed his fangs. I shuddered.

I stood up and turned away from him. No sooner did I turn my back in a show of disobedience, than I found myself up against the wall, my cheek a witness to the roughness of the brick. I stifled the whimper that brewed in my throat and closed my eyes against the excitement that stirred in my stomach when I felt Sinjin's body tight against mine.

"Do you know how many vampires are in my command?" he whispered and his breath tickled my ear.

"No, nor do I care."

His fingers ran up the sleeve of my sweatshirt until they reached my shoulder. I couldn't seem to catch my breath, but refused to admit that his touch sent a bolt of heat through me. He pulled against the sweatshirt, and it dropped from my shoulder, the strap of my tank top left to hold down the fortress. His cold fingers graced my skin and it reacted with goose bumps.

"Why do you shiver at my touch?"

I shut my eyes tight and tried to imagine myself in the heat of the desert, trying to imagine myself anywhere hot enough to melt the damned gooseflesh from my skin. "You're cold," I answered and smirked at my own response. Not bad.

Sinjin laughed. "I think it is for a different reason, poppet."

I swallowed hard. "And what reason would that be?"

His fingers started a descent down my collarbone and further still. Before he reached my breasts, I grabbed his hand and he jerked me around, pushing me back up against the wall. I forced my gaze to his. I wouldn't allow myself to cower before him.

"I think you are very aware that I would like nothing more than to bed you."

My mouth dropped open. He was like a romance novel book character come to life. "Who the hell talks like that?" I said, wishing I could've come up with something better. Not good.

"Do not be afraid of me, poppet. I can see the lust in your eyes."

I pulled away from him. "Don't flatter yourself."

He laughed and took a seat on his bed. I breathed a sigh of relief, imagining he might stay there, hoping he would stay there. I couldn't handle him so close to me, it made me think things I shouldn't be thinking.

I rubbed my upper arms, hoping to destroy the memory of his hands on me. "Why are you here? Don't you have something better to do?"

He quirked his head. "I am your keeper. I am keeping you." He smiled with fangs, and I just shook my head.

"So I'm stuck with you?"

He nodded and leaned back, completely at ease. "Shall we have a conversation? I find myself excited about the prospect of learning more about you."

I groaned. "Fine. Whatever. Just nothing sexual. What do you want to talk about?"

I felt like I was babysitting some kid and trying to keep him entertained. "Ask me a question."

I frowned. "How old are you?"

He straightened, apparently eager to talk about himself. "Six hundred nineteen."

I gulped. "Holy crap."

Sinjin laughed. "How old are you?"

"Twenty-eight."

"Holy crap," he said with a smile before changing the subject. "Was it true what you said? That the old woman refused to go with you?"

"Yeah."

I plopped down on the bed. "I'm only sitting because I want to, not because you suggested it," I said, sounding all of twelve years old.

Sinjin chuckled. "Of course."

"Why aren't you concerned about making Bella jealous with your ... attentions to me?"

He quirked a brow. "I thought you said we could not discuss anything sexual?"

"That isn't ..." I interrupted myself as realization dawned on me.

He was sleeping with her! No wonder she looked like she wanted to kill me. After the initial shock wore off, I was left with a big helping of jealousy, or was it envy ... either way, it wasn't pleasant. Why did I have any sort of feelings for this creature? God, it was infuriating.

"Bella must deal with her own insecurities."

"You don't understand women very well."

He leaned forward, looking entirely too interested.

"Let's talk about something else," I said.

"Perhaps you and the warlock."

"No," my voice was direct, and I shook my head in case he didn't understand English. "Let's not."

The door flew open then and Bella stepped inside, eyeing us suspiciously. Thank God she hadn't decided to visit five minutes ago when Sinjin was caressing my shoulder. That would have definitely ended up with my head on a plate.

Sinjin merely smiled, slow and sexy, obviously enjoying the fact that Bella was burning with jealousy. "Bella, what can I do for you?"

"I have something I ... need to discuss with you," she said and eyed me with daggers.

Sinjin stood. "Of course." He faced me. "Poppet, I will return later."

I didn't say anything, but watched them leave and allowed my heart to deflate when I heard the sound of a key locking my door.

~

"I don't care if she wants to come back with you or not," Bella snapped, her hands fisted. "Your job is to bring her back."

I frowned, shaking my head. We were sitting across from one another in the living room of the old house. I'd only been allowed to see this room, my bedroom that I shared with Sinjin, and the room in which I'd been held captive for a week. I hadn't been outside in what felt like years.

Bella had ordered me to bring back the old woman again, the one who was determined not to come back. First of all, I wasn't even sure it was possible to try and bring her back twice. Secondly, I'd touched her when she died last time and nothing had happened, so what made anyone think it would work this time?

"Don't fail," Bella warned.

I didn't care if I failed or not. I said nothing, but closed my eyes and took Bella's hands, much though I hated touching her.

Instantly I found myself in the same dark and dank room with the same smell of death. The woman was in bed and the rose stood at her bedside, not quite withered, but on its way. I wasn't going to waste time.

"Wake up," I said.

The woman opened her eyes slowly, her gaze darting around the room. She closed her eyes again, no doubt thinking I was a dream.

"I'm still here."

Her eyes widened in surprise.

"You can't see me, but I'm here. I'm not a ghost. I met you yesterday, but you won't remember. I'm here to save you."

She nodded, but pulled her covers closer to her chin. "I do not want to be saved."

"I know. We've been through this already. Last time you told me about a prophecy. What's the prophecy?"

"Prophecy?" she asked.

All I knew was this information was important. I didn't know how to use it or when I could use it, but I knew I had to get it. "When I was here before, you told me about a prophecy. You knew I was coming for you. You knew who I was."

She nodded and her eyes took on a faraway look. "The prophecy."

"What does it say?"

She coughed and I attempted to hand her the glass of water on the table, but my hand went through it. "The prophecy said a woman would come for us, that she could raise the dead."

My mind spun and I almost sank onto the bed, until I remembered how dirty the coverlet was. What could all of this mean? What did the prophecy have to do with me? "You told me before that I wasn't a witch. What did you mean?"

She shook her head. "I do not know."

She seemed confused and I had to calm down, thinking she couldn't remember my first visit as it had never happened in her world. The fact that she wasn't screaming was amazing in and of itself.

"Can you see the future?" I asked in a soft voice.

"Sometimes."

I tried not to let the frustration show in my voice. "Then the prophecy, how do you know what it is?"

She took in a great, rattling breath, her face paling into a light shade of blue. My anxiety grew; I needed answers before she died.

"The elders, they told us."

She erupted into a fit of coughing. When she was able to control herself again, tears brimmed in her eyes.

"Why does Bella want you to come back with me?" I urged, knowing I'd never get the answer from Bella.

The old woman tried to speak but her voice came out as a mere wisp of air. I leaned down, hoping I could understand. "She thinks ... I can change the course of the ... future."

Someone changing the course of the future was a good comrade to have. "But you can't?"

She shook her head. "No, she is mistaken."

The woman said nothing more as I let it all sink in. So Bella had the wrong prophet. What was Bella wanting the old woman for anyway? To change the course of history, but why?

I glanced at the woman and she was still. I couldn't help myself as I shook her and demanded she tell me more, tell me what Bella was after. But it was no use. The woman was dead, gone. Goddammit.

Bella was equally angry with me when I returned empty handed and she refused to listen to me. "You didn't try hard enough," she snapped.

I pushed myself up, ignoring the throb in my head. "It doesn't matter about trying hard enough. I just have to touch the person when they die and that brings them back. Don't act like you know what the rules are. I know no one has ever been able to do it before."

Bella's wrath exploded and she slapped me across the cheek. I stumbled back, resisting the urge to press my hand to my stinging face. Gritting my teeth against the onslaught of ire that visited me, I stared directly into the witch's eyes. How I hated her. How badly I wanted to wrap my fingers around her neck.

"Sinjin, get her out of my sight," Bella seethed.

Sinjin reached down and grabbed the front of my shirt, jerking me to my feet. Without a word, he pulled me into the hall and pushed me in front of him. I stumbled, righting myself against the wall. His jaw was clenched so tight, it looked like he'd break his teeth.

"Are you telling the truth? I will find out if you are not."

I stared directly into his eyes and lied. "Yes."

I couldn't help the smile that pulled at the corners of my lips. Bella had the wrong prophet. The whole thing was pretty comical. I wished I'd been in the right frame of mind—maybe I could've even laughed.

TWENTY

It was late. It was also the first night I didn't have my ever-watchful vampire roommate. I didn't want to stop to think where he might be—with Bella. The answer was clear and it made me ill. But as pissed as I'd been, I hadn't been angry enough not to notice he hadn't locked the door. I'd laid there for ten long minutes, my heart thundering in my chest, any moment expecting someone to come by and lock the thing. No one had.

Imagining it might be my only chance to escape, I crept to the corner of the room where I'd piled my jeans and sweatshirt before going to bed. My heart strummed within my chest, echoing in my ears as I dressed.

I figured I should arrange the bedding to make it look like I was asleep and situated the two pillows lengthwise. I threw the covers over them, hoping it would look like I preferred to sleep with the covers over my head. Okay, it was something a teenager would do, and I didn't imagine it would work—Sinjin seemed to be a pretty detail-oriented guy, but it was worth a shot.

I laced my sneakers and tiptoed to the door. Tugging on the door handle, I found it wide open. Well, my keepers weren't very diligent. It was probably a set up, but I was so desperate at this point, I didn't even give a crap.

I stuck my head out and looked left then right. The hallway was dark and as quiet as a graveyard. Thinking I'd already wasted too much time, I crept out the door. The floorboards moaned underneath me, and I froze. My attention fell to the stair well directly before me—it was so close, I wanted to sprint, but I had to force myself to go slowly, lest I make more noise than I already had.

I'd never been out of the house, so I'd have to go blindly. Reaching the staircase, I swallowed the frog, scratch that, the toad in my throat. I breathed a sigh of relief when I made it down the stairs with only the protest of a few creaky boards.

But I faced a quandary at the bottom of the stairs. I could go right or left—to my right looked like a living room and to the left, the kitchen. What was more likely to have a door leading outside? I'm no architect, but I'd have to bet on the living room. I turned to the right and forced my legs forward. No sooner did I start forward, than I walked headlong into the corner of the couch. I bit my tongue to keep the curse from my lips. It wasn't easy to navigate in the middle of the night. I was so scared, I was about to wet myself.

I'd made the right decision. A door stood before me and in my mind's eye, it shone like the Holy Grail. I bolted, too close to freedom to travel the distance slowly. Grabbing the doorknob and turning, I stepped foot outside.

I was free.

The cold night air met me like an old friend. The moonlight carved a path that led through a grassy backyard into a bank of trees. No fences, gates, or anything separating me from certain escape. Just a football field's length of grass.

This would be the toughest part of my escape. The grassy area was about four hundred feet until it reached the haven of the trees. If anyone were awake and happened to look out their window, they'd easily spot me. Lucky for me, most the windows in the house had been sealed over—vampires aren't especially fond of windows. Freedom was so close, I could taste it. And it was a taste that rivaled apple pie.

I took a deep breath and like a sprinter, well, more like a girl who'd never run before, but was hell-bent on getting away from an evil witch and two vampires, I took off.

I'm not sure why, but I ran in zig-zags, almost like my brain thought someone was going to shoot me. Weird what your body does when under duress. I reached the cover of the trees and felt the start of tears in my eyes. Had I done it? I leaned my hands against my thighs and panted. If I got out of this unscathed, the first place I was going was the gym.

Thinking I needed more distance between me and the house of horrors, I jogged in between the trees. I had a stitch in my side that wouldn't allow for running, still, I couldn't help the grin that stole my face.

Holy crap! I'd done it! Take that, Bella!

Feeling pretty confident and proud of myself, I continued forging my way through the thick forest. I had no idea where I was—away was enough at this point. I considered changing into a fox, but I wasn't sure how far Bella's spell prohibited me from using my magic. Maybe trying to use my own magic might set off some unseen alarm? I wasn't about to take any chances.

No, I was going to do this all on my own. No reliance on my witch powers. This was going to be Jolie Wilkins au natural. Getting my second wind, I started running again. I wasn't on any sort of path, and the tree branches snapped against my face and body, but they didn't slow me down. As dumb as it sounds, Rand kept me going. I just pictured his beautiful dark eyes and dimpled smile when it seemed my resolution was waning.

After intermittently running and walking for what I imagined was well over an hour, I was exhausted. I wouldn't admit that I was lost … not yet. I'd been hoping the forest would thin out or I'd come across a path—anything to make my progress easier. But the forest was just as thick and foreboding as it had been, and there were no signs of cars, streets, houses, or anything that might bring me comfort. My energy waned. I pictured Rand, but it didn't work.

Okay, I was lost.

The hoot of an owl in the foliage above nearly caused the death of me and I pressed my hand to my heart, thinking it might stop.

"Oh my God, you stupid bird."

The bird just spun his head around like he was impersonating Linda Blair.

I collapsed against the bird's tree and tried to catch my breath. Deciding I needed a break, I dropped into a seated position amid a pile of pine needles. What in hell was I going to do? I was lost, hopelessly lost. I'd never been good with directions. Just last year I'd learned to tell east from west by memorizing the mnemonic: Never (North) Eat (East) Shredded (South) Wheat (West).

God, I was going to die out here.

"It seems you have been quite a naughty girl." Sinjin's voice was like a spike right through my ear.

I screamed and jumped up from the bed of needles but couldn't see him. "Goddamn you!" I yelled, pressing my hand to my chest again. My dad had died from a heart attack—I wondered if he'd ever known any vampires.

He stepped out from behind the tree I'd been sitting under. The bastard must've been tracking me all the way, playing a game of cat and mouse. Then it was clear—the unlocked doors, no one around … he'd set it up. Suddenly I was livid. "Why track me all this way and let me think I was getting away, you asshole?"

He wore a smirk on his arrogant face. "Poppet, what language!"

He took a step toward me, and I jumped back, not wanting to be within grasp.

"I'm not going back there," I said between gritted teeth. "You'll have to kill me before I'll go back there."

He laughed. "That can be arranged, love."

"I'm not going to make this easy on you. I'll fight you tooth and nail," I seethed.

"Let the games begin."

I braced myself, but it didn't make any difference. Sinjin moved so quickly, he was directly in front of me before I knew what happened. I didn't even get a chance to gasp before his iron hand wrapped around my throat, pushing me against the tree. The bark lodged into my spine as I tried to fight the vampire, my legs and arms flailing.

He wasn't exerting much pressure on my throat because I could breathe and frolic about as easy as you please. I think it was more just a show of what he was capable.

"I tire of games, pet," he said drolly.

His arrogant tone annoyed the crap out of me, but it was no use. I stopped flailing and accepted my defeat by dropping my head.

Sinjin chuckled. "Ah, poppet, do not look so miserable."

As soon as he separated himself from me, I called on my fox. I didn't miss the pure shock that registered on the bastard's face when I dropped into a fox and scurried away, darting into the undergrowth of the forest.

"Very smart, love."

He was after me. I could hear leaves crunching under his feet, while he moved as quickly as the wind. Now I zig-zagged with purpose, trying to throw the vampire off. The protection of the forest served me well as I scurried between bushes.

Apparently, Sinjin was pretty smart. He intimated which direction I would go and landed on me like a football player would the football. I grunted which came out as a squeal in my fox voice.

Righting himself, he held my small furry body up to his chest, and even though I didn't want to, I knew I'd have to change back to my human likeness soon. It was too exhausting to maintain my fox shape. Truth was, I was already exhausted. I toyed with the idea of sinking my sharp little teeth into him but I didn't want to swallow any of his blood, afraid I'd be turned into some sort of pseudo-vampire.

I wasn't sure if Sinjin knew what happened when someone shape shifted, but he was about to find out. I shook my head, shaking off the fox likeness and suddenly felt cold and exposed. When he realized I was no longer furry and now naked, his hands coursed down my spine, pulling me into him. If he were capable of breathing, he'd be panting about now.

"You have a … delicious body," he growled.

I couldn't subdue my automatic reaction, which was intense pleasure. I wanted his hands all over me, and the idea made me livid. Here he was, botching my escape, and I wanted to have sex with him? I had to be the dumbest woman alive.

I desperately tried to envision myself in clothes but I couldn't concentrate. He attempted to push me away from him—no doubt, so he could take in every last naked inch of me. I wrapped my arms around his neck and refused to budge. He apparently didn't mind, his hands continuing to caress my naked backside.

"It is soft here, my pet," he said, tapping his foot against the bed of pine needles. "We could do it quickly."

"Shut up," I hissed. "I'm trying to focus. Stop talking."

He laughed, and I was finally able to envision myself in jeans and a sweatshirt. I smiled when I glanced down and found myself attired. Sinjin sighed his displeasure. I attempted to push away from him, but he held me tightly. "Not getting away so easily, poppet."

I pulled my knee up, thinking I could get him in the goodies, but such was not the case. He just laughed and in a split-second move, cornered both my legs between his. I wasn't going to be able to do any bodily harm to him. He was just too strong. Way stronger than Ryder.

"Calm down," he started

"Let go of me!" I yelled and batted my ineffectual hands against his steel chest. I wanted to hate the bastard, but even now, I couldn't. And I also couldn't help the intense heat I felt from being so close to him. The realization pissed me off—how could I have the hots for someone who was going to return me to Bella?

He couldn't seem to shake the grin from his mouth. It was infuriating. "Quiet, poppet. Be civilized and we can be on our way."'

"I'm not going back to Bella's with you."

He released me. "Good, I am not going there anyway."

I was too surprised to try to run away. Well, lot of good it would do me anyway. He was faster than I would ever be. "Where are you going?"

"I am en route to a petrol station three miles from here that has a vehicle waiting for me and for you."

"With Bella in it, no doubt."

He shook his head. "Sorry to mislead you, poppet, but I do not work for Bella."

I laughed with as much sarcasm as I could muster. So not only did the asshole think I was physically weak, but now he was going to add salt to the wound by assuming I was a nitwit? "You've got to be kidding. Is there a sign on my forehead that says dumbass?"

Sinjin's chuckle was rich and throaty. "No, love, there is not. Start walking and I will explain."

I didn't make any motion to follow him. "You expect me to believe you don't work for Bella?"

"Yes I expect you to believe it and no, I do not work for Bella."

He continued forward and when I didn't follow him, he turned to face me with mild annoyance. "You can come with me or you can stay in the forest and wait for Bella to find you."

Even though I had no idea what Sinjin's plan was, I made the split-second decision to go with him. It came down to the fact that I trusted him more than I trusted Bella. The other added bonus was being as far away as possible from Ryder.

I followed Sinjin as best I could through the dense forest, but had a tough time seeing him in the dark night. After fighting against branches that lashed out and caught my face and hair, I relied on my arms to guide me through the shadows of the forest. I'd rather have scratches on my arms than my face. I tripped on something and caught myself before I fell. Thank God I was wearing jeans, otherwise my legs would've been cut up like all hell.

A branch managed to avoid my extended arms and nailed me right in the cheek. "Ow, dammit, I can't see anything, Sinjin."

He slowed down and faced me. "Jump on my back, love, and I will carry you."

I hesitated, heat flushing my cheeks at the idea of being so close to him. With a sigh, I hopped up on his back, and he braced his arms around my thighs.

"Lean into me."

I rested my head against the expanse of his back and couldn't help inhaling the scent of him. It was a mixture of something spicy and cool. The coolness could have just been his body temperature. It felt pretty damn good to be so close to him—even if it was odd not to feel any heat radiating from him. It was sort of like riding on a statue.

"Are you comfortable?" he asked.

208

"You're a bit cold."

He chuckled. "You feel as if you are on fire."

He tightened his grip around my thighs making me very aware of his physical power. He was so strong, there'd be no way I'd be able to defend myself if he did decide to attack me. I suddenly wondered why I'd gone with him. Why did I trust him?

After another few minutes, something buzzed in his pocket. He stopped walking and dropped his arms from around my thighs. I slid down his body. Leaning against a tree, he fished in his pocket and produced a cell phone.

"We are en route," he said, his voice suddenly matter-of-fact and all business. "Perhaps ten minutes."

Immediately my instincts were on alert. Who the hell was he working with?

He hung the phone up and returned it to his pocket. His eyes glowed slightly yellow as he glanced at me. "Ready?"

I shook my head, crossing my arms against my chest. "No, not until you tell me what's going on."

"We do not ..."

I took a step back. "I'm not going with you until you tell me what the hell is going on."

He sighed and was quiet for a moment before shaking off his annoyance. "I was never working for Bella. I have been allied against her since I met you."

My mouth fell open. I wasn't sure what to think right away. Did I dare believe him? "Then who are you sided with?" I couldn't keep the wariness from my voice.

"That is not important now." He bent down and motioned for me to resume my place on his back. I hesitated. "The longer we wait here, the better chance Bella has of finding us, poppet."

I was quiet as I considered it. The call to avoid Bella was stronger than the call to learn what Sinjin's plan was. As soon as we were in a safer place, I would insist he tell me everything. Well, that's what I promised myself anyway.

"Sinjin?"

"Yes?" His voice almost sounded like the hiss of a snake.

"Will you promise me something?"

"Depends on what it is."

I wasn't sure why I attempted to get him, a vampire, to promise me anything. If what he said was true, he'd betrayed Bella without a second thought. Who's to say he wouldn't do the same to me?

"Promise me I won't get hurt."

"I promise you." His answer was immediate, his voice solid and unwavering.

I wasn't sure if that was good or bad, but for some strange reason, I believed him. Maybe I was just gullible and naïve. Probably such was the case.

For all I knew, he could promise to keep me safe and turn around and eat me for dinner in the same breath.

I forced thoughts of Sinjin feeding off me to the deep recesses of my mind. It wouldn't do me any good to think about such things now. It would be better to focus on escaping from Bella.

"Do you think Bella knows we're gone?" I asked.

He laughed. "I imagine she is figuring it out."

"Where were you when I was escaping?"

"Keeping Bella pre-occupied," he said, and I could hear the smile on his lips. There was no way I was asking in what ways he was keeping her pre-occupied. The answer was pretty apparent by his tone.

"How did you find me?"

"I have tasted your blood; I can track you anywhere."

I wasn't sure how I felt about that. Granted, it had helped me out in this instance, but now Sinjin could keep tabs on me. Hmm, and Ryder could too, for that matter. If I thought I wanted Ryder dead before, the thought was never as strong as it was now.

I will kill him, I vowed to myself. I didn't know how, and I didn't know where, but as long as there was breath in my body, I would find and kill that damned asshole.

"Why so quiet, pet?"

I wasn't about to share my morose thoughts with Sinjin, so I searched for something else to say. "So you what, teletransported here?"

"Yes, love."

We reached a clearing in the woods, and lights in the distance heralded some sort of civilization. I couldn't help the elation that filled me upon realizing we'd managed to escape the forest and were on our way somewhere.

"Nearly there," Sinjin said as he climbed up a bank. As soon as we reached the wide expanse of grass, he put me down, apparently thinking I could manage on my own the rest of the way. He rubbed his arms against his pants and faced me with a smirk. "You have gotten my legs hot."

I wasn't sure what to say to that. "Sorry."

"Makes me wonder in what other ways you can make me hot …"

I rolled my eyes. Unbelievable, we were running for our lives, and he was thinking about sex. Sinjin had to be the horniest creature I'd ever met. I'd heard somewhere that your average human male thinks about sex on an average of ten times a day. It wouldn't surprise me if Sinjin thought about it ten times a minute.

"Where are we going?"

"To an abandoned petrol station. There should be a vehicle waiting for us."

"Who arranged that?"

"My employer."

"Who is your employer?"

He smiled. "All in good time, poppet."

So we were playing by his rules. I could demand he tell me or throw a temper tantrum, but I doubted it would do any good. And besides, I was looking forward to getting inside the car and turning the heat on full blast.

Sinjin brushed aside a low hanging branch, and we made our way into the clearing. Amid the rubble and ruin, an old British taxicab stood like a huge, black mushroom.

"I expected something better than this old banger," Sinjin muttered. "But I suppose beggars cannot be choosers."

I laughed and watched him open the door for me like a gentleman. A blood-sucking gentleman. I crawled in, my attention immediately drawn to the dashboard as I tried to figure out how the heating worked. Sinjin sat down in the driver's seat and started the old car without a problem.

"Okay, start splainin' Lucy," I said, doing my best Ricky Ricardo impersonation. I still hadn't figured out how to turn on the damn heater.

Sinjin smiled and flicked my hand away, the chill of his skin sinking into me. He was basically dead for all intents and purposes. Sort of a weird thought when he seemed so entirely alive. What struck me as even weirder was the fact that I was lusting after a corpse. Oh, God …

He cranked a lever and depressed a button and heat sailed out of the vents.

"What do you want to know?"

"Well, for starters, where are we going?"

"I am taking you back to Randall."

That was surprising to say the least. I wondered if Rand had been working with Sinjin all this time. The thought that Rand could keep such a secret from me made my stomach churn. "Have you been working with Rand all along?"

Sinjin shook his head. "No."

Well, at least that was a relief. "What if he's no longer at Pelham Manor?" Rand certainly would've been well aware of the fact that Bella knew where we lived. I imagined returning to Pelham Manor might not be the safest thing to do.

Sinjin nodded. "I have wolves tracking him. I know exactly where he is."

"You promise you aren't going to hurt him?"

Sinjin laughed. "You and your promises …" He put his hand on his heart and faced me with a smirk. "I, Sinjin Sinclair, do solemnly promise I will not hurt him. Scouts' honor."

"You didn't say his name."

Sinjin frowned. "I just …"

"You said you wouldn't hurt 'him,' but that could be anyone. Say his name."

He sighed and held up three fingers. "I swear I will not hurt Rand … all. Scouts honor."

Randall was good enough I guess. And what was more, it was probably all I was going to get. I frowned. "Thanks."

"I am on his side."

That sounded weird, especially given Rand's intense dislike for Sinjin. "Are you sure he knows that?"

"You certainly are full of questions, aren't you, poppet? No, he does not know. He thinks I work for Bella, but he will soon find out otherwise."

I settled back in my seat and glanced out the window. I wasn't sure Rand would react to the news as well as I had. He had a definite distrust toward Sinjin, and this news would probably make him distrust Sinjin even more. "So where is Rand?"

He smiled. "He and your friend … Christina …"

"Christa."

"Ah, Christa, are in a hotel in Suffolk County, by the coast."

Suffolk County didn't ring any bells, and I had to wonder why they would've gone there. Not finding an immediate solution, I turned the heat vents so they were facing me and dangled my fingers in the stream of hot air, reveling in the feel.

"Okay, where are we now?"

"We are in Wales, on the opposite coast."

"How long will it take us to get to Rand?"

Sinjin shrugged, "Six hours or so, plenty of time for you to ask me another million questions."

"I probably have that many for you," I said with a slight laugh. "Why don't you just teletransport us there?"

He shook his head and my attention lifted to his dark hair that obscured his ears and curled up and over his collar. "I can only teletransport for very short distances and it takes quite a bit of energy."

"Can you teletransport someone else or just yourself?"

"I could do it with a circus if I could hold onto all of them. Next question."

"Okay, who are you working for?"

"It is a long story, but I suppose we have a while. I am a diplomat of sorts."

"A diplomat?" I repeated, thinking Sinjin seemed nothing like a diplomat. I had in my mind's eye the picture of an elderly man in a navy suit smoking a cigar. Don't ask where it came from, but that's what diplomat said to me. Sinjin was anything but.

"A liaison between the vampires and the Underworld community."

"I know what a diplomat is," I snapped. "I just don't really think of you as one."

"I work for a master vampire whose name is Varick Rapone."

Varick Rapone sounded the quintessential name for a vampire. As I continued to consider it, Jolie Wilkins didn't really sound much like a witch's name. Maybe Regan, I'd always liked that name. Regan Wilkins ... not very witchy either.

"You called yourself a master vampire; what does that mean?"

He grinned—he really liked talking about himself. "Master vampires are those who have survived longer than five hundred years. We are the strongest of all vampires and the highest in the hierarchy."

"So this Varick ..." I started.

"He is over one thousand; he is one of the few. As you can imagine, he is extremely powerful."

I was quiet for a moment as I let all the information seep into me. "So why pretend to join Bella ..." I stopped myself when I realized the answer. "Somehow you heard about me?"

Sinjin nodded. "I was hired to protect you. Varick knew Bella would be after you, so I was tasked with keeping you safe."

"How the hell did you get her to trust you?" I asked.

Sinjin shrugged and looked away. "I did what I had to do."

I didn't want to touch that statement with a ten-foot pole. Instead, I turned to the fact that these creatures knew about my abilities, it seemed, before I did. News travels fast, but in the Underworld community, news travels light-speed fast.

"Are you going to join Rand's side then?"

"I will see what he has to offer and then I will decide accordingly."

"How many vampires have joined Bella?"

"Hundreds, but hundreds are also undecided."

I was quiet as I looked out the window. Thoughts of an Underworld civil war coursed through my mind. It sounded like Bella was recruiting quite the army and I wondered to what purpose.

The silence became too much and I turned on the radio, trying to find something to pull my attention from the thoughts going through my head. Duran Duran's "Rio" blasted out, and I relaxed back into my seat, not caring if Sinjin was an eighties fan or not.

"Did Ryder do anything more than bite you?" Sinjin asked.

The mention of the horrible creature's name sent shivers down my spine. "No."

Sinjin said nothing, but nodded, and I fought to find some string of conversation.

"So is it true what they say about vampires?"

Sinjin grinned wickedly. "That depends, what do they say?"

"That you can't see your reflections?"

He scoffed. "Rubbish. I can see my own reflection. I could not imagine not being able to wake to my handsome face every day," he said with a smile in my direction.

I frowned. "Oh God, vo-mit."

"What else have you heard?"

"Um, that vampires can influence people with their eyes ..."

213

"Yes, that one is true."

"But it won't work with me," I double-checked. If vampire influence did work with witches, then that would certainly explain my attraction to him.

Sinjin quirked a brow. "No, it does not work with you, pet."

Damn. Fresh out of excuses. I guess I was lusting after him of my own stupid accord.

"And what else?" he pressed.

"That they're sexy." I regretted that one as soon as I said it. Statements like that just added sprinkles to a cake that was already flowing with too much frosting, whipped cream, chocolate chips, and gummy bears.

He seemed delighted I'd said it—his lips spreading into a huge smile. "Making love with me would be the best you have ever had."

"Tell me what you really think," I said with a frown, trying to get annoyed with his arrogance. I couldn't hide the blush that climbed up my neck and landed squat on my cheeks. I also couldn't help imagining sex with Sinjin. Egad. "Well, now that we're out of danger, you're back to your sexual self."

"We are not out of danger, and this is just how I am."

I ignored him. "I've heard you can teletransport, which you said was true. Um, what else? How often do you have to eat?"

"Every few days."

"Only humans?"

He grinned and quirked a brow. "Or witches."

"Be serious. Can you feed on animals?"

He nodded. "Yes, though the taste is not the best. Rodents or a dog will keep us alive for a few days. Mind you, we certainly could not survive on them alone. Human blood is truly what we need."

"How did you become a vampire?"

His eyebrows furrowed. "It is a very personal question to ask a vampire."

I dropped my gaze and suddenly found changing the radio station a prime concern. "I'm sorry."

There wasn't anything but commercials and static coming through, so I just opted to turn the stupid thing off.

"I am happy to tell you, but just so you know, most vampires might not respond quite so amiably. I was turned in England …"

"You're English then?" I guess I already knew that based on his accent.

"Are you going to let me finish my story or do you insist on interrupting?" He laughed and it was a charming sound. There was something about Sinjin. I couldn't quite put my finger on it, but he had definitely been hit with the appealing stick.

"Sorry."

"I am English. I was from a very well-to-do family and was quite the skirt-chaser in my time."

I smiled as I thought some things hadn't changed.

"Why are you grinning?"

I was surprised he could see me and then remembered vampires have excellent night vision. "No reason, go on."

"Very well. I had taken a trip to Asia, and I met one of the most beautiful creatures I had ever laid eyes on. She was dark and exotic. I immediately fell in love with her and spent many days and a small fortune on her. One night we made love and she bit me. She gave me the option to become like her or die. I chose life."

I nodded, thinking it a very odd way to be transformed. I wasn't sure if it was in Sinjin's retelling of the story, but it sounded very matter-of-fact and not at all emotional. "Where is this woman now?"

"She was killed hundreds of years ago. Which is just as well because her death freed me."

"Freed you?"

"From serving her. All vampires must serve the likes of their maker. Should that maker die, it frees them from servitude."

"So wouldn't most vampires try to kill their makers?"

He nodded. "Some do try."

From the sound of his tone, it seemed some had tried to do him in. I guess that's what made a master vampire so strong—having to survive constant assassination attempts. "Do you find you have a weak spot for Asian women?" I asked, wanting to change the subject.

He shook his head. "Quite the opposite, actually. Now I find I am attracted to petite, blue-eyed, and fair American women with lush breasts and a bottom that just sings to me."

I rolled my eyes. "You are just like Christa. Neither one of you can go twenty minutes without talking about sex."

"If I had it my way, we would be doing more than discussing bonking."

"Bonking?" I laughed. "What a horrible word."

I couldn't help the warmth that soared through me. I leaned against the seat, and for the first time that night, thought about how happy I was to be away from Bella, how truly happy I was that Sinjin wasn't one of her minions. Well, that I hoped he wasn't. For all I knew, maybe this was another trap. I pushed the thought aside; it would do me no good. I had no alternative at this point.

"Are you tired?" he asked.

"A bit."

"We have quite a long drive. You should take a nap. I will knock you up when we get there."

I just shook my head, thinking he came up with these phrases just to taunt me. "You mean wake me up?"

Sinjin chuckled.

I sighed. "I'm going to sleep now."

For some reason, I actually felt safe in his hands.

TWENTY ONE

When I woke up, it was still dark. It had to be dark in order for Sinjin not to burn up and die, sunlight being the equivalent of a vat full of acid dumped over your head.

"We are here," Sinjin said.

I rubbed my eyes and looked outside. I wasn't sure what town we were in, but after taking in the small Victorian hotel and the empty coastline surrounding it, I imagined it wasn't a large one.

"He is in room one and twenty," Sinjin said with a smile. "I will wait here until you explain the situation."

I nodded. "Thanks, Sinjin."

I opened the door and headed into the hotel. I couldn't wait to see Rand, to throw my arms around him, to let him know I was safe. I'm not sure why I was nervous as I approached Rand's room, but I was all the same. When faced with his door, I didn't bother knocking. Instead, I slowly turned the knob, and the door easily opened.

Rand stood at the windows, facing away from the door. I could just make out his profile as he stared into the night. He was mumbling to himself, although what he said, I couldn't understand. His button down shirt hung open, his hair disheveled and a few days' growth of whiskers decorated his face. He looked exhausted, yet to me he looked as beautiful as he always had. My heart sung just at the sight of him, and tears already coursed down my cheeks.

He sank onto the edge of the bed and rested his head in his hands, looking prostrate.

"Rand," I said softly.

He jerked his head up, his gaze piercing mine. "Jolie?"

Tears bled freely from my eyes as he closed the distance between us and pulled me against his hard chest. His mouth crushed mine, and I sank into him, wrapping my arms around his waist. The kiss was deeper, more passionate than one we'd ever shared. It told of the sleepless nights, the fear and the ache we'd both known.

"God," he whispered. "Jolie, you don't know how much I've missed you, how worried I've been." He pushed away from me, and I dropped my eyes, not wanting him to witness my tears.

"Are you alright?"

I nodded dumbly.

"Jolie, I …" His voice broke. "It killed me to know Bella had you …" His brows suddenly furrowed. "How did you escape?"

I fended off his question with a wave of my hand. "It's a long story. I'll tell you later …"

He grabbed my face again, kissing me as if he'd never be able to kiss me again. When he pulled away, his face was flushed.

"Is Christa alright?" I asked.

Rand nodded. "Yes, she's in the room next door. She's asleep." He dropped his gaze before bringing it back to my face. His eyes glistened. "You mean everything to me, Jolie."

I just smiled as warmth enveloped me like a comforting blanket. But the warmth was interrupted when Rand's face shadowed with anger seconds later.

"What did that bastard Ryder …?"

The mention of Ryder acted like a knife slicing right through my happiness. "He knocked me out when we heard the howl in the bushes, do you remember?" At his nod, I continued. "Then he took me to Bella. And Gwynn was sided with him all along, I'm sure you already know that now though."

Rand bobbed his head again and parted his lips as if he were going to ask me another question, but I shook my head. I was too concerned with Sinjin waiting out in the car to want to think about the hows, whats and whys of what had happened to me. "Rand, we can discuss all of that later. For now, you should know …"

"I tried to talk to you with telepathy. Why didn't you answer me?"

"Bella had a spell on me, and I couldn't use my magic."

"Did any of them hurt you?"

I could feel time slipping through my fingers like sand. "Rand, Sinjin is with me."

Any joy on his face dissolved. It was like watching a freshly painted portrait in the rain—the colors bleeding down the canvas, stealing the delineation of the subject only to stain the ground in drops of brown.

"What?" he demanded.

My heart was pounding. "Sinjin drove me here. He helped me escape from Bella, Rand. He never truly worked for her—it was all just a front."

Rand shook his head and started pacing the small hotel room, running both hands through his hair. He paused by the door, then turned on the wall with a vengeance, hitting it with a balled up fist, the plaster cracking.

His jaw clenched and his nostrils flared. "Bullshit." He turned to face me again and his face was red with ire. "He brought you here?"

I nodded. If I'd thought it was going to be hard to convince Rand that Sinjin was one of the good guys, now I was wondering if it bordered on impossible. "He's been having you tracked by some werewolves all along. That's how he was able to bring me here."

"And he said he was never working for Bella?"

I nodded, anxiety pounding within me and eyed the window—dawn was on its way, the sky growing lighter. "It's true, Rand. He works for a vampire named Varick something or other."

Rand sighed. "I know Varick, he and Sinjin are cut from the same cloth."

From the sound of it, that wasn't a good cloth.

"Sinjin has his own agenda. I'll not have ..." he started.

"Rand, he helped me get away from Bella. If it weren't for him, I'd never have escaped. You owe it to him to hear him out." I had to catch my breath. "Please, Rand, please just listen to him. Do it for me."

He crossed his arms against his chest. "Go get him."

Relief pounded through me and I wasted no time in hurrying to the door, half afraid he'd change his mind. I skipped the elevator and turning the corner, started down the stairs, walking headlong into Sinjin's hard chest.

I gasped and braced my palms against him, pushing myself back. "What are you doing?"

"I was on my way to see you," he answered with a grin, looking like a naughty child. "I have not got much time left. The sun is coming."

"You were spying on Rand and me, weren't you?" I asked. "Vampires supposedly have excellent hearing ..."

Sinjin grinned, his eyes alight with mischief. "Sounds as if I have my work cut out for me."

"If you mean convincing Rand that you're on our side, yeah you do." I shook my head and turned around, heading back down the hallway. "What are we going to do once the sun comes up?" I asked.

Suddenly I felt him pull me against his chest, one arm wrapped around my upper waist and the other across my chest. My breath caught in my throat, but I couldn't subdue the heat that suffused me.

"I have already booked a room."

His voice whispered across my ear and neck, and I had to steel myself against the exhilaration coursing within me. "Let go," I managed.

"You know I do not like it when you turn your back on me," he whispered again, and his breath danced along the naked skin of my neck like pixie feet.

I pulled his arm from around me and turned to face him. "Shouldn't you be in a coffin or something?"

He shook his head. "Poppet, do you remember seeing a coffin in our room at Bella's?"

"No, I guess not." I again started down the hallway to Rand's room, and paused before one of the hall windows, my eyes on the sky. It was still dark but now more of a blue than black. Sunrise was not far. Why did I seem more concerned about it than Sinjin?

"No need to worry about me, love." Sinjin chuckled, as if reading my mind. "Randall was pleased to see you?"

"Yes," I nodded, thinking Rand had seemed especially pleased to see me. It had been a nice welcome. I couldn't say it would be the same for Sinjin. "What's the story between you two? Why does he hate you so much?"

218

Sinjin didn't get a chance to answer. Rand tore open the door before we even reached it. His gaze drilled into Sinjin, his jaw clenched, his fists balled. "What the hell are you doing here? And don't give me any of the bullshit you fed Jolie."

I slipped past him and unloaded into a chair by the bed. Sinjin halted at the door and I wondered if Rand would allow him inside. Then it occurred to me that in order for Sinjin to enter, maybe Rand had to invite him? That's what the movies made it seem like anyway.

"No bullshit, Balfour, just the truth," Sinjin said, tilting his chin up defiantly.

Randall … Balfour … Why couldn't Sinjin just call Rand by his first name? I supposed, though, that Balfour was better than Randall.

"Let him in, Rand," I said.

Rand frowned but stepped aside. Sinjin swept in as royally as a king, like he owned the place and flashed me a smile. God, but the man was sexy.

Apparently, he didn't need to be welcomed in. Yet another vampire rumor put to rest. Sinjin took a seat next to me and sighed, extending his long legs and faced a very perturbed Rand.

"I have never worked for Bella," he began and clasped his hands together in his lap.

"Do you expect me to believe that?" Rand asked, crossing his arms over his chest to show he clearly didn't.

"I work for Varick, Balfour."

Rand glanced at him with narrowed eyes. "Why did Varick send you?"

Sinjin shrugged. "He wanted me to keep an eye on Jolie. He knew Bella would be after her and he did not want Jolie in the wrong hands."

"Why? What was he afraid of?" I asked, thinking I should somehow involve myself in the conversation.

Sinjin frowned. "Afraid of what, poppet? Why would he be afraid?"

Rand's face colored as his lips tightened into a straight line. I wasn't sure if it was due to Sinjin avoiding the question or the fact that he called me poppet.

"Don't fuck around, Sinjin. He knew Jolie had special abilities. What was he afraid she was going to do?"

Sinjin sighed as if he were not up to a long explanation. "No reason to be a wanker, Balfour. He did not want Jolie to bring the prophet back."

"What prophet?" Rand snapped.

I sighed, here was where the long and convoluted story started. "Bella wanted me to bring back an old woman whom she thought was some prophet. She believed the woman could change history but she had the wrong person." Hmm, maybe it wasn't as long a story as I'd imagined.

"I've never heard of any prophet," Rand said, chewing his lip. "Jolie, you said the woman wasn't a prophet, though?"

"No, she wasn't." But my mind wasn't on the prophet. I was more concerned with our future—what it meant that we no longer had the support of

219

the many creatures we'd been counting on. "Rand, now with Gwynn and Ryder and God knows who else on Bella's side, what does that mean for our army of recruits?"

Rand chuckled but it wasn't a happy sound. "We have no army. Half the recruits were from Gwynn's side."

"Sounds as if you need my help," Sinjin said. He studied his fingernails as if he had zero interest in our conversation.

Rand turned his angry eyes back to Sinjin. "I wouldn't say that yet," he snapped.

"And Trent's pack?" I asked. "What of them?"

Rand nodded. "Trent's pack is still with us. The wolves are the only creatures we have. Everyone else has fallen through."

"And the fairies?" I continued.

Rand shrugged. "They're still neutral. I've tried to get them to side with us but they're avoiding it at all costs. We are in a very bad position."

"I can help you," Sinjin said again.

"That would require my trust, Sinjin …" Rand started.

I stood. "Rand, stop. Think about it. We do need Sinjin's help. Just put aside your differences for a minute." I turned to face Sinjin. "How many vampires are in your lead?"

Sinjin frowned. "Hundreds and two hundred or so follow Bella."

He stood up and faced Rand, suddenly interested. "With our forces, you would be more than able to confront Bella's vampires."

"Then is that your decision?" I asked Sinjin. "Will you side with us?"

Sinjin shrugged and Rand took a step closer to him, until they were eye to eye.

"I will consider you against me if you aren't with me," Rand said between clenched teeth.

"You always were so dramatic, Balfour," Sinjin replied and his lips broke into a grin as if he were incapable of taking anything seriously. "I have been with you all along."

"Why not let me know then? Why pretend you were with Bella?" Rand demanded.

Sinjin shrugged. "I am a vampire—I owe you nothing. Varick told me to protect Jolie, and that is what I did."

"Let's forget all that now," I said, forcing myself between the two. We didn't have time to argue. "We have a major problem here and we need to figure out what to do about it. Rand, with Sinjin's vampires and the wolves, do we have a chance?"

Rand glanced at me and then his gaze returned to Sinjin. "Doubtful. Bella has all the demons, half the wolves and half the vampires."

"And if we got the fairies on board?" I asked. "Would we have a chance then?"

Rand cocked his head and tapped his fingers along his chin. "Yes, we would have a good chance." Then he shook his head. "It's pointless even discussing it. They've already made their decision."

"We have to give it one more shot if they're our only chance to defeat Bella," I insisted.

"Jolie," Rand started.

I took a step closer to him. "Please! We have to try. Who is the person who makes the decision on whether or not they join?"

"The king of the fairies, Odran," Rand said.

"Can you at least get him to meet with us?" I asked.

Rand nodded. "I can try."

Sinjin stood up and clapped his hands together. "I must be returning to my room, the sun is not far. Shall we resume this delightful conversation this evening?"

Rand gritted his teeth. "Yes."

"Very well, until tonight. If you need me, I am two doors down," he said with a smile aimed only at me. "Though I will not be able to assist you until the sun goes down."

Sinjin started for the door.

"Thanks Sinjin," I said.

He smiled and bowed. Rand scoffed and turned away from him, apparently ill at ease with the idea of working with the vampire. Sinjin quirked a brow, kissed the air and blew it toward me, then he left.

"You shouldn't trust him," Rand said, turning back to face me at the sound of the door closing.

I wanted nothing more than to avoid Rand's paranoia. So he'd been sort of right with Trent, who cares? I was pretty sure he was wrong about Sinjin. "Please, Rand, I've had about three hours of sleep."

He didn't respond and I didn't care. There was so much to do, so much to worry about, and I had no idea what to concentrate on first. It was overwhelming and exhausting all at once. I couldn't help my yawn.

"Jolie, you should take a nap."

"I'm fine," I said but just at the mention of a nap, my entire body heaved with the need to lie down and close my eyes.

"You need some sleep. It's going to take me a while to get a meeting with Odran and you need your energy."

"I don't have time," I started.

He frowned. "Jolie, we have all day."

I took a seat on the bed and sighed, starting to untie my shoelaces. I dropped the shoes from my feet and looked up to find Rand watching me. As soon as our eyes met, he closed the distance between us and dropped to his knees. He held each side of my face between his palms and there was a pain in his eyes I'd never seen before.

"I will never let anything happen to you again," he said and kissed me.

221

~

The sun streamed through the windows, and I rubbed my eyes against the onslaught of day. Forcing myself to sit, I stifled a yawn and stretched my arms and legs. The room was quiet. Too quiet. I glanced around and realized Rand was nowhere to be seen.

Eager to hear of any news, I tossed aside the blankets and hobbled to the bathroom. I turned on the cold water and washed my face, hoping to wash away my lethargy. Drying my face, I walked back into the room and my gaze fell to the alarm clock on the bedside table. Noon.

"Sheesh," I whispered to myself and tossed the towel on the bathroom floor. I'd slept over six hours. It wasn't a good feeling—we had lots to do and Rand shouldn't have let me sleep for so long.

I sat back down on the bed. What to do now? I didn't get a chance to make a decision before the door flew open and a smiling Christa swept inside.

"Jules!" she cried and threw her arms around me.

My cheeks were already wet with tears before she even reached me. "Chris, God, it's so good to see you."

She pulled away and faced me with blurry eyes. "I was so worried about you, Jolie. And, Rand, I've never seen him so completely miserable. God, I'm so glad you're back."

She wiped her eyes against the sleeve of her sweatshirt and seemed to be getting herself under control. I sniffled and wiped my eyes, trying to do the same. "God, do I have so much to tell you," I started.

"Did Bella hurt you?" she asked.

I just shook my head, not wanting to revisit any of the painful and ugly memories.

"Ah, the happy reunion," Rand's voice interrupted and I turned to see him standing in the doorway, a brown paper bag in his hand. "I brought a late breakfast."

I smiled and took a seat on the bed. Christa sat next to me. Rand handed us a bag of croissants, scones, and muffins. A breakfast of champions, as far as I was concerned.

I reached for a croissant.

"I was able to get a meeting with Odran," Rand said as he relaxed into an armchair near the bed.

"Odran?" Christa asked.

I nodded and chewed until I was able to swallow my mouthful. "He's the king of the fairies. Our plan is to try to convince him to join our side. Otherwise, it's hopeless. Bella will easily defeat us." It was the Cliff's Notes version.

"Oh," Christa nodded. "When are we meeting with him?"

Rand arched his back, stretching his arms above his head before returning them back to his lap. "Tomorrow morning."

"Fantastic. Where?" I continued.

"Odran lives in Glenmore Forest in Scotland."

"How long will it take us to get there?" Christa asked and I could already see her picturing men in kilts.

Rand shrugged. "All day and into the evening. It's not close."

"So …" I started.

"Maybe eight or nine hours."

Christa groaned. "Ugh, I hate road trips."

I stood up and the same feelings of anxiety I'd been experiencing since yesterday returned anew. "It's past noon now, we need to get going."

Rand nodded. "Odran was kind enough to offer us hospitality in Glenmore tonight. But you're correct, we should leave soon. It's going to take a while to get there."

"Why can't we ever fly?" Christa moaned.

Rand chuckled. "Because, Christa, there isn't a direct flight."

"Fine. Then I'll go pack," she said and started for the door. "It shouldn't take me long."

"What of Sinjin?" I asked, remembering we'd planned on seeing him this evening.

"Odran is our priority," Rand answered and his eyes told me not to argue with him. I imagined he was finding it difficult enough to be allied with the vampire. And anyway, Odran was our priority.

I nodded and neared the desk. Grabbing a sheet of paper, I wrote:

Sinjin,

We've headed to Glenmore Forest in Scotland. We have a meeting with King Odran in the morning. Please call Rand's cell phone tomorrow and we will give you more instruction.

Wish us luck!

J.

Then I jotted down Rand's cell number and sealed the letter in an envelope. I wasn't sure why I bothered writing the letter—if Sinjin really wanted to, he could track me since he'd had my blood. Then I remembered that Ryder could too. For all I knew, maybe he and Bella were tracking me now. I had to swallow the bile that immediately rose up my throat.

"Rand, Ryder can track me."

Rand's color drained. "He drank from you?"

I nodded and Rand shook his head. "Don't worry about that now, Jolie. We'll be safe once we reach Glenmore. Fairy magic is too powerful for Bella."

"Okay." I thought it best to leave out the part where Sinjin had drunk from me also. We needed Sinjin and if Rand knew that little tidbit, I didn't think he could handle it.

"If I ever see Ryder again, I will kill him," Rand said, his eyes deadly.

I didn't respond, didn't tell him that I was reserving that honor for myself, but pulled open the door and headed down the hallway to Sinjin's room, hoping and praying Bella and Ryder weren't hot on our tails.

TWENTY TWO

Trees, trees everywhere but not a place to sleep.

I leaned forward, my breath fogging up the window. In fact, I could see nothing but trees.

"There's nothing here," Christa said.

That was an understatement. If Rand thought Christa would sleep in a tent, he was mistaken. Sorely.

"Where are we staying?" I asked.

Rand smiled and put the Range Rover in park at the mouth of Glenmore forest. "Here."

"Here? Are we camping?" Christa asked, her tone issuing a warning that Rand's answer better not be a "yes."

"No," he said and reached inside his pocket, pulling out a gold key. It was about as long as my middle finger and just as thin.

"This will lead us to the fairy village within Glenmore."

"Where'd you get that?" I asked, in awe. A fairy key ... I don't know—it just sounded so Harry Potter.

Rand shrugged. "As soon as Odran invited us, it appeared in my palm. He said we should just follow it, and it will lead us where we need to go. Everyone ready?"

"Yeah," Christa answered, pushing open her door. "What about our stuff? How long are we going to have to walk? My bag isn't very light."

"Leave all your things here. You'll have no need for them in Glenmore. The fairies do things a little differently," Rand answered.

It seemed like he was purposely being vague and I didn't bother insisting that he enlighten us. I was still tired. It was just past 11:00 p.m., but it felt like I'd been awake an eternity. My nap hadn't done much for me.

I unbuckled my seatbelt and opened the door, feeling the cold air rush in like ghosts. Well, hopefully wherever we were going, it wouldn't take long to get there. Walking in the middle of the night in the freezing cold wasn't my idea of a good time. And knowing the unreliable UK weather, we might just find ourselves in a downpour.

Christa and I joined Rand and watched as the key poised itself in the palm of his hand and like an arrow, pointed forward.

"Wow, that's weird," Christa said.

"Fairy magic," Rand answered with a half smile.

We started walking in the direction the key initiated and found ourselves in the thick and dense forest and wouldn't you know it, raindrops started falling, plunking themselves against my head and face like Chinese water torture.

"Does the key say how long it will take to get there?" I asked grumpily, knowing the answer was a "no" but wanting to share my sour mood, all the same.

"No," Rand answered. He kept his palm out in front of us and the key pointed forward like the figurehead of a woman on a ship. It was just missing a set of huge boobs.

Ferns brushed against my legs and the moss below my feet was like walking on sponges. Well, one thing I could say for Scottish forests was they were beautiful.

After ten minutes of walking straight, I wondered if the key might've been lost. It would have had us turn somewhere, right? How long can you just walk straight? The rain had steadily increased and now the Chinese water torture was more of a downpour. And no one had brought an umbrella. Not that you could have opened it anyway, the trees and foliage were so dense.

"This is fun," Christa snapped and I couldn't keep the smile from my face. I guess I wasn't the only one in a foul mood.

The key then jumped once and faced left, looking like a pointer who'd just found a dead duck. So the thing was working. Smiles alighted on Rand and Christa's faces and I had to wonder if they had also been doubting the key's navigational ability.

"Are there any scary things in the forests of Scotland?" Christa asked, peering around her as if she thought one of those scary things might jump her any second.

"Such as?" Rand asked.

"I don't know, like bears and snakes and bobcats."

"No bobcats. But I think they do have snakes here?" I asked.

Rand nodded. "Black Adders are the most serious. They're poisonous. No bobcats but they do have wildcats."

"What's that?" Christa asked, her voice high and pitchy.

"It's basically a feral pussycat," Rand answered. "The worst it could do is scratch you."

I laughed. "I think we have more to fear from the rain than we do from animals out here, Chris."

The key jumped in Rand's palm, as if annoyed we weren't paying attention to it, and then aimed itself slightly right.

"I think it wants us to go right," I said.

"A right would take us directly into that tree," Christa said and pointed at the tall pine in question.

"Perhaps it wants us to walk to the tree," Rand answered with a shrug.

The pine was bigger circumference-wise than any other trees near it, about as wide as the width of Rand's Range Rover from driver's seat to passenger's. That was its only defining characteristic, otherwise it was just another tall pine tree.

Rand walked directly toward the tree until he stood before it. The key continued to point forward and hopped up and down as if it had to go to the bathroom. He took another step until he could touch the bark. The key lurched from his palm and thrust itself into the bark of the tree, then it cranked to the left and the inside of the tree suddenly became transparent.

"Whoa," Christa said and stepped forward, peering through the tree. I stepped beside her and could see everything behind the tree as if I were looking right through it.

"Who wants to go first?" Rand asked.

Neither of us volunteered.

"Why don't you go first, Rand?" I said sheepishly.

Rand smiled and with a salute, walked into the tree and disappeared. Christa and I faced each other and I took her hand. My heart was pounding like a son of a bitch.

"Ready?"

"Yeah," she said with a nod. The tree was wide enough for us to walk through together, so that's exactly what we did. I closed my eyes and took a step. It was like I was walking through warm water, balmy waves washing over me.

Upon coming out on the other side, I'm not sure what I noticed first: the blooming and enormous flowers growing as tall as my hips; the glowing pixies numbering in the hundreds as they flew from flower to flower; the thatched-roofed houses; Rand in a kilt; or Christa and me in long dresses. I think Rand in a kilt won out.

"What the?" Christa started, looking down at herself. As soon as she saw Rand, she started giggling.

I, myself, couldn't giggle. He looked like a wet dream come to life. His kilt was plaid green and blue and his chest was bare. He was wearing what looked like sandals with leather straps criss-crossing up his calves like what you'd see on a Roman soldier. I had to wonder if there was anything under the kilt. I mean, come on, how could I not?

Forcing my attention from Rand, I glanced down at myself and found the top of my dress was in the peasant fashion—blousy and puckered around my breasts. It had an empire waist and cap sleeves. The material was muslin, white with small yellow flowers. It was so long, I had to lift it in order to see my feet, which were ensconced in what looked like white leather ballet flats. When I leaned forward, my hair fell over my shoulder in a great mass of curls, tied back with a single white ribbon.

Christa's dress was blue and looked much the same as mine, as did her hairstyle. Then my attention fell to my surroundings. It wasn't a large village—maybe twelve thatched roof houses—well, as far as I could see. Circular globe lights as big as large dinner plates hung from the trees and aside from the glow of the pixies, provided the only light.

Flowers of a type I'd never seen before climbed up the trees, only to drop their heads back toward the ground, acting like a canopy of blooms above our heads. Their faces were broad—think sunflowers—and their colors spanned the rainbow: ocean blue, violet, fire engine red, lemon yellow. Some even seemed to reflect the dull light, almost glowing. A pixie landed on one such bloom directly above us; she was maybe the size of my thumb. As soon as she did, the flower wavered back and forth under her added weight and spilled an array of glitter-like prisms against my hair. The smell was like having a perpetual gardenia in your nose.

"Wow, your hair is glowing, Jules," Christa whispered and dabbed at my head with her fingertip. When she pulled it back, the end was covered in glittery dust.

"Oh, neat," I said.

Rand cleared his throat, apparently not as impressed with having glittery hair as we were. Christa and I smiled at one another and took a few steps toward Rand before a family of foxes trotted across the grass before us. I felt like I needed to pinch myself. Disneyland had nothing on this place.

"Have you ever been here before?" I asked Rand.

He shook his head. "It's very rare to get an invitation to a fairy village. I've been to Mathilda's but never to the king's. This is a definite honor."

"What should we do?" Christa asked, her gaze scanning our surroundings.

"I suppose we should walk into the village," Rand answered, looking as much at a loss as we were.

"I like my dress," Christa said.

I didn't get a chance to respond before a small man, maybe five feet tall, approached us. He was about thirty yards away, but it took him only seconds to reach us. Hmm, maybe fairies could materialize just like vampires.

He looked sprightly—thin and even though he didn't have wings, he bounced along as if he did. His hair was short and brown and his face was one you'd never remember—a certain blandness in his features. He, too, was dressed only in a kilt but his chest wasn't one you'd admire. It looked more like a ten-year-old's.

Suddenly I realized the rain had stopped. Come to think of it, I hadn't gotten wet since we'd crossed over into fairy territory. The weather was remarkably temperate.

"C'mon, we're jist aboot tae start supper," the strange little man said in the thickest Scottish accent I'd ever heard. Not that I really knew any Scottish people but anyway … He grabbed my hand and tugged on it and I was left with no choice but to follow him. He was mighty strong for such a little thing and seemed to be in the biggest of hurries.

"They're already blootered, aye, we been waitin' for ye but most ah them are blootered anyway."

I stopped walking and turned to face Rand, at a total loss. "Blootered?" I asked.

"Drunk," Rand said with a smile.

"Aye," the little man said and tapped his foot against the ground. He tugged on my hand again and led us into the center of the small village.

An enormous wooden table piled with breads, meats, fruits, and vegetables stood before us. It was lit with maybe twenty candelabras. The candles were halfway melted, the wax falling from the metal and forming white pyramids on the table. Forty people or so sat around it and all faced us expectantly. At the head of the table, an exquisite gold chair with the face of a roaring lion stood unattended. It was the most incredible chair, or throne, I'd ever seen. The arms of the chair ended in great golden paws, and the lion's tail wrapped around the legs of the chair, glistening in the candlelight. A red velvet pillow leaning against the seat was the only interruption in the solid gold.

"We're ta 'ave a clootie dumplin', yer in luck," the little man said, pulling my attention from the chair.

Of course, I had no idea what a *clootie dumpling* was, but hopefully it was tasty. I was a little peckish, as Sinjin would say. The little man didn't let go of my hand but directed me to a vacant seat next to the gold chair and motioned for me to sit down. I did so as he took Christa's hand and seated her across from me. He then took Rand's arm and led him to the far end of the table. I smiled and gave him a little wave. He just frowned, apparently ill at ease with being relegated to the end of the table. The little man returned and took a seat next to Christa. On my other side was a child with red hair and freckles. He smiled shyly.

"Hello," I said.

"Ello," he responded and then giggled, dropping his gaze to his lap.

Still, the gold chair remained empty.

"Can you understand me?" Christa leaned forward and asked the boy. I couldn't keep the smile from my face.

"Aye," the boy said, his eyebrows furrowed.

"Chris, they're speaking English," I whispered.

"Oh," she said and settled back into her seat.

The boy nudged me. "He's a right diddie, so he is," he said and nodded his head in the direction of the little man. By the expression on his face, I didn't imagine he liked the man. "Aye, a clipe that one is."

The man frowned at the young boy, his face growing red. Then his gaze found mine. "Doona bother aboot him, he's jist a wee bugger."

The boy turned angry eyes on the man. "Blow it out yer arse!"

Christa and I couldn't help our giggles as the man stood up and looked like he was going to come around the table to reprimand the boy, but his attention fell beyond the boy and he dropped into a low bow. As soon as he did so, everyone at the table inclined their heads and stared into their laps. I immediately followed suit and glanced at Christa to make sure she was doing the same. She was. Phew.

"Ye can raise yer heads." The voice was deep and everyone immediately obeyed, their gazes resting on the person directly across from them. I faced Christa, but out of the corner of my eye, I watched a man tower over the golden chair.

"At ease," the man said and conversation ignited along the table like fire. When I met his eyes, he was staring directly at me.

He was beautiful. His long blond hair fell about him in a mass of waves, paling against the bronze of his body. And his eyes were the color of amber. His face was angular and his lips full. He, too, was wearing a kilt. I couldn't help my eyes as they traversed his broad build and intimidating stature. His chest was completely hairless.

I had no idea what was proper protocol for meeting the king of the fairies and immediately stood, breaking into a deep curtsey. Christa, watching me, did the same. There was a round of giggles and chuckles, and I was embarrassed to realize I'd done the wrong thing. Crap, well I was a foreigner, what did they expect?

"I am Odran," he said with a deep smile and offered me his hand. That was when I realized I was still stuck in my curtsey. My thighs were already straining in the squat. I took his hand and stood, my legs wobbly. I really needed to get to the gym.

"I'm Jolie," I said. "And this is Christa."

Odran continued to hold my hand as he faced Christa and offered her his other hand.

"And our boss, Rand is at the end of the table," I added.

"Aye," Odran said and seemed completely uninterested in anything having to do with Rand. I couldn't help my smile. Rand was so far down the table, I couldn't see his reaction, but I would've bet he was frowning.

Odran held both our hands out before him like we'd won a contest or something. "Welcome."

Then he dropped our hands and took a seat.

"Thank you for your hospitality," I said and nervousness twittered within me.

"Aye," Odran said and picked up a goblet in front of me. The table fell silent again. Grasping a pitcher next to him, he filled the goblet with a thick reddish liquid that I guessed was wine.

"Mead fer ya, lass."

I smiled and accepted the goblet. I'd heard of mead. I think it was made from honey—definitely alcoholic. I was a fan of anything sweet so it sounded good to me. "Thank you."

He filled Christa's goblet and handed it to her. After filling his own, he lifted it and faced the table. "God save the king," he said and downed the drink. Unable to keep the smile from my lips, I drank to the king and his health.

As soon as Odran made his toast, if that was considered a toast, the table erupted into conversation again, and everyone started passing food this way and that. Odran simply watched them as the first plate went around. The boy handed it to me.

"Fer the king," he whispered.

229

I nodded and handed it to Odran. He accepted it but set the plate between the two of us. He handed me what appeared to be a wooden spoon. "We shall share, ye an' I," he said.

Okay, that was sort of weird, but when in Rome, I guess. He took a bite of what looked like meat stewed with vegetables and then motioned for me to do the same. I chased a piece of stew meat around the bowl, but the damn thing was near impossible to catch. As far as I was concerned, the fork was a much better invention.

Odran watched me, amusement in his raised eyebrows. He took the spoon from me and rested it against the table. Using his own, he spooned some of the meat and brought it to my lips. Okay, if I was surprised to be sharing a meal with him, I was even more surprised to have him feeding me. But, like the good little guest I was, I opened my mouth and accepted the spoonful.

I glanced at Rand, nervous he might be watching me, but the entirety of his attention pivoted on a raven-haired fairy woman. The fairy in question sat so close to him, she appeared to be his Siamese twin. Her giggling combined with his chuckles annoyed the hell out of me.

I stopped chewing and swallowed, the lump feeling like an enormous and reluctant snail as it went down my throat.

"Ye must chew it, lass," Odran said with a great chuckle.

I reached for my mead and downed it, dislodging the lump in my throat. Odran took the goblet from my hand and refilled it. If I didn't know better, I'd have thought he was trying to get me drunk.

"How long have you lived in this village?" I asked, trying to fill the awkward silence.

Odran shrugged. "This isna ma village, lass."

"We thought we were in the king's village," Christa said, sounding pissed off.

Odran just shook his head. "I couldna invite ye to ma village, it's forbidden."

I nodded, I guessed that made sense. We were just strangers, after all. It was amazing in and of itself that we were even here now. I guessed there was no such thing as terrorists in the fairy community.

"Oh," Christa said with a nod then finished her mead. Odran was quick to refill it.

"Mathilda an' Gor told me 'bout yer abilities, lass."

"They've been tutoring me in magic. I've been very lucky."

He nodded. "Aye. I only agreed ta meet ye an' yer friends because Ah've heard ah yer incredible abilities. I had ta see fer maself."

I wasn't sure what he was expecting to see. It wasn't like I walked around with a big sign that said: *I not only see dead people, but I bring them back to life.* But whatever he was seeing now, he seemed to like. His constant stare and unbroken attention was proof enough. Just a few inches from me, he downed his mead just as quickly as I had. It was like an unspoken drinking contest and even though I'm not a drinker, I couldn't seem to stop myself.

230

"More, lass?" His breath smelled of honey, and I was overcome with the need to taste his lips. He dropped his hand to my thigh and rubbed it up and down and I closed my eyes, trying to keep the sigh of pleasure from my lips.

Jolie. It was Rand's voice and my eyes flashed open. He was like a chastity belt personified.

What? I asked and my voice and my thought were none too friendly.

Don't drink any more mead. It's tainted with a love charm. Odran wants you in his bed, so unless you plan on being there tonight, I suggest you take it easy.

Okay, that explained it. Usually I wasn't so ready to jump a hot guy's bones. I immediately pulled away from Odran and searched the table for water.

"Whit are ye lookin' fer, lass?" Odran whispered into my ear.

"Water," I managed, trying to fight the power of the mead within me. Suddenly, I was pissed off. Who did this guy think he was? Okay, he was the king but seriously, WTF?

Christa handed me a jug of water and I eagerly poured myself a glass, downing it in one swallow. "Christa, have some water," I said, not wanting Odran to get any ideas about her either.

Christa nodded and poured herself a glass. "So what can fairies do?" she asked.

Odran chuckled deeply. "Whatever ye like, lass. Shall we put oan ah show fer ye?"

Christa didn't answer right away but leaned forward. "What?"

I shook my head and faced Odran. "Yes, we would love to see a show, wouldn't we, Christa?"

She nodded encouragingly. "Yeah, that would be really cool."

Odran reclined into his chair. The lion face was just above his now and in the lion's features, I saw Odran's—broad and strong. I suddenly was overcome again with the need to kiss him.

That goddamned mead was killing me. Odran, as if sensing my lusty thoughts, topped off my goblet.

"Drink, lass."

I shook my head. "Thanks, but I've had enough."

He clapped his large hands and the table fell silent. "Magnus, we shall 'ave some entertainment," he said.

Magnus stood and nodded. He was maybe five-ten and lean, also clothed only in a kilt. His dark hair was long and reached his lower butt. He wasn't quite as broad as Odran, but broad enough.

He walked around the table until he was before us and took a great breath. Then he glanced at Christa and spun so quickly, he looked like the Tasmanian devil or something. As soon as he stopped spinning, Christa stood in his place—well, that is, he took the form of Christa.

"Wow," she said with a huge smile. "God, I really love my dress."

I clapped. Even though I knew the spell—Mathilda had taught me how to change my outward appearance—it was still entertaining. "Very good!"

Magnus smiled and spun again, this time taking my form. Talk about weird to see yourself out of yourself—like an out of body experience, not that I'd ever had one. Magnus, still looking like me, walked toward Odran and trailed his hand against the king's chest.

Odran chuckled deeply and leaned into me. "I would much prefer it ta be the original, lass."

I just laughed, finding fairy magic extremely amusing. Magnus walked back around the table and spun again, this time taking Rand's form.

"Rand!" Christa yelled out with a giggle.

Magnus imitated Rand to a T—holding his chest out high and looking every inch the self-impressed warlock. Then he dropped his arms forward and pretended to be a gorilla, hopping around and grunting.

I was hysterical. The boy at my side pointed at Magnus and tears streamed down his face, he was laughing so hard.

Very funny, Rand's less than thrilled voice interrupted my thoughts.

I can't remember the last time I laughed so hard.

"Dinnae forget ta eat, lass," Odran said and spooned me another mouthful. I dutifully accepted it, but my eyes were on Magnus as I awaited his next trick.

After another half an hour, Magnus had turned himself into a giant snake, which had nearly caused the death of Christa. Then he'd made up for it by presenting each of us with a fistful of flowers. He was an excellent entertainer and although I'd enjoyed myself, I was eager to know if the fairies would join us or not. Thoughts of the impending war were never far from my mind.

Magnus bowed and the entire table lit into a chorus of clapping and cheering. The candles had burnt all the way to their stubs and it looked as if everyone had finished their dinners.

"Didnae ye enjoy that, lass?" Odran whispered in my ear.

"Yes, I did very much. Thank you."

He leaned against me again and toyed with a lock of my ridiculously long hair. "I desire ye, will ye have me?"

"What?" I asked, sounding like Christa. Then I realized what he was asking—me to go to bed with him! "No, no I will not," I said, amazed that he was even asking. Well, one thing I could say for creatures of the Underworld—they were extremely forward. "I didn't come here to sleep with you."

He sighed and pulled away from me. "Aye. We can discuss yer reasons fer comin' on the morrow."

"Why won't you support us?" I insisted.

He shook his head. "Please, lass, tomorrow. I cannae think oan it now."

He faced the table and clapped his large hands together. The table fell silent and all eyes centered on the king. "I retire an' bid ye all a good evening."

He stood and extended his hand toward me. Not knowing what else to do, I took it and stood. I sought Rand's attention, but he just gazed at his lap and shook his head as if at a total and complete loss.

"Please, lass, if ye should change yer mind, use this," he said and handed me a key. I could only assume it was the key to his bedroom. I wanted to hand it back, but thought that might be rude, so I just took it with a nod.

Everyone bowed their heads again. Except for me. I watched him and he watched me. "I hope ta see ye later, lass."

"Sorry to disappoint you."

He chuckled and strode away, his magnificent hair gracing his ass. Hot damn. I couldn't blame the mead for the current feelings flowing through me. I hadn't had any to drink in over an hour now.

I don't know how you get yourself into these situations, Rand's voice interrupted my appreciation of Odran's taut backside.

I didn't know what to think, so I didn't think anything at all.

TWENTY THREE

I woke to the sound of someone tapping on the door. With a groan, I rolled over. "Yes, hello?" I managed in a voice two octaves deeper than normal.

"Lass, the king will see ye this mornin'," a voice called out.

"Okay, I'll just be a minute, thanks," I croaked, wondering what the hell time it was. Leaning forward, I pushed the drape from the window and found it was early morning; the light still had a tinge of blue and hadn't matured into the full yellow of midday. I sat up and rubbed my eyes, yawning. I'd slept pretty damn well. Luckily, Odran hadn't tried to woo me into his bed after he'd retired the night before.

I dropped my feet to the floor, wanting nothing more than to crawl back into bed and close my eyes. Tossing the blankets aside, I was suddenly reminded I was naked. As soon as I'd been ready to go to sleep last night, my clothes had disappeared—melted off me into nothing.

I stood up, wondering if fairy magic would automatically clothe me again and what-do-you-know, it did. I found myself dressed in a butter yellow gown made of something like chiffon. The lace sleeves were long, the bust low cut and the waist still empire. Hmm, so I was dressed more formally today. Maybe because we had business to discuss with the king?

I took a few steps and faced a full-length mirror. Not bad. My hair hung freely about my shoulders in blonde ringlets and my face didn't have any of the bloating it normally did upon waking. You know how you get that sleep-swollen eye thing and basically look like a pimple? Yeah, no pimple here.

Without a toothbrush to speak of, I imagined rinsing with Listerine and could taste the stingy aftertaste of acerbic mint.

I opened my door and narrowed my eyes as a burst of dawn broke through the trees, its rays dancing on my face. The scent of dew and early morning was thick in the air. Shielding my eyes, I noticed the village was very much awake. An old man yelled at a cow, hundreds of pixies busied themselves with the gardens, pruning leaves and watering, and two young boys whitewashed the walls of a cottage across the way from mine.

"Mornin', miss." The little red-headed boy from last night skipped by and gave me a big smile.

"Good morning," I said to his retreating back.

I couldn't help the river of nerves flowing through me. Today was a very important day—really the course of our potential success in warring with Bella depended on it. And how was I going to somehow convince Odran he needed to join us? I had no freaking idea. It probably hadn't helped things that I hadn't accepted his offer last night. Not that I regretted it. But, still, it probably hadn't helped.

"This way, lass." The same little man who'd led us to the table last evening suddenly appeared in front of me as if the air had choked on him and spit him out.

Taking my hand, he led me away from the cottages, down a grassy knoll that overlooked a valley of pine trees. I found Odran sitting on a blanket that was bedecked with blue and purple tulips and daffodils, fruits of every sort, breads, and puddings. Unlike last night, I didn't await the king—he awaited me. He sat rod straight, his eyes fixated on me as I made my way toward him.

"Good morning, Your Highness," I said but skipped the curtsey this time. Hell, I still didn't know if Your Highness was even the right appellation. This royalty stuff was getting really old.

He stood. He was wearing a kilt but this one was of a different plaid, the colors of the royal sort—purple and blue. Of course, he wasn't wearing a shirt and of course, my eyes took in his chest with pleasure, heat spiraling through my stomach.

His face was stoic, his eyes revealing nothing. "Lass," he said. His eyes fell to the man who'd led me to him. Odran nodded and the man left with a little hop.

"Where are my friends?" I asked, suddenly feeling ill at ease.

Odran sighed and my nervousness turned to anxiety. "I wanted only ta meet with ye, lass."

I nodded and refused to start freaking out ... yet. So he just wanted to meet with me. That was still in the realm of normal. I mean, he did seem to have some sort of connection with me, based on last night anyway. Okay, granted the mead had been tainted but even without that, I'd say there was something between us.

"Okay," I said, my voice sounding none too sure. "I imagine you know of Bella's plans?" I figured I might as well jump right into it.

"Aye, lass, aye," Odran said and reached for my hand. "Sit."

I quickly took a seat on the edge of the blanket, wrapping my arms around my legs. Odran sat beside me. Stretching his long legs out before him and crossing them at the ankles, he leaned back against his elbows and exhaled.

"Are you going to answer my questions now?" I asked, not sure what his plan was but not wanting him to sidestep mine.

He turned to me and a smile brightened his entire face. It was so disarming, I nearly dropped my defenses. But I knew better. Odran couldn't be trusted.

"Aye, lass, but furst let us break our fast." He lifted a bunch of red grapes and pulled against the vine in a tug of war. It was like I was having breakfast with Bacchus or something. Once he freed the grape from the vine, he held it up to my mouth.

235

"I prefer to feed myself, thanks," I said and took the grape between my fingers. I dropped it into my mouth and the flavor burst into tiny drops of delight on my tongue. It was the sweetest grape I'd ever tasted and my stomach groaned with hunger. Odran eyed it with quirked brow and the flush of embarrassment claimed my cheeks.

"Lass, afore we discuss yer reasons fer being here, cannae we discuss jist one other thing?" Odran asked.

I nodded. "As long as we can talk about you joining Rand and me, yes."

"I doona need yer answer right away, lass, boot I want ye ta consider livin' with me."

I choked on nothing. "What?"

"Not here, ah course," Odran continued, completely ignoring my outburst. "Ma village is mooch larger an' more … coomfortable than this one, lass. Ye wouldna be unhappy there. Ye wouldna want fer anything."

Then it occurred to me—why would Odran want me to live with him? It wasn't my pretty face, and it wasn't my witty conversation. He wanted me for my talent. As usual, the creatures of the Underworld were always looking out for themselves.

"Why?"

"I find maself taken with ye, lass."

What a load of … "Taken with me?"

"Aye, lass, yer fair face an' amicable company …"

"That's the biggest load of crap I've heard in a long time," I snapped. Odran's eyes widened in surprise. I guess he was used to women jumping at his blatant lies. Well, I was human and used to players. Hell, I'd dated one. "Why don't you drop the act, Odran, and tell me what you really want from me."

"Why, lass, ye doona do yerself justice."

I shook my head. "Okay, granted, I know you want to have sex with me, but having sex with me and wanting me to join your village are two different things. You're not smooth enough, Odran, I can read you like a book."

He sighed. "I shoulda known ye wouldna be easy, lass."

"Okay, so why don't we try this again. Starting with the truth, this time."

Odran nodded. "Very well. Ye have a unique ability. I want that ability. Ye would strengthen the fairy power, lass." Then he smiled. "An, as ye say, I would like ta bed ye."

Well, at least I was getting the truth now. But that didn't change the fact that it pissed me off. "Well, regardless of what you would like, I'm not interested. Thanks all the same."

Odran chuckled. "Think on it, lass. I know yer offended now, boot think on it. The fairy community is the oldest ah the creatures. We've the most power an' we can offer ye safety."

My eyes narrowed. "Speaking of how powerful you are, let's discuss why I came here in the first place. You are aware that Bella will consider you an enemy if you don't join her?"

He sat up straight and grabbed another grape, rolling it around in his hand aimlessly. "Aye, Ah'm not worried 'bout Bella, lass. She couldna defeat us." He wound his elbow back and launched the grape into the air. We both watched as it hit the bark of a tree and disappeared into the undergrowth.

"Okay, well that's fine and good but what about the other creatures of the Underworld? Half of them are against her and she'll wipe them out."

He faced me again and his eyes were sharp, predatorily so. "Aye, an' she plans ta become queen herself."

Wait, what? I wore my shock. "What are you talking about?"

Odran shook his head like I was stupid or something. Hmm, I could say that Scottish men didn't hold quite the attraction for me that they had yesterday. "Doona ye think that Bella would've come here ta try ta get us on her side, lass?"

Well, crap and a half ... no, I hadn't considered that. "She did?"

"Aye, threatened us might be the better word. Her plan is ta become queen ah all creatures ah the Oonderworld."

"And you as king?" I put the final puzzle piece in place.

"Aye, lass." He picked up another grape and launched it again, this one missing the tree and disappearing into the pine needles.

"And? What was your response?" I demanded.

Odran chuckled. "Ma response, lass, was ah no. I doona need ta join with anyone, we're powerful enough as it tis. We prefer ta keep ta ourselves. Let the other creatures war among themselves. If they kill each other, it matters noothing ta me."

Okay, that didn't sound good. And it surprised me. You'd think that creatures of the Underworld would have more of a care for one another, but the more I got to know them, the more I found that wasn't the case.

"You don't care if the other creatures destroy themselves? What of the Lurkers?"

"Lurkers?" he asked with a laugh, shaking his head. "We've never dealt with them, lass."

"Okay, then what about the other creatures of the Underworld?" I repeated. "You don't care what happens to them?"

"They matter noothing to us. They are the squabbles ah children."

It was beginning to look like there was no light at the end of this tunnel. Frustration and fatigue beat down on me until my shoulders sagged. "So you won't join us?"

Odran held my gaze, strong and relentless. "No, lass, I willna."

"Because you don't care what happens to us?"

He shook his head. "I doona care what happens ta the rest ah them. I care what happens ta ye."

"Because you want to use me for your own needs," I finished as any warmth I might have harbored for him dried up within me like water in the desert.

"Those are yer wards, lass, noot mine."

"If I agreed to help you, would you consider it then?" I asked, my tone suddenly hopeful.

"I willna consider it at all, lass, it would mean the death ah many ah ma men. I doona think yer side is capable ah defeatin' Bella. An' puttin' the lives ah ma men under yer lead ... I willna think on it."

"Rand is very powerful," I said, my lips tight. "We also have one of the strongest vampires who has hundreds in his lead. And I thought you believed me to be powerful?"

"Rand was taught magic from the fairies, lass. Vampires are destroyed by the light ah the sun an' ye, lass, ye are powerful boot not in fightin'. Ye are powerful in creatin', not destroyin'."

I stood up, furious. Furious with Odran, but more so with myself. How stupid I'd been to actually believe this asshole would help me. What a waste of time. And what would we do now? Fight Bella and die? Give in and join her?

"How can I prove to you that I'm powerful enough?"

Odran shook his head. "Ye couldna, lass."

I wasn't taking no for an answer. The futility of my situation echoed through me until I could feel it in every part of my being. Odran was our only chance to beat Bella. "There must be some way I could prove myself to you. You name it."

He was quiet for a minute. "I would believe in ye if ye could defend yerself against ma best fairy ... in magic."

Well, crap, that sounded doable, didn't it? It wasn't like he was asking me to defeat someone, just defend myself. I'd think my magic had advanced enough that I could handle it. "Defend myself? Against magic?" I repeated.

"Ay, lass, then I would believe in yer magic. But tis silly discussin' it. Ye couldna take on a master ah magic. It'd surely kill ye."

I ignored him. In fact, I'm not even sure I really heard the "kill ye" part. My mind was completely stuck on the fact that I'd found a chink in Odran's armor, a way to get him to join us. That was all that mattered. "Let's just say, for the sake of argument, that I did take on your fairy and was able to defend myself from him. Would you join us then?"

Odran was quiet again. Finally, he nodded and my heart swelled. "Aye, lass, I would join ye if ye could defend yerself against ma fairy."

I guess everyone did have his or her price. "Then I accept."

Odran's eyes grew wide. "Nay, lass, I thought ye were speakin' in generalities. Tis too dangerous. Ye would be killed. I'll not 'ave that oon ma conscience."

I narrowed my eyes. "Are you taking back your word, Odran? Does the word of a fairy mean nothing?"

His face colored and his jaw was tight. "I am no fibber."

"Then it's set."

"Lass ..."

"My mind is made up, Odran."

He stood up and towered over me. "Ye are too big fer yer britches," he said in a thunderous voice. Color stole his cheeks and just as quickly, bleached away into golden skin. His lips relaxed into the slightest hint of a smile. He ran a finger down the side of my face. "Sooch courage."

Well, courage or no courage, all I could do was hope and pray that I'd be able to defend myself against fairy magic. We needed Odran on our side, but I also wanted to live.

~

Twenty minutes later, I stood in what looked like a Roman amphitheatre—like the Coliseum. Only much smaller. Instead of holding fifty thousand spectators, this one could probably hold two hundred, maybe. I guess that included me and the fairy who was going to kill me.

The buzz of excitement filled the air. As soon as I walked into the arena, the crowd grew silent and as one, turned to watch me approach their king. I imagined there were fairies here from neighboring villages because the fairies in Glenmore alone never could've filled all the bleachers. Odran sat in his throne looking as stoic as a statue—staring straight ahead, his eyes focusing on nothing. I had yet to see Christa or Rand.

"Where are my friends?" I asked.

He dropped his gaze, but his mind was still elsewhere, his eyes just as vacant as they had been. "Comin', lass."

I nodded and glanced around, extremely uncomfortable with the fact that I'd have an audience. I'm not sure why, but it seemed like it made the task at hand that much more real. Or maybe I was just embarrassed with the idea of losing in front of two hundred people. Course, if I lost, I'd probably be dead, and it's hard to be embarrassed when you're dead.

"Lass, please reconsider this foolishness."

I shook my head immediately. "If you won't reconsider joining us, then I won't reconsider taking on your fairy."

I'd made up my mind. Well, really, it seemed the only way to get him to join us and when you're stuck between a rock and a hard place ... you get it. Maybe I was just being stupid, but defending myself didn't sound like it would be too difficult. It wasn't like hand to hand combat like it had been with Ryder. Yeah, piece of cake.

"What's going on?" Rand demanded.

I turned to find anxiety written in his wide eyes and tight lips. The little man who'd met me this morning had led Rand into the amphitheatre.

I started toward him. "It was the only way, Rand."

"What was the only way?" He grabbed my shoulders, shaking me as if trying to get the words out faster than I could say them. "What the hell have you done?"

"She's agreed ta defend herself against my best fairy," Odran said.

Rand glanced up at him, fire spitting from his eyes. "No, your fairy will kill her."

A surge of anger spiraled through me. Why did everyone doubt me? I wasn't sure if my own sense of bravado was misplaced or stupid, but either way, it hurt to be constantly reminded that I wasn't powerful enough merely to defend myself.

Odran nodded glumly. "Aye, Ah've told the lass boot she is determined."

Rand faced me again. "Jolie, you will die, do you understand?"

"I just have to defend myself," I repeated what I'd been telling myself over two hundred times already.

Rand shook his head. "It doesn't matter. His strongest fairy could kill you without even trying." He faced Odran again. "Call this off, Odran, Jolie won't fight your fairy."

Odran shook his head. "I cannae call it ooff, it tis doone."

"Goddammit!" Rand yelled and then immediately fell silent, his eyes pensive. His jaw was so tight, it twitched. "Let me take her place."

"Rand, no." This was my fight. "I have to do this."

Odran shook his head again. "I grow tired ah this argument. Either step aside or I'll 'ave ye restrained."

Rand's eyes were wild. "Jolie, run. Run as fast as you can."

No sooner did he say it than two fairies grabbed his arms, pulling him away from me. Rand's face was an angry mask, outrage etching his lips and eyes. He broadsided one fairy with a burst of magic but as soon as he did so, another four surrounded him, all of them livid. Tears blossomed in my eyes as I watched him struggle to free himself.

What in the hell had I gotten myself into?

"Run, Jolie," he yelled, still flailing against his captors.

"Remove him," Odran ordered and then faced me. "Doona attempt runnin', lass. Ye have made yer bed."

And now I would lie in it. I said nothing but nodded, resigning myself to my fate. I watched the fairies drag Rand from the pit and disappear with him around the wall of the amphitheatre. It was just as well. It would be easier for me to focus with him absent.

"Where's Christa?"

"I didna think it right fer her ta be here, lass."

"Thank you," I said, thinking at least he'd done me a good turn there. I couldn't handle the possibility of Christa watching something bad happen to me. Suddenly it occurred to me that I really hadn't thought this one through. Defending myself didn't sound like death. Why hadn't I listened when Odran had said I could be killed? Goddammit, I'd thought he'd been exaggerating.

I was a freaking idiot.

Half of me wanted to beg him to change his mind, to let me go. But then I'd sealed my fate when I'd demanded he stand by his word. And now? Now I could even end up dead. Or, as everyone else seemed to think, I would end up dead.

I didn't know what was happening when two fairies took me by both arms and walked me into the center of the pit. Coming from the other side was a man, a fairy man. He was tall though not as tall as Odran. His hair was a dark red and fell to his knees. Muscles littered the landscape of his body like afterthoughts. But it wasn't his muscular build that really got me. It was the tattoos. They looked Celtic in design and ran the length of both arms and legs in a band of black criss-crosses. The largest one, in the shape of a cross, occupied the majority of the fairy's chest, the black standing out against the otherwise white of his skin.

"I am Dougal," the fairy said in a deep voice.

"I'm Jolie." I was surprised I could find my voice.

"Dougal," Odran called from the sidelines. He motioned Dougal forward with his index finger. When Dougal reached him, Odran whispered something in his ear and the man nodded. God, hopefully it wasn't strategy.

I was dead, a goner.

Jolie, just focus on protecting yourself. Focus on nothing else, do you understand? Rand's voice broke through my thoughts.

At the sound of his voice, tears sprung to my eyes. *I'm sorry, Rand. I didn't realize what I was getting into.*

That doesn't matter now, just focus on protecting yourself.

Okay, I will.

I don't know what he plans on doing, but don't be frightened; don't let anything take your focus away from your own protection. Whatever he does, you must ignore it.

I lifted my gaze and noticed Dougal had finished his silent communion with the king and was returning to his side of the pit.

"Begin," Odran commanded.

I did nothing as Dougal approached me, his eyes fixed on mine, his stride purposeful and intimidating. He didn't wear a smile, but neither did he frown. He waved his hand in the air, starting near his shoulder and bringing it down to his leg. As soon as he did so, the sleeve of my dress ripped itself from me.

Jolie, protect yourself, dammit, I thought.

I pictured a blue glowing orb circling me and as soon as the thought left my mind, I could see the perimeter of my haven. The fairy just laughed and opened his hands, launching what looked like a glowing ball of energy toward me. Luckily, it burst into a fizz of nothing upon encountering my circle.

Dougal frowned and strode to me, placing his hand on the transparent blue sphere. His fingers sunk through it and with a balled fist, he shredded my cocoon like it was as delicate as the skin of a grape. I backed away, bile thick in my throat and cried out when he grabbed hold of my dress, yanking me toward him. My blue sphere disappeared, taking with it my protection.

He lifted me by my neckline and with a flick of his wrist, sent me flying through the air. I yelped and hit the ground a good fifty feet from him, my back and elbows absorbing my fall. I stared up at the sky, willing the air to return to my lungs. The sting coming from my elbows bore evidence to the fact that they were bleeding. I inhaled deeply and forced myself up, knowing time was a luxury I didn't have. The air burned as it filled my lungs, and tears caught at the corners of my eyes. Crawling onto my hands and knees, I stood and braced myself for Dougal's next attack.

He held his hands shoulder-width apart and what looked like a current of electricity emanated between them. With a malicious smile, he pulled one arm back as if to launch the bolt of electricity. I immediately pictured a stone wall before me. A buzzing sounded from the other side of the wall as the electricity erupted against it.

The stone suddenly crumpled and I swallowed a cry of alarm. Dougal faced me with a sinister smile and holding his palms heavenward, fire burst within both of them, the flames long and blue. He tilted his head to the sky and cried something I couldn't make out, something guttural and foreign. The sky, seemingly in response, grumbled a great and rumbling sound as dark clouds eclipsed the blue sky. The clouds grew and swirled together. A drop of cold rain splashed against my head. Then another, and another until it beat down on me, as if the blue sky were crying over its demise.

Dougal neared me, the rain glancing off him like he was carrying an invisible umbrella. He held his hands up to the heavens again as lightning struck the ground beside him. His tattoos glowed and he closed his eyes, as if inhaling the residue of the lightning.

The sky thundered and a bolt of lightning graced the ground in a dance of electricity. Dougal dropped to his knees, face heavenward as another bolt hit him right in the center of his chest tattoo. He shook violently. I felt a scream tear from my lips and stared at him in incredulity as smoke whispered from his tattoos. As soon as the smoke appeared, flames of blue engulfed Dougal, swirling around him and reflecting against the crazed look in his eyes. I half-wondered if maybe his magic had gone wrong but no, he'd planned to be aflame.

His skin began to buckle with what looked like scales. And his fingers arched, his nails elongating into talons accompanied with the sound of snapping, like someone stepping on dried twigs. His spine seemed to grow underneath his skin, the bones breaking and reinventing themselves anew. His neck was now maybe five times longer and his face … I couldn't handle the fear coursing through me as his teeth became razor sharp incisors that were as long as my hands. I had to look away.

I shielded my eyes, too afraid to bear witness to whatever horrid creature Dougal was becoming. I knew without a doubt, whatever creature it was, its sole purpose was to kill me. Now very much aware of the fate awaiting me, I shook with my own fear. I raised my head when I heard a round of applause from the bleachers and beheld a dragon directly before me, a dragon glowing in blue flame, immune to the rain.

I screamed and the creature brought its head right down to me, staring at me with the eyes of a lizard. Its massive snout was the size of a small car and its forked tongue lashed out of its mouth, tasting the air.

Shivers seized me and tears mingled with the rain as they coursed down my face. No matter how I tried, I couldn't force my attention from the beast. Its body was covered in dark yellow scales, the tail maybe thirty feet long. It didn't have any wings but had long claws on all its four paws. It waddled toward me, its tongue continuing to sniff me on the air.

I pushed the wet clumps of hair from my face and imagined a wall of protective energy. The dragon flicked it with his claws, but the wall refused to budge, seemingly standing against the incredible beast with its chest puffed out in pride.

The dragon released a shrill cry and the wall shook like it was as frightened as I was. I dropped to my knees, shielding my head with my arms and closed my eyes. I needed all my focus and energy on my protection, not on the dragon. At the sound of the dragon breaking down my defensive wall, I opened my eyes. The dragon was a few inches from me, wearing a definite smile in its hideous eyes.

I screamed, nearly drowning in the onslaught of rain.

The dragon reared up above me and took a great intake of air, its chest billowing out. Then it threw its head toward me and breathed a river of fire from its mouth. I huddled in on myself and imagined my glowing orb of protection. The fire bounced off the orb, and the dragon took another breath. He sprayed fire down on me again, and I could feel the potency of my shelter waning. I covered my eyes with my hand and continued to visualize the defensive barricade of my orb, picturing the walls to be as strong as steel and as thick as the trunk of a huge tree.

"Dougal, dinnae kill her!" Odran screamed from the bleachers.

I glanced at the dragon and realized there was nothing capable of reasoning within it. The man was gone; all that remained was the beast.

I was as good as dead.

I felt the heat of fire again as the dragon breathed down on me. My defenses were steadily growing weaker, exhaustion starting to claim me. I scrunched my eyes tighter and imagined my orb glowing with a brighter light as it reinforced itself. Another blow of fire rained down on it and the heat was fierce against my back. Before I had the chance to envision strengthening the orb, the dragon breathed another blast against me. This time the heat was more potent, singing my back as if a giant were putting out a cigarette on me.

My heart throbbed in my chest as I forced myself to concentrate. I imagined my orb again and focused all my attention on it, feeling the energy surround me. The next blow of fire wasn't as hot. But the blow after was. I didn't have time to regroup before another fire onslaught caught me off guard—the heat so intense, I could smell my hair burning. I ran frantic hands over my head but found it wasn't aflame. It was just in my imagination.

The magic wasn't real.

Another blow of fire pelted down on me and my skin singed, the pain like the stab of thousands of knives. I focused on my orb, trying to strengthen it, but another blow of fire disabled me. Now I could smell my skin burning.

It's all in your head, Jolie, I told myself. *It's all in your damned head.*

Another blow and I shuddered against the pain.

I was dying. I could feel it. The shouts of the audience were a soft droning, like the buzz of flies and my eyelids felt increasingly heavy. My energy was dissipating, and I didn't have the wherewithal to focus on my own protection. I couldn't last much longer, and the truth of it was that I just wanted to give in—anything to end the pain.

Another river of fire danced over me and I dropped my head to the ground, no longer able to hold it up. The dirt was rough against my cheek. My whole body was aflame now. I didn't need to open my eyes to know it was true. I was going to burn to death, whether it was real or not didn't matter. It felt real and either way, it was going to kill me.

Do not give up.

I didn't recognize the voice in my head. It was a woman's voice, strong and sure.

You can beat this. You have the strength within yourself.

I shook my head, feeling another flame of fire lapping at my skin, burning through me. Killing me slowly.

Believe in yourself, Jolie, you have more ability than you know.

And like a wave of calm, the pain within me completely dissolved into nothing. I opened my eyes and found my cheek against the rough earth. Out of the corner of my eye, I could see the dragon breathing more fire down on me, but I couldn't feel it. My eyes found Odran who was focusing on his lap, shielding his face from the spectators who were silently watching the dragon.

I pushed up to my knees and felt the blow of fire on my back but couldn't feel the pain. There was something within me, something strong and something angry. I stood and wavered a bit before I found my balance. I faced the dragon just as it blew another fire stream. The flames merely danced over me, entertaining more than threatening.

I took a step nearer the beast and when it blew fire again, I held my hand up and the fire merely crystallized into drops of ice as soon as it met my palm. If it was possible for a dragon to look dumbfounded, that's exactly how it looked. I continued walking toward it, something driving me forward.

The fire meant nothing to me.

The dragon inhaled until its chest looked like it might explode and breathed a torrential downpour of liquid fire atop me. The heat of the fire momentarily stopped me, but I had to continue forward. Tiny pinpricks of heat and pain coursed over me, but I ignored them. Only a few steps separated me from the dragon.

The dragon, apparently realizing I was immune to the fire, threw its face down at me, its mouth open and teeth shining. It wrapped its jaws around my upper shoulder and bit down. I screamed against what I imagined would be hideous pain but opened my eyes when I found I could feel nothing.

The dragon tossed its head this way and that as if tearing my shoulder apart, and I clamped my eyes shut, imagining Dougal as nothing more than a fairy, denying him his dragon appearance. I felt myself collapse to the ground. When I opened my eyes, Dougal lay before me unconscious … or dead.

The sound of silence from the bleachers was telling. I knew what it meant. I'd defended myself. Now the men who sat around me would be going to war, that is, if Odran kept his word. I moved like I was in slow motion as I faced Odran who stared at me open-mouthed.

I felt myself go down again, and braced my arms against the ground. I inhaled great gulps of air as tears coursed from my eyes. How did I manage to defeat a dragon? The question rang through me and I had to push it aside, knowing I'd never find the answer. Either way, I'd won. I might be half-dead, but I'd won. We actually had a chance to defeat Bella now.

I'd never been prouder of myself.

"Lass." It was Odran. He reached down and pulled me into him, cradling me against his massive chest. "Ye did it."

"Is … is he dead?" I asked, my voice still sounding distant and odd.

"Nay, lass, nay."

I nodded and my eyes fell to the opening of the amphitheatre as some people left and others remained. Then my eyes found the familiar face of Rand as he made his way toward us, pushing aside anyone unlucky enough to get in his way. He reached me in seconds, his eyes never straying from mine.

"Odran, get the hell away from her," he said as I collapsed into his arms.

"Wait," I said, lifting my eyes to Odran as he started to walk away. "Odran, wait."

He turned to face me and his eyes were angry. "Lass?"

"I defeated your fairy."

He was silent before he nodded, his eyes furious. "Aye, lass, we will join ye." Then he turned on his heel and strode away, reminding me of a great lion. A great lion retreating.

"Rand, did you hear that?" I said, facing him again.

"Yes," he whispered with a grin. "You did it."

His arms tightened around me as I collapsed into him, sobs tearing through my throat.

I did it.

I didn't know how and I had no idea whose voice I'd heard in my head or if I'd invented it or what. But all that remained was the fact that I'd done the impossible. And I never could have done it without Rand.

His fight was my fight. We were in this together from here on out. And I couldn't say that bothered me. Even with Bella's army looming above, I believed in us … I knew we could win.

245

I looked into Rand's eyes again and they glistened with unshed tears. His lips were tight. There was something in those eyes—a warmth. Love. I could see it as clearly as the moors of Pelham Manor after a cool rain.

He and I would have our day—I didn't know when and I didn't know how, but someday, Rand and I would find what we both wanted. I didn't just believe it; I knew it was true.

Rand had changed my life—in some ways for the better and in some ways for the worse. I guess nothing is ever one hundred percent black or white. But, either way, he had been my ever-fixed pillar of strength. He'd taught me to accept my abilities and he'd taught me how to use them. Without Rand, I'd still be sitting in my shop in Los Angeles thinking my cat was the best kind of company.

Are you okay?

I glanced at Rand and nodded, sinking into the chocolate beauty of his eyes. *Everything's perfect.*

Perfect? He chuckled. *Well, I don't know about perfect, but I've certainly put you through a lot.*

I didn't drop his gaze. *I wouldn't change it for the world.*

Pondering my life, I'd never thought it would've taken the turn it did. The Jolie of just six months ago was a different person to the Jolie of today. I didn't fault the old me—I didn't resent my apparent acceptance of the status quo or the fact that I thought I was happy with the lonely life I'd led. I loved the person I used to be, but I also loved the person I now was. I was strong, independent, and capable.

I was beautiful.

And I was ready for whatever life decided to throw at me next.

Bring it on.

H. P. Mallory is the author of the Jolie Wilkins series as well as the Dulcie O'Neil series.

She began her writing career as a self-published author and after reaching a tremendous amount of success, decided to become a traditionally published author and hasn't looked back since.

H. P. Mallory lives in Southern California with her husband and son, where she is at work on her next book.

If you are interested in receiving emails when she releases new books, please sign up for her email distribution list by visiting her website and clicking the "contact" tab: www.hpmallory.com

Be sure to join HP's online Facebook community where you will find pictures of the characters from both series and lots of other fun stuff including an online book club!

Facebook: https://www.facebook.com/hpmallory

Find H.P. Mallory Online:
www.hpmallory.com
http://twitter.com/hpmallory
https://www.facebook.com/hpmallory

Printed in Great Britain
by Amazon.co.uk, Ltd.,
Marston Gate.